Churchill's Rogue

John Righten

My thanks to Kate, Jules, Alan, and Jacky for translating my scribblings into the Queen's English, and Chris and Davy for the Rogues website.
In memory of Alex, 'My Dad'
1949 – 2013

The 1930s epic: The Rogues Trilogy

Churchill's Rogue, The Gathering Storm & *The Darkest Hour*

The 1960s thriller: The Lochran Trilogy

Churchill's Assassin, The Last Rogue & *The Alpha Wolves*

The 1990s odyssey: The Lenka Trilogy

Heartbreak, Resilience & *Reflection*
&
The Benevolence of Rogues & *The 'Pane' of Rejection*

For the latest updates on all my novels go to
https://www.rightensrogues.co.uk
facebook.com/theroguestrilogy
Instagram rightensrogues

John Righten, real name John Enright, has delivered medical aid to orphanages and hospitals across the globe, including Romania during the revolution, South America and Bosnia during the war. His Rogues novels are based on the characters he encountered during his many dangerous missions, when he enlisted unlikely support from those he terms 'benevolent rogues'. John has worked in over forty occupations, ranging from a gravedigger, a cocktail barman, and a tree-surgeon, to a professional poker player, and government "Transactor". He has ridden a British Army motorbike across India to support several children's charities and worked in a mental health facility in Manhattan. He is married to Kate and has two sons, Logan and James.

Along with his autobiography and a play, John has written three trilogies: The 1930s based epic adventures, The Rogues Trilogy; the 1960s thrillers, The Lochran Trilogy; and the 1990s odyssey, The Lenka Trilogy.

Churchill's Rogue was shortlisted for the inaugural Wilbur Smith Adventure Writing awards. *Heartbreak* won the Page Turner Audio Award.

'I abhor war, but it will come and we must be ready for it.'

Winston Churchill

Chapter 1: Brief Encounter

December 1937, Kent

'Do you know many Governments want you dead?' asked Churchill.

'No,' replied the Irishman, taking his seat in his former adversary's study.

'Five, according to my sources in British Intelligence.' The Statesman kept his focus on the sturdy oak tree in his garden that barely moved as the wind started to build. 'Oh, and there are a few in British Intelligence who would also like to see you dead.'

Churchill was only acknowledging what the Irishman already knew, as Ryan had killed one of their agents years earlier.

'British Intelligence, a bunch of inept adventurers, drunks, traitors, womanisers and fantasists judging from my encounters with them.'

'Are you interested in who the five are?'

'No,' replied the younger man.

The Statesman was not one to wait for an audience's

approval, continued, 'You've clashed with Fascist bodyguards to the military junta in Argentina, Italian cavalry officers in Tangiers and a Japanese execution squad in Manchuria.' The younger man remained impassive. 'And let's not forget that you hospitalised a further two German so-called "advisors" to Mussolini's army in Ethiopia in thirty-five.'

'They were where they shouldn't have been.'

'Ethiopia?'

'In my way.'

Churchill knew only too well that this was not false bravado.

'One detail in the dossier I had compiled on you intrigues me. Why are you on the Norwegians' list?'

'Some off-the-cuff remark I made about herring, no doubt.'

Churchill ignored the man's irreverent attitude. 'Of course, there are those in your own country who want you dead, too.'

'So, apart from a few disgruntled alcoholics in your secret service, I'm not *officially* on the British Government's list. Dear me, what is the Empire coming to?'

Churchill ignored the man's flippancy. 'Irrespective of the Norwegian question, I'm puzzled as to why you are you are often referred to as 'The Englander'?'

'I guess it's the most damning insult my enemies can think of.'

Churchill had read of a great many men who moved in the shadows, but the Irishman's anonymity was protected by a bewildering array of reports, each giving him a pseudonym that depended more on the author than the subject: 'The Englander' was recorded in reports from Germany; 'The Scrapper' in British dossiers; 'The Guardian' in the most recent communiques intercepted from China, and 'The Saviour' in despatches from Latin America earlier in the year. One Irish communique referred to him quite simply as a woman's private region. Descriptions of him varied from the romantic to the absurd. He was reported as anywhere from five foot eight up to seven feet tall. His hair anything from 'deadly black' to 'fiery red,' even 'sun-kissed strawberry blond'. At least the descriptions of his eyes were reduced to a choice between grey-green and blue. The real Sean Ryan hid somewhere behind these phantoms.

'Well, we can't have the good name of the country besmirched by someone knocking the heads off Fascists, can we?' For the first time, the Statesman broke into a mischievous smile. 'I cannot think of anyone with such a diverse list of enemies,' said the Englishman, standing by the window, staring out onto his beloved garden, besieged by the encroaching frost of winter.

Churchill turned to face the man helping himself to the nameless whiskey in the crystal decanter on the table. He studied the man. On the first morning of that now-long past Anglo-Irish meeting, a Government aide outlined the make-up of the Irish delegation and when he got to the man now sitting opposite, he simply referred to him as the Scrapper.

His features were set like a rock by the shoreline. The nose was straight and sharp, but wide at the nostrils. His firm jaw had provided him with good protection in numerous fights over the years, while his ears were tucked in beneath his ruffled, thick, matt-black hair.

3

Churchill was not up on the latest trends, but all the men who ran around Whitehall with files had immaculately waxed hair, in the manner of film idols like Errol Flynn and Robert Taylor, and combed in a manner that flopped down signposting one eye. The Irishman's hair was swept back as if put in place each morning with one sweep of the hand (which it was). Fashion was of no interest to the man.

Standing at six-foot-two, his body had grown and then solidified like a boxer who had reached his peak and could add no more muscle. He wore a navy-blue fisherman's jumper, no shirt, black trousers, and British army surplus issue boots. He had not shaved that morning, though the driver Churchill had sent to his lodgings had offered him time to do so. His stubble showed no hint of red, common with even the darkest-haired Celts.

The Statesman remembered one aspect of the description of 'The Englander' in his dossier. A British agent had observed him in a fight with two Italian officers in a bar in Tangiers, and provided an almost lyrical description of him, as having 'steely blue eyes' and being 'like a wild animal on the hunt'. Perhaps the Irishman was right about the 'fantasists', or else the agent was infatuated with the Irishman, which would be unrequited, as the file contained the names, or in some cases just descriptions, of several female dalliances. He had done more than fight his way around the world.

Sitting only a few feet away, it was obvious that the man's eyes were grey-green. His pupils were small, even though the room was not overly well lit, as if he had manually adjusted them like the exposure on a camera, to

4

let in as little light as possible.

He was a man who took everything in, while his playful flippancy told one nothing and served as a mask to disguise his thoughts. He used it as a magician or a thief might, as they flamboyantly released a dazzling white handkerchief from their top pocket, while removing your wallet from your coat. As he watched the younger man approach the house thirty minutes earlier, Churchill noticed his walk was light for such a big man. The Irishman moved as he had done years earlier when he prowled around the men at the negotiating table in the main dining room of 10 Downing Street. He had the stealth of a large cat, akin to the panther that Churchill had stumbled across one evening when he served as a young soldier fighting in the Sudan. The animal wandered alone, watching everything, trusting no one.

This panther was larger and more dangerous. Churchill had fought beside many seasoned fighters in his earlier years in Cuba, the Sudan and later, South Africa, but two things singled this man out – his eyes and his stealth. The alertness and intensity of his stare, and the guile in his movement coupled with his size and no doubt considerable experience as a fighter, sent a clear warning to any opponent: I'm ready! In a rage, he would be a handful for any number of men. This was the man he had received many reports about in the last few months, none complimentary, all stressing his threat. This was a man who thrived on danger – this was the man he sought.

'Have you not enemies enough?' he asked the man.

'My ambition is to piss off the Vatican in time for Christmas.'

Churchill rarely swore, unless in temper, but the

cheek of the young man reminded him of his own youthful swagger and he once again surrendered a smile.

'My good fellow, such youthful arrogance would try the patience of Job.'

The Englishman had met the man once some fifteen years earlier, but over the last ten minutes, it was the first time he had heard him speak. If you paid it little attention, you could easily have mistaken the voice as that of an Englishman – as a girlfriend of Ryan's once exclaimed, 'the arrogance helped' – apart from when his voice was raised, releasing his West-of-Ireland brogue. The Irishman's accent had softened and become more measured following his travels over the last ten years, and a lighter and smoother tone had come to the fore. So much so, that foreigners often mistook him as a native of his former enemy's country; hence the sobriquet, 'The Englander'.

'I believe your only family is a sister, but do you have friends?' asked Churchill.

'A few might confess to be, depending how close the gun was to their head.'

'I'm more fortunate, as I have the love of my family,' imparted the politician as he moved towards his favourite armchair, whose wooden frame had politely bent as required over time to accommodate his extra pounds. He looked down as he ran his hand along the embossed design on its arm. 'But now I too am deficient in the friends department and, like you, I am an outcast in the country I love.'

Churchill reclined as he pondered the recent events that had led to his political and, more painfully for his family (and therefore for him), social isolation. He seldom had an opportunity to engage in robust debate in the House these days. His protestations against the Nazis were met with anger and ridicule by his opponents. With each act of appeasement, the nation breathed a sigh of relief, thinking that the Nazis' appetite for conquest was finally sated. He was of the view that it only encouraged the beast to come back for more. But each time he tried to awaken his countrymen to the ever-growing danger, he was rebuffed.

Leaning forward, he barked at the young man, 'Mind you, I have not reached your position where previous acquaintances are vying with my enemies to kill me,' and broke into a laugh, 'at least as far as I know.'

'An old comrade once informed me that I lack social skills, but it keeps the bastards at bay,' replied Sean, who smiled for the first time since entering the room.

The Irishman noticed a genuine delight in his former adversary's laugh: it was honest and unabashed which, in his limited experience, was rare for a politician. Ryan remembered that after the Anglo-Irish Treaty was signed, the Englishman had teased his boss, Michael Collins. He remembered every word spoken between the two men whose enmity was finally put to one side by a piece of paper they helped to negotiate, which created the Irish Free State.

"With this act today, Mr Collins, fiery-headed Irishwomen can turn their formidable rage away from our shores and once more back towards their men. As indeed they should!" he quipped.

"My Ma is a redhead and you're very welcome to join our family for dinner anytime, but don't expect to get a word in edgeways until you're back on the ferry home," replied Collins.

Sean remembered the night they signed the agreement, when he and the others in their delegation drank Guinness together in a little bar on a side street off The Strand. Lord Birkenhead, a counter signatory, declared, "In signing the treaty I've signing my political death warrant". Collins shrugged, "I've signing the treaty I've signed my *own* death warrant."

Two years later, Collins, aged thirty-one, was assassinated on a road on the outskirts of his home town, Cork, by his former colleagues in the Irish Republican Army (IRA). The Treaty plunged the country into civil war, and as the last of Collins' bodyguards, Ryan was one of those right at the top of the IRA's death list.

Now sitting opposite him, Sean had a better look at the man he had not seen since that day, sixth December nineteen-twenty-one. Then the man was greatly respected in his country of birth and across the globe, despite the debacle of the Dardanelles. Today that same man was distrusted, even loathed, by many of his fellow Englishmen. Yet, apart from being older and having put on a few pounds, he was unchanged. He was still proud, assured and not afraid to shout from any platform from which he was given the opportunity to speak. This was the same man who cared little for what people thought of him, except for his family and close friends. Sean thought the older man rather enjoyed his notoriety.

He was larger around the waist than he should have been for a man of sixty-three. His black waistcoat pulled violently at the lower buttons and his pinstriped trousers strained at the stitching. Though still a very active man, judging by his movement across the room, his enjoyment of the finer things in life was evident. His dicky-bow gave him the look of an academic, though he was not regarded as academically bright by Randolph Churchill, his father. Black and white photos in the newspapers gave the impression that he was bald, but on closer inspection you could see that the hair on top of his head and on the sides was moistened with some kind of oil and mercilessly pressed up against his scalp. He had that steadiness of jaw, the look of a man that had seen battle, victory and loss, and survived it. His eyes were resolute and intent with purpose. Yet, when he smiled, his face became that of a mischievous boy, one that a parent would regularly scold but would have to adopt the most severe of faces, as their heart would not be in it.

Both men continued to weigh up the other, while marking out their positions. After a few minutes, Churchill broke the silence as he removed the glass stopper from the decanter and took a sniff, which produced a frown. He turned to Inches, his loyal butler, who up to that point had been standing silently, but uneasily, at the door. 'Inches, this bilge is for my last guest of the day. Time for the fine scotch!'

He turned to the man opposite, and asked, 'Will you take a Bushmills with me?'

'No,' answered the Irishman and holding a hand up to Inches as he approached with the requested bottle on a silver tray. 'Though it's a fine whiskey, it leaves a bitter aftertaste,' he added.

'Aftertaste?'

'I prefer a Jameson from an unoccupied Dublin than a whiskey distilled from an occupied Belfast.'

'Let's settle on a neutral ground and agree on a Scottish whisky?' replied Churchill without a pause. 'Can we agree on Johnnie Walker?'

'I prefer a single malt, but I'm not one to cause trouble,' replied Sean.

The Statesman huffed, as he lifted a bottle of the blended malt from his desk, 'How do you take it?'

'As a double.'

Churchill opened the wooden box that contained his favourite cigars, *Romeo y Julieta,* from Havana.

'Smoke?'

'No thanks, maybe once I tire of alcohol. I'll probably buy a box when I'm eighty.'

'I never thought you an optimist,' replied Churchill, as he began the first of many attempts to strike one of his specially made extra-long matches, for the cigar perched between his lips.

Peering out from between two of the sofa cushions, another pair of eyes watched the two men.

'That's Jock. He owns the establishment. You two don't seem overly friendly towards each other? Do you like cats?'

'I love cats, but the Jocks are more of a problem. As fellow Celts, we don't sit comfortably sharing the same space.' The ginger cat remained curled up, oblivious to the other occupants in the room.

The Englishman had been intrigued by the serious young man who had stood guard by his boss all those years ago. Whether through age or perhaps because their war was over – at least officially – he was at ease, unafraid, and sure of himself. How different he was then, during those three days of discussions. He remained on guard, even when the ink of the signatories was absorbed by the parchment. On that fateful day in 1921, the younger Sean Ryan was the only member of both delegations after the Treaty was signed to refuse a drink.

But the politician in Churchill was now delighted that he had reached a compromise with the Irishman, so they could finally share a malt. Churchill was also pleased to see the man was not a 'pioneer', as the Catholic Church referred to Irishmen who took the pledge not to touch alcohol throughout their lives. He refused to trust a man who did not have a single redeeming vice.

Churchill poured himself a double scotch, though at this time of day he would have preferred a glass of Pol Roger Champagne, the 1928 vintage.

'Your old boss, The Big Fellah, I think they called him,' referring to the late Michael Collins. 'His greatest attribute was that once he had secured his objective, he laid down his weapon and then worked to protect the freedoms that had been won. I have seen too many men, clouded by hate, vengeance, victory or greed, carry on the fight, only to lose all that they have gained.'

Churchill nodded to Inches to leave the room. The man hesitated, wary of leaving the man he served alone with such a dangerous looking individual. The Statesman noted his concern with an appreciative nod but firmly waved him to go. Inches did as he was bid and left the two men to discuss Churchill's project in private – the details of which would soon reach Berlin.

'You have an Irish disrespect for authority.'

'In our history the English represent authority, so you're right.'

'I believe you have that same quality as Collins. That

is why I asked you to come here this morning. It's time to bury the past and let old enemies unite against a common foe.'

'You'll be disappointed if you asked me here for a hug.'

'I asked you here to join me to confront a deadly foe, one that if victorious will destroy the very liberties that we have fought to protect. A threat that sadly remains invisible to our countrymen.'

Winston poured them both another glass of single malt, before saying, 'We have a shared enemy.'

'Teetotallers.'

'Narzees!'

July 1934, Berlin

General Vaux, one of the most respected leaders in the Wehrmacht, knelt in the mud, his uniform soaked from the torrential rain, his hands clutched behind his head. Next to him was a younger man, an army clerk, also kneeling, but with his head bowed. The day before, the young man was accused of gross insubordination for failing to return an officer's Heil Hitler salute. His accuser sat in the back seat of the black Mercedes, watching in silence, as the two SS recruits positioned themselves behind the general and the clerk.

Throughout the four-hour drive to the clearing in the forest, the young army clerk had begged for his life. He tried to explain to his accuser that his regular migraine attacks sometimes resulted in temporary deafness. His accuser remained impassive – news of his disability only added to the man's worthlessness. Like the young man,

General Vaux had his wrists secured to his seat, but he did not struggle, retaining a dignified silence.

The general had fought bravely in the First World War, defending the German border until he received orders from Berlin for his troops to lay down their arms. He accepted defeat without bitterness. With America having joined the Great War a year before, he knew the surrender of the German army was inevitable. Though he had never confessed it to anyone, he was glad to return home in time to be there when his young wife, Greven, had their first child.

In the intervening years of the Weimar Republic, Vaux had risen to the rank of general. He was respected by his peers in the German army as well as his men. He was a devoted family man and a man of honour, who believed in the democratic ideals of the new Weimar Republic. He had been awarded numerous medals and, recently, to his great surprise, the new National Socialist Government had awarded him the Cross of Honour for bravery in the last war. This did not stop his outspoken opposition to Hitler's personal bodyguard, the SS, when it was incorporated into the Wehrmacht. It was this that led to his arrest by the National Socialist Government on the personal orders of its Chancellor, Herr Hitler.

The Mercedes was parked by the clearing. Its engine was still running to provide heat for the two men inside. The elegant machine was jet black but for the sides, which were blood red from the base of its windows down to the footplates. Mounted on each wing were small flags carrying the emblem of the Third Reich, the *Hakenkreuz*, the black cross, with its arms at ninety-degree angles. Within a year of the Nazis taking power and bringing an end to democratic rule, the swastika had already become a symbol to be feared.

The car possessed several extras that added to the opulence of the vehicle and its purpose. Its dashboard was of the finest mahogany with a walnut trim and its steering wheel was enveloped in a black leather sheath with the *Totenkopf*, the Death Skull motif, mounted on its centre plate. The ivory dice-shaped buttons that operated the radio were disconnected, but a second set had been installed in the right-hand armrest of the backseat so the passenger seated there had control. The playing of music coupled with the curtains on its windows ensured that the cries of the victims inside remained unheard and unseen.

The passenger seats were covered with red velvet. Exposed metal on the inside of the vehicle was plated in gold gilt, while that on the exterior was chrome-plated. An additional light had been fixed into the roof above the back seat and pointed in the direction of those sitting opposite. In the two armrests on either side of the seats facing forwards were built-in cigarette trays; the major never smoked in the car, but he put these to use when he had 'guests'. On each of the armrests opposite were leather wrist straps. A restraining strap was also bolted into each of the side panels of the passenger doors. The adjoining seats were covered in a brown leather sheet that was now dotted with the blood of its two most recent passengers.

A few metres away, the two troopers pointed their Lugers at the backs of the heads of the men kneeling in the mud. The major wound down the window, letting a few drops of rain jump onto his black uniform.

He leant forward from the shadows at the back of

14

the car and shouted towards the men awaiting execution, 'Run!'

But neither man did.

General Vaux spoke. 'Even if we could, we would not, nor will we crawl,' he pronounced, hoping that the young man, trembling and kneeling next to him, would obey his final order.

Out of the corner of his left eye, he looked at the young man and knew that even if he had wanted to run on his crippled feet, fear had paralysed him.

'You deny me the thrill of the chase; so be it,' replied the officer from the car whose voice could hardly be heard with the rain pounding on the leaves above.

As the Mercedes drove out of Berlin, the major ordered the two troopers to remove the boots and socks of the two prisoners. He produced a pair of bolt-cutters he kept, having recently tortured a Jewish locksmith to death in his own workshop. The troopers secured their limbs. The clerk had screamed, struggled and passed out before the cutters engaged.

When it was the general's turn, he uttered not a word nor expressed any emotion, except the brief clenching of his teeth as the big toe from each foot fell into his hat. It was not that his superior rank made him braver or able to take more pain. It was his acceptance of his fate. He was determined not to provide any gratification to the sadist in front of him. The general focused his mind, not on what was being done to him, as the younger had, but on composing his last words.

On reaching the clearing, unable to stand, both men were dragged from the car and thrown into the mud.

'If you murder us today, you send our country down a path that will lead to the eventual destruction of our nation,' pronounced the general in a firm, composed voice that did not betray the excruciating pain shooting through his body. A gun barrel jabbed against the back of his head. The general was afraid, but not for his own life. He was resigned to his fate when he was dragged by the troops standing behind him from his bed that morning. No, his fear was for his wife and children, who he knew would be arrested and perhaps executed by Hitler's SS shortly after his execution.

'Fire!' came the order from the car.

The two troopers pulled the trigger on their Lugers. Six times they aimed their pistols and fired, and six times nothing happened. After each attempt, the failed executioners prodded the barrels of their guns even more violently into the backs of their crouching victims. The first failure caused the executioners a mixture of frustration and embarrassment, as the major had selected them that morning to test their worthiness to join the SS. By the sixth failed attempt, this had become blind fear. Now that all their attempts had failed, the impotent executioners turned towards the darkness inside the open window of the Mercedes. All that met them were two narrow eyes, with black empty pupils; the rest of the man remained in the darkness.

The troopers turned around to look at the back of the general's head, his short wiry grey saw hair steadfastly refusing to be flattened by the torrential rain. The men on their knees knew this was only a temporary reprieve. The younger man was sobbing as he buried his chin into his chest. The only visible effect one could see on the older man beside him was that his fingers, still clasped behind his head, were white and bloodless, pressed tightly to his skull. The skies roared, sending lightning flashes into the surrounding mountains, as if angered that the promised sacrifices to the gods had not been made.

The major's driver, Grossmann, opened the front door of the car and stepped into the thunderstorm. Indifferent to the torrential rain and the deafening clashes of the black clouds hurling javelins of light at the mountains and the tallest trees of the forest, he rose to his full height of six foot six. The goliath doubled as a personal bodyguard for the officer who remained seated in the shadows. His soft-felt garrison cloth cap, though it was the largest size available, was ridiculously small for his large, bald, cannon-ball-shaped head, but this did not deflect from the intimidating presence of the man. Grossmann took two steps to lay his plate-sized hand on the chrome handle of the right-hand side passenger door and opened it.

The giant held the door open while standing to attention. As always, his passenger took his time to emerge. The major did everything with care and deliberation. He placed his left black leather boot on a mound of earth rising out of the pools of water surrounding the car. He turned his full body towards the open door and positioned the heel of his other boot firmly down on the exposed tiny rock island. Once he was sure of the firmness of his footing, only then did he rise from the car and expose himself to the natural light that peeped through the storm clouds. Grossmann was the taller of the two men now standing by the vehicle by a good three inches and far broader, but it was the other man who always drew people's attention, until interest turned to fear.

Like his driver, the officer wore the black uniform of the Gestapo, the Nazis' secret state police, beneath his long black leather coat. The four pips on his collar protruding above his coat showed that he held the rank of a major, *Sturmbannführer*, in the Gestapo. He was tall and thin, his face was deathly pale and unmarked, a creature who preferred to remain in the dark. His eyes were green and narrow, lifeless and hooded. His skin appeared stretched, making it unnaturally smooth, as if his skull had growth but its membrane had ceased to grow with it. His blond hair was thin and sparse, like a cheap doll whose maker had suddenly realised that his reptilian creation would terrify a child and added some flimsy threads as an afterthought; adding only to its grotesqueness.

Grossmann had been assigned to him for the last four years. In that time he had rarely witnessed him expressing genuine emotion. Only when he was inflicting pain on a prisoner did his worm-like blue veins press against the surface of his skin excitedly. His stance was straight, rigid and unyielding. His skeletal body lacked the warmth of fat. His wrists protruded far beyond his cuffs and his fingers were long, thin and claw shaped, like that of a puppeteer poised above his little theatre holding the strings to manipulate the figures below. He wore his tight black leather trench coat easily, like a second skin easily shed.

Apart from the stripes of his uniform, everything about him – the arrogance in his look and in his voice, the way he positioned his feet wide apart with his hands clasped behind his back – declared that he held absolute power over all the men in that little clearing in the middle of the forest.

Above them the cracks of thunder clamoured even louder and the intensity of the forks of lightning stabbing the earth increased, clamouring for the promised offerings to the gods to be kept.

The major removed his cap and secured it under his left arm as he circled the small gathering. Grossmann marched back to the front of the car and took the black umbrella from the front passenger seat. His commander waved him away before he opened it, and instead directed him to stand behind the two failed executioners.

The major stood facing the two men kneeling on the ground, but the younger prisoner was weeping and too scared to look up. He addressed the general, whose eyes met his, while calmly he undid the clasp that secured the revolver in his holster.

'Your God has granted you a temporary reprieve. This gives me the opportunity to tell you a little of your final resting place.'

His monotonous voice was like that of a museum guide – neither boastful, sarcastic nor enthused – but one that delivered information in a manner that made it clear that the facts were irrefutable.

'Did you notice the mushroom-shaped pile of boulders ten metres in front of you? Yes, of course you did, though I believe that only we two were the ones to notice its unique shape.' He nodded at the men around, who only now squinted at the rock formation. 'In my early days as a member of the Hitler Youth, we regularly hiked in these forests. You see the ruins of the Red

Castle,' he said, as he pointed to a windowless stone building twelve metres to the left, 'and this was known as the Bear Trap.'

He strode over to the unusual formation of stones. 'But this is what I came to see.' He ran his open hand along the stone tablet that rested on top of the mound. 'This, so the legend goes, is the *Teufelstisch*, The Devil's Table.' Nodding as he inspected it, he glanced at the two crippled men and said, 'If you could move a little closer, you would observe the crevasses that cut deep into its core. It is alleged that they are the result of the steel cards laid down by Satan when he played a hand with goblins.' He patted the stone once more, and whispered, 'What I would have given to be dealt a hand in that game,' allowing himself a little smile.

Since removing his revolver from its holster, he had kept it sheltered under his hat from the torrential rain, but he was peeking at it like a magician, building up the expectation of his captured audience. 'Remarkable. Though my gun has been covered until now, I believe I too have been brought down in my endeavours to deliver justice.'

The troopers looked surprised. Even Grossmann appeared to be, as the major had cradled the gun so carefully that even the rain could not have reached the weapon's mechanism.

'Your God is merciful today.' He looked to the heavens, as raindrops bounced off his face as quickly as they could. 'This weather will be the death of us all,' he said, as he returned his Luger PO8, the German officer's weapon of choice, to its leather holster.

He stared across at the terrified farmer, wearing a

20

black leather apron, standing in the porch of the farmhouse on the edge of the clearing. The major trudged towards him, doing his best to negotiate the stepping stones so as not to splash any more mud on his brilliantly polished leather boots. The farmer avoided the officer's gaze. The major had no interest in the man, only the object that had originally caught his eye as he stepped from the car, a pickaxe leaning against the porch. The major picked up the implement and weighed it in his hands.

The major stared at the small group in the clearing, who were transfixed and waiting for his next move. He strolled back towards the failed execution party, standing to attention now too afraid to blink. When the pickaxe rose into the air, two pairs of frightened eyes followed the point of the metal tip as it came down and cracked open the general's skull. The heavens crackled once more, diverting everyone's attention to the executioner, as the lightning illuminated his grin.

The general remained in a kneeling position, his body convulsing violently. The young man next to him wailed and prayed that he would faint before it was his turn. The major placed his mud-coated leather boot on the nape of the general's neck to apply leverage as he wrenched the axe violently until it broke free. The general's mouth opened and closed, but only a jumble of incoherent sounds came out, before he toppled into a large pool of water on the ground. The officer lifted the pickaxe once again. The young clerk stared up before it came down and split his forehead in two.

Despite the blow the dead clerk was still kneeling. The major applied the sole of his blood-and-mud-splattered leather boot against the man's face and again worked the axe head from side to side until it pulled free. The troopers retched, before the taller of the two collapsed on to all fours.

The officer stood in front of his victims. He would have liked more time, but his orders from Berlin were to return as quickly as possible. He was pleased to receive his instructions earlier that week, but he was more than the leader of an execution squad, much more. He handed the axe to the nearest of the two troopers, the shorter man, who was trying to swallow his own vomit in an effort to compose himself. 'Carry on, until I order you to stop.'

Grossmann watched over the troopers, until his commander ordered him back to the car. He remained impassive throughout the execution; he knew what brutality his superior was capable of.

The general's body lay lifeless in the mud, but the clerk remained on his knees, his body convulsing uncontrollably.

The two troopers peered down at the bodies and though one was moving, it was a reflex action. But they knew better than to question their orders – their lives depended on it. The Gestapo officer watched as the troopers began to swing the pickaxe down on corpses. They were ordered to deliver twenty blows each in rotation.

The Gestapo officer reclined as he watched the troopers raining unrelenting blows down upon the two now-unrecognisable bodies. Ten minutes later, he smiled when the metal head of the farming implement broke from its wooden handle, spun through into the air, and landed in a puddle with one bloody end protruding.

The smaller of the two spent troopers stood holding what remained of the handle. He stared at the car, desperate for new instructions. The officer emerged from the car, having once more selecting the firmest mounds of earth and rocks for stepping stones. Grossman followed. They strode towards the men. The major looked down at the battered bodies and then back to the two troopers. He breathed a sigh, not of regret, but of a man who believed his work was done – the troopers would be punished for their failure, later.

The major negotiated his path so that the shine on his boots remained, until he reached the axe head resting in the waters beneath a willow tree. Peering down, he saw the general's Cross of Honour, partially visible above the surface of the water. One of its four metal points had snapped off. The major stood silently, watching as the blood was washed from the tip of the axe into the puddle. Transfixed, he stared at the blood red serpent circling the medal in the land. Placing his heel on the highest honour in the land, he pressed it into the mud.

The major retrieved the axe head. He turned towards the farmhouse, and he threw it on to the deck of the wooden boards of the porch. The farmer was kneeling on the damp slates of the wooden porch, vomiting over his leather butcher's apron.

'When we advance towards Moscow, let's hope that our armaments are not forged by those who manufacture farming tools,' shouted the major.

Grossmann nodded.

The major rested his right boot on a fallen log and wiped the blood and fragments of flesh from the leather with a handkerchief. It had been freshly washed and ironed, before Vaux's wife tucked into her husband's top pocket that morning. The major shook his head at the crimson stains on his black trousers.

He shouted to Grossmann, 'Fetch the farmer's apron, have it cleaned and delivered to my train.'

The major turned to the two soldiers, 'You are not fit to wear the uniform of the lowest rank in the Wehrmacht, let alone that of the SS. You disgraced the Fatherland today. I will consider what further punishment will be required.'

The major climbed into the Mercedes and ordered Grossmann to drive off, leaving the troopers behind in the rain. He had no intention of sharing the car with them, even if they had fully carried out his orders. The major found their odour, a mixture of damp clothing, sweat, vomit and cheap cologne, nauseating. They would need to be cleaned thoroughly before their execution.

The major reclined into the plush red leather seat of the car. He thought of the other purges taking place across the country.

He addressed Grossmann, though he could only view the back of his shaven head, 'If our fellow officers have done their duty as we have done today, the Führer will sleep easily tonight.'

The dark clouds above clapped once more, and seconds later its accomplice, lightening, lit up the clearing, as if to take one final snapshot of the macabre scene.

Chancellor Hitler did sleep easily that night. All week, moderate members of the German Army and members of the previous Weimar Government who opposed the rise of Hitler's National Socialist Party were being arrested, put on trial, and executed. Alongside them were leading members of the Nazis fascist rivals, the *Sturmabteilung*, the SA. 'The Night of the Long Knives,' as it came to be known, cleared the way for the Nazis to arrest, imprison, torture and eventually murder all those who opposed them. Now it was Germany, but soon it would be all central Europe.

This was the time when Major Klaus Krak began his meteoric rise through the ranks of the Gestapo. For though he was feared, he was not respected by his Gestapo colleagues. Some referred to him as the Ghoul, others as the Reptile. These names never reached the popularity of his other nickname, partly because if anyone was heard using either of them, not only would he have them arrested, he would also ensure that their families joined them. Only one name was tolerated by Major Klaus Krak, a name born from fear rather than mockery. A name associated with the dreaded mythological guardian of hell. He did not seek admiration. He had no need of love. Neither did he demand respect. He sought only to be feared. He was known by his enemies – he had no friends – as Cerberus.

December 1937, Kent

The glass tumblers of both men were still half-full, but Churchill summoned Inches, his butler, with a little silver bell, to refill the Irishman's – if only to reassure his loyal servant that he was still alive.

Inches arrived with fresh tumblers and placed the redundant decanter on his tray. He had come to respect

25

his employer, not just because of his worldwide reputation as a statesman, albeit he was now a pariah in Parliament, but because he always treated him, and his family, with the utmost consideration. True, Churchill had a fierce temper, he had seen it, but the Statesman had never turned on those in his service. When Inches first took up the position as Churchill's butler, he would enter the study, to find his new employer surrounded by men and women running about with maps and papers, telephones ringing continuously as if stimulated by the power and energy in the room. The room was a tornado of activity while the man sat in the centre of the room; a rock in the epicentre of turmoil.

Now in that same room, apart from his family and a few loyal friends, and the occasional messenger from former colleagues in the Admiralty, he was alone. Visitors were rare and dignitaries when they came, ventured only to observe, rarely to listen. His employer though did not give a damn, as he continued to sound the clarion call warning of the Nazis' threat. Inches respected the man even more. That was the greatness of a man, to stand up for what he believed was right when his contemporaries opposed him or, even worse, turned their backs.

Having topped up both men's glasses, knowing his boss could drink with the best of them no matter the hour, he felt relieved as the men seemed to have reached what his boss would refer to as an *entente cordiale*. Inches stood back from the table and thought he might need a little fortitude himself later, perhaps a glass of Madeira tonight. Churchill looked up at his loyal servant and dismissed him with a gentle nod. Outside the room, Inches recalled a comment by Eddie Marsh, Churchill's first Private Secretary, 'The first time you meet Winston you see all his faults and the rest of your life you spend discovering his virtues.'

The Irishman knew that from the moment he entered the study he was being assessed. Sean had little interest in making an impression, good or otherwise, but he was intrigued to know why he had been summoned and why here in Churchill's home and not to his parliamentary office. It may have been because of his reputation, but Sean judged that Churchill would not worry too much about that; it was more likely that the subject of their discussion was not sanctioned by Her Majesty's Government. Sean set his empty tumbler down on the antique oak table, an heirloom from Churchill's ancestor, the Duke of Marlborough. Now the men were alone the conversation resumed.

'Yes, like you, I've clashed with the Nazis, only with a little more violence,' replied Sean in response to Churchill's opening gambit. He sat forward in the armchair. 'For different reasons, we now find that we share an enemy, but it does not make us allies. Yes, we can bury our differences, share a drink, reminisce about the past, but I don't trust you. You were one of those politicians who unleashed the Black & Tans upon my country. Many Irishmen and women were shot in cold blood,' though he did not mention his own family, 'I see no reason why we just don't continue to fight the Nazis in our own manner and leave it at that.'

'You believe you can continue to fight the *Narzees* alone, while your other enemies redouble their efforts?' Churchill turned around, stretching his right arm across his mahogany desk to retrieve a large folded piece of paper. 'Yesterday I received this communique.' He passed it to Ryan, and continued, 'The IRA has doubled the bounty on your head.'

Sean did not know that the contract on his head was now two thousand British pounds, but he was not surprised after the loss of two of their men when they tried to garrotte him in a Liverpool dockyard, last month. It was the fourth attempt on his life by the IRA in as many years.

He ignored the piece of paper placed on the table before him, 'I understand why many of my countrymen wish me dead. After all, I was there when the Treaty was signed with the English. The man I was twenty years ago, would have killed the man I am today.'

The Irishman stared into Churchill's eyes. The Englishman held his gaze. Believing he had made his position clear, Sean sat back.

'You hold the naïve arrogance of someone who has never failed. I have had my successes, but I have survived my failures,' responded Churchill, in a clear, powerful voice.

'In my line of work you don't get a second chance to learn from failure: you fail you die.'

'You are a young man who seizes the world by the throat. That means that failure is inevitable. If you survive that failure – and it will happen, as sure as night follows day – I ask this,' edging forward, his voice growing louder, 'will you continue the fight?'

Churchill had responded in a manner that accepted the younger man's declaration of past grievances, but he did so without apology, and he had set down his own marker. He was the man of greater experience; and as

28

with all great men and women who walked on the international stage, he had failed on many an occasion, and it had cost many lives. He blamed himself, and he never shrank from his responsibilities. One of the man's many qualities was to not expunge himself of the memory of these failures, but to learn from them. He was also resilient, he had to be, as his numerous past mistakes were well documented in the history books: the debacle of the Dardanelles when he had to resign as First Lord of the Admiralty; his opposition to Independence for India, or his recent objection to the abdication of Edward VIII, which united the whole House against him. Each time he picked himself up and prepared himself for the next challenge.

'You have rage, and you have channelled it in the same direction as my own.' Churchill finally managed to ignite a match and took his first puff of a cigar that day. He took a smaller note from his waistcoat pocket and deposited it on the table in front of the younger man. 'Together, we can aim your skills to where they are most needed, while striking our enemy hard.'

The Irishman looked at the smaller piece of paper, but he left it lying on the table. The man's inaction could not have delivered a clearer message than if he had shouted and banged his fist on the table. He required more information before he would open the folded note. Churchill was impressed by how the man had foiled his attempts to manipulate him; a skill that he had employed successfully on the world's most able leaders. The Stateman's had met a man who excelled in one of the areas in which he was deficient – patience.

Churchill was enjoying himself. He challenged the

man head on to coax him from his lair.

'John Donne wrote "that no man is an island". Do you think you can provide safe refuge for those who flee the gathering storm?' He paused, providing the Irishman the opportunity to comment. He did not. Churchill continued. 'No man is an island, but Britain is an island and we will fight for the freedom for all who seek sanctuary on our shores. Bring those who are persecuted to our shores, and I promise you that we will protect these women and children. You have my word.'

Sean had no expectation that the British Government would honour the Statesman's word, but Churchill had shown himself to be a man of great integrity in his Treaty negotiations with The Big Fellah.

'What your armies did in Ireland is nothing to what the Nazis will do. I have seen for myself what they are capable of. But unlike Michael,' he sat forward once more, and this time raised his glass in a toast and drained it, 'no matter what the outcome, I'll never drink a Jameson with you and I will never be subordinate to you or any British officer. But your whisky is excellent and I believe you are genuine in what you say. The least I can do is to pay you the courtesy of listening to your plan.'

As Churchill spoke, Sean leant forward to retrieve the folded piece of paper and opened it.

'You and others of your roguish nature, who you may or may not know, are smuggling refugees out of Europe before they fall into the hands of the Nazis,' said Churchill. 'On the note I have given you are the names of a woman and child that require your help. My contacts are of the firm belief that both will be arrested and worse will follow if the Hun or its puppet regimes capture them.'

Now that he knew the objective, Sean needed to mark out his boundaries. Both men were sitting forward, but the game they had played to reach this position was over.

'I'm not interested in smuggling out munitions experts, spies, or potential spies. I will decide the cause I serve and it's not the Empire.' It was time to ask the one question that puzzled him the most, 'Why me? You have your own field operatives, dysfunctional misfits that they are, to do this?'

Churchill cut the younger man short. 'I'm well aware of your views. This is about getting people to freedom. I'm not promoting a covert war, enlisting spies, promoting acts of sabotage or embarking on a programme of assassinations. To do so would only escalate Hitler's advance across Europe, and the reprisals on the local population would be unimaginable.' In a solemn, almost despairing voice he added, 'You know of the horrors the Fascists have committed in Spain.'

Sean took a long swig from his glass, before nodding.

'Now, I know now why you summoned me, here. If you send your own agents, when they are caught, for the idiots would be, it would embroil your government in a very embarrassing diplomatic incidence. Goebbels' propaganda machine would go into overdrive. Any friends you still have in America would not be impressed. It might even lead to war.' Churchill reclined into his armchair, allowing the other man to continue.

'But I'm an Irishman. If I'm captured the hands of the British Government are clean.' Sean shrugged, 'I'm as expendable as yesterday's razor blade.'

'I usually extract two good shaves out of mine,' noted the Englishman as he took a sip of whisky – he never gulped his drinks despite the rumours circulated by his opponents who painted a picture of him, falsely, as a drunk. He picked up his smouldering Havana cigar once more from the ashtray and rolled it delicately between his fingers, respecting the hours of labour that had gone into making it. He allowed the Irishman to run with his train of thought as he was clearly warming to the plan.

'It would also damage any attempts by some politicians in Ireland to negotiate with the Nazis for access to Irish ports,' continued Sean.

'I fear such a deal, and I sense you do too.'

'Ireland is similar to England, in one respect.'

'And that is?'

'Its politicians rarely reflect the values of the people.'

'If I were a young man, I would be off to rattle the cage of the Hun like a shot.'

There was vigour in the Statesman's voice, exposing the former soldier's yearning for adventure had not been diminished by his years.

He slumped back in his armchair and, lowering his voice once more, 'But my battles must now be ones of state.'

Sean had never thought of himself as a young man, even when he was. He was thirty-three and any innocence that he possessed had been stolen long ago, on that wretched night when the British raided his family's home. But he was a young man compared to the man who sat in the armchair opposite, a man who apart from his political achievements had fought with honour in both the Sudan

32

and India. He too once had a price on his head of twenty-five pounds, placed there by the Boers for escaping from one of their prisoner of war camps.

The Statesman may have lost the respect of most of his countrymen, but he had secured that of the Irishman.

Sean lifted his glass to Winston, 'I respect your intentions, but it is in want of a plan. Tell me though, why help this particular woman and her boy?'

'Though I'm out of favour, I still have some contacts. I will not divulge my sources, but their names were passed to me by a contact in the Admiralty.'

'The Admiralty, well that is better than the security services.' Churchill was surprised to hear the man say anything positive about the British services. Sean read the Englishman's questioning look. 'You've a powerful navy – and it's never given me cause to sink it,' exclaimed Sean as he got up from his armchair.

The Irishman never liked to stay in the same place too long. He rose and strode over the window. Though he did not possess his host's love of gardening, he too noticed how the creeping frost was killing everything in the garden. He reread the note in his hand.

With his back to the Englishman he gave his answer. 'I will use a few contacts I have to find out what I can about the woman and if your story rings true. If it does, then I'll decide if I'm the right person to get them out.' He turned sharply. 'If I'm to help them, I'll need papers, money?'

'Agreed.'

'Your contacts can prepare escape plans if they wish, but I'll decide on the best way to get the woman and the boy out.' Churchill nodded. He re-examined the note.

'Three names. Three addresses?'

'The woman, her son and your contact in Budapest. The first address I'm told is the last known address of the family. The second is that of the British Consul in Budapest who will relay messages between you and our contact. The third is the address of a family who have a farmhouse just on the outskirts of the city. They will hide you until your contact has located the woman and the boy.'

'To help families flee the Nazis. That's your only motive, to help this family?'

'Yes. But it's only the start. There are hundreds, maybe thousands more, but if you're captured, there's no point in putting others in even greater risk by giving you any more names. We believe, as I mentioned, that there are other rogues like you causing the Nazis aggravation who may be able to help with others.'

'Makes sense,' and with a smile he added, 'If I'm captured, will you assign one of these dubious characters to get me out?'

'I'm afraid my resources are limited to saving the innocent.'

'Quite right. If my rescue implied that I was innocent, I'd never live with the shame of it.'

The Irishman returned to the table and refilled his tumbler from the bottle. He drained his glass in one swift movement and put the empty vessel back on the antique mahogany table. He looked at the Englishman, refolded the note, and slipped it inside his coat pocket.

'I believe your sentiments are true as you have more to lose than gain by this. But, you're a wily old bugger, and as I say, I'll check out the family.'

34

Churchill nodded, 'If you are the man, I have been led to believe you are, I would expect nothing less.' He rose swiftly, marched over to his writing desk and removed a large brown unmarked envelope from the top drawer. 'I have saved a little income from my writings to aid you.'

Sean took the envelope and without opening it slipped it inside his black leather jacket. The two men were standing facing each other for the first time.

The Irishman spoke first: 'The papers call you a warmonger.'

'They are wrong; I strive to uphold the freedoms of this great nation in the hope it will be an example to all.' He solemnly added, 'But for the foreseeable future we will both have to live our lives based on the *Narzee* threat until we defeat them or die in the attempt.'

'I read that you nearly you nearly lost your seat some while back.'

'I won it by only thirty seats. If I'd lost, it would probably would have removed me permanently from the political stage.'

Though they had agreed on the objective, Churchill was pleased that the Irishman wished to return to the game, as he could unsheathe his ripostes.

'But though I'm not known for my diplomacy, I would find it hard to believe you could muster thirty birthday cards, let alone votes.'

Sean grinned, 'Alas true, but when all is told, you're as much of a rogue as I am.'

Churchill smiled and nodded, 'It doesn't make one a genius to recognise that.'

Neither man offered his hand as they parted.

Churchill ambled over to view the barrenness of his garden from the rain-splattered bay window.

His thoughts were of the arrogant young man who would, it was clear, take on anyone that threatened him. He was pleased that the most recent dossier on him had not exaggerated the threat he possessed. But he needed to see this for himself. If this was the man to take on the challenge, he had to meet him face to face. The enemy was fierce and to stand against them required men like the Irishman, and women, equally so. The lives of those on the list, and those that were in his drawer, depended on it.

The Irishman stepped towards the door, a little clearer on why a car had been sent to his lodgings in Kilburn a few hours earlier summoning him to Chartwell. But thinking he might catch the man off-guard, he turned towards the Englishman, 'Why?'

'Why what?'

'Why are you *really* doing this? You fight battles for the good of Empire, so why help a young woman and her child. There something about them you're not telling me. So you might as well tell me now.'

'I have no knowledge of them other than what I have told you. They are in severe danger, is that not enough reason to help. The Nazis we hear are committing unspeakable acts against Jews, gypsies, Slavs, homosexuals and those who dare question their dominance. God help us, I received a dispatch from one of our agents this morning, that now even the disabled are being persecuted. This is more than nations flexing their muscles; this is an abominable attack on humanity. Caught in the middle of this is a young woman and a little boy?'

Sean had heard the politician speak on the radio with great passion, but this was the first time he had detected anger in the Englishman's voice. The Irishman now knew that he was right to come him. He had attempted to catch him off guard to discover if he really believed in what he disclosed; after all, he was a politician. But the Englishman's passionate response removed any doubts the Irishman had. As he turned the brass doorknob to exit the room, the Statesman called over to him.

'Why did you decide to accept my offer to come to my home today?'

That was the question Sean had been waiting for since he had first entered Churchill's study thirty minutes earlier.

He glanced back, 'It's not often I'm invited to share a good whiskey,' then he paused, as he believed the man deserved a straight answer, 'Years ago, I *was* a young man standing guard behind The Big Fellah when we first met. You were the great politician, but the only one of your number who had fought on the front line, as we had done. In the months before he died Michael referred to you as "friend". After all these years, I guess your invitation aroused my curiosity.' As he opened the door to leave, he said, 'And as my Ma used to say, "The cat can look at the King".'

Churchill thought of his mother, Lady 'Jennie' Randolph Churchill, 'My Mama, too had a saying: "Curiosity killed the cat".'

Churchill stood by the window in his front room, as he watched the Irishman stride past the waiting car swigging from the crystal decanter, he swiped from the sidetable in the hall.

Nodding to himself, as he tried once more to strike one of the long matches against the stone window ledge, he muttered 'My dear mother, it will take more than curiosity to kill this cat.'

Chapter 2: The Battle for Madrid

April 1937, Madrid

'Back off, cowboy!' shouted the Russian who was face-to-face with Jake, the American. They only acknowledged each other when they were on the verge of a fight.

'Try it Vodka and you'll be using your teeth for chess pieces.'

Lenka had had enough of the two of them. 'Jesus, will you two ever stop? Just watch those windows.'

Jewel moved at her usual slow pace and addressed Lenka, 'I don't understand why Major Talbotá is assigning these two to guard me?'

'It's madness to put me and the Neanderthal together,' protested Jake, without looking at the Russian.

The Russian turned to the Australian nurse. 'It's just a cover as I'm really making sure the cowboy doesn't get his head trapped in the gates to the city.'

Jewel smiled at their adolescent banter.

Jake and Vodanski had lost count of their clashes. These encounters had broken out into fights on two occasions. Both times they had been blind drunk; if not, one of them would have been dead by now. They were evenly matched and it would be hard to say who would have won, but it was a common conversation amongst the other units in the International Brigades.

'Lenka's Rogues,' as the other battalions referred to

them, were based in the library of the Banco de España, in the centre of Madrid, on the main drive of Paseo del Prado. The front windows of the building had been blown out by Nationalist mortar shells, and been replaced by rocks, with books stacked behind them to stop any bullets that did get through. Despite the pockmarks of ricocheted bullets, the white stone building was mostly intact, as the city had not been the target of bombing by Germany's Condor Legion. The Republican northern Basque region had borne the brunt of that.

The unit was officially under the command of Major Talbotá and was, in terms of countries of origin, the most diverse of those formed to defend Spain's democratically elected Republican government. Its men and women risked their lives for a multitude of reasons. Some to advance their own revolutionary ideals, others saw Franco's military coup as an attack on democracy itself.

Jake left Manhattan in search of adventure. Lenka left Krakow to defend liberty, as she had spent her whole life fighting abuse and oppression, firstly as a child in an orphanage protecting the other children, and later warding off threats to the same orphanage that she now ran. It was more complicated with Vodanski, but once in Spain, he remained because he was exiled from his own country.

Jake Flynn, whose parents had changed their surname from Frankenberg during the Great War, was over six foot three, with a mane of blond hair and the physique of a swimmer, having a large chest, powerful arms and narrow waist. He had that carefree manner that was unthreatening but masked the steel within. With his farm boy looks and broad grin, he had at school been known as the 'Cowboy', except that he was born in Brooklyn and had never been on a farm in his life. Though he was raised by a loving but poor family of German descent, it was a tough city and it gave him an edge. The edge came from never being sure where the next meal would come from and that once you had it, the fear that someone might try to steal it. Those not from the cities call it cynicism, but it was a mentality based on suspecting the worst, so you were ready for it. Jake had it in abundance.

He enjoyed fighting and with his build and agility, at the age of sixteen he was top of the boxing bill in his local gym. The makeshift posters advertising his next fight put up in local sports halls and bars every Thursday night became collectors' items in college girls' dorms by the Friday. He reached semi-professional as a boxer, but his real skill was with a gun.

His boxing coach had ambitions to be a writer, and he tried to build on the young man's female following by giving him the title 'Single Fare,' a dreadfully jumbled pun based on the fighters blond locks, his bachelor status and the fact that his opponents always got a one-way trip home in an ambulance. The frustrated coach vainly persisted, but every time Jake laid out an opponent, the audience of mainly women just carried on screaming 'Jakey! Jakey!' as they punched their arms into the air.

Jake enjoyed goading the Russian, referring to him as 'the Dancing Bear' or, more usually, the 'Neanderthal', dependent on his mood. Despite being born on opposite sides of the world, and of different cultures, ideologies and upbringing, the men had much in common. Both were tall, powerfully built, independent, anti-authoritarian and loved the thrill of the fight. Though they had never met before arriving in Madrid, both had resided in the brothels of Paris and were regulars in its gambling houses in the weeks before they joined the fight against the fascists. Sharing the same appetites, it was natural that as they first met, when they took up positions on the roof top of Madrid's central Police Quarters to fire down on Nationalist mercenaries, that they despised each other.

Vodanski was slightly taller than Jake, by no more an inch, but it was enough to taunt the American. When anyone was trying to find Jake, he would imply he did not know such a man and then once the person despaired after providing various descriptions, he would finally respond, 'Oh you mean "Tiny".' He was also implying Jake was shorter, and not only in height. Lenka shut them both up one day in the middle of one of their heated exchanges, when she shouted out that neither man 'had anything worth writing home about'. Jewel was dressing a flesh wound on a man's arm at the time and trying not to laugh, but failing, much to the irritation of her patient.

The Russian was broader in the chest and arms. Overall, he was more powerful than the American, but not as nimble. Whereas the American's speed would enable him to avoid an enemy landing a punch, the Russian would pick his ground to fight and hold it. When he could not avoid an enemy's blows, he would absorb them as a bull would a punch – with similar repercussions. Then, when the opportunity to counterattack presented itself, he went for the most vulnerable point, which usually resulted in death. Like many Muscovites, Vodanski had a serious, sometimes solemn, demeanour. No one in Lenka's Rogues had seen or inflicted as much death as he. But his sobriety concealed a very dry sense of humour that took people by surprise.

The younger, less confident, less experienced fighters in the Republican forces were drawn to the Russian. In battle they would tuck themselves in behind him, as if taking refuge behind a granite boulder. Jake would often counter the Russian's iconic status with the young men by declaring, within earshot of Vodanski, that women preferred to take cover under his wing. The sparring was incessant. The Russian bellowed to Jewel, as she stood beside the American, that young women were naturally drawn to 'the biggest girl'. The American also directed his response to the Australian nurse: 'I hear the Neanderthal fantasises about me all the time, but my answer will always be no!'

If the sparring erupted into violence, afterwards both men would be a little embarrassed because the women never lost sight of who the *real* enemy was.

Jewel and Katherine, the other volunteer nurse, only took a break from tending the wounded to scrub blood from the wooden floors or to sterilise equipment with what alcohol the Rogues could secure for them. Lenka, similarly, never lost focus; whether in her role as head chef or preparing for the next enemy attack. She was as proficient with a carving knife as she was with the dagger sheathed in her left boot. To Lenka, fighting personal battles was an indulgence.

A young recruit in the Red Army, Vodanski was a brave and courageous soldier and was known as the 'Hero of Kiev' or the 'Slayer of the Devil of Feston'. But his independent streak was soon brought to the attention of Trotsky's Bolshevik commanders, and he was exiled to a Gulag. When the Spanish Civil War erupted, his superiors thought it would be a good idea to release him only to send him to the front line to fight their Fascist enemies in Spain. The thinking in Moscow was that he would be killed, and his death would be a good recruitment symbol for the international communist cause. After all, it was sending its heroes to die in an anti-Fascist war.

However, Moscow did not want Vodanski's life to be left to fate. He was put under the command of Major Allegro, known as 'Suicidal Al', as no one ever lived long enough to be labelled a veteran under his command. All did not go according to the Bolshevik's plan. Upon the arrival of the Hero of Kiev, Major Allegro ordered Vodanski to launch a full-frontal attack on a heavily fortified Nationalist outpost. The major handed Vodanski a Mauser with a broken firing mechanism and a small, damp, cardboard box, filled with six mouldy bullets. Vodanski looked at the equipment and thought of the three tanks guarding the fortified position. Having weighed up the odds, he launched the major through the first-floor window of Communist headquarters.

After paralysing Suicidal Al he continued his fight against the Fascists alone. Then he met Lenka.

Lenka was five foot six, but with her waif-like frame she seemed smaller. Her matt black, short hair was curled just a little at the end above her collar and when she washed it, it lay where it fell. Once, a foreign journalist for *The Woman's Week* approached her in the lobby of the recently renamed 'The Internationale' and asked her where she had her hair styled. Lenka replied that she was

44

there to fight Fascists, 'not to prance down a fucking catwalk'. The woman gathered up her notebook and pencil and fled to the hotel bar.

A few hours later, the reporter marched up to Lenka, who was negotiating for a case of twelve bottles of Napoleon brandy from an American journalist who had just written a very popular book about the First World War, called *A Farewell to Arms*. The reporter, fortified by a half-litre bottle of Rioja, asked Lenka if she knew that everyone referred to her as 'the Polish Tramp'. The label was probably a reference to the number of lovers Lenka had had, rather than her lack of fashion sense.

If the reporter had any ambitions to strut along the catwalk herself, they were short-lived, as The Polish Tramp knocked her front teeth out. The one-punch fight delighted the large, bearded man Lenka was negotiating with. He pushed the case of brandy towards her, and when he stopped laughing, declared, 'Dear Lenka, the Molotovs are on me.'

The Rogues joined forces not because they were the best fighters in the Republican battalions – though they were – but because they had been thrown out of every other unit. Jake had been kicked out of the Abraham Lincoln Brigade for insubordination. Vodanski from every Communist battalion for confining his commander to a wheelchair for life. While Lenka had to form her own unit after kicking a Republican colonel in the groin within two hours of arriving in Madrid.

The relationship between the American and the Russian was akin to the ends of two magnetic iron bars of the same polarity forced together by a greater force – it was the respect they had for Lenka that overcame their mutual hostility and made them a formidable force.

Late one February night in 1937, someone started banging on the door that led to the library of the Banco de España. Lenka opened the door, her revolver cocked in her hand. Though it was dark, she could see a tall blonde nurse holding up an injured woman. The Nationalists had tried various ruses to infiltrate the building before. But she lowered her weapon when she saw the pain on the injured woman's face. She helped the nurse, whose white linen scarf and nursing apron was drenched in blood, carry the semi-unconscious woman to a camp bed in the centre of the room. With such a serious wound, Lenka did not understand why the nurse's pace was so slow.

Having gently lowered the patient, the nurse began to fill a bowl with hot water at the kitchen sink. The left side of her face was severely burnt and by the look of her scars, Lenka knew her injuries had occurred some time ago. Her left arm and hand were withered. She dragged her left foot behind her as she walked, as it was turned inwards and at a forty-five-degree angle to the other.

Together, Lenk and the nurse bathed the woman's wounds. Afterwards, the blonde woman held her hand and constantly reassured her patient until she fell into a deep sleep three hours later.

'I'm Jewel,' said the nurse, now that Lenka was preparing food for them. 'Thank you for your help. I found the poor woman lying in the street on Gran Via.'

She kept left side of her face hidden when she

46

spoke. She explored the large lobby as her patient slept. 'So his must be where Lenka's Rogues are based?'

The Polish woman looked at her and smiled, then said, 'Yes, I'm Lenka.'

'My God, you're Lenka! The leader.'

'No, that's Captain Talbotá.'

Jewel raised her eyebrows, as if she knew better.

Lenka continued, 'Are you from the general hospital?'

'No, I work in a little makeshift hospital we just set up with Katherine, another volunteer nurse, in the gardens of the Campo de Moro a mile away. We don't have a permanent base; we go wherever the fighting is fiercest and help where we can.'

'Why there?'

'Everyone is now being pushed back into the city, so we followed and set up our hospital in the gardens, as we didn't know where else to go.'

'You're vulnerable to attacks from all sides, there. Best you set up your medical unit here, we'll protect you while you work.'

'That's very kind of you, but we need to be near the fighting.'

'Well, we will need your help too, as we suffer more injuries than any other unit. Even when there is a lull in the fighting in the city, we'll keep you busy.'

'Please don't be offended, but though Katherine and I will help anyone, we are here for the civilians.'

'We'll bring the injured here.'

The Australian looked at the injured woman sleeping soundly now that the injection of morphine had taken control of her body.

'I won't say no, as I think our patient will need care for a while.'

Lenka nodded and smiled at Jewel. The nurse quickly turned the left side of her face away. The Rogues leader was never one to hide her emotions. She stormed over, grabbed the nurse and hugged her. Lenka lived by her instincts and after watching the Australian tend her patient, she knew she was a good person.

Jewel was shocked. The only physical contact she had was when she treated a patient, or when Katherine applied antiseptic to cracks formed on her scar tissue that she could not reach. The pain that surged through her body from Lenka's unexpected embrace was easier to deal with than the bewilderment that she now felt. No one had held her like this since her brother, but even this did not prepare her for the greater surprise that followed. The small dark-haired woman released her, then cupped her jaw in her hands.

'Everyone here looks each other in the face, so no more of this nonsense.'

Only when Jewel looked like she understood the rule, did Lenka drop her hands from the nurse's face.

Upon being released, Jewel's instant reaction was to turn her head away, but she fought against it and looked at Lenka.

'I'm not used to people looking at me and smiling.'

'Well get used to it,' she said, and with that Lenka grabbed a blanket and draped it over the injured woman, who was now sleeping peacefully.

Within weeks, Jewel and Katherine had transformed the Rogues' headquarters into the best field hospital in

Madrid. It was also the best equipped. When the Rogues went into combat, Katherine had made it clear that they had to secure any medicines they could find.

'My priority is to come back alive,' pronounced Jake, who revelled in challenging the Scottish nurse.

'I don't want anything to happen to you, either,' replied Katherine.

'Really, so you don't hate me after all?' exclaimed the American, making sure that Vodanski, who was nearby, could hear.

The Russian was helping Jewel turn a patient over. Jewel looked up at Vodanski and whispered, 'There is a very thin line between love and hate.'

The Russian replied, 'I almost feel sorry for him. She'll eat him without salt.'

Katherine feigned a puzzled expression, 'Hate. Why should I hate someone that I barely notice? I need you alive, so you can carry the medicine back. You're no good to me with your brains blown out.'

Jake did not look over at Vodanski, but he heard him bellow, 'I was wrong. She applies the salt to the open wound first and only when he is writhing in pain, does she eat him. Once she has spat out the remains of the Cowboy, I will offer myself for sacrifice.'

Jewel tried not to laugh as Vodanski playfully held his sides and forced out a hearty laugh, rousing one patient from of a two-day coma.

In their confined living quarters, soon the Rogues saw the full extent of the Australian nurse's injuries. Occasionally, one of them would catch sight of Jewel's semi-naked body in the moonlight, as she would slowly wash herself, believing that all were asleep. When they did, it was just another reminder; amongst the many they saw every day, that life was cruel and impartial in its brutality.

Two-thirds of her body has suffered horrific burns. In some places, particularly her rib cage and upper left femur, the skin was so thin it was like gossamer stretched over the bone. She never told anyone what had caused her burns, even Lenka, but it was clear to those who seen burns on that scale, that she had not received treatment at the time of her injuries.

Jewel averted her eyes when she encountered looks of revulsion exhibited by the ignorant and those of disgust by the cruel. But what caused her the greatest pain were the looks of pity, and the chorus of sighs, that followed her throughout her life. They noted her damaged shell but failed to see the young woman inside. But with the Rogues, she never felt pitied. In fact, for the first time since the death of her brother, and apart from her friendship with Katherine, she found people who did not shrink away from her scars. They cried, laughed, talked of major events and insignificant things. She felt she belonged – she even felt loved.

Jewel and her brother, Michael, had been brought to Spain by their Aunt, ten years earlier, after the death of their parents. They grew to love the country, but they never expected to die for it – a Nationalist firing squad executed Michael on the day the civil war erupted.

She had trained as a nurse and was helping the causalities on the Republican side until that day when Lenka answered the door.

Jake or Vodanski were always close by to help her

and Katherine lift a patient, especially in the sweltering heat of the summer, to ensure they did not develop bedsores, or for a wound to be treated. The two men fought each other every waking moment; she wished they did not fight, but she took a guilty pleasure from their verbal sparring. Sometimes, when the two men were going head to head hurling abuse at each other, she would release a loud unrestrained laugh that would extinguish their rage.

The Australian nurse was happy within the confines of the Rogues, but she hated the war and the suffering she witnessed every day. Particularly, the bewildered look of the injured children who had no comprehension of why anyone wanted to kill them.

Now, she and Katherine had to witness the suffering of the innocent on a far greater scale as the Fascists tightened their stranglehold on the city. Civilians had no defence against the aerial bombardments that was now daily. When the bombers departed, the snipers would appear, positioned on the rooftops of the city. They waited silently for a stumbling target to appear from the debris. Then the sniper would breathe out (to relax their body), before pulling the trigger. Then breathe in again, once the target dropped lifelessly onto the rubble.

Jewel and Katherine would appear amid the street-to-street fighting to tend the wounded, sometimes even the enemy when they came across one of them. One Russian officer found Jewel cradling a wounded Nationalist soldier. The officer threatened to shoot her unless she stepped aside so he could kill the man. Jewel refused. Vodanski appeared, spun the Russian officer around, delivered a knee to his groin, along with a left and right hook to jaw before he hit the ground. When the Russian officer later regained consciousness in the hospital, Jewel was piecing his nose together.

It was not that incident that made the major decide to assign his two best men to her side, but the attempt on her life when six crack troops from Franco's best legion tried to storm the Banco de España. Jake, and Clara, a new addition to the group from Frankfurt, opened fire on them as they zig-zagged across the main street to reach the oak door of the Rogues' hospital. Vodanski searched their bodies. He found a newspaper clipping containing a picture of Jewel tending a man lying on a street, on each of them. The photo had been taken, perhaps intentionally, from her right side.

Intrigued, Vodanski went in search of the commander of the assault force, who had abandoned his men in the gun battle. The Russian discovered him in a café underneath the Rialto, a cinema on the Plaza del Callao. Their encounter was brief. Vodanski thrust his knife up under the lieutenant's jaw into his brain. He discovered an envelope in the dead man's tunic. Inside was a letter from the Nationalist headquarters in Burgos, ordering the assassination of the woman in the newspaper clipping. Unwittingly, Jewel had secured sympathetic international press for the Republican cause. It has been decided by one of Franco's senior officers that she must die.

Vodanski returned to the hospital and told the Rogues the grave news. Major Talbotá – who Jake referred to as Major Bloater – said that the Australian nurse 'had to be protected at all costs'. The major, a pragmatist, believed that the Rogues' morale, already low after nearly two years of fighting, would not recover from Jewel's death – for once he was right.

The major ordered that Jake and Vodanski be assigned to Jewel as her permanent bodyguards. Both men could see the sense in the major's orders and for once they decided to carry them out. Jewel was not as accommodating. When she was told that an assassination squad had been sent to kill her, she carried on ministering to a young man she had tended since his legs had been blown off three days earlier.

'Are you sure all the men are dead?' was all she asked.'

The last few weeks had seen the two nurses working around the clock in shifts as the Germans had launched an aerial bombardment of the city. The field hospital was full, as Jewel and Katherine tended twenty or more men and women and two children who were packed into the lobby and on the floor of the kitchen. If her two friends wanted to follow her around that was fine, and she thanked Jake and Vodanski for their concern, but she was not going to change her routine or her number one priority, the health of her patients.

A week later, Chris arrived. 'Where do I put my rucksack?' he asked as he entered the Rogues' hospital.

'Use it to start building a wall between those two idiots,' replied Lenka, nodding her head towards Jake and Vodanski, who were arguing again. Chris saw the two men squaring up to each other and thought they were arguing over politics, as he picked up references to *Das Kapital,* and *The Bible,* in between the profanities. But neither man had an interest in politics. Their argument was over which books up on the library's shelves would make the best firewood that night, as it was expected to be bitterly cold.

'Welcome. You must be the Scotsman that headquarters told us was coming.'

'Please, call me Chris.'

'I'm Lenka. I believe you're trying to find your sister. We will help you, but in this unit you do exactly what I tell you until we have a new commander-in-chief, as our leader Major Talbotá has shipped back home,' and she went back to cleaning and reassembling her rifle, which she did before and after each skirmish.

Lenka was officially in charge, since a four-inch enemy mortar landed on the toilet at the back of the telecommunications building with Major Talbotá still inside it. Incredibly, he survived, but now he was sitting on a toilet without a door. A sniper shot off a large piece of the inside of his thigh along with his testicles. Jake told Chris that the major often took up a 'defensive rear guard action,' when the enemy launched an attack on the front of the building.

'She was always in charge, Talbotá was just her glove puppet,' added the American.

He returned to his argument with the Russian. Finally, each came to the view that the best thing to put on the fire would be the man standing opposite.

Later, while Lenka was making dinner on the stove in the corner, while the others laid a tablecloth on the floor, and sat down.

Chris thought that as the new recruit he should start the conversation, 'Lenka is quite a woman, fighting, cooking . . .'

'Great lover, too,' interrupted Jake.

'Sadly, she is not always attracted to gentlemen and has found herself in the beds of unclothed American pigs,' added Vodanski.

In her absence, Jewel jumped to the defence of her friend's honour. 'She told me, that each of you was a major disappointment to her.' She smiled at the horrified reaction on both men's faces. 'To make up for your shortcomings, you boys must really learn to cook,' as Lenka had banned them both from the kitchen.

Lenka sat down and filled her plate with Polish stew, a recipe from her friend, the remarkable Olen, her 'able assistant' who was looking after the children in the orphanage in Krakow. 'What have I missed?' she asked.

'Very little,' said Chris.

Although the Scotsman had not meant it in a derogatory way, the other men grunted. Jewel's laughed so hard that soon all those sitting around the pot of excellent stew, including the Jake and the Vodanski, joined her. Chris smiled, having realised what he said.

'Are you all drunk?' asked Lenka.

She was even more bewildered when Jewel put her arm around her shoulder and said, 'Just ignore us.'

That night, over a fine bottle of Napoleon brandy, Jake continued to educate Chris about the Rogues.

'You'll never get used to it. Lenka's been ordering me about for a year. She's even pussy-whipped this ugly old bear here,' pointing his thumb at the Russian without looking at him.

'Fucking Pole, I love her though, as she kicks the Yank like a flatulent dog,' interjected the Russian.

Lenka could hear them well enough and decided to ignore them as usual unless the exchanges reached the point where they about to kill each other.

After dinner Jewel turned to Chris and said, 'I'll make some tea. Would you like some?'

'Yes, please,' he said, as he held her gaze and smiled. New recruits to the Rogues either looked away or stared like idiots at her scars. The Scotsman not only looked at her like Lenka, Jake, Katherine and Vodanski, but there was a warmth to it that surprise her.

Jewel thought she was imagining things and returned to asking the man about his search. 'All we were told was that you are looking for your sister. We have no description of her. We don't even know her name.'

The Scotsman heard a familiar voice as Katherine entered the room. She had not been there when her fellow countryman arrived, as she was in a nearby church, applying fresh dressings to a priest who had been shot by the Communists while trying to say Mass. The Scotsman turned to look at the blonde-haired young woman standing in the doorway.

She smiled and spoke first: 'It's Katherine', before racing towards him, leaping into the air and landing in her startled brother's arms.

Chris Kildare was a tall and muscular, similar to Vodanski, with the same short clipped jet-black hair. But he was a quiet, unassuming man, who over the following months joined the others in supporting the two nurses as they attended the injured. What struck the others about the Scotsman, as they watched him help Jewel and Katherine, was his awareness of his immense strength.

The nurses were appreciative of Jake and Vodanski's assistance in the make-shift hospital. However, Katherine was scathing of Jake's help at times, as he and Vodanski, being such powerful men, sometimes lacked delicacy. One day Katherine rounded on Jake and pushed him out of the way, just as he had finally decided that the best way to lift a man who had had all his limbs blown off, was by his head.

'Dear God! It's like watching a gorilla in wearing oven-gloves try to change a nappy.'

With Katherine tending his wounds, the patient's horrified expression turned to one of immense relief. Later that week, before the wounded man was put on the next ambulance to France for further medical treatment, he thanked the Scotswoman profusely, while swearing loudly at the American at every opportunity.

Apart from his considerate approach, Chris was also able to read a pained face and know exactly where to position his hands to ensure that he caused the minimum of distress. Even when he shook someone's hand, he would do so as if gathering up a child's, as if conscious that he could easily break your fingers. No one was accepted so readily by the Rogues, who were not known as the most welcoming of people.

Vodanski crashed through the plaster wall of the Metropolis Building on the southern tip of the junction of Gran Via, with his pan-sized hands around the throat of a Moroccan mercenary.

'Great, I'm pissing around for two hours edging my way around corners to get here, but the Neanderthal comes through the fucking wall.' muttered Jake.

'All image, typical American,' replied the Russian, but addressing Chris directly as he lifted himself off the dead mercenary.

As with Lenka and Jewel, Chris had become part of the third-party conversations that the other two men would engage in. Lenka found their schoolboy behaviour ridiculous, but Chris would mimic the exchanges with Jewel as they found the verbal sparring between the two men hilarious. The Australian nurse would laugh so much that sometimes she would rest her head on his shoulder. He bathed in her wondrous scent, and the silken caress of her hair.

Lenka looked at the hole in the wall and the towering Russian who made it, then commented, 'Make sure he's dead.'

Vodanski stamped his boot onto the mercenary's face.

'Do you want me to check his pulse?' asked the Russian, with his size 13 Soviet-issued army boot embedded in the mercenary's skull.

Jake wrenched the gun from the dead man's hand, 'This is the latest model. A Mauser Karabiner 98k. The Germans are upgrading their shipments. He must have been good to be given one of these. Do you think he was the one who shot the nuts off Major Talbotá?'

'Maybe I should have thanked him,' sighed Vodanski, glancing down at the corpse and feigning a look of regret.

Lenka glared at Vodanski, raised her gun and fired it, removing part of his right earlobe. The Russian threw himself to the side, grabbing the knife from his boot when he landed. Then he heard gunfire, followed by the sound of breaking glass and the cry of someone behind him. He turned just in time to glimpse the man falling from the window directly opposite.

The Polish fighter lowered her rifle, and left the three men to investigate the next room.

'I wish I had bought her that machine gun for Christmas,' huffed the American, shaking his head.

'Fucking Pole,' shouted the Russian, trying to stem the blood gushing from his ear as he scanned the floor for his ear lobe. Later, he guessed that it was likely to be embedded in the head of the bullet fired from Lenka's gun, which was now in the neck of the sniper lying dead on the street below.

Screeching pulleys signalled the lift's ascent.

'Take your positions. I think we have guests,' shouted Jake.

The three men took cover and aimed their rifles at the concertina gates to the lift-shaft. When the lift got to their floor, the third, it contained a wooden box. Lenka returned and raced towards the lift. She threw the metal gates open. In the wooden crate were two sticks of dynamite, each with a short fuse now alight. She could see beneath them were German 'thrower' grenades, because each had a handle that enabled it to be directed with greater accuracy than the standard issue egg-shaped type.

Lenka grabbed the dynamite, lifted the knife from her boot and swiftly lopped off the smouldering fuses.

'God, you're a woman and a half. I'll find a priest and we'll be wed before you can say Van Gogh,' declared Jake, not missing the opportunity to mock the Russian.

Vodanski was still cursing about his ear, but he

refused to acknowledge the American's jibe. He marched over to the open lift, grabbed one of the throwers and tied one end of the circle of rope draped over his shoulder around its long steel handle.

'About forty-five feet,' shouted Jake, and the Russian measured the rope by winding it around the base of his arm and his shoulder, estimating each loop as four feet. An average-sized man would have measured three.

The Russian threw the rope, now tied to the grenade, out of the open window facing the street. Without waiting for it to go taut and then swing back towards the window on the ground floor, they all ran towards the rear wall, but away from the lift-shaft. They threw themselves on the floor and grabbed hold of a water pipe running along the skirting board. Chris was confused, but he had learnt never to question their actions during the fighting. He followed their movements without hesitation when one of their plans, as now, was underway. When the explosion came, pieces of white alabaster and dust rained down on them. The three longest-serving Rogues scramble up and raced to the lift. Chris followed. They knew that any member of the attack party below that had not been killed would try to move away from the source of the explosion, driving them towards the lift shaft.

'Return to sender,' shouted Jake, as he relit the fuse on the dynamite and threw it back on top of the box of throwers. The Rogues machine-gunned the steel cables that holding the lift, sending it hurtling down the shaft.

The explosion blew out the front wall of the ground floor of the building. The first and second floors collapsed.

Lenka was the first one to abseil down the lift-shaft on Vodanski's rope. When she landed, she immediately adopted a crouched position, scanning the room, rifle at the ready, searching for signs of movement. There was none, not even the usual reflex movement of a body in the last throes of life or the death rattle, which she had heard most nights in the hospital. She stood up and surveyed the devastation. There were about fifteen bodies, maybe more, as it was hard to tell from what she could see amongst the rubble. Heads and limbs were strewn everywhere, some embedded in the remaining side walls or hanging by muscle fibres and flaps of skin from the broken beams. They had not stood a chance. They were attacked from the front by the grenade, then from the back as the lift loaded with explosives exploded. Finally, if anyone was still left alive, they would have been crushed when the two floors collapsed on top of them. Chris was the last to abseil down the lift-shaft. As he did so, it struck him, and not for the first time in his three months fighting alongside Lenka, Jake and Vodanski, that he was part of the deadliest combat unit in Spain.

The Battle for Madrid had been raging for two-and-a-half years. Franco's goal was to take the capital, but in that time the Nationalists had made little progress. But as the leaves turned brown on the apple trees in 1938, the Fascists were making gains. This was not only because of the superior firepower offered by Germany and Italy to the Nationalists, giving them command of the air, but also because the Moscow-led Communists were purging the Republican army of all those who did not adhere to the pro-Stalinist line.

As the Nazis had done in 1934, those they thought disloyal were rounded up and shot. These ruthless purges not only deprived the Republican forces of their most experienced and committed fighters, but their brutality matched that of Franco's army. Now, civilian support for the Republic fell away, as there seemed little difference between the two opposing forces.

The International Brigades' had been disbanded. The war was raging on all fronts, and though Lenka's Rogues remained focused on defeating the Fascists, it was clear that the Republican forces had lost.

Jake still had contacts with the Abraham Lincoln Brigade, especially those who were like him, adventurers, sharing a romantic dream of fighting evil and living life akin to the heroes in the novels of the modern author Ernest Hemingway. But he was one of the last remaining American fighters, as most of his former unit were either dead or had become disillusioned and returned home.

The initial rumours when Vodanski first joined the Rogues, that he had been sent to spy on the Rogues, were proven unfounded. In his two years with them, he had never mixed with the Communists and recently they had issued an arrest warrant for him, after he had broken both arms of one soldier who marched up to him and waved *Das Kapital* in his face, and denounced him as a traitor. No one had attempted to serve the warrant. Jewel held no politics that anyone knew of and had never been heard to make a single partisan comment against Franco's armies, even after they had executed her younger brother.

The fighting drew closer. Nationalist snipers had taken control of the Telefónica on Gran Vía. They christened it the 'Hawk's Nest', because for the first time their snipers had an unhindered view of the great oak doors of the Rogue's headquarters.

Even the predatory Lewis gun, which for two years had stood outside the Telefónica pointing away from the city, was now trained on the Banco de España. In the heat of battle, a soldier would often need to urinate on the gun to prevent it overheating and jamming. Rumour had it that German military advisors were now the suppliers of the makeshift cooling system – and that someone had scrawled '*LENKA*' on the gun's casing.

Unfortunately for the Nationalist snipers, the Telefónica was Jake's favourite building in Madrid. Its modern design reminded him of Manhattan, and he made it his personal mission to save this pseudo bastion of American influence. Throughout the first day of the Nationalists occupation of the Hawk's Nest, the finest marksman in Madrid trained his Remington rifle on anything that moved. The Fascist occupation lasted less than a day. That evening the occupiers' nerves finally unravelled when their commander received a bullet to the temple during his speech declaring that Madrid would fall by nightfall.

It was a hollow victory, as all Republican victories were now. But to celebrate, and therefore claim the success of retaking the building, the Communists blasted out revolutionary marching tunes over the tannoys positioned on the Gran Vía. Jake seized the Lewis gun and riddled the loudspeakers, bringing the recording from the last annual parade in Red Square to an end. Vodanski shook his head, muttering, 'Philistine!'

The following day, a rotund little man wearing an ill-fitting lieutenant's uniform, with a peaked cap two sizes too large for his head, and two troopers, even smaller in height, arrived at the door of the hospital with a note for the leader of the Rogues. Jake took the note and turned and handed it to Lenka. 'They must think you're Snow White.'

It was from Russian headquarters, stating that the Nationalists had launched a major offensive on a village called Guernica in the North. As with all information from Communist headquarters, it told the recipient little, only that the unit was to proceed with haste through enemy lines and head north. There was no information on what kind of attack had taken place, how many were dead, or even what was to be done once they reached the town. The stories that circulated around the city were usually Soviet propaganda, and Lenka was no longer taking orders from the Communists. But something troubled her about the message. The little fishing town of Guernica held no strategic importance to either side.

Lenka decided that they needed to know the extent of the attack and see if this was the beginning of the final Nationalist push that they had been threatening for so long. She asked (which was the same as an order) Jake and Vodanski to go north to investigate and, if it were true, to help, any way they could.

'I'll go on my own,' replied Jake's.

'No, the transport I have in mind can accommodate two and you might need all the firepower we can put together when you get there. You two idiots are the best fighters we have.'

'You will keep Jewel in the infirmary?' asked Vodanski.

'Yes, Chris will watch over her.'

Chris nodded, and everyone knew that with the Scotsman there, Jewel might as well have a wall built around her.

The diminutive lieutenant was far from satisfied that the orders he had given them were the subject for debate. 'You all go now!' screamed the officer at Lenka.

Lenka stood eye to eye with the officer. 'We don't take orders from anyone, particularly a bunch of robots who want us dead, but are too scared to do it themselves.'

Jake stepped forward and glared down at the lieutenant. 'Fuck off, Grumpy.'

'What did he say?' demanded the lieutenant addressing Vodanski directly, as he could speak Polish but no English.

The two soldiers behind the little lieutenant moved their hands towards their Fedorov automatic rifles.

'Fuck off, Grumpy,' growled Vodanski in their native language, as he squared up to the soldiers whose faces were now on a level with his chest.

The lieutenant and the two soldiers retreated through the door and hastily made their way up the street.

Jake turned to Lenka. 'What do you think, a ploy to lure us out of here and slaughter us?'

'Why bother? With the Nationalist blockade thrown around the city, they'll cut us down sooner or later.' She paused, before adding, 'But we need to know if this is the big push?'

'I'll go alone, I don't need a clown for entertainment,' declared the Russian, being the first to take the opportunity to start a new argument.

Lenka looked at both men, and said, 'We have no idea what you will face, so this requires brute force and ignorance in abundance.'

'Okay. Ignorance can come, but tell him not to get in my way,' exclaimed the Russian who, without looking at the American, picked up his rifle, collected his backpack and strode out of the room.

'Take one last look at his ears, as they will be symmetrical when you next see him,' countered Jake.

He collected his Remington, knapsack and the blue-coloured bandana that he always wore around his neck, the one his younger sister, Stacy, gave him as a going-away present. Then he saw the other red one beneath it, a present from his eldest brother when he bought his first motorbike and picked that up too. He ambled towards Katherine, wearing a broad smile. She returned his smile, but it failed to disguise how worried she was.

Fleeting lovers meant nothing to Lenka, but the two men were from her unit were more than that, they were friends. She raced out after them and grabbed them both by the arms.

'Morons, I have a way to get you past the cordon.'

'Well, as you put it so kindly, lead the way,' replied Jake.

She led them along the main avenue up to a small park, the Plaza de Isabel, and into what appeared to be a hangar at the back of the Teatro Real, the city's dilapidated opera house. The men were intrigued but said nothing.

Inside was a huge object, the size of a pick-up truck, hidden under a mouldy green canvas. The two men stood apprehensively on either side of Lenka's well-kept secret.

Lenka pulled the canvas sheet away, unveiling what had been hidden underneath since before the war, and waited for the inevitable protestations.

'Fuck . . . that!' exclaimed Jake, emphasising each word slowly and with great deliberation.

Vodanski's raised eyebrows expressed his thoughts. In front of them stood a dull yellow-coloured cylindrical metal body with what appeared to be a gigantic propeller screwed on top. It had a tail with a smaller propeller on the end that looked like it was made from a metal dustbin lid.

'OK, you win. What is it?' asked Jake.

'It's called a helicopter, and it's going to fly the two of you out over the Nationalist forces.'

'Like fuck it is!' cried Jake, but this time his reaction was neither slow nor deliberate.

The Russian never agreed with anything the American said, but it was clear he too was far from excited by Lenka's plan.

Jake had far more to say on the subject as he paced around the object. 'Actually, I have seen something like this before.'

Lenka waited for the sarcastic remark.

'It was stuck between an elephant and a spaceship, with kids sitting on it. A carousel we called it, only it moved.'

Both men examined it as if it were a ticking bomb. They had to bend down so as not to knock their heads on the overhanging, limp rotors as they opened the cockpit doors. After wiping away the cobwebs and dust with their hands, they inspected it, trying to determine what, if anything, held it together. Through the holes in the almost transparent canvas that formed the body of the machine, they could see a combination of welded steel pipes and plates bolted over the joints. It did indeed look like the first prototype of what would at some later stage be a helicopter. But that stage was a long way off.

'If my nephews . . . played with it in the garden, I'd give it . . . five minutes, max,' commented Jake, who was laughing heartily – a common reaction in those suffering from nervous tension.

'A man called Federico Cantero Villamil built it,' interjected Lenka. 'It's called the Libelula Española.'

'Where is he, now? I want to ask him what drugs he's on?'

'They say he fled Madrid.'

'This must have been just after he stood back for the first time and saw what he created,' noted Jake.

'They say that *if* the engine works . . .' replied Lenka, who at this point betrayed her own doubts.

'If? If? If my auntie had bollocks, she'd be my uncle!' snapped Jake.

Lenka pressed on, but Vodanski's silence was as discouraging as the American's tirade. 'They say . . .'

'Are these the same people who say the world is flat, and the moon is made of cheese?' interjected the American once more.

Vodanski played with the little side door of the yellow cabin, before it came off in his hand. He spoke, but without emotion, to undermine the American.

'We can't afford to waste good men on this, but after all these years we have finally found a use for the cowboy.'

Jake pulled a large rusted metal flake off the door on his side. 'The only way this would get in the air is if you launched it off a cliff.'

'Look! It's the only way to get you both out of Madrid,' said Lenka, half-heartedly.

'Both? Where's the cowboy going to sit, on my lap?' asked the Russian, whose calm demeanour collapsed. 'I didn't get that fucking close with my wife.'

'Sensible woman, probably saving herself until she finds a man,' replied Jake.

'Then the bravest one of you should go!' barked.

'That will be me then,' said Vodanski, who would do anything to rile the other man, even if it killed him — and he had no doubt that this would.

'Lenka, you can manipulate this idiot here with your crude psychology, but there is no way I'm getting into that death-trap with a one-eared Harpo Marx at the controls.'

Lenka had spent her life manipulating men, so with one down, she was not going to give up on the other.

'Well, it's a shame then that we don't have a marksman to finally take on the Condor Legion for a change. They won't be expecting you.'

'Neither will St Peter, when we turn up at the Pearly Gates, five minutes later,' added Jake. He threw his hands up in the air and said, 'Ah, fuck it! It will be worth it just to see the surprise on their faces, before spreading me over a ten-mile radius.'

Jake and Vodanski were fearless. Lenka never had any doubt that both men would at least try to fly it, just as they would never baulk when it came to a fight with the Fascists. The greatest challenge as always was getting them to work together. Fortunately, Lenka knew how, but she wished she had failed as she too doubted their chances of getting airborne, let alone reaching the northern coast.

Dawn the next morning, the two men squeezed themselves into the rickety flying machine. The cockpit was so small that both men found that they had to lean towards each other to close the doors. Lenka was joined by Jewel, Chris and Katherine, who were sure the flying machine would never leave the ground, were trying not to laugh. Lenka tried to fasten them into their seatbelts, but they came away in her hands.

'Maybe you could put an arm around each other?' she added, while trying to suppress a rare laugh.

Neither man smiled nor uttered a word. They just glared at her through the concave windshield with the tops of their heads almost touching.

The Russian had the handwritten flying manual on his lap. Jake turned to Lenka. 'I bet Van Gogh was reading it all night?'

'I just found this under the seat,' shouted out the Russian in Lenka's direction.

'Shit!' muttered Jake, who tucked his head down to try and look out the window.

Then, after the eighteenth attempt, the Russian kicked the helicopter's four-stroke engine into life. It sounded like the generator they had back in headquarters, which did not bode well as it conked out every ten minutes. A side door came away from its hinges, taking any confidence that the passengers and observers still had along with it. As Lenka watched, Chris reattached the door. She now held the view that the men had more of a chance of breaking through the forty-thousand-man cordon if they pole-vaulted it.

The helicopter shot forward, bouncing across the

dirt floor of the barn on its skids, like an overfed, waddling goose making a dash for freedom. Lenka, Jewel, Katherine and Chris dived in all directions, as the helicopter's rotating blades chipped off large wooden chunks from the edges of both doors. The resulting noise of the building doors collapsing and the whining of the rotating blades brought cries from residents of nearby houses. Either that or it was the screams of both men inside what Jake referred to as 'The Flying Yellow Casket,' as they flew north towards the sun.

'The Flying Yellow Casket' soon encountered a swooping Heinkel 52 fighter, keen to explore it. Unfortunately for its pilot, neither he nor the ground crew had not checked that the plane's gun magazine was loaded – after all, it was only a reconnaissance flight. When the pilot flew up close, too late, he realised his mistake. The third bullet fired from Jake's Remington hit the plane's fuel tank. The Luftwaffe's ambivalent attitude that morning resulted in one failed test flight, one less plane and one less pilot.

Jake mused that if there was an afterlife, the Heinkel's fate might have brought some solace to the rifle's first owner. He had bought the rifle in a pawn shop in Paris. The shop owner told him an elderly American had brought it in and confessed he had taken it from the hands of a fellow US infantryman in 1918. Scribbled on a note tied around the butt were the words, 'I'm sorry, but I need the money. This was my best friend's rifle. He suffered an excruciating death because of a German gas attack. Forgive me.' There was no signature. Jake lost the note, but he did not need it to remind him of its words.

Without fuel after eight hours flying, 'The Flying

Yellow Casket' landed, or rather collapsed, in a field outside Bilbao. Vodanski had quickly grown to love the thrill of flying the machine, in addition to scaring the life out of his passenger. In its final moments, he managed to control it, so he could rest it on a clear patch of ground. Upon touching down, the supports of both skids came straight through the helicopter's rusty-red metal floor.

By foot, horse cart and even sitting together on a stray donkey, they reached the small fishing town of Guernica. Before they reached the outskirts of the town, they already had confirmation from many locals that the *Luftwaffe's* Condor Legion had bombarded it. When the two men entered the town, the carnage they saw stayed with them for the rest of their lives.

Everything that was not moving was coated with white dust, except for fragments of blackened charcoal where fires had continued to smoulder. The scene of flattened homes and schools was devoid of colour, only broken up by the rare strand of blue sky reflected in the waters released from shattered water pipes.

Though it had been a week since the attack, people were staggering past Jake and Vodanski, as if in a trance, carrying the dead. Others cried, and some stood silent, unable to comprehend the savage destruction of their town and its inhabitants. There were still body parts littered around. It was impossible to know how many bodies there were, as many had been ripped apart by the explosions. Stray dogs attempted to gnaw remnants of flesh from bones, before being scattered by children throwing stones at them, trying to salvage some dignity for what remained of family and friends.

Both men had witnessed death, but this was on an

72

unprecedented scale. It was as if some celestial power had decided to obliterate the little town and any memory of those who lived there. The American and the Russian knew they were witnesses to a new level of war; except it was not a war, but the indiscriminate destruction of an entire populace and with not a single casualty incurred by the enemy.

Without a word, both men laid their weapons and knapsacks on the ground. Jake took the bandanas from his bag and passed one to Vodanski without looking at him. They tied them over their mouths, as the stench of burnt and decaying flesh was overpowering in the sweltering sun. They joined the other survivors and villagers from nearby towns and dug through the debris of a house where women and children had huddled together in their last moments and began the horrifying process of trying to prise their bodies apart. They worked alongside men and women equipped only with shovels, pickaxes and their frayed hands bloodied after a week of clawing at the earth. They knew they were not part of a salvage operation but a burial party.

That night Jake and Vodanski sat by a fire, built from wood they had collected from the forest; there was nothing left to burn in the town. The Russian stared into the flames.

'Dante didn't have to write about hell on earth, we are in it,' as he passed the one of the rats he was roasting in the flames to the American.

Jake tore a piece from it. Their differences remained, but for now they knew who the *real* enemy was.

Guernica was the first example of the carpet bombing of civilians. The Germans called it *Blitzkrieg* – lightning war. In Berlin, it was hailed as a tremendous success, with over a thousand civilians recorded as killed in a single two-hour raid. Hermann Göring, head of the Luftwaffe, revelled in the glory. It was his idea to use Spain as a training ground to blood his new pilots and test out planes like the Messerschmitt 109 and the Stuka dive-bomber, alongside Junkers and Heinkels. It was also a rehearsal for a new system of aerial bombing using incendiary explosives.

From a military perspective, with Republican forces routed, the Fascists strengthened their power base in Europe. Within the month, General Franco signed a lucrative agreement with Hitler to supply iron ore from the Peninsula's mines for his armament factories. From a political perspective, it was an even greater success. Democratic countries around the world condemned the fall of a fellow democratic government but that was all. The Nazis were ready to unleash the largest and best equipped army on Europe.

'The Revolution has devoured its own children,' pronounced Lenka.

'Who said that?' asked Jake.

'Danton, the French revolutionary.'

'Which unit is he in?'

'Isn't he in the Philosophers Light Infantry Battalion?' interrupted Vodanski, but speaking to Lenka, as he sat down on the stone floor to help himself to goulash.

He turned to Jewel, and said, 'The Cowboy's

stupidity knows no bounds.'

It had been two months since Jake and Vodanski had set off for Guernica. The cordon around the city had been tightened, though occasionally it was broken when Republican forces launched counterattacks. In one breach, the two returning Rogues seized the opportunity to enter the city. During their absence, there had been major developments that had convinced Lenka it was time to leave Madrid. The Communists were rounding up former allies, and denouncing them as 'Fifth Columnists', before placing them in front of a firing squad. The other deciding factor was that the German and Italian bombing of the Basque areas of the north had escalated, and children in their thousands were being evacuated to France. It made little difference to the Nazis that the convoys consisted mainly of children as their fighters strafed them with machine gun fire. Lenka decided that it was a better use of her fighting skills to protect the next exodus of children making their way over the Pyrenees, than fight a war that had already been lost.

Lenka broke the news to the Rogues over dinner and asked if any of them wanted to join her. Jake was first to say yes, as he had had enough of the politics. 'I came here to fight Fascists, now the Communists say that's no longer enough. Fuck 'em!'

To the others surprise, Vodanski replied that he would join them.

'Like the rest of you, I'm regarded as a Rogue; no country claims me or wants me. The Stalinists sent me on a one-way trip, so if I can protect the children, I'll join you. But after that I'm heading home.'

The others remained silent. Then Jake spoke, 'Well,

once we get the children to France, it's time I went home (he did not add 'too'). Two years is a long time for me to be in one place.'

'America has signed a Non-Intervention Agreement, and it has banned all Americans from coming to Spain to fight,' said Lenka. 'So, don't expect to be welcomed with open arms.'

Jake was determined not to be dragged down by the downbeat mood of the others and replied, 'True, but we got dragged into the last European war. I lost three uncles fighting in that, so I understand. But it will change, as I believe in Roosevelt. If the Nazis are stupid enough to take us on, we'll unleash hell,' replied Jake.

Despite his rousing response he knew that J. Edgar Hoover, the head of the FBI, would make life very difficult him.

Then everyone heard the one response they feared most.

'Some of the patients are in no condition to be moved,' said Jewel, softly. 'I have to stay with them.'

Lenka knew it was futile, but she had prepared a reply: 'The children in the convoy will also need help.'

'I know, but there are three children here too.'

Katherine's reply was also dreaded, particularly by Chris and Jake, 'I'm staying too.'

Lenka persisted, but she always found that women were so much harder to persuade than men. 'Jewel . . .'

'Please, no more. The children will need protection and there are no better people in the world that can give them that than you, Jake, Vodanski and Chris. I can't protect them; even if I could fight, I wouldn't. We each have our roles to play, and my place is here. All of you go,' she said, and turned to Chris. 'That means you too, as the convoy of children needs all the protection it can get.'

The others looked at Chris, but again they knew what his answer would be.

'I'm staying,' announced the Scotsman.

Jewel looked up at Chris. 'They won't do anything to me; I'm no threat to them anymore, the war is lost, but you and Katherine are foreigners and you're a known fighter.'

'The longer I can hold them back, the more time you two have to nurse your patients and prepare them for the journey.' He turned to his sister and said, 'I can't afford to lose you again.'

Katherine rested her head on her brother's shoulder and whispered, 'When Father died, I'm so glad I went in search of my little brother.'

The Russian was the first to break ranks, 'I'm staying.'

'Nothing to do with Van Gogh,' one of those rare occasions where Jake acknowledged the Russian was in his presence, 'but, I'm staying.'

'Shut up all of you,' yelled Jewel's, startling the others, as they had never heard her raise her voice before. Tears flowed unevenly done her cheeks. 'I know the dangers but I will stay in the hospital, so I'm safe. The children need you, now.

Chris turned to his Russian and American friends. 'I'll make sure nothing happens to them. Help Lenka.'

Nothing more was said. That night, during one of the last of the Republican counterattacks, Lenka, Jake and Vodanski evaded the Nationalist patrols, and broke through the cordon thrown around the city.

Eight days later they joined the convoy of children who were leaving the beautiful Basque town of San Sebastian. The refugee convoy was frequently scattered from the roads by the terrifying clatter of machine guns, as Stukas swooping down on them, until two weeks later it finally crossed the French border.

The march involved four hundred children, the largest to date, but it was the last. The Fascists had secured Madrid. All of Spain was now in General Franco's iron-grip. After over two years of intense fighting, and now that all the children from the convoy were being dispersed to safer parts of the globe, it was time for the Rogues to return home. But thinking of those they left behind, their hearts were never so heavy.

Chapter 3: 'Shoot the Bitch and then the Boy'

January 1938, Budapest

Wrapped in his sleeping mother's arms, Tóth shook her gently to wake her up. 'Mama, we must go now; the train driver has started the engine.'

It was getting harder to rouse her each morning. The more frequent piercing pains in her head, the fumbling in the dark during the day, and the fear that the Nazis would find them again exhausted her. Since they fled their home in Debrecen, and made their way towards the capital, they had avoided hotels. At the end of each day, her son would select the safest place to hide and she would lay them down for the night. Even then, only when Tóth's breathing adopted a constant rhythm, did she know he was not feigning sleep for her sake and she could close her eyes. Then, in the recesses of her mind, the nightmares would agitate, getting ready to renew their attack.

Magdalena knew she was on the verge of a breakdown, perhaps even madness, but she fought hard to keep her sanity until she could deliver Tóth to his father.

'Mama, it's time to go, the station is empty, no one will see us,' pleaded her son, trying to reassure her.

Her eyes flickered open, only to remind her that there was nothing to see.

'You're a good boy,' she replied, as she raised herself. 'Have you got our bag?'

'Yes, Mama.'

They had spent the night curled up in front of the locked luggage room, which was down the stairs in the right-hand corner of the train station. She had wrapped them up under a cashmere Coco Chanel blanket her husband had given her for her birthday last year from in Paris.

She focused on getting them on the train and finally to safety. 'Check again. Look at every part of the station, as the Germans will be watching all the terminals for us.'

'Mama, there is no one here,' he said. He took his mother's hand and picked up the one small but heavy bag they had had time to pack before they fled their home in the middle of the night. Unbeknown to them, the Gestapo had been watching their house and had observed them leave.

The Irishman peered above the head of the unconscious man lying face down on the table next to him. He saw the woman and her son for the first time and watched the pair as they emerged from the basement stairwell. After covering a further ten feet, the two figures came into the full glare of the opulent gas-lit chandeliers that adorned the concourse of the magnificent nineteenth-century train station. The woman had strong chiselled features, a slim attractive figure wearing the very latest fashionable clothing from what he had seen in his recent travels through the wealthier cities of Europe and South America. The boy was about seven, maybe eight, and had a freckled face, which was surprising, as his hair, like his mother's, was as black as coal. He was dressed in a blue blazer, long grey flannel trousers, classic brown brogues and wore a sober claret-coloured knitted tie.

But there were several things that were not right. Despite her exquisite clothing, she wore no face powder or lipstick, suggesting that she had been in a rush or that she only possessed fine clothes and had decided that without make-up she might not stand out so much. She wore flat shoes, which again did not complement her outfit. Their clothes were dishevelled and dirty. Her white frilly collar and similar cuffs had scuff marks. The boy's clothes too showed signs of wear, particularly his trousers, which were threadbare at the knees, no doubt from running and falling over. His shoes were well polished, but the double layers on the base told him they had recently been soled and heeled, but with rubber rather than leather, implying that their financial circumstances had recently changed.

If money was tight, then she was a smart woman making sure that they had the proper footwear to run if they had to. In a train station, most people would have hurried past them, probably not noticing any of these things, but no one could have missed the most obvious thing about them: the woman was blind. The Irishman assumed this was recent, as the bandage wrapped around her head had yellowing pus stains around the eyes. If he were closer, he would have noticed specks of blood.

The assassin on the balcony above the railway concourse had the boy in his sights. It was a clear shot. After that, he calculated it would only take two seconds, no more than that, to shoot the woman, as she would be paralysed with fear, thinking, rightly, that her son had been killed. But his orders were clear, the woman would be the first to die.

A week earlier, the man who had hatched the assassination had calculated every permutation of the woman named Magdalena and her son's death. He did so without writing anything down – like others in the hierarchy of the Gestapo he rarely wrote anything that would, if it fell into the wrong hands, incriminate him.

He sipped Earl Grey tea from a fine bone china cup, as he sat by the window on his specially adapted train as it sped across the Hungarian border and back into Germany.

In deciding the order of their deaths, he visualised how the woman and her son would react to the death of the other. The woman, hearing the gunshot and fearing the death of her son, would naturally dash to her boy. But she was blind and would be in a panic, a combination that meant her next movements would be unpredictable. However, if the mother was shot first, the boy would instinctively run to her. For the sniper, the boy's movement would be easily predetermined. Yes, a far easier shot. This, after all, was the easiest part of the mission.

The sniper, the best of the latest recruits to his Alpha Wolves according to Berlin, would require his complete attention to complete the mission. Yes, the woman first. Very good, he thought, and he took another sip of his favourite refreshment. He looked out of the train window at the beautiful snow-covered landscape. Smiling, he registered nothing of the scene, his mind filled with violent images.

The station, as with many major train terminals in Europe's capital cities, was magnificently grandiose. Former Kings and Queens of Europe required the finest of buildings to welcome dignitaries, usually family members, when they arrived. It had a soaring semi-circular glass window above the ornate entrance that invited passengers to gaze up in awe. However, unlike other European train stations, the roof had no supporting columns. This meant that apart from stationary trains, luggage trolleys and vendors pushing their carts, there was an unrestricted view from any angle of the concourse.

In the sniper's crosshairs, Tóth guided his mother by the hand across the open concourse, struggling with the bag with its leather strap that hung heavily on his left shoulder and across his back.

As they approached the train, Tóth reassured his mother that the station was deserted, apart from the train driver and the conductor who were eating sandwiches and were drinking small bottles of beer. Like his mother, all week he had been racked with the fear that they would be recaptured. But when he saw the doors of the last carriage were open, for the first time in days he believed that they might finally escape.

A hand darted from behind the luggage trolley and seized Tóth by the throat. A tall, thin man stepped out from behind the cases. He tightened his grip around the boy's throat, silencing his attempt to warn his mother. The man in the dull cream raincoat lifted Tóth into the air. As he did so, Tóth's right hand slipped from his mother's and then from their bag, letting it fall loudly to the ground.

'I wouldn't want you to miss this,' whispered the tall,

thin man as he lifted the boy towards his gaunt, white face, broken only by a broad grin exposing his yellow tobacco-stained teeth. The man turned the boy towards his mother, while still gripping him by the throat. Tóth was only inches from her fingertips, as her arms stretched out in desperation to reach her son. 'Tóth! Tóth! Tóth! Please answer me!' she cried, but he could not reach her or answer her. Tóth watched helplessly, finding it so difficult to breathe that he could hardly struggle. The tall, thin man with black hair, waxed flat to his head, pointed his Hungarian army issue revolver directly at his mother who was still screaming in panic. His captor again whispered into his ear, releasing once again his stale ashtray breath, 'My captain's orders for today were very clear, "Shoot the bitch and then the boy".'

The attention of the tall, thin man who held the child by his throat was caught by something falling from the balcony. It was a body. It was 'the Lady-killer' from Berlin. The expert assassin. The handsome sniper. The body had fallen a good twenty feet, head-first, and landed motionless on the cold polished stone of the concourse. Crimson splatters landed metres away, while an expanding circle of blood formed around the body. The tall, thin man turned to his right, looking for instruction from the Gestapo captain who had earlier positioned himself at a table by a café at the far side of the Station, tucked into the side entrance out of general view.

From here the captain was well positioned to observe their mission, while continuing to eat his breakfast. It was also where, the night before, he had told the two assassins that the success of their mission would bring great rewards from Berlin. But the captain was motionless, lying face down on the small cast-iron table. He turned back to look again at the corpse of the sniper, as he tried to work out what was happening.

All this happened under the cover of the noise of the taxi engines, which suddenly stopped. It made no difference now, as the last assassin failed to spot the knife spinning silently through the air, high above the concourse, before severing his oesophagus. Life immediately left his body, releasing his grip on the boy's throat.

As the man collapsed, Tóth fell on the ground, as his legs were still limp. Quickly, he scrambled back up on his feet and raced into his mother's arms. He clung to her, crying from a mixture of relief and fear. Wiping his tears, he saw a fearsome-looking man racing towards them. He seized his mother and closing his eyes. But the man sprinted past them.

Tóth watched the man press his boot on the man's head and pull out the knife from the man's throat. He wiped the blood from it on the dead man's tunic. The man turned and walked lightly towards them. Tóth just held his wailing mother closer, but he moved himself so he was now between her and the lethal stranger. The man bent down and gently took the boy's hand in his right hand and the mother's in his left hand. Raising them up, he nodded once. Then calmly said, 'My name is Sean. You are safe now. Stay close to me and no harm will come to you.'

The evening before, Sean sat laughing and drinking in a farmhouse belonging to the Budgakov family. They had made him a very welcome guest for over a week. This was where London had told him to remain undercover until they had news on the whereabouts of the woman and the boy. Before leaving England, Churchill had been supplied with the name of Paul Budgakov, who would be Ryan's contact in Hungary, though the Irishman was to learn that the young man was based in Berlin. The farmhouse belonged to Paul's aunt and uncle, Christina and Larne. Both had little love for Germans, even though Larne had fought alongside them in the Great War.

They worked hard, rising early and only returning home late in the evening to sit down for a family dinner, a ritual that Christina insisted must always be observed. Larne fully supported his wife, as it also gave him the opportunity to interview any prospective partners for his children. Suitors were very welcome to join the family at the table, providing they were brave enough.

Each morning Sean awoke a little the worse for wear, due to the flagon of home-produced wine they emptied each night during the meal. But he was up before dawn broke to join the household as they got ready for the long day of toil ahead. The Irishman helped where he could, mainly by shattering huge boulders in the fields with a sledgehammer that the men of the family had tried to clear over the years.

Sasha, their youngest girl, was nearly eighteen and by far the prettiest of her sisters. She had her mother's strong features, clear complexion, beautiful, long, auburn locks and bright green eyes. She also had a cheeky confidence and mischievous nature that added to her sexuality. Sasha had no qualms in positioning her chair next to the tall, attractive stranger at the dinner table each evening.

Sean looked at her and smiled, flattered by the attention and not for the first time reflected that young women always find disreputable men intriguing, despite that he was a good fifteen years older than her.

Sean was more interested in her mother, who looked like an older Sasha, but by far less than their twenty-year age gap, despite the harshness of the work on the farm and having borne six children. She was a strikingly good-looking woman with a powerful personality and a sense of humour to match. However, Sean dutifully kept his attraction to her to himself. The three sons and the other two daughters, unlike Sasha, bore the same bulbous nose as their father and hazel eyes of their mother and were very similar in appearance, set apart only by their height and sex. They reminded Sean of a set of Matryoshka dolls he had seen on a stall in Moscow. There was a time when he travelled the world, turning his hand to whatever work he could find – until the questions began.

Larne was a powerful man, as you would expect from a farmer whose ancestors had farmed the land and its coarse terrain for over a hundred years. He had the demeanour of a man content with his life, who had found a good woman, and together they had raised a family of whom they were immensely proud. Larne exhibited that same pride when he showed the Irishman his tractor and later his new barn, which he and his three sons had built and where Sean slept each night. He had a hearty laugh, released loudly and often, which would coax even the most tired of bodies to release a smile.

For the first time since he had sat at his parents' table as a boy, Sean cried with laughter. All week they had spoken and laughed in his company, often accompanied by generous slaps on the back. Their joviality was infectious. Sasha spoke a little English and told Sean that she would teach him some of the local language. Only on the last night did she confess that she had tricked him into using phrases like 'more dog piss, your highness,' rather than 'more wine, please.' This explained the raucous laughter, helped by the consummation of much of the produce of their small vineyard.

Larne was proud of Sasha, and now, she had outwitted the Irishman, an experienced man of the world, a man nearly twice her age. She was his favourite, and her siblings knew it but loved her just the same. He smiled at his wife, for their daughter had inherited her mother's guile.

Each night after Sasha had gone to bed, Christina would continue to work on a double-sized quilt. It was to be a surprise for her youngest daughter's eighteenth birthday, for the day when she would find a man and raise a family of her own.

On their last night together, Sean looked at Larne – a man who possessed everything he did not – and smiled. Scanning the table, his smile broadened. This was the happiest he could remember being for many years.

That night, one of the sons, Theo, arrived with a note from his cousin Paul. Sean moved away from the table to read it on the little bed that Christina had made up for him in the barn that he shared with Tobias, the Budgakov's Alsatian. Each night the Irishman would stagger to his bunk, collapse, and drift off to sleep. Tobias would lie next to him on the dusty barn floor. Sean would fall asleep to the rhythm of the constant growls of the very affronted canine. He was a very temperate animal, with pious views on alcohol, thought the Irishman.

The note read that the woman and the boy were believed to be heading to the Nyugati Pályaudvar train station, the terminal for trains serving the west, and that he should proceed there tomorrow. It contained nothing else. No details of when they were expected to arrive. What train they intended to catch, or indeed how it was known that the station was their destination.

The next morning, the Irishman firmly shook Larne's hand and thanked him for his hospitality, and then he did the same with his sons. He placed a kiss on Christina's cheek and similarly on those of the two eldest daughters, which made them blush. Sasha playfully offered her right cheek, but she turned her head quickly at the last moment to plant a kiss on his lips. She did not blush but looked up at the tall man's grey-green eyes, which were a foot above hers, and grinned.

The Irishman set off on the ten-mile trek into town, having refused Larne's offer of a ride on his cart. He did not wish to expose them to any further danger. He stopped at the main road and turned around for the last time to see the family at the top of the path. They were a hardworking family, with great ambitions for the future. They waved, before setting off to do their chores for the day.

Sean prayed that he was wrong about the war and that it would never come. He thought of his own family, who had lived in a farmhouse like theirs – before the British came.

The Irishman hiked along the dirt-road that led to the Gellért Hill, which brought you into the centre of Budapest. A few hours later, the Irishman saw a man sitting at the side of the road. The description matched that of Paul, given to him by his family. He was a young man, thin and wiry, in his early twenties with black unkempt hair. Physically, the description matched the man perfectly, but it did not provide the detail that told one what mattered just as much: his emotional state.

Paul lacked the confidence of most young men of that age. He seemed permanently in flight, never at ease, always edgy, always eager to move on. Sean was now only a few feet away and could see he was surprisingly well dressed for a student. He had a pallid complexion, oily mousey-brown hair and wide brown eyes with thin eyelids and an over-enlarged lower lip. He reminded Sean of a trout he'd once seen in a tank in a fish restaurant bewildered by the invisible force that held it back, but unlike Paul seemingly unaware of the danger it was in. Sean was to discover that whenever they met in a bar or restaurant, he always had a cigarette smouldering between his fingers and a glass of wine; although Sean had never seen either make the journey to his mouth.

Though he was waiting to intercept the Irishman, Paul was nevertheless startled when he first caught sight of the frightening, stern-looking man, though the physical description London had given him was accurate.

'I'm Paul, your contact . . . you must be Mr Ryan . . . err, was everything fine with my family?'

'Yes, good people, but drop the mister bit. Call me Sean.'

'Yes, err . . . Mr Sean.'

Sean thought he should help him, as conversation, along with relaxing and staying inconspicuous, was clearly not the man's strong point.

'Any news of the woman and the boy?'

After what seemed an age to the Irishman, as Paul had selected a spot that had the two men standing in the open road without cover on either side, he finally pieced together the man's rambling update. Paul had given Sean a letter from the British Embassy in Budapest that had arrived yesterday morning. Its postmark was over a week old. He opened it and saw it was from Magdalena Ilona. She wrote that she, with her son Tóth, had abandoned their apartment in Debrecen. They had taken what possessions they could carry and were making their way to Budapest, the only way to secure a connection to Western Europe from Hungary. However, they requested help as all trains from Hungary, along with those from Poland and Russia, had to pass through the German capital, Berlin. They would hide for a few days in the little town of Pomaz. Then head into the city and go to the British Embassy in the hope that London that been given enough time to make arrangements to smuggle them out of Budapest.

Paul immediately contacted London. He was told to leave a reply that they were booked on the first train to Vienna every morning that week. A few hours later, he received a call from the Embassy that a woman with a young boy had collected the note but left no response.

Sean quicken their pace towards the town as Paul spoke. By the time the young man had recounted the details of London's escape plan, they had reached the Citadel overlooking the city. They headed down towards what the locals called the Duna, but foreigners called the Danube.

When they reached the river, Sean told Paul that the

plan was shelved and he outlined his new plan, including what he wanted Paul to do before morning. The young man was already fidgeting, but by the time the Irishman had finished, passers-by were staring at the anxious man sweating profusely and looking on the verge of collapse.

'But . . . what . . . will London . . . say?'

'Bollocks to London!'

The Irishman's original plan was in line with London's, insofar as it was to smuggle the woman and her son out on a train from Budapest. He knew after reading the note from the night before that if they were making their own way to the station unaided, there was a very good chance they would already have been spotted. Even if they had not been intercepted, security checks would be increased on all trains leaving the city as it was the obvious way to escape to the West. Before crossing the Elizabeth Bridge, Sean stopped, shook Paul's hand and told him where he would meet him in Vienna. Paul hesitated, uneasy with his new instructions. But between arguing with the Irishman, whose eyes were fixed sternly on him, or answering to London, he thought it safer to drive to Austria.

Ryan avoided the main streets and made his way hurriedly through its narrow alleys. He arrived outside the station just before midnight. Quickly, he whipped the blanket from his knapsack. To Christina's annoyance, he had refused the offer of her best woollen blanket and settled for the one that Tobias slept on. During all the handshakes and hugs he received as he was leaving, the disgruntled animal placed his paws on the Irishman's foot, bared his teeth, and growled at him.

The Irishman usually got on well with animals,

unlike humans. When he last visited his sister, her new husband and their young family, having smuggled himself into Dublin, she asked him how he made so many enemies. He replied that he did not see it as a failing, but more of a gift, as those he crossed soon proven to be arseholes. She hugged him, and uttered with resignation, 'Unfortunately, little brother, you think everyone is an arsehole.'

Ryan lay down in a doorway, out of sight but with an unrestricted view of the front and side roads on the left and right leading to the station. He had no intention of sleeping, but if the police or members of the Gestapo, who Larne believed had taken up a covert presence in the city, discovered him. Wrapped in a badly chewed-up blanket, he would be mistaken for a tramp.

Though covered, it was a cold night as the rain had splashed onto the concrete step that was now his bed and had turned to sheet ice. He stayed awake all night, curled up but with his eyes firmly fixed on the three entrances to the station. The main passenger entrance would naturally be the most popular access, while the smaller side entrance on the right of the terminal was where taxis would drop off passengers. But if the woman was smart, she would use the staff entrance on the left-hand side of the station. He knew his best chance of getting them out of the city would be if he could spot them before they got to the station and guide them away. He had to, as he could see the silhouette of a fat man wearing a peaked cap sitting in a chair by the upstairs window above the main entrance.

When dawn broke, the Irishman's worst fears were realised. Another man, a taller, thin man, woke the fat man at the window, and they both moved from their position. The woman and the boy must have been spotted. Ryan cursed, guessing they must have already been hiding inside the station before he arrived.

Jumping up, he grabbed his knapsack and slipped Tobias' blanket inside, before ripping out the dagger he had sowed in the lining. Moving quickly towards the train station and saw the first of the morning's taxis pull up outside. The Irishman hastened along the icy cobblestones towards the left side of the station building, which unlike the other entrances remained in the shadows away from the rising. Slipping under the arch leading onto the main concourse, he saw the overweight middle-aged man in uniform wearing a peaked cap. On his arm were four stripes, indicated he was a captain in the Hungarian Army. He also wore an armband that Ryan had never seen before, a white cross with four arrow points with the letter H printed in black in the middle.

This was the man overseeing the operation, and he had selected the best spot to observe the station concourse, while remaining safe in the shadows. There was no getting past him and no backing out as their mission was already underway. Ryan realised that whatever happened next was going to be noisy and could not fail to alert the other assassins. He waited for the taxi-drivers outside to rev up their engines, as they had to do on bitterly cold mornings, so they would start when the first fare of the day arrived. A minute later, a crescendo of pistons kicked into motion. Ryan hastened towards the fat man.

Ryan pulled a chair out from the table next to the captain and sat beside him.

'*Raus! Alle Raus! Du kannst mich mal!*' shouted the officer. Although Ryan's knowledge of the language was limited, he was familiar with the terms 'out' and 'bastard'. Ryan checked for any activity, but it appeared that the man's abusive language so far only had a disinterested audience of one.

Ryan smiled stupidly at the captain, pretending not to be able to understand German. This was easy to do as not many Hungarians spoke or understood it. To add to the performance, he pretended to be mentally impaired and not to comprehend the meaning of the fat man's shouts and the frantic waving of his hands. Frustrated, the captain shoved him violently, still yelling at him. The Irishman ignored him, as he focused on the two assassins he had spotted. One was hiding behind the luggage trolley, but the more imminent threat was the one on the balcony. He had a rifle trained on the concourse, waiting for the targets to emerge into the open.

The captain shoved him harder, but his shouts were drowned out by the train engine as its driver continued to stroke its furnace into a rage. Ryan appraised the situation and, satisfied that the two assassins were focused on their mission, he grabbed the man's strudel from his plate and landed a right hook to the left side of his head, knocking him out cold. Ryan seized the man's half-empty bottle of beer, just before his head crash landed onto the empty plate. Peering over the unconscious man, Irishman picked up his bag.

'Nice talking to you, but I must dash. Train to catch,' he said, before finished the captain's breakfast in two quick mouthfuls, and walking briskly towards the staircase leading to the terraced balcony.

Sprinting up the top of the staircase, he saw the sniper crouched down in the most comfortable and therefore best possible firing position. His rifle was protruding through the solid white stone railings of the balustrade and balanced on his bent left arm. The forefinger of his right hand was resting on the firing mechanism, but not the trigger. A professional. He had made sure that he had a solid wall behind him, to minimise the risk of an attack or disturbance from the offices along the terrace. Though he was positioned slightly off the centre of the landing, he still had a perfect view of his targets and anyone who attempted to enter the terrace from the staircase.

The sniper wore neither a helmet nor a cap, exposing his blond hair and army crew cut. He wore a Hungarian uniform like that of the unconscious captain below, and it had the same armband. Some snipers would have trusted their own vision rather than use a sight over such a short distance, confident that they could easily take out their targets over less than a hundred metres with perfect visibility. But this man's rifle had a sight. He was leaving nothing to chance – a professional. Ryan knew that he would be spotted as soon as his boot hit the landing, and if judged a threat, he would be dead within seconds.

Ryan's first thought was to crawl his way along the floor using the cover of the solid stone base of the balustrade that bordered the walkway. Reaching the assassin depended on the man assuming a shooting position and being fully focused on the view from his rifle sight. If not, once again, he would be dead within seconds.

Then he saw the sniper place his finger on the trigger. His targets were in the open.

He lowered his bag onto the last step, and wrapped Tobias' blanket around his shoulders, emptied the remains of the captain's beer over himself and assumed a crouching gait. Coughing violently and swaying unsteadily, he announced his entrance on the terrace to the sniper.

Steiner immediately caught sight of the noisy tramp staggering to his right along the landing. He viewed tramps, alongside Jews and cripples, as the vermin of society. He hated them all, and he would happily shoot the lot of them if he had the chance. The sniper often played with shooting scenarios, and he thought he could shoot the tramp after he took out his targets. Yes, he would have loved to put a bullet in the old tramp's head once his targets fell, but he was a professional. He had his assignment and business always took precedence over pleasure. His job had its benefits, apart from the rush of adrenaline when he saw his target throw its hands in the air and fall. One reason he chose to be a marksman in the infamous Alpha Wolves was because of its reputation amongst the wealthy young women of Berlin. Add to this, that he was one of the most dapper of the soldiers in the Nazi elite unit, and it was no surprise to him that the women of the city's clubs flocked to him. He revelled in his nickname amongst the other snipers, the 'lady-killer'.

Lying there looking over the station, he focused the cross hairs of his gun sight on the Hungarian, the assassin on the ground – or so the man had been told. Putting a bullet in the brain of the 'Idiot,' now that would take precision with such a small target. He laughed at his own joke. His orders were to kill him immediately after he had killed the woman and then the boy, before he had time to take the envelope from his coat and drop it on the woman's body.

Steiner had travelled by train from Berlin two nights ago. Opposite him, the fat captain ate his way through an entire hamper during their journey to Budapest, as he outlined the plan in the secure carriage of the train designated for their sole occupation.

The Idiot had been offered up by the Hungarian authorities 'to take the fall,' as his commanding officer called it. He would have a sealed envelope concealed in his raincoat. It would contain forged documents from the French government and a letter indicating that he was one of their agents. It detailed that his mission was to murder, at random, a Hungarian woman and child at the station that morning. Then he was to jump on the first train back to Paris. The letter continued, "The public execution of an innocent Hungarian family will be blamed on Nazi Germany by our propaganda people. This will irreparably fracture the new and mutually beneficial relationship between Germany and Hungary."

'Crude, but effective,' noted Steiner. 'What story was concocted for the Idiot?'

The captain smiled as he took another swig from the open bottle of beer, one of six by his feet. 'The Idiot is to be fed some nonsense that as soon as you, or he, it doesn't matter who, kills the woman,' Steiner smiled as he was in no doubt who would kill her and her boy, 'he is to slip the envelope into the woman's bag. Inside it, he has been told, are papers that say she is a Communist spy, callously using her son as cover. On her body will be the

98

letter and a few secret papers, and the newspapers would be informed that she was fleeing with stolen defence secrets for the enemies of the country.' The captain laughed again, sinking his badly rotting teeth into a pickled egg. 'Of course, we haven't bothered with any of that, as the Idiot will do as he is told.'

'The Hungarians have someone that dumb?'

'Every country has someone that dumb, as there are always men wishing to be heroes, who will believe anything in their desire for fame and fortune.' He laughed again as he applied more salt to the final remnants of a leg of pork in his hand. 'It seems the Hungarian army, and he's from some paramilitary fascist force within it, has its fair share, but they have selected one that also speaks German, so he can be our translator up to the point you put a bullet between his eyes.' The captain sank his teeth into a pig's knuckle that he had now just unwrapped from an old newspaper he produced from his over-night bag. This only added to the sniper's disgust. Steiner did not have much regard for people who failed to meet the perfect ideal of the Aryan race – after all, he did.

'Of course,' the captain continued, as he picked at a piece of fat that had wedged in between his teeth, which made the sniper look away once more. Once he had dislodged the culprit from his back molars and swallowed it, he returned to the fate of the idiot: 'he has been told to return to barracks, where he will be rewarded handsomely for his service to the state.'

That evening, the three-man assassination team had met for the first time in the city's main train station. Steiner and his captain had already changed into Hungarian army-issue uniforms. Each uniform fitted perfectly as they were made by the Gestapo's own tailors-in-residence in their Berlin headquarters. The Idiot was in civilian clothing and had met them off the train. After his offer of a handshake was ignored, he led the Nazis over to a table by the station café. Steiner kept his distance from the Idiot, whose clothes stank of cigarette ash. He knew the *real* plan, and he had no interest in anything the man had to say, before he set off to find the best position to eliminate his targets.

Ten hours he stayed in this position overlooking the centre of the train station. Surveying the station through his rifle sight, he even toyed with the thought of putting a hole in the bloated captain just for fun. He was not looking forward to having to share a train with him on their return to Berlin and watching him nauseatingly stuffing his fat face once more. But he was a professional, the best sniper in the Gestapo, and he had been specially selected for this assignment at the highest level, he was told. As for his targets, it had not occurred to him to ask why they had to be executed – it never did, though he always hoped that those that were to die were Jews. He dropped his eye back down to the eyepiece of the gun sight on his rifle and waited for his targets to appear. It would only be seconds now as his captain had taken his position by the café. Then, he felt someone grab his ankles from behind and the final thing he saw was the yellow stone floor racing towards him.

As Ryan tipped the sniper over the balcony, he sliced the strap of the rifle with his knife to free it from the gunman. His intention was to use it to shoot the second man who had just jumped out from behind the packed luggage trailer and was now lifting the young boy into the air by his throat. But the sniper clung on to the rifle, taking it with him to his death. The distance between him and the remaining assassin was around thirty metres, but there was no wind as the doors to the building were closed. Visibility was clear, and the trajectory was downwards. With a combination of judgement, experience and luck, he launched his dagger with all the force he could summon at the man holding the boy by the throat.

The second assassin, in civilian clothes, was the same height, had the same cropped military haircut but not the intense composure of the immaculately attired sniper. Some might think he was the brawn to the other assassin's brain, but he was assigned with the most responsible of the tasks, to slip the papers he had been given into the woman's jacket once she was dead. He had no idea why they had to be killed; indeed, he had not even thought to ask why. His one thought, was his major's last words to him: "Obey the Germans instructions, without question."

His German was good, as he had learnt the language of the country he admired since he was a boy. Now, with the dominance of the Nazis, surely his countrymen would see what he had always known, that Germany was their rightful master. That was why he wore the fascist armband, a H blazoned on a white background. He was delighted to be chosen for a mission of national importance, as there were other German speakers in his regiment. More so, as up until he was told of his new assignment, he thought his major did not even like him, as he had heard him once describe him to another soldier in his unit, as "only good enough to be a target on a rifle range". Finally, he had recognised his talents.

He knew the other assassin, the immaculately attired man, Steiner, could also recognise a fellow professional, as did his captain. They would be a formidable team together. Perhaps after the death of the woman and the child they would make a special request to their Nazi superiors, so he could return with them to Berlin. He grew excited by the thought that he might even be assigned to the SS.

His eyes bulged, his grin broadened, as he gripped the boy throat's like a fisherman raising his catch. He enjoyed the thought of killing the woman – women never trusted him and always rejected his advances – but he cared little either way about killing the boy. What delighted him more was the praise he would receive from fellow marksmen in his regiment and soon from Steiner's colleagues in the SS. But all that was immaterial now, as his hands instinctively threw themselves up to find the Irishman's knife was embedded in his neck.

The Irishman did not wait to see if his weapon had hit its intended mark, as he immediately tied Tobias' blanket to the balustrade and leapt over. Abruptly, coming to a stop, he dropped the remaining four metres, using the body of the sniper to cushion his fall. The blanket broke away from its mooring, along with a section of the balustrade, and both came crashing down onto the concourse. Ryan regained his focus on the three people on the station platform by the luggage trolley. He let out a deep breath, as his target was in the last throes of life.

The woman was cradling the boy in her arms as they

knelt on the stone floor. The best Ryan had hoped for was to wound the man while missing the boy and have enough time to run across the platform and finish the assassin before he had time to recover. The Irishman kept a watch on all three entrances to the station as he scrambled onto his feet and sprinted towards the woman and the boy.

Ryan raced past them. He about to smash his boot down on the end of the blade, but there was no need, as the crimson circle seeping from the man's body was already over a metre wide. The Irishman retrieved the knife, wiped on a dry part of the dead man's tunic, and turned around. Raising the boy's hand and then the blind woman's hand, he lifted them up.

He nodded before calmly saying, 'My name is Sean. You are safe now. Stay close to me and no harm will come to you.'

The roars of BMW engines announced the arrival of three military motorbikes entering the great hall of the station. The first rider was trying to steer his machine directly at Ryan, while trying to manoeuvre his machine gun, which was held by a strap over his right shoulder, into a firing position. The Irishman shouted to the boy, 'Run with your mother over to the fat man,' and pointed towards the captain who was flopped over table but was starting to stir.

Tóth did as he was told. He grabbed his mother's hand and raced with her in panic towards the café. As they ran, the boy glanced over his shoulder. The stranger was sprinting towards the motorbike, bearing down on him. The rider had the throttle fully open as he bore down on his target. The stranger jumped, placing one foot onto the connecting bar between the luggage trolleys, and leapt into the air towards the motorbike. His boot of hit the rider in the face, propelling him into the air. The bike crashed onto the smoothly polished floor, slipping sideways into the luggage trolleys. The rider landed on his back and slid along the polished floor until he came to a halt when his head split open on a metal bollard. The petrol tank of the motorbike exploded on impact with the trolley, launching flaming clothing and open cases across the platform.

The second rider gunned his motorbike at Ryan, firing with his machine gun held in his left arm. But he lost control of his bike as he tried to avoid the flames. He was thrown from his machine, which skidded off the platform onto the train tracks. The rider sailed through the air and impacted directly with the metal safety barrier at the end of the platform. He remained motionless, draped across it.

A third motorbike rider was hurtling at full speed towards the woman and the boy who had nearly reached the exit on the left side of the station. Ryan knew he could not reach the rider before the woman and the boy fell under the wheels of the motorbike. For the second time, he had to find something that would reach his target before he could. He saw the five-gallon can of lighter fuel that the conductor had left on the steps to the buffet carriage, before he had run off in the direction of the engine when the mayhem started.

The Irishman grabbed it, ripped the lid off with one pull and launched its contents over the flames towards the speeding bike. A stream of flames shot through the air and engulfed the rider along with his motorbike, and both erupted into a ball of fire when the petrol tank exploded.

Ryan ran towards the boy and swept him and his mother up into his arms as burning debris rained down on them. Once he reached the archway, he saw that the captain was awake but still dazed.

The dangerous stranger addressed them once again in a clear voice that did not betray the pain from the bullet in his shoulder and the other in his right side, 'Stay here, I need to have a word with someone.'

Whether it was the dramatic disposal of the men who had tried to kill them, his calm commanding voice or just sheer terror – neither moved until he returned minutes later.

The train driver was still standing by his engine in shock at what he had just witnessed, when Ryan grabbed him and dragged him up into the engine room. There he found the conductor huddled in the corner, his arms wrapped around himself, clutching an empty bottle of beer. A few minutes later, the first plumes of smoke emerged from the train's funnel as it started to pull out of the station.

In the meantime, Tóth set off on his own mission to extract the man's blanket from the rubble. He did so and returned to his mother, just as the stranger leapt from the train and raced towards them. He rushed past them once more, leaping up the stairs like a big cat leaping up a tree to retrieve a recent kill it had hidden. Within seconds he returned with a small knapsack.

Tóth handed the man the blanket, and with a frown he said, 'It's very smelly'.

'No matter. Smart thinking kid, it's going to be cold,'

said the man releasing a smile.

The heat from a blazing motorcycle launched a stack of gas cylinders into the air, where they exploded, blowing out the glass from the gigantic stretched windows above the entrance of the building.

The captain regained consciousness. He opened his eyes and surveyed the devastation before him; only minutes earlier the station had been completely under his control. As he tried to focus on the scene, he saw the bloody body of what looked like the sniper he had brought with him from Berlin. There was no sign of the Idiot, but dotted around the burning station were motorbikes and riders, members from the covert SS unit based in Budapest, the first of the elite units of assassins, The Alpha Wolves. All had been based in the city, under his command. All were ready to mobilise as soon as Berlin gave the order and were disguised as Hungarian military personnel with the connivance of senior government officials. Apart from the sniper, he had personally selected these men for this mission.

But now, the Nazis' elite unit lay all around him, dead, unconscious or writhing in agony. His only thought was how he would explain this to his commander in Berlin, Cerberus, a man who punished failure with death.

The captain needn't have worried, as all his worries were at that moment resolved. He heard a man say in German, '*Guten Morgan,*' and he lifted his head to look up. But the last words he ever heard were in English – 'End of the line!' – before a fist smashed into his broken nose. His head snapped back, severing his spinal column.

Chapter 4: No Vices

August 1934, Berlin

With his rigid right arm stretched arrogantly in the air, Cerberus remained in position for longer than his senior officers. The two senior officers returned his salute, but with the shorter movement of the lower arm, leaving the upper arm fixed. Himmler returned to his black leather desk chair, while his deputy, Heydrich, went to sit in the black leather armchair opposite. General Vaux's executioner dropped his right arm but remained standing to attention. This was the pinnacle of his career, the moment he had dreamed of but for others where the nightmare began.

Cerberus was in the presence of one of the most powerful men in Germany, second only to Hitler. Rudolf Hess was the Führer's official deputy, but everyone knew that the real power resided in the humourless little man sitting upright in his huge armchair. On the sleeve of his black uniform were the three white stripes on a red banner with a black swastika stamped on a white circle. This was Reichsführer Heinrich Himmler, Chief of the Police and head of all security services in the National Socialist Republic of Germany. A man of ruthless ambition, who saw himself as Hitler's successor. Like the Roman Emperors he sought to emulate, he held the power of life and death over millions.

The Reichsführer's office was in the new headquarters of the Secret State Police, the Gestapo. It was an imposing building on Prinz-Albrecht-Straße only a few minutes from the Reichstag. A year earlier, it had been the home of the democratically elected Weimar Republic. The headquarters of the state security police lacked the history and majesty of the surrounding buildings now under the control of the Nazis. It had no marble columns, no majestic lions or swooping eagles about the main entrance or in its hallways. But its grey concrete slab exterior and its dull, ivory-coloured plaster walls and stone floors, perfectly met its objective: to secure, isolate and intimidate all who entered.

'Cognac, Major Krak?'

'I do not drink alcohol, Reichsführer,' replied Cerberus, who had not been invited to sit on the empty red padded mahogany chair next to his commanding officer and mentor, Obergruppenführer Reinhard Heydrich.

'Abstinence, very good, one should have a clear head for the battles ahead,' replied Himmler, exhibiting neither pride nor approval.

'Major Krak is always on duty,' added Heydrich.

Himmler was a pudgy little man, and everything about him gave the impression that he was restricted in growth; not only in height. His restrained, black moustache dared not stray from beneath the shadow of his nose. His chin was weak, cowering under his lower lip. His eyes, which were small and pinched, were framed behind his perfectly spherical lenses. Yet his uniform was strikingly dramatic, as is the case with military officers who pay an extraordinary amount of attention to their attire in the belief it will add to their gravitas. The Führer took a personal interest in such matters. This was typical of all those who Hitler had made Reichsführer. Hermann Göring was the most ostentatious of all. He wore a white uniform draped with medals awarded to himself. Stripped of their ornamentation, you would not give any of them a second glance if they cashed your cheque in a bank.

Himmler carried on the conversation as his valet, whom he did not acknowledge, poured cognac into two of the three glasses.

'Major Krak,' said the Reichsführer, fixing his eyes on the tall, thin man with a translucent complexion. 'It is the nature of Berliners to provide nicknames for all things. This building is already referred to as the Ministry of Truth. But you are not from Berlin?'

'Munich, Reichsführer.'

'The cradle of National Socialism. It seems only yesterday that the Führer and I and my predecessor led the Sterneckerbrau Beer Hall putsch.' Himmler never mentioned his rival for the Führer's patronage, Göring, by name. 'My predecessor once described our business here as, "not to do justice, but to annihilate and exterminate".'

Obergruppenführer Reinhard Heydrich, Director of the Reich Security Main Office, Leader of the Secret Police and of the *Sturmabteilung*, the SS Security Service, turned to his protégé.

'Once again you have shown yourself to be a loyal servant of the Reich.' He spoke without emotion and, if you did not know the man, with the curl of his lip you might think he was being sarcastic.

If Himmler had the power to take life, then

Heydrich was his executioner. He was known as 'Himmler's brain' and he, like his protégé, was a tall, thin man, with green eyes and skin bleached of colour. A secretary in the typing pool was overheard months earlier whispering to a colleague that the Obergruppenführer, 'drove the sun in when he stepped out into daylight'. She and her colleague were arrested and were somewhere in the basement of the building. Cerberus had learnt much from his mentor.

The men's expressions were always measured, rarely revealing or releasing an uncontrolled emotion. Cold analytical calculation was their master. The heart was never to be trusted. The most frightening aspect of the three men emerged when they smiled. It signified neither joy nor warmth but a perverse pleasure, usually as a result of some misfortune inflicted on a rival or an opponent

'Yes, you have performed admirably, Cerberus,' said Himmler, who gestured the man to sit down. 'May I call you Cerberus?' he enquired, but he was not seeking approval. 'The Führer is proud of your commitment to the Reich. Vaux represented the old decadent Germany,' added Himmler. He smiled for the first time. 'It was not expected that you would personally take control of his execution,' his smile broadened, 'as these things can be messy. It is best you leave this to your subordinates in the future.' His smile disappeared. 'A discrete distance is required.'

The senior SS officers were the architects of the purge of the Wehrmacht launched that week. But it was Cerberus, on Heydrich's orders, who had concocted the evidence against its generals; a combination of forged letters and forced signed confessions. He was particularly proud of the evidence he had manufactured for General Vaux, along with the forged signature stating that he was plotting a coup d'état while in the pay of foreign powers.

Both senior officers withdrew cigarettes from sterling silver cases. Each was embossed with the SS Death's Head symbol, the *Totenkopf.* Himmler offered one to Cerberus, but Heydrich put his hand up, saying, 'Cerberus has no vices.'

'I live only to serve the Reich,' replied his protégé.

The other men nodded their approval. To serve the Reich was to serve the Führer, which was to serve them.

Himmler spoke in the manner he used to conduct interrogations before he adopted a *'discrete* distance,' 'What is the function of the SS?'

'The *Schutzstaffel* is dedicated to protecting the Führer,' replied Cerberus.

'The Führer is the Third Reich. Any threat to the purity of the Reich is an attack on the Führer himself. Would you agree?'

'Of course, Reichsführer.'

'We have no time to lose. Plans must become reality. The first concentration camp is to be opened in Dachau with *accommodation* for five thousand,' he said, without adding the term *people.* 'All Communists and functionaries from the previous government who pose a threat to state security are to be interned there. It will be the first such camp for political prisoners, serving as a prototype for others in Germany and future occupied territories.'

Himmler wrote on a note on the pad as he spoke. He was constantly drafting speeches and treated meetings with his officers as a rehearsal.

'We are embarking on a policy of racial hygiene.

How can we mould a world to our pure form when it is infected by Jews, Communists, homosexuals and the *deformed*? Never again will the Jewish-Bolshevistic revolution of sub-humans be able to undermine the *Volk*, from within or through foreign emissaries.'

Cerberus was delighted to hear that those who were not of Aryan purity would be eradicated. They were the malignancy that he and others in the Party believed had led to Germany's surrender in the last war.

'Those who are found to be of Teutonic blood will be assimilated into the *Volk*. In addition, the Slav nations will provide us with *Lebensraum*, the living space as declared by the Führer that we require. Its people will also serve us.'

For Cerberus, the moment was greater than he had even imagined. He had been taken into the confidence of his superiors. Words were spoken that were only for the chosen few. He had never expressed his views so openly, except to those who were about to die by his hand.

'You know of my ambition to build an elite force within the SS?' asked Himmler.

'*Deutsche Männerorden*,' replied Cerberus.

'Yes. For which you were honoured with The Order of German Manhood,' pronounced Himmler. 'You have been an able warrior for the Gestapo and I want you to become part of the SS and the Security Service,' the latter known by the initials SD. That Cerberus had been awarded a rank across all three services was a unique honour.

To be admitted into the SS meant that checks had already been carried out that proved he had German ancestry, with no Jewish blood, going back for the required three hundred years.

'You will continue to wear the black uniform of the Gestapo,' continued the Reichsführer. 'Your new role is aligned to the political rather than the military wing of the SS, but your unique role encompassing the SD provides you with influence beyond our current borders.'

'It will also ensure that you remain in the background and keep a discrete distance,' said Heydrich. As your enthusiasm to deal personally with your prisoners is well known. If your methods are discovered, you must not be. It will be traced to the party and, at least for the present, we must be viewed on the international stage as a determined but just government.'

Himmler sat forward and clasped his thin, pale fingers together. 'Reinhard and I have spoken to the Führer, and we have agreed your objectives. First, you must destabilise all European governments in advance of invasion. Second, you will seek out and eliminate all individuals or groups who pose a threat to us.' Both men continued to watch the major for his reaction. 'Now, you see what an honour the Führer and I have bestowed on you. You will be the iron fist that delivers the first blow to our enemies. Do not fail us.'

Cerberus scanned the faces of both men. As the implementer of this new programme, he would secure the career advancement that even he had never thought possible.

'It is the greatest honour to destroy the vermin that threatens Germany.'

Himmler continued, 'We require more than brute force. We need you to build a shadow army of informers. You will extract confessions, false or otherwise. You will monitor, identify, and expose the weaknesses of the governments that oppose us. You will discover and manipulate the fears of the people in their factories, the soldiers in their armies, their agents in the security services, and their teachers as well as the children in their schools. You will instil panic and suspicion within families and between neighbours. No area of existence,' (Cerberus noted he did not use the term resistance), 'must be shielded from us. This is why you will prepare files on all who may oppose us, so those you do not eliminate directly will be put on the gallows when their country falls to us.'

'I am proud to say, Cerberus, that you will lead the first of the death squads, The Alpha Wolves,' said Heydrich.

Cerberus was once again surprised to hear his commander use such direct terms, but the lack of a more euphemistic phrase for death squads again underlined that he was now part of an elite circle within the regime where there was no need to speak guardedly. 'You will be given carte blanche to find those who oppose us and eliminate them,' he added dismissively. 'We need not know the details as you have our full confidence.'

Heydrich broke into a broad smile, exposing his long, thin teeth beneath his dead eyes.

'We have given you your objectives; you will provide the method and the application.'

Himmler remained expressionless, like an accountant going through his ledgers. He laid his spectacles down on his desk and stood up.

'Come to the window. I want to show you a little project of mine.'

Heydrich bid his protégé forward toward the telescope mounted on a tripod by the bay window.

Standing beside the telescope, Cerberus stayed out into the garden. It was green but lacked the bloom one would have expected to see from the roses planted by the head gardener the previous autumn. However, the recently extended high concrete walls would ensure that even the green stalks that held up the underdeveloped buds would be shorter and even more anaemic next year. The few red petals that had stretched out in search of sunlight lay withered on the path.

Himmler kept the telescope mounted on a tripod by the main window. He summoned Cerberus, and said, 'Look!' The major bent down to look through the lens, resting his hooded eye against the instrument's rubber eyepiece. 'You see the building under construction on the top of the mountain. I made a few modifications. It will be a very exclusive concentration camp, where you will bring some of those you capture for interrogation before execution.'

Cerberus adjusted the gauge until the fortress came into view. As the new head of the SS's new assassination unit continued to train his eye on the fortress, Himmler continued. 'It was built by Frederick I in 1739, as a private prison for his son after he reluctantly commuted his death sentence for treason. It was never used for its purpose, as the King died a year later, but it has remained a prison ever since.'

The major could see it clearly, now. It was perched on the mountain above the trees and lakes like some large and imposing grey vulture. It had four red-roofed turrets positioned on its granite stone walls. He noted the new constructions. The huge brick wall that lined the perimeter was nearly complete, along with buildings behind it to the left of the fortress. Towering above it was a thin red brick chimney stack. Higher still, flew the red, white and black symbol, the swastika.

'If the purpose of the new building is to intern prisoners while awaiting interrogation, there is no reason to extend it, said Cerberus as he straightened up. 'I will extract all the information from those that fall under my hand.'

His senior officers smiled, thinking he was making a joke. He was not.

'Your methods are proven, but this is more for experimentation. Now, leave us,' commanded the Reichsführer, who returned to his armchair without looking at the man.

Cerberus clicked his heels, raised his right arm and with a vehemence that surprised his superiors, he declared, 'Heil Hitler.'

Himmler and Heydrich repeated the words, before both men lowered their heads to unfurl the huge blueprint on the desk. In the top, right-hand corner, were the words "Amsterdam: Magyarnite-Chemlabs".

December 1937, Kent

Inches led the young woman into the study. He sensed both her surprise and her disappointment. There were two chandeliers that you would expect to see in the home of one of the country's most famous statesman, but the rest of the room resembled a typical English country house.

The light-yellow flowered cotton curtains and magnolia walls reflected the full light from the three bay windows down one side, giving the room a feeling of openness and warmth. Watercolour paintings of British landscapes hung on the walls, but there was nothing to reflect the man's military campaigns or that of his great ancestor, the Duke of Marlborough. Rather surprisingly, the only military presence was a bust of the last little corporal who had threatened to dominate Europe, Napoleon Bonaparte, but he was now exiled to the Statesman's roll-top mahogany desk.

Two vast, imposing but plain, beige-coloured settees faced each other on either side of the open fire. Each was decorated with an abundance of yellow and blue cushions to brighten them up. But their presence was a functional one, allowing guests to make themselves comfortable and children to spread out their toys and play. This was the room of a man who enjoyed the company of his family and made his guests at ease, rather than of a man trying to impress.

'Sir, I'm a little confused. You want me to be the senior British officer in the field?' She was known for expressing her opinion and seeking clarification no matter where she was or who was present, much to the chagrin of her superiors. 'Particularly, as you're not known for the advancement of women,' added Lieutenant Amelia Brett of His Majesty's Royal Navy.

Everyone was struck by the young woman when they first saw her. She was tall, with her clothes always tightly wrapped around her hourglass frame, but it was her pale porcelain skin that was most striking. Her scent was light, a mixture of rose water with a trace of lavender.

117

Yet, nothing about her was natural: she was physically perfect, and nature always, cruelly, leaves a blemish. She was the archetypal English Rose, but she had an aloofness that one observer noted gave the impression that she was sculpted from ice. Her high cheekbones were framed by blonde curls that turned dutifully in under her cheeks Her nose was delicate, though sharp. Her hourglass curves were supported by her firm ballerina-shaped legs tilted slightly forward by her three-inch stilettos. Most women would have hated to be seen purely as an object of desire. She neither hated it nor loved it, but she knew it and used it.

'Yes, I'm typical of my sex, so on such a sensitive operation I know that men won't suspect you for a moment,' responded Churchill. He repeated his proposition. 'If I can clear it with the Admiralty, will you take on the task?'

'Yes,' replied the woman without the slightest hesitation.

Amelia controlled her emotions because she knew the old man was renowned for his mischievous approach. Churchill had goaded her, but she had bravely made her point while keeping her temper in check. His auditions were notoriously short, as he knew what skills were required, and she had passed. Now the exercise was over, he returned to character. 'Thank you for not scolding an old man. I was wrong to oppose all women being granted the vote, as my Clementine often reminds me. However, my dear, men will not change overnight and some never change at all. I would suggest that you use our ignorance to your advantage,' he smiled, 'but I believe you already do.'

Churchill outlined his plans, including why he required a woman of her capabilities. He would provide all the resources at his disposal to assist those trying to help refugees flee the Nazis. To do that, he required someone with her communication and logistic skills.

Lieutenant Brett had heard of Winston's outlandish schemes. The security services' eavesdroppers in Admiralty House had intercepted a communique from Washington in which President Roosevelt had commented that "Winston had a hundred ideas every day, of which only four were any good". She did not think this was one of today's four.

'Sir, I may be a lieutenant in the navy, but if I am not the senior officer, how do I lead . . . sorry, steer these Rogues?'

Churchill laughed heartily, 'My dear, there is not a man or woman alive that could lead these Rogues, as you aptly refer to them. No, your role is to coordinate the operation, provide them with what resources I can muster, guide them to their target, and arrange for all those they are attempting to save to be given safe passage to England.'

'Do I report to you?'

'No, Lord Sloane.'

'Has that been agreed?'

'It will be.'

'I take it I liaise directly with the Irishman?'

'No, radio contact will be difficult, as everything the man touches blows up. You will liaise with a Polish woman who has a network of radio operatives in several countries.'

'Trustworthy?'

'I believe so; she is a woman of letters. That that weighs well with me.'

'Letters?'

Churchill did not respond but returned to the report he had on his lap, an action which indicated that the meeting was at an end. She remained seated.

'Sir, forgive me, but I still don't know why you selected me?'

Churchill was now consumed by the dispatch he had secretly received from his contacts in the secret service. It provided the latest numbers of bombers within the Luftwaffe. It was the second time that day he had been asked such a question, and without looking up he replied, 'You are the only one who responded to my request to the Admiralty for help.'

'Thank you, Sir,' she replied, rising.

But the former Minister of the Admiralty had already moved on to another folder marked HIGHLY CONFIDENTIAL and was examining the designs of a new plane being developed by Reginald J. Mitchell. He pondered on whether enough of these nimble fighter aircraft could be manufactured, and if pilots could be trained in time to defend Britain from the might of the Luftwaffe.

Churchill enjoyed sparring, particularly when it was delivered with mischief and wit. Part of the duel was not to let your opponent choose the weapon of engagement or the battleground. A few hours earlier he had let the young Irishman circle and jab with the youthful weapons of sarcasm and irony, while he took the well-fortified centre ground of knowledge and experience. The

Statesman was the pre-eminent exponent of the art of verbal jousting in all its forms, and though his next encounter would be with a much duller opponent, he would nonetheless relish it.

Ten minutes later, his final visitor of the day, Lord Ogilvy Arbuthnot-Sloane marched into the room, with Inches following behind carrying a tray of tea and scones. By the room was empty.

It was still drizzling but to Churchill the landscape was clear. He was standing on the patio wearing his grey homburg, its hatband decorated with the swan and goose feathers that he regularly retrieved from the bank by the pond in the garden. He was inspecting another arrival to Chartwell that day; a mechanical digger. His latest purchase was one he intended to operate himself to fashion one of three lakes he planned to add to the beauty of the already resplendent scene. The Statesman made it a point to never ask anyone to do a job he would not do himself, no matter how difficult, dirty or dangerous the task.

He also liked to keep his nemesis in the Admiralty waiting, knowing his impatience would lead to angry outbursts and the disclosure of information he would later regret.

Churchill strolled through the open bay windows of his study to find Lord Sloane sitting back on the leather upholstered chair. He removed his hat and mischievously waved it at his unimpressed guest, like a matador would raise a red cape to startle and then enrage a bull. The Statesman ambled over to his armchair and flopped into its arms to face the man opposite, a man whom he knew despised him.

Lord Sloane had completed two tours in Afghanistan, though a little later than Churchill, and so had missed all the fighting. But he was resourceful. During the Great War he carried out covert operations in the Balkans, and later in Ireland he led the British forces unit interrogating captured rebels rounded up after the Easter Uprising. His political career took off, just as Churchill's started to wane. For the last ten years he had worked his way up, using his aristocratic connections and those made at Harrow. Now he was a junior minister in the Admiralty. He saw Churchill's career as a counterbalance to his own. One of the rumours doing the rounds in Whitehall, instigated by him, was that in the next cabinet reshuffle, Chamberlain would offer him Churchill's old post as First Lord of the Admiralty.

Ever since Harrow, he had been labelled with the unfortunate nickname of 'Peanut'. His forehead seemed constricted compared to his extremely elongated and expansive jaw. He also had a small but pronounced chin, which only added to his already exaggerated features. But it was not his appearance that kept people at a distance, rather his temper, which erupted regularly and violently. After the birth of their second child, he told his wife that as she had now delivered on their marriage contract, she would now sleep in a separate bed; she only asked if she could do so on another floor. Those who worked for him, even his chauffeur of ten years', disliked him, unlike those who served the man opposite.

Churchill updated Lord Sloane with the morning's events, and once he had done this, he prepared himself for the man's tirade.

'A Paddy, eh? You consort with that sort, now, do

you?'

'Do not underestimate the Irish. After Bloody Sunday, we thought we would never contemplate an Irish Free State, yet within a year we were sitting around the table with our fountain pens, eager to sign the Anglo-Irish Treaty.' The lord grunted, 'Did you see the Irishman? He refused a lift back to London, so you may have seen him on the road as you drove in, carrying a crystal decanter.'

The aristocrat remembered a lone man striding along the pathway. 'Yes. The rough-and-ready type, but those people are all like that.'

Churchill repeated the question: 'Did you recognise him?'

'Why would I?'

'You should pay more attention; you have met him before.'

Lord Sloane's thick owlish eyebrows perked up. The Irishmen he remembered were those he interrogated in Dublin Castle, and he looked in robust health. The only others he had met were from the Irish delegation that came to London a few years later when he was a junior parliamentary secretary. It had been his job to brief the ministers negotiating on behalf of His Majesty's Government on each member of the Irish contingent.

'You mean he was one of those present when the Treaty was signed?'

It was an agreement that Churchill was a major party to, a document that the aristocrat believed shamed Britain.

'He was one of Collins' bodyguards.'

'But I thought that all those who were present on

the Irish side when the Treaty was signed were assassinated by the IRA during the civil war that followed, including Collins?'

'Not all. If you remember there were two enormous carthorses standing behind Collins and an equally tall, but leaner younger man?' Lord Sloane nodded, though Churchill would be surprised if he recalled any of them. 'Over the three days, the younger man prowled around us like a caged cat; I never once heard him utter a word.'

Lord Sloane stared at the ceiling. As always Churchill ignored the man's indifference and continued, 'As is always the case when foes are forced together, eventually tensions ease and once the agreement was signed all those in the room toasted the signing of the Treaty.' Churchill continued to goad the man, saying, 'Including you.' Lord Sloane visibly bridled at this. He had no wish to be reminded that as a young man, his political ambition took precedence over his ideals. 'That is, all except the young man,' added the Statesman who could not resist pressing the point. 'Even the two carthorses guarding Collins raised a glass.'

The aristocrat exploded, and as usual the first target were staff.

'Don't just stand there, man!' he shouted, turning his fury on Inches, who was standing by the door of the study, and waving his full glass. 'Fill it up!'

Inches was about to move forward, but his employer shook his head once, before leaning forward and filling the aristocrat's glass up to the top.

Churchill continued, 'At first, I thought he was a spy for Éamon de Valera, but a few days later Collins told me that he trusted the young man with his life, and that if we had moved to arrest him or any member of his delegation, it was I and those by my side who would never have seen daylight again.'

The aristocrat shrugged. 'Collins was all bravado. I cannot see how a boy from the bogs could have gotten the better of us, particularly with my military experience.'

'You're right and I had my trusty Mauser automatic pistol to hand,' he responded, referring to a pistol that had served him faithfully in the Sudan. After dislocating his shoulder during the India campaign, he found it easier to handle than the other option for his regiment – a sword. 'But I believe that before the Irishman fell, he would have levelled Downing Street.'

The bloodshot eyes below the man's wild eyebrows bulged.

Churchill continued goading the man, 'Surprising that you can't remember him, for in your briefing to the British side it was you that christened him the Scrapper!' Though his face was now red and blotchy, Lord Sloane refused to rise to the jibe. It would not be long now thought the Statesman.

'Did you see the woman that just left?'

'Rather fetching, I thought.'

'I have asked her be our contact with the Irishman and later others.'

The aristocrat was riled once more, 'Dear God, that's no job for a filly. If this nonsense is to proceed, then I will pick one of my best men.'

Churchill smiled genially at Lord Sloane. 'I have no ministerial authority, and you can do as you wish. But this is a private matter, and I have volunteered this information out of common courtesy to His Majesty's

Government. All I ask is your permission to use the expertise of the woman. After all, you are a "minister" in the Admiralty and she comes under your authority.'

Churchill allowed pragmatism to prevail over his mischievous nature, as he decided not to use the prefix "junior" to his position, as this was the point when he sought the man's help.

However, the aristocrat's temper was as short as usual.

'Don't you dare play games with me, Winston, I'm far too clever for you!'

Churchill remained calm. 'She can be useful to us both. I hear she is a very competent communicator, and I have no doubt that she will ensure you are kept informed of all developments, before me.'

Lord Sloane knew that despite being a pariah in government circles, Churchill still had some powerful friends. He also knew that the man's stock was higher internationally. However, he had personal reasons to make sure that his old foe's latest scheme was enacted, despite knowing it would fail.

'Put your head on the block if you wish Winston, but when this all backfires, it's nothing to do with His Majesty's Government.' His voice rose as he banged his fist on the table, spilling tea from the china cups that remained untouched. 'This madcap adventure will finally completely scupper your tilting boat.'

Churchill nodded, but he knew the man would never give anything up for nothing.

'Winston, there is one condition,' declared the Minister, trying to regain control of his temper.

'The names of those on your list.'

'Of course.'

'Here they are,' and he wrote the two names on a piece of the finest quality paper from St. James on the Strand and handed it over.

Lord Sloane looked long and hard at the names but remained silent, before he slowly folded the note and slipped it in the top, left-hand pocket of his blue, pinstripe blazer.

'What is the significance of the woman?'

'I don't know; her name and that of the boy came from our American colleagues, I believe.'

'Still trying to curry favour with the Yanks?'

'I'm half American myself, remember.'

As he had reached an accommodation with his guest, he moved the conversation onto a topic that would rile him. He was looking forward to it.

'I know you and others are unhappy that I have spoken out in the House about the threat of Herr Hitler and his thugs.'

'You're out of tune with the thinking of Government and the people of England. It would be better, Winston, if you shut up.'

'You, and others see Germany and Italy as our natural allies.'

'Frankly, yes, Europe is a mess. We need order and we welcome strong government, especially as Hitler is all that stands between us and Stalin. The Frogs and the Belgies are next to useless. Indeed, you yourself were once sympathetic to Herr Hitler.'

'No, I believe that Germany, a once great nation, had a right to lift itself off its knees after the war. But this does not mean that I am blinkered to the threat that Herr

127

Hitler and his *Nazees* pose. I oppose and mistrust the Communists as much as I do the Fascists, but Hitler is the immediate threat.'

Lord Sloane erupted, 'The country wants peace, and you are in no position to direct its fate! I'll have you know that at this very moment we are near reaching an agreement with Herr Hitler to avert another war.'

'Really?'

'Lord Halifax is doing his utmost on behalf of His Majesty's Government to reach an accord with Chancellor Hitler.'

So the rumours were true, thought Churchill.

'You're an embarrassment. An old man, out of touch, desperately trying to position at the centre of stage. You can proceed with this foolish endeavour, and it blows up in your face you will have plenty of time to write your history books, paint your pictures, before you disappear into oblivion.'

The Statesman allowed the man that he had schooled with at Harrow to grandstand, but he did not like him or those whose company he kept. One of Lord Sloane's few friends was Sir Oswald Mosley, politician and Sixth Baronet of Ancoats, who had formed the British Union of Fascists, known more infamously as the 'Blackshirts'. Two years earlier, Lord Sloane had attended Tom's – the nickname used by his family and closest friends – secret marriage in the home of the Head of Nazi Propaganda, Joseph Goebbels, in Berlin.

Churchill remained resolute. 'Be careful that your judgement is not clouded by some notion that peace can be kept by Britain and Germany carving up Europe between us. It is the nature of Fascism and Communism to dominate, but only one voice can be heard in such company. Britain is a democracy, and I will continue to shout and embarrass the Government with all the energy I can muster to ensure we remain so.'

Lord Sloane tried to interject, but Churchill denied him the floor.

'Do not ignore the abuses by the Fascists that are becoming clearer by day, and do not think for one moment that the *Narzees* will treat us any differently if we bow to them.'

To Churchill's surprise, Lord Sloane's anger disappeared from his voice and he smiled as he finished his whiskey.

'Winston, you exaggerate,' he said, and his smile broadened, 'but let me assure you that I am looking to the future.' He rose and collected his hat and tweed jacket from Inches, without acknowledging the man and made his way to his chauffeur-driven Bentley.

A week later, a call from Lord Sloane was put through to Churchill in his study: 'Ogilvy here.'

Churchill was surprised to hear the man announce himself so informally. 'I have a good man, in fact my best, to deal with your Budapest project.'

'Too late, the Irishman has already engaged with the enemy, and freed the woman and the boy. They are believed to be heading to Vienna, but I've no idea where they are and I cannot reach them. All we can do is sit back and await news.'

Churchill waited for a response, but Lord Sloane did not answer. Then he heard the click as the man replaced the receiver.

Chapter 5: Sean's Story

April 1916, Cork

It was April 1916, and members of the Irish Volunteers had occupied the General Post Office in O'Connell Street in the heart of Dublin. An event that became known as the Easter Rising. It had been over a hundred years since those fighting for an Irish Republic had gathered to fight a conventional war against the superior firepower of the British Empire. Before its leaders surrendered six days later and were put against the wall of Dublin Castle and shot, reprisals were already being carried out across Ireland. The tail of the British lion had been pulled, and it was angry. The day after the rebellion was crushed, British Army trucks drove at high speed into the Blackrock area of Cork looking for rebels.

Thomas Ryan was one of the teenagers who had thrown rocks at the armoured vehicles that cordoned off all roads leading in or out of the city. That night the soldiers rampaged through the town, arresting anyone they thought was sympathetic to the rebels or had been part of the mob. Any resistance was met with immediate and brutal force by the Black & Tans, a British army force who had recently arrived in Ireland to crush the rebellion. The hastily formed military unit brought together ex-soldiers, many of whom had been kicked out of the army, with ex-criminals. Their ruthlessness had already alienated any support the British had hoped to gain from the Irish people.

Five Black & Tans from the unit targeted the Ryan's family's little farmhouse. They had been directed there by a boy who had a playground grudge against Thomas. It was very likely they would have targeted the house anyway, as British troops were breaking into houses along the River Lee with looting the main objective. They kicked down the door of the house that Thomas shared with his parents Megan and Joe, his younger sister Marisa and his little brother, Sean.

Religious artefacts lined the walls. On the right-hand side of the door was a little plastic font. All visitors were expected to dip a finger into the holy water it contained and make the sign of the cross before entering. On the other side of the room was a picture of the Virgin Mary and child, each crowned with a halo. Sean would look at the depiction, puzzled that the bright rings had not attracted the Roman legionnaires attention years before they paid Judas his twelve pieces of silver. The inquisitive boy was of a practical nature, and religious symbolism was often lost on him.

The young Sean infuriated his brother just as much as the presence of the British. The boy was also the bane of the Jesuit brothers who ran the local school, as he was always up to some mischief. That school day was a typical one for the young Sean. The first class of the day was religious education, and the school was given the honour of a rare visit from the Bishop of the Diocese who addressed Sean's class and pronounced that he was happy to take questions on 'the faith'. To the consternation of his Jesuit teachers, Sean was the first to raise his hand.

'Father, in The Lord's Prayer, we are praying to our Lord and only to him?'

'Correct, my son.'

'So, when we say, *"And lead us not into temptation"* then we are praying to the Lord to not make us sinners. So, he's the one who makes people sin?'

Sean received the usual response, a beating and a month's detention. Later he discovered his brother at the back of the school with Maureen Kilkenny. Just as Thomas had worked his hand under her bra, his little brother pulled on his black school jacket exclaiming 'Tommy, I'm too young to be an uncle.'

Maureen took fright at the thought and ran off, doing up her blouse as she did so.

'You little bastard,' screamed Thomas, who not for the first time, headed off after his brother to give him a good beating – his second of the day.

His parents and sister, Marisa, doted on Sean and the women of the family used to grab him and comb his thick, black hair. He hated that and ruffled it up immediately afterwards. He preferred to run his hand through it once, after he washed it in the morning to sweep it back, and that was all the attention it received for the day.

Thomas was a volatile sixteen-year-old and at over six feet in height, quite a handful for his age. The young man met the first soldier to enter the house with his right fist, sending the soldier flying across the kitchen table, scattering the homemade soda bread and raspberry jam across the wooden floorboards. Thomas stood ready to take on the three soldiers circling him. Then Joe, his father, ran towards the group of men to stand between the raiders and his son. He was trying to bring an end to the conflict, as the Black & Tans trained their revolvers on his son. Megan had run in the opposite direction, grabbing Marisa and Sean by their hands.

A revolver appeared at the open window behind the men and the leader of the assault team who up to that moment had remained outside and unseen, emptied its chamber. Four bullets hit Thomas in the middle of his back. He turned as he fell to his knees and stared at his mother.

'Ma,' he cried before he hit the ground.

His father looked in disbelief at the dead body of his eldest boy. He dropped and cradled his son, before the fifth bullet hit him in the back and the sixth sliced across his throat.

Joe launched himself at the arm holding the empty revolver extended through the open window into the room. He grabbed it as the holder of the weapon kept pulling the trigger. The wounded man pulled at the murderer's outstretched arm, dragging his head through the aperture, and smashed the shooter's face down onto the stone base of the window frame. The three soldiers ran towards the man holding their sergeant and bludgeoned the mortally injured man with the butts of their rifles.

The bloodied Irishman, who should have been lifeless on the floor from his injuries, continued to beat the sergeant's head against the stone windowsill. The three soldiers continued to pound their rifle butts down into the man's skull. The sergeant grabbed a revolver from one of the soldiers, seized the Irishman by his hair and rammed the barrel of the gun between the man's broken teeth and emptied the chamber.

Megan watched the murder of the men of her family while cradling her remaining children in the corner of the room by the fireplace. Marisa had pulled her white linen apron over her eyes and was weeping. But her only living son never once averted his gaze from his father and brother's murderer, as he now entered the cottage through the splintered front door.

The sergeant railed at his men.

'Fucking Irish, we come here to civilise the bastards and this is what we get.'

He pulled the tablecloth from the table, sending the pot of tea and gammon that Megan had prepared to join the rest of their untouched meal across the floor, and wiped his battered face.

'The bastard's broken my fucking nose,' he roared, as he repeatedly stamped his boot on the head of the dead boy who lay on his back by the door, his eyes open and fixed on his mother.

Megan released her children and lifted herself uneasily to her feet to plead with the man to stop desecrating the body of her son. As she staggered uneasily towards the sergeant, the full force of an infantryman's rifle butt shattered her jaw, sending her to the ground. A second soldier delivered a kick to her head, but she was already dead. Marisa screamed and cried as she begged the soldiers to stop.

The sergeant spat out fragments of teeth and blood.

'Fuck them all, hold the boy and let's see how much

spirit the little bitch has,' as he held the cloth to his nose while trying to hold his head back to stem the flow of blood. His left eye was completely closed, and the swelling had severely bloated his face, so he looked like he was wearing a cheap Halloween mask.

Marisa released her little brother and staggered up.

'Run Sean, run!' she shouted, pushing him towards the backdoor, while standing between her brother and her family's killers.

Sean ran – but straight at the sergeant, only to be intercepted by one of the soldiers who whisked him up in his arms. The more the boy struggled and kicked, the more the soldier laughed. The sergeant moved towards the girl who was trying to control her crying. He punched her in the face, sending her backwards across the wooden floor towards the fire. He strode over to her, crouched over her semi-conscious body and started to tear at her blouse and cardigan.

The sergeant grinned at the boy; he wanted to make sure he had a good look at what he was about to do to the last surviving member of his family. The boy stared back, expressing neither fear nor anger. He no longer struggling. It was as if he were conserving his energy.

The intensity of the boy's blue eyes unnerved the sergeant. He had seen that look before, on the wild dogs that used to prowl around in winter outside the house where he was raised in the desolate hills of Dartmoor. As a boy, he had watched them as their jaws latched onto their prey and their piercing blue eyes focused only on their kill.

The memory of the pain he suffered all those years ago made him put his hand on the inside of his left thigh below his groin, where a wild dog had once sunk its fangs into him.

A female had been hiding behind the log pile beside his house, having watched the movements and rituals of the household for the last few days. She had selected the nearest position to the trail he made each day to collect firewood and bided her time until he was only a few metres from her. Once he had swept up a few small logs in his arms, only at that moment did she pounce and sink her fangs into the inside of his thigh. She continued to stare down on him, as she dragged him through the snow away from his home. Not once did she avert her gaze from him, even when his father opened fire from the porch and bullets pierced her thick winter pelt. It was only when the sixth bullet removed most of her head, leaving her jaw and incisors embedded in his thigh, that the boy was finally free from the stare of her fixed blue eyes. From that day, he was always drawn to the colour of someone's eyes.

Marisa was lapsing in and out of consciousness but tearing at her attacker's face whenever he released a hand to rip another article of clothing from her legs. Having forced her legs apart, the sergeant found that he could not produce an erection. It was not because of her struggles – as this was nothing new to him – but the intensity of the boy's stare.

Sean continued to glare at the sergeant, even though the soldier who was carrying him under one arm, had joined the other men emptying the wall cupboards and helping themselves to food and drink. As the troops filled their sacks, while scoffing down food and smashing crockery, not once did the boy avert his stare from the sergeant. For the sergeant and the boy, the rest of the world no longer existed.

The sergeant leapt up from the girl. The bloodied man stormed over to the boy, grabbed him from the trooper's hold and lifted his face up to his.

'Do I look like fucking Errol Flynn to you,' yelled the sergeant to the amusement of the three other men as his trouser buttons were still open and one of them waved his little finger to the other two. Any other time the sergeant would have half-killed any of his men who mocked him, but he only had one objective; he just wanted to kill the boy. 'Is that why you can't stop looking at me, you little Irish fuck?'

The boy's cold blue eyes remained fixed on the sergeant. Then, the sergeant remembered the colour of the family's eyes, as he was watching them through the window – particularly the girl's. She, her mother and the youngest boy all had grey-green eyes. He turned to look at the dead woman's eyes, which were still open, and they were grey-green. He looked across the room at the girl and though closed now, he was certain they were grey-green when she was screaming.

'What kind of devil are you?' he shouted as he flipped the boy back with his left hand, so he could hit him across his face with the full force of the back of his right hand.

The impact launched Sean across the room. He landed by the open fire. The boy was barely conscious, having caught his head on the edge of the iron coal bucket. Though blood was running down his left cheek and quickly spread across his freshly starched white school shirt, he desperately tried to remain conscious as

138

he turned and fixed his stare once more on the sergeant.

Believing that the boy was dead, the sergeant joined his men as they ransacked the house, stuffing as much food, and anything they thought they could sell, into the sacks they always carried with them on their raids. The sergeant, through his one eye that was starting to close, caught sight once more of the boy's icy blue eyes staring at him. The boy was judging him, condemning him; how dare he, the little Irish scum. Again, he exploded and ran at the boy, launching a kick towards his stomach.

The sergeant did not see the poker that the boy had hidden under him, until it speared him below his groin, severing the main artery. If it was not for the inept response of his men, they might have saved him if they had applied pressure to his wound, but his men were poorly trained and were now frenziedly kicking the boy.

Like his sister, Sean drifted in and out of consciousness, but each time he opened his eyes he could see the sergeant rolling around the floor screaming in agony. He was gripping the handle of poker, desperately trying to extract it.

When Sean woke the next time, he saw the man was still, lying on the floor but screaming even louder. His men just standing indolently in a circle around him. His sister had crawled over and was cradling him in her arms. As her tears landed on his face, he forced a smile before passing out.

Minutes earlier, as the little boy lay by the fire after being thrown across the room, he knew that he did not have the physical strength to pull the sergeant away from his sister. Instead he would have to anger the man so he would come at him instead, and Sean knew how to do that. He also knew that once the sergeant came at him, he did not have the strength to drive the poker, which lay beside him, into him. Instead, the man would have to come at him at such a speed that he would impale himself. To do that meant sending the sergeant into such a rage that he would rush at the boy and be blind to the weapon in his hand – again the young Sean knew how to do that.

When the boy came to, he saw that more troops had arrived. Sean looked around the room and there was still no movement from his mother, father or brother. He watched as his sister was wrapped in a blanket and in the arms of a serious looking British officer. The officer was saying to his sister, 'You're safe now.' He repeated this over and over to her, as he carried her towards. Marisa looked over at her little brother and tried to smile. She was alive. The little boy closed his eyes, and his icy blue eyes slowly reverted to their natural colour.

Chapter 6: Death in the Forest

January 1938, Budapest

Having lost the protection of the night, three figures moved within the creeping shadows, desperate to avoid the exposure of dawn. Making their way to the river, the tall man at the front moved silently from one archway to the next. When he thought it was clear, he would signal to the woman and the boy to join him. This delightfully sunny morning was like the beautiful day before, apart from the deafening crescendo of sirens that rocked the city from its sleep. Fire engines, police cars, ambulances were heading frantically towards the train station, engulfed in flames.

Each vehicle as it passed sent the three figures deeper into the shadows. People were running towards the raging fire, many to help, but some sought the best vantage point to survey the disaster. The children on the streets were excited by the spectacle of it all, releasing giddy sounds mimicking the noises made by the emergency vehicles. The adults' cries betrayed their innermost fears. 'Communists,' shouted one man. 'Nazis,' shouted another. The commotion was deafening but a welcome distraction for the three silhouettes edging their way towards the river.

When they reached the Danube, Sean helped Magdalena and Tóth into the rowing boat that Paul had secured for them. The young Hungarian had carried out all that was asked of him as part of the Irishman's revised escape plan. There were also two loaves of bread, a pound of cheese and a foot-long smoked sausage hidden and a flagon of water, hidden under a dull-coloured blanket left at the back of the boat beneath the wooden passenger seat. Two oars rested in their cradles and a crushed-up, empty box of Gauloises was wedged in between the wooden slats of the raised platform where the rower would sit – the agreed sign to signify that this was the boat that Paul had secured for them. The young Hungarian was a bundle of nerves, but he was a good 'fixer', thought the Irishman.

Seated in the boat, they were now exposed to the cold wind that advanced across the river, neutralising the warmth of the sun's rays. Magdalena and Tóth were shivering, despite the blanket the Irishman had wrapped around them. The boy was grumbling to his mother that it smelt like an old wet dog whose owner was a drunk. Ryan surveyed the riverbank one more time and once he was satisfied that the two men fishing on the quay were there solely for that purpose, he pulled on the oars and move the little boat out from the shadow of its moorings and steer it towards the centre of the river.

Two hours later, the wind died as the sun rose higher in the clear blue sky. The ice crystals that had formed on the river's winding path turned to ripples. On the banks of the river, fishermen speculated about the sensational events that had occurred hours earlier. No one paid any attention to the little rowing boat making its way along the river.

The Irishman continued to pull on the oars gliding through the smooth waters, as the backdrop of large terraced buildings gradually morphed into one of smaller cottages, dotted with churches.

Hours later, as the sun slipped behind the castle on Kuckländer Hill, the gatekeeper of the Danube Bend, ripples flattened and the river once again became a black, glassy sheet of ice. Now that its brasher cousin, the sun had retired, the subtler moon appeared, and took centre stage on the dark blue canvas. Its appearance bathed the landscape in silvery light, illuminating the three silent figures in the tiny boat gliding through the water.

The Irishman looked up at the nakedness of the full moon and prayed for clouds to return to cover its dignity. He rested the oars in the still waters and smiled at the family cuddled up, asleep under the blanket. As he had done thorough the voyage, he lifted the fallen blanket from the floor and draped it back over them.

The woman slept uneasily, while the boy gripped on to her as if to protect her from whatever demons were tormenting her. Ryan wondered what was it that positioned a woman and her son at the centre of a power play between the two most powerful nation states in Europe. But his thoughts did not interrupt his rowing rhythm, or his surveillance of every yard of the riverbank, particularly when the road came into view whenever there was a break in the trees. As he continued to row, hundreds of pairs of small white and green torches, of various sizes, would peer out from the pitch-black darkness of the riverbank. He prayed that all belonged to the animals of the night.

143

Tóth stirred before his mother. He looked up to see the fierce-looking man was still rowing, as he had done whenever he stirred on their journey that day. The boy was sweating, having awoken from a violent nightmare. Then he remembered the gunmen, the motorbikes and the explosions. It was all real and far more frightening than any nightmare. The man stopped rowing and produced some bread and cheese and handed it across to him.

'Have some breakfast, there's sausage too,' he said as he broke off a chunk of each and handed it to the boy.

The man swallowed a thick slice of sausage he had cut with the knife he had tucked into his right boot. Still chewing, he sat back and continued to row. Tóth wanted to devour it all, but he broke the bread and cheese in half again once and put them under the smelly blanket for his Mama when she woke. In the darkness with the moon behind him, he could not see the man's face, but he had a feeling he was smiling as he rowed.

Having devoured his share of the food, Tóth briefly cuddling up to his mother once more. Now that the damp smell had been burnt off by the heat of their bodies and the night breeze had aired the cloth, the blanket reminded him of Riga, the little terrier that they had had to leave behind when they fled their home.

His head resting on his mother's chest as she slept, her breathing interrupted only when her nightmares returned. The boy tried to focus on the puppy, but he kept looking at the silhouette of the man rowing. He knew his name but, though he had saved them, he did not trust him. After what those men had done to his mother, he trusted no man. Even his father had taken Lens, his

144

sister, and gone to Amsterdam and left them alone.

Yet, for the first time since his mother had been taken from him, he fell asleep without seeing that terrible image of her being dragged away by the police. In fact, there was no image, only the words the man had spoken amid the chaos of the train station, "I'm Sean. Stay close to me, and no harm will come to you."

Tóth woke up the next morning to see the man bending over his mother. He leapt onto the man's back and beat him with his fists.

'Leave my mother alone,' he screamed.

Sean stood up, even though the boy was still hanging from his back, rocking the boat as he did so.

'Easy kid, I'm just bathing your mother's eyes.'

The man turned so the boy could see that his mother was smiling. The man bent his legs to let him down onto the boat as he continued to reassure him, 'It's OK, kid. It's a concoction my mother used to treat my cuts with when I was a boy.'

He presented his hands, so he could see that one was holding a small bottle of a very pungent liquid that smelt like iodine, and the other held some cotton cloth.

'Tóth, it's all right,' whispered his mother as he collapsed into her arms.

Sean hoped the balm would help a little, but he was careful to only smear it on her eyelids as pus was seeping from her eye sockets once more. Moments earlier, before her son awoke, she had allowed him to remove the bandages wrapped around her head so he could bathe her injuries. He expected to view the damage to her eyes, only to find that they had been gouged out by her interrogators. Sean was amazed that the intensity of her pain had not killed her. God knows how she had survived; perhaps the love for her son and her concern for his safety had kept her alive.

Sean began to row. He stared at them huddled together, and understood why they were terrified of everyone, including him.

Sean moored the boat up under a bridge in a little cove and told them they would have to wait here for a few hours as the terrain was flat and they would be too exposed in the full glare of the moon. Before he stepped out of the boat, he added that he would be back soon, as he had to find some more food.

True to his word, he returned a couple of hours later with bread, cheese, milk and even some fresh meat cuts. Magdalena told him she not eaten meat since her arrest, yet she had refused his earlier offering of the sausage, and now despite her hunger, she once again refused his offering of a slice of ham.

'You're Jewish?' asked Sean.

'Yes,' she replied as she felt around the now opened cloth containing the fresh provisions with her hand. Sean handed her a lump of cheese to add to the piece of bread she was clasping. Then she stopped as if she remembered something, and said, 'But my husband isn't.'

'Where is your husband?'

'Ferdinand is in Amsterdam, and our daughter Lens is with him.'

'Lens is in a world of her own, playing with her dolls all the time,' interjected Tóth, but then he looked down as he spoke in a sombre voice, as he squeezed his mother's

146

hand, 'We miss her though.'

'Why did he leave you?' pressed the Irishman.

'His company relocated its Budapest offices to Amsterdam, fearing a German invasion.' She pondered for a moment and in a subdued tone added, 'Little good it did. The Germans now own his company, Magyarnite-Chemlabs.' She did not want to say anymore, as Tóth was listening and changed the subject. 'Why have you helped us?'

'Let's say you have friends in high places,' replied Sean.

Then he realised that word play would only add to their anxiety and after all they had suffered, they deserved straight answers. An honest dialogue might also provide some answers to unravel the mystery of why the Nazis wanted them killed. 'Your names were given to me by the British. They asked me to help get you both out of Hungary and take you to Vienna.' They looked perplexed, and as they offered no response, he continued. 'I checked you out. You're a teacher, married to a wealthy chemist.'

'I still don't understand. You were asked, not ordered. So, if you don't work for the British, why help us?'

'I have no love for the Gestapo and when I heard of your plight, I thought I could help.'

'The Gestapo?' replied a startled Magdalena.

'The fat man and the sniper were German for sure and as it was a covert operation; that means the Gestapo.'

'But they wore Hungarian army uniforms,' interjected Tóth.

'The fat man shouted at me in German and the sniper also cried out in German when I threw him from

147

the balcony. People always return to their native tongue when they face death.'

'What about the man who seized Tóth?'

'I'd say he was a local. More of a blunt tool, perhaps an interpreter for the Nazis, but that's a guess. Though the fact they put him in the line of fire of the other assassin also tells me that he wasn't one of them. They wouldn't want to risk leaving one of their own behind and their involvement being discovered.'

'The man who grabbed me spoke Hungarian,' nodded Tóth.

His mother put her arm around her son and pulled him close, remembering how close the man, wherever he was from, had come to killing him.

Sean's honest responses did not tease out the answers he had hoped for. He changed tack, as any information they could provide might save all their lives, no matter how direct and insensitive his questions now were.

'When they tortured you, what did they want to know?'

The woman held her son tighter.

'For hours, the Hungarian police kept asking me about Ferdinand. Then the Germans arrived.' From under the bandage that Sean had wrapped around her eyes, a tear appeared. 'As he began the interrogation, the German officer took a teaspoon to my eyes.' The boy gripped his mother's blouse. 'But he didn't seem interested in my answers.' She tried to stifle back the tears as she continued, 'He just seemed to . . .' she began to weep, but added, 'enjoy . . . it.' She bowed, as if she had suddenly become aware of the incomprehensible thought

148

that she had been blinded simply for someone's pleasure.

'Why did they arrest you?'

'I don't know. I'm only a teacher. I work with children who are mute and now, without anyone to communicate with them through signing . . .' She broke down once more. 'The Nazis have left them isolated from the rest of the world.' Tóth squeezed her arm, as though trying to transfer some of his strength to her.

Sean knew he was causing them tremendous pain but pressed on as none of this made any sense. 'How did you escape?'

'After the major . . . had left,' she said, dabbing her cheeks with her silk handkerchief.

'How do you know he was a major?' asked Sean quietly.

'I know nothing of these things, but the Hungarian police called him Sturmbannführer and Tóth told me . . .'

'It is the equivalent of a major,' interrupted her son. 'I know all the ranks, as I have a collection of toy soldiers.' The boy added, 'The Germans always lose.'

Sean smiled at the courage and defiance of the boy.

'How did you escape?'

'Once the German had taken my eyes, he left. The police kept me locked up, for how long I have no idea. Then another man came to my cell and ordered me to gather my things, as he was to take me to another prison. Before I reached my bag, I was dragged by my hair along the floor of the building and eventually thrown into the back of the car.'

She turned her head towards the water to see nothing. 'The driver must have been awaiting more orders as we stayed there. Soon he began to snore. He

149

must have thought that because I was blind, that I wasn't going anywhere, so we seized the opportunity to escape. I carefully opened the car door to ease myself out. Standing by the car, I stretched out to find a wall, so I could work my way along towards the noise of the street. As I began to move forward, I slipped on the snow, but a woman grabbed my hand. She whispered to me that she was from the British Consulate and that she had been waiting for me to leave police headquarters in the hope that she could somehow ferry me away. She helped me into another car and drove me to the Consulate. There I was reunited with Tóth, who had been brought there by my friend Maria.' She squeezed her son's hand and solemnly added, 'Maria was arrested as she returned to her home.'

'When we heard this, we decided to leave immediately. Before we left, I sent a letter to the British Embassy in Budapest. I wrote that we would make our way to Budapest and then to the British Embassy in the hope that arrangements would be made to help us escape to England. Thankfully, when we reached Budapest, there was a letter waiting for us at the Embassy which Tóth opened. It contained two open train tickets for England and new identity papers. We headed to the train station and hid there overnight, so we could take the first train this morning.' Magdalena paused. 'Not much of a plan, as we must have stuck out like a sore thumb as we made our way across the city to the station during the day.'

'Well, it was better than mine to wait outside all night. I should have guessed that you were already inside.' Sean smiled. 'You're an amazing woman to survive and keep this little lad safe.'

The boy proudly glanced up at his beautiful and

courageous mama.

Magdalena searched the false papers in her bag. Having found them, she lifted them up for Sean to take.

To an untrained eye they would suffice, but they would not fool a border guard or a ticket inspector.

'Why do you think the Nazis did not simply try to arrest you?'

'I have no idea.'

The more questions Sean asked, the less he understood.

'Why did you think the British would help you?'

'At first I didn't think they would. I wrote letters to some friends of Ferdinand in the US State Department a few months ago. I guess the Americans couldn't officially be seen to be getting involved in a European problem, but perhaps they contacted the British thinking they were in a better position to help. Whatever the reason, thankfully they sent that woman to wait for me outside the police station.' She lifted her head, and said, 'Please don't be offended, but if they really want to help us, why send just one man?'

'I'm just the brawn,' but he did not mention expendable.

They had no idea why the Nazis were trying to kill them, or even why Magdalena was arrested in the first place, so his questions had confirmed only one thing; this was no simple rescue mission. They were two sacrificial pieces – the opening gambit in a high stakes game.

'Perhaps you can help to identify the armband the Hungarian assassin wore. It had a pointed black cross on a white background with a large black H in the centre . . .'

'The Arrow Cross,' said Magdalena. 'They were a

151

paramilitary force of Hungarian Fascists, gaining in strength and numbers every day and are have been absorbed into the army. They are running in next year's elections, and they may win. To wear such a symbol would mean no one would dare challenge them. Our country is fragmented. After the Great War, our neighbours took two-thirds of our country and the Nazis and the Soviets are like vultures ready to swoop down and take what we have left.'

The fear in her voice was replaced by anger. She was a tough woman, and Sean's admiration for her grew. But the more she told him, the more troubled he became. You did not need a paramilitary force, or trained assassin to stop a blind woman and a boy getting on a train. Even the fat captain could have swept them both up while still eating his strudel.

Magdalena's shoulders slumped due to the exertion of reliving so many painful memories, and soon she fell asleep along with her son. Sean covered her with Tobias' blanket and started to row, as the clouds had formed a screen across the moon.

After a few more hours rowing, the Irishman moored the boat under a small wooden pedestrian bridge that spanned the narrowest part of the river. He woke his passengers and told them that there was a main road ahead and he would check to make sure it was clear before they went any further. It was the first of the lies he told them that day.

Ryan had to find somewhere out of sight, so he could remove the bullet in his left side and the other in his left shoulder. The others only grazed him. He had not attempted this before, because he could not risk passing out. While Magdalena and Tóth had slept, he had been discreetly applying his mother's lotion to his bleeding wounds as the effort of rowing had kept them open. Though the pain was no worse than when the bullets from the motorbike rider's machine-gun entered him, he knew they had not reached vital organs, but he knew he could wait no longer and he had to extract them before they poisoned his system.

Up the hill behind a boulder and out of view of anyone passing along the road, he took his knife from his boot and covered it with some neat alcohol he kept in his knapsack, to sterilise it. He worked the blade into his flesh between his third and fourth ribs to remove the first of the bullets. It took only a few minutes as the bullet had not penetrated too deep and was wedged between two ribs near his sternum.

Ryan poured more alcohol over the blade. Tentatively, he approached the second wound with the sharp end of the knife. The one in his shoulder would be the hardest, as he could not see it, which meant he had to dig blindly into his flesh for the bullet with the point of the blade. The pain shot through his body each time he manoeuvred the knife into his exposed nerves. It took two agonising hours – at one stage, as he feared, he passed out – before he extracted the bullet.

He lay back on the boulder behind him, exhausted, his shirt drenched in blood and sweat. After a few minutes, he sluggishly bent his head forward to look at the bullet covered in his blood now sitting guiltily in the palm of his hand. After taking a few minutes to recover his energy, with another almighty effort, he applied his mother's potion to a piece of cotton gauze and secured it with medical tape over the gaping wound. Then, only after checking that the terrain was clear, did he close his eyes to sleep.

An hour later, Ryan was woken by the sound of someone scampering up the hill. He folded his battered black leather jacket to secure the new cotton dressing over his wound and held his knife posed in his right hand. Tóth appeared, wheezing heavily. Having appeared from the bushy clumps that dotted most of the hill, the boy was now struggling with the steepness of the incline and the assault course of rocks that covered the highest part of the slope. When Tóth was only a few metres from the top of the hill, he saw the road and flopped to the ground to crawl to up to where Sean lay.

Sean lifted his hand up. The boy flattened to the ground. Quickly, but subtly, the Irishman fastened his leather jacket so all the blood stains were covered. Once he was sure, he waved Tóth forward.

The boy took a good long look at the road and was relieved to see it was empty. The boy leapt up and climbed onto the largest of the rocks next to the man. For the first time in weeks Tóth became a little boy again, excited by the world rather than afraid of it.

'Are you English?' asked Tóth.

'I'm Irish, but sometimes I do stupid things and I'm often mistaken for being English,' but his little barb at the old enemy was lost on the boy.

'Mama and Papa taught me English,' he said, looking down at his feet. 'Well, my father used to, but he had to go away.' Then he brightened and his feet began swinging. 'I wanted to learn English, because one day

Mama and Papa, Lens and I will go to America.'

'Well, you'll fit in easily as your English is as good as any Yank.'

'Yours is not too bad either,' replied the boy, laughing. Suddenly, he was seized by what was a very important question: 'Is it true that the Americans only eat hamburgers?'

'No, they also eat French fries.'

'Do you always make jokes?' asked the boy who enjoyed this lighter side to the Irishman's character, though he noticed that the man now had a waxy pallor.

'Not always; sometimes I have to sleep.'

Tóth was laughing as all children and only a few adults do; unrestrained and caring little for what others thought.

'Do you play football?' asked the boy.

'Yes, but when I was your age, my game was hurling.'

'What's hurling?'

'It's an Irish game where you go on the pitch and batter the hell out of each other with large wooden sticks for eighty minutes, providing you're not knocked unconscious first.'

'Is that all there is to it?'

'Well, they say you have to hit a ball into a goal, but that's just what we tell our women to make them think it's a sport.'

'My Dad is a great footballer,' replied the little boy with immense pride.

The boy fell silent and kept looking at his feet, swinging like a pendulum. He was clearly building up to the reason why he had launched his assault on the hill to

155

reach the Irishman.

'Have you a home?'

'I did once but not anymore.'

The boy seemed uneasy at the man's answer. 'Don't you miss it?'

'No, all the people I knew are gone.'

'Do you have any family?'

'A sister.'

'I have a sister,' the boy said excitedly as he looked up, but then he dropped his head down. 'But you know that.'

Sean knew the boy was desperate for answers but was struggling with how to ask the questions.

'Are you a soldier?'

'I was once. Not now.'

The boy looked at him, and asked, 'Are you a mercenary?'

'No.'

'My mama asked, but I still don't understand why you are helping us?' he asked without averting his gaze from his now motionless shoes.

'Many years ago, when I was only a few years older than you, I failed to stop men from doing terrible things. I swore that if I could, I would never let it happen again.'

'Are the English paying you to help us?'

'Well, over the years I have travelled across different countries, and sometimes I get paid to help people.'

'So, you are a mercenary?'

'I take money to help people escape from dangerous situations, not to kill. What money I'm paid covers my food, lodging and transport.'

'But you do kill. I saw you!'

'I'm sorry that you had to see that. Sadly, yes. Sometimes in my line of work I make enemies.'

'We have no money,' blurted out the boy who immediately wished he had not, fearful that the man would leave them.

'Don't worry, kid, most of the time I help people for no payment, though in your and your mother's case, you have a guardian angel in England.'

'Is he a good man?'

'I don't know. But what he is doing now, is a good thing.'

'Who is he?'

'That's a secret and I believe he would like it to remain so.'

Sean waited for the question that boys always ask any man that they believe had fought in a war.

'How many men have you killed?' asked Tóth, no longer smiling, with his eyes peering down at the mud on his shoes.

'Too many,' replied Sean truthfully. 'But, don't let anyone tell you there's any glory in it.'

The boy stayed silent, focused on the scuff marks on his brown brogues, before scanning the hills.

After some minutes, the troubled boy spoke, 'All the powerful men we meet, want to hurt my mother.' He stared down at his shoes. 'I never want to be powerful, and I never want to hurt anyone.'

'Some men and women become powerful and use that strength for good. I believe you will grow up and be one of them.'

Tóth looked up at the Irishman, 'Thank you for saving my mother and me,' he hesitated, 'but you bring violence like the other men.' He after a pause he added, 'I don't want to be like you.'

'I understand kid; I wouldn't want to be me either,' replied Sean, with a knowing smile. As he rose, Sean felt his wounds drag on the dressings. Quickly, he ruffled Tóth's hair to distract from seeing the spasms of pain on his face. 'Come on, let's go back down before your mother starts worrying about you. Also, I want you to meet some friends of mine. Be careful of the youngest lady though, she'll try to marry you.'

Sean and the bemused boy then set off back down the hill.

The mood in the boat was mellower, as the boy believed that the man was on their side. Magdalena felt it too. Sean dripped the oar into the icy waters and started to pull. She reached forward and moved her hand in search of his breath. Coming forward on the rowing stroke, she touched his stubbly cheek.

'You're a good man. We trust you,' she said. Then she added, 'but if you have to choose between us, save Tóth.'

Magdalena released his face, sat back, and pulled some darning wool from the pocket of her long tweed coat. She ran her fingers through her son's socks, feeling for the holes, now they had dried after washing them in the water. Despite her ordeal, she was determined to remain a mother to her son. No one would take that from her, not even the Nazis.

A few hours later, Sean moored the boat by a tree that ran below the Budgakovs' house. It was three in the morning, but the paraffin lamps hanging from the beams in the dining room were still lit. The Irishman crouched down behind a tree and watched for any movement and listened for the slightest sound. All was silent, and eerily so was the forest. The only scent in the air was from the log fire, and there was no sign of smoke rising from the stone-brick chimney, now. The Irishman drew his knife and made his way up the grassy slope to the house. Tobias was not barking. He would surely have picked up the scent of the villain that stole his blanket by now.

Ryan was ten yards from the house, but now the overwhelming smell, one he knew well, hit him. He charged forward at the door. As he expected it burst open easily, for the house and its wood were brittle, soaked, baked and dried repeatedly from years exposed to the extremes of the seasons. As he landed on the floor, knife at the ready, he prayed beyond reason that he would look up to find the family looking down at him, having risen earlier than usual to begin their chores. Instead, he was met by a horror that he could never have imagined.

He looked up to find Larne and his sons hanging from the beams by chains around their necks. All were facing towards the table. On the table were the naked bodies of Christina and her daughters. All four were slit open from their throats to their stomach. From the orientation of the women's bodies, and the position that the four chairs now lay in, he calculated that the men had been forced to watch as the women disembowelled, probably after being violated.

There were sixteen distinct circles, each the size of a large shilling on the bare wooden floor, where the women's blood had dried around the wooden legs of the stools. The chairs must have been kicked away some time after the blood had dried, which suggested that it had gone on for some considerable time.

Ryan heard Magdalena and Tóth making their way up the hill behind him. He spun around to find the Tobias, pierced on a wall hook next to the door. He stepped quickly to the doorway and pulled what was left of the door behind him.

'My friends are not here. They must have gone to visit relatives. Let's not lose any time and return to the boat.'

'What is that terrible smell?' asked Tóth. Sean was silent as he hurried them both back towards the slope. 'But weren't they expecting us?'

'Yes, I think they probably were,' replied the Irishman.

Sean noticed before he crashed through the door, that it had not been forced and once inside there were no signs of a struggle. The Budgakovs had been expecting them – that was the problem.

Magdalena knew from the Irishman's clipped instructions that something terrible had happened, but she trusted the man and did not ask questions. The only thing now was to get Tóth to safety. She never mentioned it to Sean, but as they climbed the hill to approach the house, she had tried to hold Tóth back. The stench of death was unmistakable.

Once the woman and the boy set off down the slope, rather than racing down the hill with them, Sean turned back towards the house. He grabbed any blankets he could find and ripped curtains from the windows and sheets from the beds, and with great care he began to cover the bodies. The stench of the opened bodies was over-powering, but he kept to his task. He knew that if the murders returned, they would know that they had been there and that they were close by.

But though Sean was not a spiritual or religious man, he wanted to provide the family, a family that he had no doubt had been murdered because they had harboured him from the enemy, with some dignity in death. The first body he covered was Christina. He pulled a fresh linen tablecloth over her body and then he lifted her shawl over her contorted, horrified face. Sean lay his hand on her ice-cold, alabaster cheek and wiped the trails of dried salt that had flowed from her eyes. He was certain that everything she had given life to and nurtured had been violated and murdered in front of her.

After lifting the men down from the chains, he covered Larne with the tablecloth. Then the two eldest girls and the three boys, with blankets from their beds. Finally, he came to Sasha's. He carefully rested the beautiful handmade patterned quilt, which Christina had finished, over her. He knew she would have physically suffered most of all before they finally killed her. In war, murderers always violate and corrupt the beautiful, and those with promise. Those who are inaccessible to them in times of peace. With a mixture of rage and sorrow, he tenderly pressed his forehead against hers for a moment and closed his eyes as he did so. Then he rose and gently lifted the end of the bedcover over her face.

A few minutes later Sean re-joined Magdalena and Tóth in the boat. As he rowed away from the riverbank, he watched the boy curl up in his mother's arms and drift off to sleep. Magdalena did not sleep. Aware of the danger, she held her son tightly to her.

Since leaving Ireland as a young man, Sean understood that whenever he rested, death would arrive unannounced, for friend and foe alike. As he rowed, he thought that perhaps once the woman and the boy were safe, he would stop running, turn and accept his fate. But when the time came, he would take down as many of the Budgakovs murderers and Magdalena's torturers as he could.

Though he had only slept for a few hours over the last two days, Sean rowed steadily but continuously, only stopping to drink some water, until they reached the river's edge by the Weiner Prater Gardens of Vienna. He moored the boat beneath a bridge, and the three made their way towards the British Embassy in the centre of the city.

Paul had driven away from Budapest right after Sean had destroyed the train station, just in time to escape the cordon hastily thrown up around the city. He had reached Vienna a day earlier than Sean, in part because he was driving a new Mercedes-Benz 150 Sports. The Irishman had collected a note from Paul, which he had left for them at the British Embassy. The note told them to meet him in the plush Café Griensteidl when they reached Vienna. After collecting his message, the woman and the boy had taken advantage of the Embassy's washrooms. A kind woman who worked in the post room and had a boy about the same age as Tóth provided them with some spare clothing.

Meanwhile, Sean was led to a transmitter where he tried to reach the contact he had been given in the Admiralty. But he was told that she was with her family in Cheltenham and could not be reached. He left a message for her and then once Magdalena and Tóth were ready, he headed to the café. After reaching the café and passing through its beautiful oak and glass doors, they sat at one of its ornate white-veined marble-topped tables. Sean had brushed aside the one shown to them by the maître d' and selected one away from the centre, by the kitchen doors. The Irishman positioned himself with his back to the restaurant's beautiful marble walls. He had a perfect view of all the entrances and exits and the heavy, blue cotton curtains that were drawn across one of the alcoves on the far side of the room. They had moved slightly when they had first entered the restaurant.

Magdalena was more accustomed to such surroundings than Sean, though it pained her not to be able to see them, and she ordered lemon tea and a variety of exquisite Viennese pastries by name. Tóth was delighted, as it reminded him of more peaceful times and the very glamorous tea-rooms overlooking the main square in Debrecen. This was where his father would take the four of them for lunch every Sunday. It was also where his father, while his mother sat silently, told him that he had to leave for Amsterdam and that he was taking Lens with him. Tóth clasped his sister's hand when she started to cry.

An immaculately dressed waiter, wearing black flannels, a black bow tie, brilliantly polished black shoes and a bright white apron and a similar starched high collar shirt, served them. He was overly civil to the woman and the boy, as if he was sympathising with them for having to share their table with the rough-looking man. Sean looked at his dark blue woollen jumper, faded trousers, scuffed boots and knew that if he was not so intimidating, he would have been asked to leave.

After Magdalena had given the waiter their order, the Irishman growled at the man. The waiter left immediately, leaving Tóth laughing heartily.

'Even where you have no enemies, I see you have to make them,' noted Magdalena. Sean and Tóth saw her smile briefly, before it disappeared behind the teacup she lifted to her lips. The man and the boy exchanged a quick smile and then a nod, indicating that the older man had been suitably chastised and that he had accepted his rebuke.

Paul appeared at the oak doors, looking as flustered as usual. Sean decided it was best to intercept him, and he led him to a table at the other side of the room and away from the blue curtains. Sean noticed that the young man's demeanour was drawing even more attention from the other diners than he. Having made sure that he could observe the other diners seated at various tables, the Irishman began his questions. He asked the Hungarian what he knew of events following the fight in the train station. However, it was only after another waiter had handed the young man a glass of wine and lit his cigarette, that he had composed himself enough to speak.

Paul told him that with the train station ablaze, it seemed every fireman in Budapest was trying to douse the flames. The police secured the area for two blocks around the station, checking everyone's documents, and began emptying passenger's bags on the pavement. As if they

164

were expecting Magdalena and Tóth to fall out.

After the police checked his papers, Paul did not wait around and jumped into his car and drove straight to Vienna. He arrived yesterday morning and had been at the British Embassy ever since making arrangements to transport the woman and the boy to England as soon as they arrived. After he discovered that his message had been collected by a woman with a boy and 'a big, fearsome, scruffy-looking man,' he had made his way straight to the café.

Paul looked at the Irishman, and said, 'That was the receptionist's . . . description of you . . . err, not mine,' as he handed Sean the train tickets along with forged ID papers for Magdalena and the boy. It took Paul half an hour to update Sean, and that was only after repeated but polite reminders by the Irishman to be concise.

After the Hungarian had finished, Sean had one question: 'Who supplied the forged documents?'

'London and they had them delivered by a courier marked TOP SECRET.' Sean frowned, as it might as well have been sent direct to the spies in the Embassy (they all have them), marked 'FOR THE IMMEDIATE ATTENTION OF THE ENEMY'.

The Hungarian had selected an exquisite restaurant for their last meal together. With its splendid red velvet booths, its beautifully designed mahogany chairs and dark wood panelling, it exhibited a splendour that would have made the Hapsburgs feel at home. After their recent traumas Magdalena and Tóth were delighted to be in such civilised surroundings, but Sean was uneasy. It was not the place to meet if you did not wish to attract attention.

Every European city has a glamorous establishment

that comes with a reputation for intrigue. It attracted diplomats, journalists and spies, who loved to experience the grandeur normally reserved only for the rich and powerful, if only for a few hours.

But this was not the time to remonstrate with the young man, as Sean had to inform him of the fate of his family. The Irishman held back the horrific details of the manner of their deaths, but it made no difference. On hearing the news, Paul fainted. The waiters stopped serving and looked over at the fearsome-looking man who was lifting the smaller man up off the granite tiled floor. All were firmly of the belief that the huge ruffian had punched the poor sensitive young man to the ground. The Irishman brought him back onto his feet, but he held the young man firmly by his shoulders and told him, 'Grieve, but later. We must concentrate on the living, or your family died for nothing.'

Paul summoned all the strength he could, while Sean kept his arm around him as he led him over to Magdalena and Tóth.

The boy nodded, carried on eating, and did not notice the fragile condition of the young man who now joined them at the table. Magdalena stood up and searched for the man's hand and shook it. She thanked him for his help, but was surprised that he did not say anything, and how cold and limp his handshake was.

Sean informed the woman and the boy that they must go with the young man. Magdalena lifted her hand to find the Irishman's face and when she did, she whispered, 'Thank you.'

She left her hand on his cheek for a few seconds, before trying to gather her son's hand. As always, he

166

found hers first.

When they reached the front doors of the Café, Tóth stopped.

'Mama, wait.' He released his mother's hand and ran back towards the man. 'From my mother and I, thank you,' he said and held his hand up to Sean. The Irishman shook it firmly. The boy laughed, as if all the fear of the last week had evaporated. He turned to go, but after taking a few steps he ran back to Sean and hugging him around the waist as hard as he could.

'Take care of your mother, and when you grow up become powerful, remember to be a good man,' said Sean, ruffling the boy's hair, but not to conceal his pain this time.

The boy looked up at the man. 'Maybe it might not be so bad to one day be a little like you.'

'Not if you want to have tea in plush surroundings like this, it won't,' replied Sean, as he looked around at the waiters, who were glancing over.

Tóth ran back to his mother, took her hand and led them both out the door. Sean barely noticed the driver, as her chauffeur's cap was pulled firmly down. The driver opened the car door. Once Paul had made his way unsteadily into the back of the car, the vehicle was driven away.

For some time, the Irishman stood by his table just looking at the empty doorway. It had been a long time since he had grown that close to anyone. He smiled at the thought that perhaps not all feeling had died within him after Ireland. The maître d' interrupted his thoughts, as the waiters refused to go anywhere near the dangerous-looking man. He handed him a note. *'Dankaschön,'* replied Sean as the maître d' backed away while not taking his eyes off him. Sean opened the folded piece of paper; in English it read, 'CAN YOU DRIVE A BUS?'

He noticed in the far corner of the café, another customer, a short, dark-haired woman, had appeared and was rolling a cigarette. She looked up at him as she did so, slowly running her tongue along the paper, never once taking her eyes off him. Then she slipped the complete but unlit cigarette in her top pocket of her waist-length brown leather flying jacket. She rose and strode over to Sean. Standing in front of him, she glared up at him.

'So, you're the Irishman who doesn't like Nazis,' she said, pausing for a reaction from the man whose intimidating presence had terrified those around them. There was none, only the intensity of his eyes on her. She slipped the cigarette between her lips and lit it. Defiantly, she matched his stare.

'My name is Lenka.'

Chapter 7: Jewel's Story

January 1915, Melbourne

Jewel's mother died giving birth to her little brother Michael. Her father died a year later in the Gallipoli Campaign, December 1915. Many Australian and New Zealand families lost men, some say nearly 120,000 dead and the same again in casualties. The blame was laid on the instigator of the ill-thought-through campaign, the First Lord of the Admiralty, Winston Churchill.

When the little blonde girl was aged four, she and her little brother were put into the custody of their only immediate relative that anyone knew of, an elderly great-aunt on the borders of senility. By the time Jewel was seven, she was looking after her great-aunt as well as her little brother.

That year, their official guardian died and the local authorities decided the children should be farmed out to any family who would provide them with food and lodgings. Jewel was heartbroken to be separated from her little brother; her only friend. Their separation was brutal. They were lifted from their beds during the night. Neither was given a chance to say goodbye or even hold each other for the last time. Distraught and struggling, each child was loaded into the back of separate pickup trucks and driven away.

After a three-day drive, Jewel was dropped onto the

wooden steps of a ramshackle farmhouse, along with the post – a bundle of red-labelled reminders for unpaid bills. Mrs Blunt, the farmer's wife, handed her a cloth and told her to wash the farmhouse's wooden floors. Jewel spent the remainder of her childhood years working hard for the Blunt household, and never complained. Her only concern was the fate of her little brother.

The farmhouse looked like it had been abandoned. The outside had not been painted for two decades or more. Much of the surrounding greenery was weeds, and the rest was dried bushes and roots. For a farm, there were, surprisingly, no animals wandering about, no dogs or cats, but she could hear noises coming from the barn. Equally surprisingly, there was no garden or allotment at the back for growing herbs or vegetables. The farm's sole purpose was to grow wheat, and that was the only thing that thrived.

Mr and Mrs Blunt had bought the homestead twenty years earlier, when they moved from Sydney for reasons that they never volunteered when their neighbours made polite enquiries. When one neighbour pressed further, they broke off contact with all the neighbouring farms. The only person they spoke to in the area was the storekeeper when they had to buy vegetables, spices, and spirits.

The Blunts had three sons, who terrorised Wanadoo, a town four hours' drive away. If the boys went to school, it was usually to hassle some poor girl or to extort pocket money off their classmates.

Mr and Mrs Blunt and their three sons barely bothered Jewel except to assign her work. Her chores started at four in the morning and lasted well after dusk. It was hard work, but not unusual work for farms in the area. However, the brutal treatment of the young girl was not usual. She never went to school and if neighbours were concerned about her welfare and turned up at the house to ask about her, they were met with savage abuse and ordered from the property by its owners.

Mr Blunt and his sons would lash out at her. Everything had to be done immediately, in most cases as soon as they had thought of it. The mother took a special dislike to the girl. Some nights she would drag the girl from her makeshift bed of hay in the barn and strike her with her husband's belt, often without bothering to manufacture a reason.

The young Jewel made the barn her sanctuary, but one that she happily shared with the other occupants. No matter how tired she was each night she would brush Benjamin, the only horse on the farmstead, and Nellie the goat and wash down Mr and Mrs P, the pigs and their latest litter, and provide extra food for the array of rabbits and chickens whom she called her family. Jewel was like most young girls, full of play, often dressing up Nellie, which did not last long as the goat ate any hats made from bits of cloth and hay rested on her head. She desperately wanted to play with other children, but there were none.

Acts of kindness or attempts to be part of the Blunt household were angrily repelled, but being a strong, optimistic girl, she refused to be broken. After all, her brother would need her support one day, and in the meantime, she channelled her love towards the animals, showering them with warmth and affection.

The poorly maintained house and barn were the only buildings for miles, but at night the atmosphere within each could not be more different. From the barn laughter could be heard, from the house only voices raised in anger.

It was the middle of autumn, 1925. Jewel had reached her thirteenth birthday, or thereabouts. There were no calendars in the house and as she was not allowed to go to school, it was impossible to know. She had kept a diary, but a year earlier Mrs Blunt found it. It was one of the few things that Jewel had time to grab when she was taken from her great-aunt's home. Since then, she had hidden it, but kept a meticulous record of the animals' births, deaths and illnesses. She loved books and there were no other books, not even in the main house, but it was only years later that she was properly learnt how to read and write properly. The night Mrs Blunt used the diary to light the fire in the house.

The brothers started to take an interest in Jewel. She was growing into a very beautiful young woman. One evening, Jewel had pans of water boiling away on the stove for the evening meal and had gone to the barn to check on a new litter produced by Mrs P. She heard the large rickety barn doors open and looked up to find the two eldest brothers standing unsteadily. Jewel was terrified as they staggered towards her. They circled her, leering menacingly, stinking of alcohol, each waiting for the other to move first. They started to goad each other on. The elder of the two grabbed at her shawl. Jewel leapt past him and dived through the gaping arms of the other.

The girl ran into the house, but it was still empty.

The brothers pursued her, both falling over as they did so. For the first time, she noticed that one of them had torn a sleeve off her dress, exposing her bare shoulder. In their drunken haste, they wedged themselves in the brittle frame of the front door. The younger broke free of his brother, breaking three panels of the door and part of the door frame away from the wall as he did so, and leapt at her.

Jewel evaded his arms once more and ran past him, making towards the broken door, but this time the elder brother caught her square on the face with the palm of his powerful left hand. She found herself propelled through the air until she smashed her head against the kitchen stove. Jewel tried to lift herself up from the floor. Blood streamed down her face from the impact with the oven's metal door handle. As the brothers tore her clothes off and tried to turn her over, she caught sight of the light reflecting off a chopping knife that had lain on the cooker but had fallen onto the wooden floor. Jewel grabbed it, slashing wildly until she hit one of them. The elder brother screamed as he threw his hands up to his bloody nose.

The next few moments marked her both physically and emotionally for life. The brothers grabbed the saucepans full of boiling water from the top of the stove and rained their contents down on her. She screamed. Her flesh melting away as she tried to crawl across the splintered wooden floor. With kicks flying in and more scolding water pouring down, she lost consciousness.

Jewel was woken by noises coming from the house. It

was a mix of shouting, swearing and occasionally, even laughter. Had she woken from a terrible dream? But then when she tried to move, pain ripped through her, and every breath tore at her melted skin that had fused with the cold, compacted earth. She laid there for hours but wanted nothing more than to disappear under the soil. The animals were silent. Benjamin and Nellie were both tethered as usual, but their ropes were taut as they strained to look at her. Mr and Mrs P were penned in, but their snouts were wedged between the slats of their pen.

Jewel heard a man's footsteps coming towards the barn and she knew by the heaviness of his steps it was the Mr Blunt. She heard the noise of the barn doors being pushed open, followed by heavy steps. A man's boot appeared in front of her face. Rough hands seized her body and ripped her it from the dirt. She screamed as parts of her skin that had meshed with the hard ground were torn away from her bones, exposing the nerves. The man carried her over to Benjamin's stall, opened it with one sweep of his hand and threw her unceremoniously onto his soiled bedding.

Mr Blunt then led the animal out and harnessed him for the plough, as he did every day, to work for the next fourteen hours. The animal was shaking his head as if bewildered. Perhaps, she thought, he was wondering why she had not brushed his coat the night before, or was it that he recognised her scent, but not her.

Jewel worked at the farm for two more years. It would have been a miracle for an adult to survive such an attack, even with the best of medical attention, but somehow the young woman had. Each night she would make her way

174

to the barn, though far more slowly than before. Her left leg was permanently deformed from the severe burns and she was susceptible to regular infections, as she had never been taken to a doctor. Her left hand had shrivelled from the burns into the shape of a claw. She continued to tend her animals each night – she was of the firm view that they should not suffer because of what the men had done to her. No one mentioned the attack, though at least for the first few weeks the two brothers refused to look at her for fear of catching her eye. The young men's look eventually turned from embarrassment to disgust.

Their father and mother, along with all three brothers, returned to their previous treatment of her, looking through her, unless it were to shout orders or berate her. The only other time the sons paid her any attention was when they drove back from the town drunk and made their way to the barn. These incidents became rarer, for each time one of them entered the barn in the middle of the night, Jewel would roll over so they could see her scarred skin down the left side of her face. If they persisted, she would pull back her faded blouse to reveal the burns across her shoulders. They would curse her, but all that mattered was that they left her alone and, wherever Michael was, he was safe.

It was a sweltering day in July 1927 when Jewel, aged about fifteen, answered a knock at the front door of the farmhouse. It startled her, as no one ever knocked at the door of the Blunt household – the neighbours no longer dared even approach the house.

It took a while for her to make her way across the room, so she repeatedly kept calling out, 'Sorry, I'll be with you in a minute.'

The young woman opened the door, not knowing who to expect, except that it could not be the men of the house – if one of them was too drunk to open the door, they would have kicked it in.

Standing in the doorway was the silhouette of a woman in a wide-brimmed hat that eclipsed the sun, with a taller man standing behind her. The woman removed her straw hat, releasing rays of sunshine into the bleak house.

Jewel got a better look at her face. She was in her late thirties with a beautiful, sun-kissed face – a face that had seen much and yet had welcoming lines that told you that she laughed often. She broke into a large beaming smile, but it disappeared just as suddenly and was replaced by one of shock.

'There is no one here, I'm afraid,' said Jewel softly, not wishing to meet the woman's gaze. 'The house is empty.'

The man stepped forward. 'But you are here.'

He was handsome, taller than Jewel but maybe a few years younger than her. He looked at the young woman and with tears streaming down his cheeks, uttered just one word: 'Jewel.' It was the first time that she could remember that anyone had called her by her name. The young man bent down, releasing more sunlight into the room, until his eyes were level with the young woman's face and repeated her name, 'Jewel, it's me Michael, your brother.'

The kindly lady took the young woman's right hand in hers. 'I'm Elizabeth, your father's sister. I went to live in Spain before you were born. I'm here to take you and

176

Michael to Spain to live with me and my family.' She tried to smile, but tears were now flowing freely down her cheeks. 'Oh, my child, what have they done to you?'

Jewel was confused and glanced sideways again at the young man. His features were like her little brothers, but this was a man, but he had that same magnificent red hair. The day after her mother died, her father returned from the hospital and presented her little brother to her. She remembered him saying, 'His hair is a bonfire of flame' and 'take care of him'. The boy who claimed to be her brother, fell onto her and hugged her. He was sobbing inconsolably. Jewel could not remember the last time anyone had held her so close, but his strong embrace caused her great pain. She caught that familiar scent . . . 'It's . . . you . . .' it was impossible to believe, 'Michael!'

The woman and man led her gently by the hands, to show her the bright yellow Ford Model T parked in front of the crumbling shell of a house. Pulling up in front of the conspicuous car was the dull brown pickup truck. Jewel's aunt grasped her hand tightly as they approached the young woman's abusers.

'You bastards!' screamed the tall young man.

He was about to run at the three men jumping down from the back of the truck, but the woman caught him by the arm and held him back.

'Please Michael, I understand, but we need to protect, not avenge your sister.'

The young man wiped away tears, now of rage, and took his place to the left of Jewel, who offered her withered hand to him. He carefully took hold of it as if it were the rarest of flowers.

Mrs Blunt and her husband emerged from the front

of the vehicle. Their sons armed themselves with thick sticks of the firewood they had purchased in town and formed a wall in front of the woman's glitzy automobile.

The girl looked at her brother and then pulled at the kind lady's hand, as she said, 'Please, I'll go back in, just take my brother with you and care for him.' As the woman grasped her hand tightly, Jewel saw that her tears were running along her laugher lines.

Elizabeth strode with even greater purpose towards the Blunt family. With the sun was to her left, her shadow stretched towards them. The lady released Jewel's hand, and, to everyone's surprise, grabbed one of the brothers' clubs, wrenched it from his hand and threw it with all her might into the distance. Her strength was nothing to that of the now-disarmed man, but her determined look and courageous act stunned him. The woman pushed each man away from the car, like they were cattle blocking her way to a gate. Jewel looked at them and for the first time, the men who had terrified her, crippled her and abused her appeared small and insignificant. Mr Blunt backed away towards his truck, closely followed by his sons.

Mrs Blunt remained standing in front of the driver's car of the model T. She looked down at Jewel and spat towards the girl, but Jewel's aunt held out her hand and caught it. She took a white lace handkerchief from her brightly coloured orange handbag and used it to wipe the yellowish spittle from her hand. Then she folded the handkerchief and placed it back into her bag. Mrs Blunt met the girl's aunt's still unflinching gaze, but then turned and shoved her brood towards the house.

Michael gently helped his sister into the red leather backseat of his aunt's car and then slipped in next to her.

Elizabeth opened the driver's door, lifted the hem of her red and yellow, flowery cotton dress and eased herself down into the driver's seat. She turned the ignition on and looked over her shoulder to give Jewel a most wonderful smile. Then the sturdy little yellow car slowly drove away.

Chapter 8: The Orphanage

February 1938, Vienna

'Do I look like a fucking bus-driver? If you want someone to take your bags to the station, hail a taxi,' growled Sean at the short, dark-haired woman smoking a cigarette and standing in front of him in the middle of Café Griensteidl.

'You don't look like a bus-driver, but you speak in the manner of one. Drink?'

'Yes, please,' he said, and walked back to the table with the woman.

Sitting at the table, Lenka honoured her offer: 'Any particular brandy?'

'Yes. A double.'

Lenka shouted across their order, including another bottle of red wine to the nearest waiter. Within minutes, he returned unsteadily with a tray of drinks.

'I have thirty children to smuggle out of Poland,' said Lenka.

'You've been a busy lady. You've kept your figure though.'

'Oh, another comedian. They're in an orphanage. I'm told you do this kind of thing. Will you help?'

'Of course, I just need to find a large enough wheelbarrow.'

Lenka frowned as she wondered why all the men she

knew made stupid jokes. But she continued and told him about the orphanage and that the children there, most were disabled, some mentally, others physically and some both.

'The Nazis want to exterminate all those who do not meet their ideas of perfection. Have you heard that they have built clinics in Germany where you can bring your child if it has a disability, or even judged a little slow, so you can have it, "humanely relieved of its burden".'

A few months earlier the Irishman had razed to the ground a similar facility. The Nazis had secretly built in the hostile terrain of the fjords, that even the Norwegian Government did not know about. But Sean decided not to divulge anything to the woman for now.

'Best way to tell a Nazi is that they will always have a euphemism for murder,' added Lenka. She then jabbed the stub of her cigarette into the inch-thick glass ashtray, 'Fuckers!'

This caught the attention of a waiter and a large party who had just arrived for an early lunch. They stared across at the wild-looking couple, then quickly looked away again.

Lenka banged the base of her pack of Black Spot cigarettes on the table and put the one that jumped furthest from the pack between her lipstick-free lips. Sean was to learn that she always found the most direct route to do anything. She offered one to the Irishman.

'No thank you. I was a sickly little child with asthma, so I never liked smoke.'

'You look fit enough now,' she replied, but thought it was unusual for a man to admit his imperfections.

Perhaps, she thought, the Irishman was inferring

that in a different time, in a different country, he might have been volunteered to be 'humanly relieved of his burden'.

'Recently, the Germans have been making border raids into my country. I've told the Polish authorities and they think the Nazis are trying to goad them into war. Extra troops have been deployed on the borders, but the raiders are professionals. By the time we raise the alarm, the damage is done and they have disappeared into the mountains. It doesn't seem to be widespread. Our orphanage has been singled out for special attention for some reason.'

'In what way?'

'I have been away for some time.' From what was left of her tan, Sean judged that it was not because she had been in jail. 'The raids began the week just before I returned. They burnt our barn down and killed the cow, her calf and the chickens that supplied us with much of our food. On their last raid, they removed five of our most handicapped children and took them to God knows where. They also told all the staff to leave or they would be taken away the next time.'

'How many staff do you have at the orphanage?'

'Dr Levi, Gilda and Sophia are all from the local hospital. They volunteer their time to help Olen, my little helper, and I keep the home going.'

The Polish woman swigged back her double brandy in one swift arm movement and the thick glass clattered back down on the white marble table. Most of the diners at the now full restaurant jumped, but none looked over. 'Olen told me that the German officer in charge of the raiding party had gathered all the children together. He told them that Himmler had ordered the construction of a special hospital to treat them and that his "Wolves" – whoever the fuck they are – would be back to take them there.' Her rage was building. After she refilled both of their brandy glasses from the wine bottle left on their table, she drank a large measure and again slammed her glass down only this time, shouted, 'Bastards!'

This caused the four waiters dashing between tables in the now very busy café to look over at their table. They nodded to each other and approached the table. Sean glowered and grunted loudly. The waiters stepped back. Lenka suppressed a smile. Before coming to the café, she had made some enquiries about the Irishman. One of her French contacts who, to his misfortune he confessed, had clashed once with 'The Englander', described him as 'mad, bad and dangerous to know'; now she believed him.

The maître d' summoned his waiters back and, looking over at the 'wild couple', put his finger to his lips. Lenka in turn gave him the finger. The waiters grinned at each other and went back to taking orders from their tables.

Sean asked Lenka about her background; it was the best way to detect a spy, as they always told too perfect a tale. Lenka made it clear that all that mattered was the children, and she had no time to indulge in stupid small talk with him. This convinced Sean that she was who she claimed she was – any spy would be eager to tell all they had learnt. But she talked of the war in Spain, a story told with passion, mostly anger. This part could have been faked, but after an hour of questions and four double brandies, he decided to at least listen to her escape plan for the children.

Lenka, too, kept her eyes firmly focused on the Irishman. This was not to see if he was who he claimed to be – the description given to her by London matched him perfectly – but for signs that he had a brain and was not just brawn. He was tall, nearly as tall as Chris, Jake and Vodanski, and only a little broader than the American but less than the Russian. His eyes were grey-green, warm, even kind, a look that was enhanced by his laugh, which came easily when he was with friends, as she observed when he was with the woman and the boy.

But when the anxious young man appeared later, the Irishman adopted a persona that was intense and focused. Lenka had to admit, he exerted a formidable presence. She noticed how when the anxious young man started to cry, the Irishman transformed himself once more, throwing his arm around the man to support him, his voice softening while his body relaxed so he appeared less threatening. What struck her most of all was his movement. He was light, almost graceful for such a large man, like a large prowling cat. She had never seen anyone who moved so conscious of his surroundings while his eyes missed nothing. This he now confirmed by saying, 'By the way, for future reference, curtains move when you peek out from behind them.' He added, 'They also don't stop bullets, so next time find something a little more solid.'

'If you knew I was watching you, how come you didn't drag me out?'

'Not while Magdalena and the boy were there, but if you hadn't appeared when they left there would have been polish stew on the menu.'

'Don't be fooled by my size or my sex.'

'If I thought for one moment you were a threat to the woman or the boy, don't think being a woman would have stopped me blowing your brains out – that's if you have one.'

'When this is over, try it, and I'll nail your balls to your head.'

'More brandy?' asked Sean, but he did not wait for an answer as he filled both glasses, before he returned to pressing her for more information.

'When did you first make contact with London?'

'When I returned from Spain, I sent messages to London through the Polish Embassy, informing them of the Nazi raids.'

'The Brits, why? Its government has its shirt tail up and is offering its hairy arse to Herr Hitler.'

'We, like the Czechs, are powerless, caught between Hitler and Stalin. We're a brave people, but our cavalry can't match tanks. But England has always championed our independence, and I hoped it would offer sanctuary for the children.' She shook her head. 'But you are right, I got nowhere. Then I wrote directly to Winston Churchill.' Lenka looked inquisitively at the Irishman, remembering the telegram. 'You know the old warhorse?'

'The name rings a bell.'

'A week later I received a communique from London acknowledging my request. Three days later I received delivery of a British Mk III Suitcase Transceiver so I could be in regular contact when,' she stopped herself and added, '*we* are on the move. A few days ago, I deciphered another communique, saying that you were heading to Vienna and that you might be able to help.'

'Good looks, wit and charm, keeps me in popular

demand.'

This was not how London described the man, but Lenka was still making up her mind as to whether he really was stupid, arrogant or simply making fun of himself.

'Why not just put your children on a train to England?' asked Sean.

'You don't know much, do you?'

'I'll take that as a compliment, as most people think I don't know anything.'

'The Nazis are doubling security checks on all trains coming from the East. Jews and those with disabilities are, at the very least, being sent back,' and then in a low voice she added, 'while others are marched away.'

'I take it *we* are not driving all the way to the English Channel?'

'No, once we get over the border, we will head to Berlin and take a train from there,' she said and sat back and waited for the man to explode, as she had when London informed her that was to be their destination.

'Berlin! You must be fucking joking.'

'A special train is being organised by some wealthy benefactors, to take immigrants to London. It is due to set off from Berlin in a week or so. It's our best hope.'

'Once we are out of Poland, why not carry on to France?'

'I have some forged papers, but they won't stand up to the intense scrutiny that the Nazis will give them at borders. The Czechs will not care too much, as they have other things to worry about. But, according to the latest intelligence from London, the Germans are not too stringent in their checks on their southern border, as their

187

focus is France and Poland. London believes the children are equally at risk from the Austrian and the Italian authorities, as they are believed to be sympathetic to Hitler. The Swiss may turn us back to protect their neutrality.'

The Irishman stood up. 'Come on, let's go, if we're going.'

As they picked up their knapsacks to head to the train station, she turned to the Irishman and asked, 'Do you just go with any woman who asks you to go off with them?'

'Only the foul-mouthed ones.'

'I see why they call you 'The Englander', as I hear the Irish have charm.'

As they got to the door of the restaurant, Sean smiled and announced, 'Ladies first.'

'A little late for charm, isn't it?'

'It's my English persona coming to the fore, as there might be someone outside waiting to shoot me.'

Lenka stepped onto the cobbled street. She glanced up at the Hofburg Palace opposite. But unlike the other visitors to Vienna, she was not thinking of the splendour of the city's imperial palaces or its magnificent opera houses. Her thoughts were on the Irishman beside her, towering above her five-foot-six frame. Though they had been drinking hard, he never relented in his probing, while at the same time giving nothing away. London and perhaps the majority of those who encountered him greatly underestimated him. Certainly, whoever wrote the telegram from London, delivered to the orphanage a few days earlier, had: 'THE IRISHMAN HAS BRAWN,

CAN DRIVE AND IS RESILIENT. HOWEVER, HE IS OF LIMITED INTELLIGENCE AND SHOULD NOT BE PRIVY TO ANY INFORMATION BEYOND THAT REQUIRED.'

She had no doubt that he knew he was held in low regard by those in authority and that he played to it, using their ignorance to his advantage. He was certainly physically powerful, but what made him dangerous was his brain; she would have to keep her wits about her with the Irishman.

They boarded the train at Anhalter Bahnhof to Kraków, using forged papers that Lenka had managed to secure through her contacts. Sean was relieved to see they were not supplied by London. The carriage was packed with German troops off to fortify the Nazi forces already massed on the Polish border. The soldiers were noisy and brash. Sean had witnessed young men heading to the front line before, and often over-excitement usually masked nervousness.

However, the regular and unforced laughter exhibited by these young soldiers suggested a mood of confidence rather than fear. Lenka seemed to care little as she was used to being confined in small spaces awash with an abundance of testosterone. She placed her feet across Sean's lap and closed her eyes.

The Irishman sat there and endured the soldiers' sniggering and rude comments. Sean only knew a few words in German, but the rude gestures they made to each other told him enough.

After a few minutes, Lenka lifted her head, picking up one of the words spoken by one the soldiers. Sean had seen in the café that she did not give a damn what anyone thought, but now he was to learn that she was fearless as well as uninhibited. In perfect German, she turned her head to the abusive trooper and told him to 'go and fuck yourself'.

The recipient of her retort blushed and was lost for how to react in front of his colleagues. The other troopers were similarly unsettled, as she and maybe the brawny man who had not spoken might be German citizens. Ryan tensed up waiting for two, maybe three of the eight men to make the first move, but each was waiting for one of the others to take the lead. Fortunately for them, no one did.

It was nightfall and everyone was asleep, including the German troops. Sean looked down at the woman who was now fast asleep on his lap, with her arms wrapped around him. He found her feistiness incredibly attractive. Thinking she was asleep, and almost without thought, he bent down placed a gentle kiss on her hair before turning to look out of the window. He did not wish to miss his first look at Poland, even if it was shrouded in darkness, as the signs indicated that they would soon reach the border.

Lenka mumbled in English, 'And you can fuck yourself too.' He looked at his reflection smiling in the glass. He was starting to like this woman.

About a mile from the border, the German troops alighted.

Ten minutes later, as the train pulled away from the platform, Ryan watched the eight troopers standing on the platform pointing the barrels of their rifles at him.

On the other side of the border the carriage filled up again, this time with Polish troops. The Irishman guessed they were about the same age as the Germans, but the mood was very different, a mixture of sobriety, fatigue and apprehension. Most of them went to sleep as soon as they flopped onto their seats, but two stayed awake and occupied their time playing cards. They neither spoke to the two strangers or each other.

Over the last twenty years Sean had seen young men excited by the prospect of going to war, believing that death was for others. But these young men were preparing for invasion by an army that had already struck fear in their stronger allies – the French and the British. The enemy was stretched right along their borders, and Polish troops they did not know when or even where they would finally launch an all-out assault. That is the basis of fear: the realisation that your fate is no longer in your hands.

The Irishman noticed that two of the soldiers wore crucifixes around their necks. He remembered an article he had read in the *New York Times* a few months ago. It stated that in the last year church congregations across Europe had dramatically increased. He was not a religious man, believing it would take more than prayer to make peace with an enemy whose very existence was dependent on war. The young Polish men, from the household cavalry by the looks of the spurs dangling from their backpacks, knew it too. It explained why the heady optimism that you would normally have expected to see in men of that age, had been replaced by the despondent expressions of men expecting to die.

Before they had left Vienna, Sean had put in a call to Paul at the station.

'Paul, did Magdalena and Tóth board the train?'

'Yes, the driver dropped me off at the Embassy to collect their papers and then we went straight to the station.'

'Are you sure they got on the train?'

'Yes . . . I didn't leave until it pulled away from the platform . . . heading off in the direction of . . . the Hook . . . of Holland.'

'Good. Paul, I need your help once more.'

'Err . . . yes, of course . . . but it won't get me into trouble again with London, will it? They weren't happy with . . . me . . . after you revised the escape plan from Budapest.'

'It worked, didn't it?'

The young man fumbled for words, but Sean decided that he did not have time to wait for a 'Yes'.

'I have to transport all the children from an orphanage in Kraków to England . . .' There was no response. 'Paul, are you still there?'

'Yes . . . err . . . how many children would . . . that be?'

'Thirty, I'm told, maybe more by the time we get there.'

For a few more minutes the Irishman explained his plan to the even more agitated than usual Hungarian. Sean put down the receiver and turned to Lenka. 'I think I may have pushed the poor bastard towards insanity, but he's a good man and he will do what I ask.' Lenka would not understand his next comment, but the Irishman expressed it, anyway, 'At least for the sake of those he lost.'

When the train pulled into Kraków central station they were met by Lenka's little helper, Olen, who was sitting on a horse and cart trying to giddy up an uninterested mare. She was about fifty, maybe fifty-five – she was not sure herself; but all four and a half feet tall of her, if that, was full of vigour and optimism. When she saw Lenka she ran up and hugged her, as a mother would welcome home a long-lost daughter.

She wore an apron all the time. Sean was later told by a gathering of children around the dinner table that she kept it on when she went to bed. Sean himself saw that even when she changed it for a clean one, she did it quickly under the cover of the other, as a sunbather would change under a towel so no one glimpsed their nakedness. When she put on a new apron, within minutes you would not have known it was a clean, as she was continually cooking or cleaning and repeatedly wiping her hands on it. Her hair was tucked under a scarf, another part of her adopted uniform.

Sean noticed that when Olen was not busy cleaning the house, feeding the children or nursing them when they were ill, she would run after the children, grab one of them and whisk them up into the air. He had never seen anyone so delightfully happy.

'This is the wonderful Olen I mentioned,' said Lenka proudly. 'She is mute and a little innocent. Others say she is simple or has the mind of a child; I prefer innocent, but she is the engine that keeps the orphanage going.'

Olen looked up at Lenka, who she hugged once more, before stepping back to sign a message.

Lenka turned to Sean, 'Christ! The Nazis raided the orphanage again a few days ago. They took Gilda and Sophia with them.'

Olen hugged Lenka once more, but not in greeting, but in fear; fear for their children.

Sean jumped up onto the cart and reached forward to take the reins of the horse, but Lenka stopped him. 'The horse will take us back, but Olen likes to sit in the driving seat.'

A local hotel in the town allowed Olen to go back and forth from the station on their horse. It needed the exercise these days, as the hotel no longer had guests to ferry back and forth from the station.

Two hours later, Lenka took the reins to draw the cart to a halt in a little village to buy some further provisions for the long journey they were soon to take. A further hour later they pulled up outside her orphanage.

As a family home, the grey building was nothing unusual. It could amply hold maybe a family of eight, perhaps ten at a push; but it had to accommodate around thirty, sometimes even forty children, several with severe disabilities.

Sean noticed a flag on the roof. It was an apron with a smiling face drawn on it. Olen tugged on his hand, slapped her hand on her chest and smiled up at her work flapping above the chimney. Sean smiled at the woman. Olen was more than a wonder; she was a force of nature.

Next to the house lay the remains of the barn the Nazis had burnt down. Sean knew it was probably only the deep snow that covered the ten or so metres between the buildings that had saved the orphanage and all within it. He could see that Lenka had been right; the children were the target. Thieves would have taken the animals to sell or keep for themselves. But he could see the carcasses of the livestock had been locked inside before it was doused in paraffin and set alight. The aim of the raiders was to starve them out.

The snow leading up to the white stone building was a foot deep. All the lights were on and Sean could hear the laughter of children congregating in the corridor behind the front door. As soon as Lenka leapt off the passenger seat into the snow, which reached high above her woollen stockings, the children burst forth from their home and ran towards her. You could hardly see Lenka in the throng, and when she handed out sweets, the weight of them all caused the ball of joy and emotion to collapse into the snow. The Irishman grinned, as the laughter of the children, many physically disabled, was infectious.

Sean was enjoying the celebration, when a very serious boy appeared in front of him. The boy wiped his right hand down the side of his shorts and then extended his left arm up to offer his hand in welcome. The Irishman bent down to acknowledge the boy and his position – clearly, he was the top man in the orphanage – and shook his hand firmly as one would a superior. This satisfied the boy who retained his serious-looking face as he then ran off towards the ball of children rolling in the snow towards the house.

The Irishman was unloading the cart when the boy reappeared. He looked up at the Irishman and handed him a little shape made from a folded newspaper. Sean looked approvingly at the paper model of a lion.

Sean bend down and gave the little modeller a

thoughtful nod. 'This is very good indeed. But I need you to sign this work of art. It's what artists of world renown do.'

The boy frowned and then, without collecting his creation, he ran back towards the house, past the ball of children that was rolling around with Lenka. A minute later, he negotiated his way around the ball of joy once more, now wedged in the corridor, and ran back to the stranger who was unloading the last of the supplies. The boy put out his hand, and the man handed the lion who produced a blue crayon. In large letters the boy wrote, 'LEO' on both sides.

'A perfect name for a lion,' said Sean.

The boy seemed suitably pleased and ran off to join his friends.

Then, a young woman, aged about fifteen with a branch pared down for use as a cane, sauntered over towards the Irishman. He guessed by the weakness in her legs that her severe limp was the result of polio. Later, Lenka confirmed this to be the case for her, and four other children in the home.

'Leo had a very tough time before he came here, so he's a bit defensive,' the young woman said. 'But he's kind, and though he's only five, he's very protective of us all.' She smiled, 'You must be special as it's not like him to go up to someone and give them a gift of one of his animals. He's our resident artist.'

'Boys are always looking for a male mentor. I'm surprised he hadn't chosen Lenka; she's got bigger bollocks than I have!'

'Be quiet. She's got a fierce temper; she'll kill you if she hears you,' she whispered, glancing at the house to hide her smile. She then delicately bent down to pick up the paper bag full of fruit to bring into the house. 'I think it's more than that; it's his way of saying thank you for bringing Lenka back to us. I thank you too.'

'No one brings Lenka anywhere; she brought me.'

The young woman smiled again. 'I believe you're going to make us laugh a lot, even Leo. Mind your language though, as Olen will punch you in your aforementioned profanity if you swear in the presence of the children.'

'Quite right too! I promise to mind my Ps and Qs, my Bs and even my Cs.'

The young woman trudged back towards the celebrations, but stopped and turned, 'Oh, I'm sorry, I'm Ursula, by the way.'

She carried on traipsing back up the hill. Sean watched the young woman, who eased herself past the ball of delight, which was rolling towards the kitchen. Ursula resumed her task of kneading the dough she had started to prepare for when the ball dismantled for dinner.

Having brought all the provisions into the house, Sean hung a nosebag of oats on the horse. He patted its neck, as it was old now and it had meandered its way from the village up the winding path that led up to the orphanage like a tired old man. Once the horse had its fill, Sean unhooked the nosebag and placed it in the cart, only to find Olen was standing next to him – this was unusual he thought, as he only ever received this amount of interest from his enemies.

Olen looked up at him and then with trepidation to the snow-covered path leading to the house. Sean removed the knapsack he had just loaded on his back and lowered it to the ground. He knelt down, 'Come on. Up you get, granny.'

Olen slapped the horse on its hind quarters to send it on its rambling way back to the vacant hotel. Then, smiling and jumping up and down like an excitable little girl, she leapt up on the man's back.

On seeing the two, the ball of children disintegrated and began to laugh and clap with hysterical delight. Sean trudged towards the house, holding Olen's legs tightly to his hips as she waved her left arm at the children like they were her royal subjects. Sean did not see it, but Lenka looked at him in a way she had not looked at a man in a long time.

After devouring a wonderfully tasty goat casserole and singing songs, Lenka whisked all the children upstairs to bed. After kissing and hugging each of them, she returned to the kitchen.

Sean was helping himself to wine and drinking from one of their chipped coffee mugs that was missing a handle.

'Your house could do with a coat of paint,' he said.

She looked at the plaster falling off the wall, but the floors were always clean, as if falling plaster and dust evaporated before it hit. When not chasing children, Olen would flay the floors with a besom with life-threatening sweeps.

'No point? We're not staying.'

'So, this, I take it, was where you were raised. Barring Ursula, are all the children deaf or mute or both?'

'Yes. Many orphanages say they don't have the specialists required to look after them and, as everyone knows Olen, they view her as a specialist in the field. Of course, she isn't, she just simply loves each and every one of them.'

'That makes her a specialist in my book.'

'You surprise me; you're soft in the heart, as well as the head?'

'Do they all understand English?'

'Mostly. I wrote to Churchill when I was a girl and asked if he could send us any English books.' Sean looked at the books that lined the shelf. They covered subjects from cooking to brick laying; there was even one on the Duke of Marlborough. 'Through his benevolence, we know more about England than our own country.'

Lenka poured some wine into another cracked mug for herself and topped up the Irishman's drink. She drank the contents in one gulp, as did Sean.

They looked out of the window to watch Olen building a snowman to greet the children when they arrived at the breakfast table in the morning.

'Do you think Olen is aware of the danger?' asked Sean.

'Yes, but she thinks the best of everyone. Ever the optimist is Olen. She is innocent in more ways than one.' They continued to watch Olen who was now sitting on her own in the snow looking at the sky and waving at the stars. 'She is my only family,' revealed Lenka quietly, and then she took a long drink after refreshing their mugs. 'Right! Time to look at the bus,' she said as she filled their containers with the last of the measures from the bottle. 'You may need this,' before they drained the contents of the mugs.

Lenka approached a smaller barn. She opened both

doors as wide as possible. Inside was what looked like the abandoned shell of a bus.

'I didn't think it was worth covering it with a canvas, before I went to Spain.'

'Quite right, it might have collapsed under the weight.'

The Irishman reminded Lenka of Jake's cynicism when she first showed him and Vodanski the rickety helicopter in Madrid. They shared that same gallows humour, and she imagined he would come up with some derogatory name for the vehicle in the same way that Jake had scrawled 'The Flying Yellow Casket' in the dust on the body of the helicopter. But she was surprised when Sean lifted the bonnet of the bus and began tinkering with its engine and nodding, saying, 'Hmmm, a couple of metal braces and a rivet here and there. It should hold.'

Sean swept away the cobwebs to have a better look and, much to the loud consternation of its inhabitants, he removed the raven's nest from the roof rack. He leapt into the driver's seat and, on the eighth attempt, with the choke fully out and the throttle pedal flat to the metal floor, a burst of thick black smoke shot out from the exhaust.

'I'm impressed,' confessed Sean as he waved his arm frantically, now that Lenka now completely disappeared inside the smoke.

She yelled to be heard above the clattering of the pistons, 'The engine's good, Olen turns it over every week and she's very good with a wrench. The body's not too bad, is it?'

Lenka was disappointed in herself for not applying a film of grease where the body had been welded before

200

she left for Spain. The seals connecting the chassis and the body were riddled with rust.

With another blast of smoke, the Polish woman disappeared again from view, but Sean shouted, 'Tell Olen she's brilliant and I'll lift her up on my back and take her for six laps around the kitchen table before breakfast.'

Lenka's face appeared from out of the darkness, but her joy had faded into the haze.

'Do you think it will it take us all to Berlin?'

'In all honesty, we would have more of a chance if we manufactured some documents and put the children onto a train.' He knew what her reaction would be, but he felt he would say it anyway: 'Then, if we split into two groups, one may at least get through.'

'All of us or none of us.'

'You asked, and I gave you my honest opinion.' He turned the engine off, rested his arms on the steering wheel and looked at Lenka. 'I would have given the same answer if I was in your position.' She shrugged, but his words did nothing to alleviate her fears. Sean continued, 'How much time do you think we have?'

'Ursula said the Germans warned them that they had better be gone by the end of this week.'

'Two days.'

'They may come sooner. They seem to be taking an interest in more than just us. A couple of days ago, a group of Germans in civvies were seen surveying an area nearby, in a little town called Oświęcim – a town the Germans called Auschwitz.

Ursula and several of the children were there collecting potatoes for the farmer in exchange for some

201

milk and eggs for their labour. As the Germans walked around, she overheard one of them say that they intended to build one of their "treatment centres" there. The ignorant bastards think that just because some of the children are mute, that everyone was deaf.'

'It's going to be tight, but we go first thing in the morning. What is the terrain like?'

'We're expecting a heavy snowfall tonight, so every road will be treacherous. But while you prepare the bus, I'll drive into town to the school and try to secure the snow chains from the headmistress. She is a friend of ours, so it won't take much to persuade her that our need is greater.'

Rather than heading north-west taking the direct route to Berlin from Kraków, Lenka outlined an alternative route. They would head south-west to circumvent the Polish-German border. This would take them through the Sudeten Mountains, the intersection between Poland, Czechoslovakia, and Germany. The plan was to enter Germany from Czechoslovakia, in the hope that the Nazis would have less of a presence there than on the more heavily fortified Polish border. The problem was that no one knew what the Nazis would do next. She knew, as did Sean, that the success of her escape plan depended on one key determinant – luck.

Sean was uneasy about traversing the mountains. 'The main road looks like a sheer drop in places?' he asked, pointing to the Karkonosze Mountains on the map, bordering the Valley of the Kamienna River.

'True, particularly at the hair-pin bends. If we fail to negotiate them, we're finished.' Lenka was not one to hide the dangers or the weaknesses of her plan. 'Then there is Shooters Gallery.'

'How much cover will we have?'

'Well, apart from the mountains, it is all forest, but as we drive down and around the hairpin bends towards the border point and the town of Szklarska Poreba, we will be exposed. The area is renowned for its glassmaking in addition to some of the best skiing in the region, and furnaces need wood. Szklarska Poreba means "glass forest clearing".'

Irishman did not need to say anything as she had described Shooters Gallery.

'A ski resort; it will be a busy time of year,' he replied in a cheerful tone, trying to lift her spirits.

'I'm hoping that might be to our advantage as a school party heading to the slopes won't be out of place,' she replied.

Though, again, she seemed far from convinced now that she had said it, as several of the children could barely stand.

'You haven't held back on the risks; anything else?'

'When you asked about the sheer drop on the sides of the road, the greatest threat is not that the roads are not wide enough, but that they are covered in snow for a third of the year. This means we won't blend in with the other tourist buses until we come down from the mountains.'

'The Nazis won't be looking for us, as no one in their right minds would dare negotiate the mountains by vehicle at the height of winter.'

'I understand now why London thought I was the man for the job,' sighed Sean. 'And all this to reach Nazi Germany,' he shrugged.

Lenka did not share the Irishman's gallows humour. She cupped her face in her hands, knowing that the success of her plan was based on huge assumptions, including that the roads high up in the snow-covered mountain were passable. Since she first mapped out the route, she had had her doubts. The plan seemed more hopeless now that she had shared it with someone.

'I guess the one thing you are trying to avoid is heavy armour?' added Sean.

'In such inhospitable terrain, it's unlikely that the Germans will have tanks or armoured vehicles up in the mountains to block the roads if they see us. If I'm wrong, it would only take one vehicle to block our path or ram us off the road.'

Lenka looked at the Irishman. 'It's likely though, that we will meet the Nazis' 'mountain Rangers'. They patrol the border.'

She remembered how London had signed off the telegram about the Irishman: 'HE IS A LONE WOLF. WHEN THREATENED, HE WILL READILY RESORT TO VIOLENCE'. She added a postscript, 'But remember before you start shooting anyone, Polish troops wear similar white camouflage jackets and trousers covering their uniform as the mountain rangers.'

'No problem, when I meet anyone, I'll ask them; politely mind you,' producing an insincere smile, 'if they're a murderous Nazi? If they say yes, then I'll cave their skull in with a tyre-iron.'

'I don't think your knowledge of Polish and German is up to it. But the Nazis wear an arm band depicting the edelweiss flower.'

'Okay, I'll march up to them, turn them sideways,

and if it's a flower or bird shit on their sleeve, I'll knock their fucking head off. Happy now?' feigning another smile.

Sean remembered something about the edelweiss flower that his sister, Marisa, once told him that she had learnt at school. It was claimed that the flower was said to be unique to the Alps, as it only grew there due to the very high altitude. The Nazis were the masters in the use of symbolism. The symbol announced their supposed mastery of even the most inaccessible of locations.

'Anything else? As my blood is up and I'm keen to run off into the hills and pull the turret off my first Panzer tank of the day.'

'Look, we have a bus load of children and any stupid heroics will only put them in danger,' as Lenka's jaw jutted up. 'Fuck around with any of your gung-ho shit and this will be sticking out of your eye-socket'; she had lifted her boot and removed the serrated dagger and waved it in his face.

'Despite the foreplay, I don't give out on the first date, but when this is over perhaps a little candle-lit dinner somewhere?' responded Sean, producing a genuine smile.

Lenka ignored him, but he was just as infuriating as Jake and Vodanski. She shook her head at the thought of how unbearable it would be if the three were to meet.

'There's a pass in the mountains we have to negotiate, it's called Shooters Gallery. Many have lost their lives . . .'

'No need to explain, I understand. Let's try to get some sleep, if we are to make an early start. Where am I sleeping?'

'My room,' grabbing the surprised but delighted Irishman by the hand and dragged him back to the house and up the stairs that led to the loft at the top.

The next morning, Lenka woke from a restless night's sleep to find the Irishman gone. She rushed downstairs, naked but for the blanket she pulled off the bed. Lenka raced past a none-too-surprised Olen who was collecting all the spoons from the drawer so all the children could sit in the snow and have breakfast with the snowman – Ursula, having lost the argument to have breakfast served in the kitchen. There was no sign of Sean, but Lenka heard hammering.

In the barn, she found the Irishman nailing metal sheets from an old disused water tank that had once supplied the house onto the sides of the bus.

'If we're going to be target practice for snipers, a bit of body armour might even the odds a little.'

'Will it not make the bus too heavy, going up the mountains?'

'Maybe, but I have a crowbar to prise them off if they slow us down.'

'It will scare the children when they see it. They'll know we will be heading into danger.'

'They'll know anyway, but you're right, the little ones will be scared,' he said and looked again at the armour-plated vehicle. 'I'll think of something.'

Sean looked at Lenka and dropped the hammer and nails as he made his way over to her. Her unkempt black hair and the fact that she was wearing only a blanket added to her wild sexuality.

'No time for that,' retorted the now officious

woman, as she turned back to the house. Suddenly, she dropped her blanket and ran towards him. Sean opened his arms to embrace the beautiful firm naked body, he had caressed for most of the night.

Lenka continued past, shouting, 'I forgot my shopping bike.'

She disappeared into a little shed in the far left-hand corner of the barn. Sean mumbled, 'Great, a fuckin shopping bike, that's my rival.'

He heard a four-stroke engine kick into action. What he saw next was an image that he prayed would stay with him for the rest of his life. Lenka burst out of the little hut, naked astride a motorbike with a sidecar.

The Irishman was rarely stuck for words, but managed to mutter, 'I think I'm in love.'

'Me too, it's a four-stroke V-twin-engine Sokó 1000,' yelled the naked woman.

Lenka sat upright, revving the throttle, almost purring at its power. Sean was deaf to it as her black locks stopped just above her shoulders, exposing her pert breasts. Her legs were stretched to their maximum, so her toes just about reached the ground. Her position reminded him of when she had climbed on top of him a few hours earlier. The moment did not last. The entire exhaust pipe shot backwards into the crumbling wooden slats of the barn, before by the brake clutch came off in her hand.

Lenka was undaunted and was delighted to be astride her old motorbike. Though the no-longer-muffled noise of the engine was deafening. Sean could just about hear her shouting, 'God knows how many are left, as they only made about two hundred and this one is over twenty years old.'

'I'd say there's about one, but probably fuck all by lunchtime,' he yelled, as he made a mental calculation that twenty feet now separated the bike from its exhaust pipe.

He turned back to find Lenka gleefully revving the engine of the motorbike that he viewed as the equivalent of a clown's car.

'It can reach speeds of nearly ninety miles per hour . . .'

'Over a cliff?'

'. . . but it's better for off-roading.'

Lenka was ecstatic. She jumped off the bike and ran past Sean towards the house. The damp air of the morning alerted her to her nakedness, and she turned around and grabbed her blanket, which lay on the floor of the barn. Then she ran back towards the house.

'Lucky I'm not the sensitive type,' Sean muttered, before giving the motorbike's tyre a playful kick.

He mounted the stairs of the bus to flatten the spikes of the nails he had hammered through the outer plates to secure them to the sides of the bus.

When Sean returned to the house, the freezing children had returned to the kitchen to continue their breakfast served by the now fully dressed Lenka, along with Olen.

'Take a seat,' offered Lenka, but with the wickedest of smiles, pointing at the spare children's chair at the end of the table. 'Seating arrangements are based on matching the chair to intellect.'

Sean sat on the stool, placed the heels of his boots in the rung below the seat, bringing his knees up to his ears. The children convulsed into laughter. Sean's antics reminded Ursula of how her dad used to clown around when they all sat at the table. That was before the car crash that killed her parents.

While Sean ate his breakfast of water and oats and three apples, Celina – one of the little girls, who was mute – sat on his lap and pulled on the chest hairs that stuck out from between the buttons on his threadbare, rumpled, white, cotton shirt. Having finished his breakfast, Olen dragged him from his stool.

'She's waiting for her six laps around the table,' announced Lenka, raising her eyebrows and smiling at Sean.

Sean adopted a playful frown, pursed his lips. 'It was a joke.'

But he did as he was bid, though he scowled at Lenka each time he cantered past. The children giggled, and nudged each other, as they had never seen Lenka smile at a man before.

Within two hours, Lenka had headed into town, persuaded the headmistress to let her borrow the snow chains and returned to the orphanage on the horse and cart. While Sean attached the snow chains to the bus, Lenka gathered all the children together and informed them, through signing – the universal language of the home – that they were all going on a wonderful adventure.

Sean strode into the kitchen and deposited two roughly made metal boxes on the dining table, and said, 'I have made three little sentry boxes for the three smallest soldiers.'

But there were only two babies in the wicker baskets

that Lenka deposited on the table. Ursula told him that at a couple from the town had come to the orphanage that morning and offered to take one of the babies and raise it as their own.

'Ah well, let's keep the spare one,' before winking at Lenka. 'Who knows, one day we might find a use for it ourselves,' before releasing a mischievous smile.

'Fuck you!' shouted Lenka.

Olen seized up a wooden spatula and waved it – and not for the first time that morning – at Lenka for using profane language.

'That would be an essential requirement for the process for it to work,' replied Sean. 'But I didn't come all this way to be abused,' before winking at Lenka. 'Okay, maybe I did.'

Ursula tried to hide her smile, as Sean wrapped each baby in a little blanket he had made by cutting one large one into four pieces. Lenka and Ursula watched as he lowered each child into its new cradle to test it for size. After adding more padding until he was finally happy, he then took the little bundles out again. 'Right, I'll bolt these cradles into the seats behind me.'

Turning to Lenka, Ursula whispered, 'Are they all mad in Ireland?'

Before Lenka could answer, Sean shouted, 'Yes, I'm the only sane one,' as he strode out of the kitchen with a metal crib under each arm.

Ursula turned to Lenka. 'Do you think you will have a family one day?'

'If it means committing myself to one man, then to hell with that. They're good for sex . . . well, actually most are fucking useless.'

Olen hit her playfully on her backside with the spatula. Ursula had been raised by Lenka, so she was used to her swearing. But she never knew how her painfully honest declarations were often very funny. She did not wish to anger Lenka and gripped her bottom lip between her teeth to stop herself from laughing.

Lenka continued, 'And carrying things . . . though use a donkey if you can. They're less trouble and are satisfied with just a carrot afterwards.'

'But the Irishman's different, isn't he?' asked Ursula.

'Balls!' but turned and smiled out of the window as she watched the man traipsing through the snow towards the bus with the cradles under each arm. 'When you are a little older, you'll find that men are either stupid, big kids or just mad. The Irishman is different, as he's all three. Watch him closely, for even if you live till you are a hundred, you'll never meet one as crazy as him.'

Olen spun Lenka around and fluttered her hands like a butterfly over her heart.

'I don't like him, let alone love him,' protested Lenka whose mood changed.

She stormed off towards the bus carrying some extra warm clothing, leaving both women to smile at each other.

The house was a hive of activity. The children knew they their journey was about to commence, but they were intrigued by what the playful giant was doing hammering away at in the barn where the old bus was parked.

Once everyone had packed and brought their bags and cases downstairs, Ursula led everyone out to the front of the house. All, that is, except Anzelm and Celestynka, two of the youngest, who had been confined to bed with measles for the past few days. That morning Olen signed to Lenka she would stay with them until Dr Levi arrived the next day to take them to hospital. Lenka had hoped that one of their neighbours would have offered to look after them, but no one did. Olen removed her favourite shawl and draped it over Lenka's shoulders. She was crying but Lenka did not shed a tear when her little helper told her that had to stay. But it was the closest that Lenka had ever come to doing so.

Outside the house, the scurrying children stopped when Sean drove the bus out of the opened doors of the barn. They shared anxious glances when they saw that the body of their old bus was covered in metal sheets.

The Irishman leapt down and stretched his arms out wide, 'Roll up! Roll up! To ride on 'The Sleepy Armadillo'.'

Through a combination of whispers and signing, the children became excited at the thought of jumping on the Irishman's theme ride. Those that could broke into a run as they scampered towards the bus. Ursula followed, hiking slowly through the snow with the support of her makeshift cane, while holding the hand of one of the children, Mala, whose legs were braced by callipers. Leo was the last to approach the bus, as he had stood at the back to studiously monitored the processor to ensure that everyone was accounted for.

The children were wearing little backpacks filled with food and clothing and gathered by the front of the bus. Olen made her way through the children and once she reached the Irishman, she ran over to him and seized him, plunging her face into his belly. He whisked her up and gave her a full-on kiss on the nose and lowered her back down, leaving her giggling like a little girl. All the children mobbed Olen. Her cheeks were damp with their tears along with her own. Leo stood by the door of the bus. Olen held out her arms to the severe looking sentry, who gave her a sensibly handshake. She spat into her handkerchief. He screwed his face up, still standing to attention, as she wiped away his tears.

Only when Ursula had climbed up the metal stairs of the bus, did Leo join the others. But he clipped the top step and toppled backwards. Sean grabbed him, released him into the air, spinning him as he did so, and caught him. To everyone's surprise, Leo appeared to smile as he took a seat on the bus.

Lenka started the engine, but this time no one screamed with excitement. All the children had their hands and faces pressed against the windows, peering through the narrow gaps between the metal sheets to smile at Olen. They wondered when they would see the little old woman that Lenka referred to as her little helper, but whom they called 'mum'. 'The Sleepy Armadillo' slowly crawled away.

Olen signed to Lenka that all would be OK, or she would smash the Nazis in their 'thingy's'. Lenka signed back, to say to remember to give the letter to Dr Levi to hand into the Polish Consulate in the city when the children were better. They would contact her and she would come back to collect her and the children.

Lenka rested her flat hand on the windscreen. As she did so, she remembered ten years earlier, the first time she had met Olen. The mute woman had been running the house for her elder brother, until he died. Her brother had not left a will, so the authorities seized the house. She was left destitute, much to the anger of the townsfolk. Even if she was not mentally impaired, being a woman, the law offered no protection.

In return for doing cleaning jobs, the townsfolk took it in turns to give her food and a bed for the night. Apart from the occasional abuse from some of the young boys, the town felt protective of her.

Lenka had heard of Olen, but had never met her, and on hearing the news that she had no permanent home, she went into town to find her. She discovered Olen playing alongside some young children, sitting around a puddle in the road. She approached the woman and asked her if she would help her run the orphanage, in return for food and lodgings. She explained that the home had benefactors, mainly relatives of the children, past and present, and the town's shops donated any surplus food, but she could not pay her much. Olen gave Lenka the longest and tightest hug she had ever had in her life.

Since that day, Olen was content, until that morning when Lenka told her she was going to fight the Fascists in Spain. She wept until the children appeared for breakfast. She had never hurt anyone and though she could not understand why Lenka wanted to fight, she made her a huge cake with a little marzipan figurine of a young woman with short black hair, fists raised like a boxer, mounted on the top.

Olen ran by the side of the bus pretending to be happy, ignoring her tears and waving her arms like miniature windmills, as 'The Sleepy Armadillo' rocked from side to side along the pot-holed path towards the main gate.

The Irishman followed on Lenka's motorbike, having re-affixed the exhaust and welded the rust-riven side car. He blew Olen a kiss as he passed her. But Sean's heart was as heavy as everyone on the bus, as he steered the motorbike out onto the main road. He looked back at the lady waving frantically, standing alone by the gates as black crowds erupted above.

Olen stared out into the night, now that the storm had grown tired of the orphanage. Upstairs the sickly children had eaten some of their sandwiches. The fire that the Irishman had lit in the kitchen continued to spread warmth throughout the house. Olen knelt by the window, she started to pray. She prayed for the children she had helped raise and that they would be safe on their journey. She prayed for Lenka and prayed that God would forgive her blasphemy and allow her into heaven one day. She prayed for the animals they had lost in the fire, and that God had amply food for them in heaven. She prayed for the Irishman who made her laugh. Olen looked up at the stars through the steam on the window and with a finger she drew a heart around one of them and smiled.

She put her finger once more to the glass and wrote

LEE KA XXX

The sledgehammer landed on the outside doorknob with such force that its inner counterpart was propelled along the hallway and stopped only when it hit the base of the stairs. Olen jumped up and ran towards the kitchen doorway. There were six men in white uniforms standing in the corridor. She noticed that they wore a badge with her favourite flower, the edelweiss, in the centre. It was a flower she had only ever seen in a book when she was a child, a flower she always hoped that one day she would bend down to smell and discover its scent. Now the flower gripped her with fear. These were the men who had taken away the lovely Gilda and Sophia.

Olen watched as the man at the front raised his rifle. The bullet hit her with a thud straight in the chest. She felt no pain. Her limbs went limp, and she fell to her knees. Olen turned her head to look for the base of the stairway that led to the children. She leant the weight of her body in its direction, so she would fall in the path of the soldiers.

The Mountain Rangers ignored her and spread out to search the ground floor. She could hear glass breaking. Struggling to breathe, she tilted her head back to look up the stairwell, praying that the noise of the angry men would not wake the children.

Two of the rangers returned to the hall and stepped over Olen's body and headed up the stairs. Olen held her hand on her chest wound, turned onto her front and began to crawl up the stairs behind them. The men now disappeared into the rooms. The men were shouting. She tried to warn the children, by slapping her bloodied hand against the wall. It only served to increase the flow of blood seeping through the fingers of the other hand over her wound. Olen heard more gunfire. She could not comprehend what was happening.

Someone seized her ankles, dragging her down the bloodied stairs, along the corridor, over the doorstep and then launched her into the snow. She landed on her side. She raised her head. That smell. The same smell of blue paraffin that the men had used to raze the barn.

Her eyes flickered. A tall handsome man, with short sun-bleached hair and a distinctive scar over his left eye appeared. The man dropped his boot on her side and pushed her onto her back. He knelt on one knee beside her. Slowly he slipped on his black leather gloves. His face was inches from hers. He lifted her head up by her blood-soaked hair. He roared, 'Where are the . . .' then he stopped. He looked at the compound of blood and tears that masked her face, but then he noticed what Lenka called, 'her look of innocence'. In frustration, he turned to one of his men and shouted out '*Verlangsamen*!' (retard), while releasing her hair. Her head dropped back into the snow.

The captain was right, not for dismissing anyone that was not 'pure' like him, but because the woman would never tell him where the children were, even if he had the forethought to place pen and paper in her hand.

Furious, the captain spun around and stomped over to retrieve one of the sets of skis they had spiked into the snow. He fastened them to his mountain boots. Three of the other rangers continued to cover the house in blue paraffin. Two others lifted Olen up by her arms, so she could watch as the orphanage disappeared under the flames. The heavy blanket of snow that had refused to disperse when the storm resumed its assault could not save it. Olen was crying, distraught by the incomprehensible spectacle of the huge fire, praying that Anzelm and Celestynka had escaped.

The captain who had shot Olen, stood in front of her, eclipsed the fire. Her nose and jaw were broken. She stared at the blurred man raising the rifle. She might have been able to summon up enough strength, in one last defiant act, to spit a mixture of blood, teeth and salvia onto his white camouflaged trousers, but the thought would never have occurred to her.

'The Sleepy Armadillo' lumbered along the snow on the main road leading to Szklarska Poreba. The children were giddy, since one of them spotted a road sign that read CZECHOSLOVAKIA 280 km. They had never travelled this far from the orphanage before, let alone crossed the border into another country. The bus was making good progress despite negotiating the icy winding road. They had covered over a hundred kilometres in the last five hours, but now that they were heading up into the mountains, every turn in the road brought tension for the drivers for fear of encountering a German raiding party.

Sean and Lenka had changed places. She was scouting ahead on the motorbike. Every time the children lost sight of her, strained to look through the windscreen, they became anxious. But when they squinted through the gaps between the metal plates, the magnificent beauty of the mountain range held the children in awe, especially now that the tops of the trees were blanketed in snow.

At one point, they had to stop as Sean and Lenka had to shovel a large cover of snow from the road with shovels Sean had put in the boot. Through the open door of the vehicle, several of the children saw some animal tracks amongst the leafless, white-coated trees. Their imaginations ran wild with fanciful ideas of tigers, polar bears, mammoths and even vampires. But the tension inside 'The Sleepy Armadillo' was palpable as Sean started the bus. The snow had settled on the exposed glass above the windows like a sheepskin blanket and now inside the bus all was dark.

The road disappeared under the heavy snowfall. Sean decided it was best to find cover and to park the bus for the night. They could continue, but to drive the vehicle through the darkness meant putting its headlights on full beam, which would attract attention from mountain patrols for miles; perhaps from the air if the skies cleared.

It was time to prepare a hot meal for thirty hungry mouths as all the sandwiches had been devoured hours earlier. While Sean shouted that they needed to park up and start cooking. Ursula signed his message to the children. He watched for the reaction in the driving mirror. Thankfully, sleepy heads began to nod.

'I'll be mother, as Lenka needs a rest,' whispered Sean. 'So, if that's OK with everyone, we all work together to make sure she can catch some sleep? But that's our secret.'

Ursula translated his message, and again the children nodded. The children loved Lenka, but they also loved secrets and they were intrigued to see what the Irishman would cook for dinner.

Sean parked the bus in a secluded spot in the forest on top of the mountain, just off a bend in the road, so he had the best possible view of anything coming up from both sides.

Lenka drew her motorbike up alongside the bus. She jumped off and announced, 'Right, I'll start cooking.'

'Don't worry, all in hand,' countered Sean who appeared from the back of the truck, carrying a bag of cheese wheels, some meats and some vegetables.

He squatted down on a snow-covered bolder under the thick brush of a conifer tree a few metres from the forest. Gathering dry wood from the boot of the bus, he let a fire. Satisfied it had taken, he mounted a large pan of snow on a metal tripod to boil some potatoes for a stew. Once all this was underway, he watched the knowing little smiles exchanged by the children, whenever Lenka tried to pick up or do anything. Just before she did so, one of them would intercept and carry out the task, much to her bemusement.

Leo, having observed that all his friends were working diligently and applying themselves fully to their tasks, helped Ursula re-tighten Mala's callipers. Working together, Leo nodded at the Irishman to affirm that all was proceeding to plan. Sliced carrots into the boiling water, Sean scanned the hastily erected camp and saw that some of the children were starting a snowball fight. He smiled, children are remarkably resilient, and he remembered Tóth and how protective he was of his mother, despite all they had suffered. At least they were safe now. These children had suffered too, many because of their disabilities had been abandoned. Now they had been forced from the only home they knew, and though he had not said it to Lenka, he believed that because of her reputation, all of them were being hunted by the Nazis.

Lenka, exasperated, turned to Sean and said, 'Right, well, nothing for me to do here so I'll go and find some eggs and milk for the morning and some fuel if I can.'

Sean looked up at her, 'It's best you get some sleep.'

'Shove that. The children need breakfast.'

Though Sean had known her for less than a week, he

knew there was no point in arguing. Lenka leapt back on the motorbike and disappeared down the road. The children all looked over at Sean and he shrugged his shoulders as Ursula joined him and eased herself down to sit next to him.

'Well, my plan was bollocks!' confessed Sean.

'I probably won't sign that to the children,' replied the young woman as she started to help him peel carrots.

After checking two deserted houses for food, Lenka guessed that the inhabitants of all the farmhouses in the mountains had fled. Nazi incursions must be taking place right along the border and the orphanage was not being singled out after all. She watched as the clouds dispersed to allow the moon to expose life in the mountains.

'Christ,' she muttered

Looking around, she saw a small light in the distance. She gunned the motorbike towards it. As she drew closely, she realised that the light was flames coming from a farmhouse. Twenty minutes later, she drew the vehicle to a stop behind a tree, thirty metres from the burning building. As she dismounted, she saw the spare metal cradle in the sidecar. She was furious with herself for driving around with the damn thing all day, using up valuable fuel. Grabbing it, she threw it to the ground and cursed.

Lenka struggled through the snow, which was twice as deep as that surrounding the orphanage. As she got nearer, she strained her eyes to see if anyone remained inside. There were no signs of life. The fire was contained to in the front room, because it was built from granite rock and clay and ceiling supported by thick wooden beams, but its structure was badly damaged, perhaps due to grenade. She edged around the house, until she reached the back door.

Lenka wrapped Olen's shawl around her face as the embers landed on her like blowflies. She slammed the sole of her boot against the old door and jumped to the side knowing that flames would leap forth in search of oxygen. The door flew open but was hit something. Once the flames had receded, she peered inside. On the other side of the door was the charred body. Man or woman, it was impossible to tell which. She squeezed her way through the gap, avoiding the parts of the two collapsed, burning wooden beams that had crushed the dining table. There were more burnt bodies, positioned alongside the front door facing the walls. They must have tried to escape whoever killed the person at the door. Lenka knew the signs; she had seen similar incidents in Spain in the aftermath of Nationalist raids.

Lenka heard a cat crying, but it was hard to hear with the crackling of the burning timbers above. As the flames had not progressed beyond the stone stairs, she seized the chance to take a quick look upstairs. Farmers would often store surplus food in the loft when *predators* roamed around outside. The supporting beams built into the plaster on the upstairs landing were starting to smoulder. The smaller bedrooms had been ransacked but only now did flaming tongues seep through the thick oak floorboards

She shuddered at the caterwaul she heard above the cracking timber. Curiosity won over her fears as always, and she edged open the door of the main bedroom. The room, though filled with smoke, remained untouched and whoever had ransacked the house had not got around to checking it thoroughly, perhaps because whatever exploded in the building had brought the main wooden rafter across the back of the door. The opening was not wide enough for a grown man to squeeze through but it was enough for her.

Inside the room, there was no sign of the cat. She sighed and thought perhaps her mind was playing tricks, as she was tired and hungry. There were adult clothes in the wardrobe and drawers. As the heat of the fire drew nearer, she thought it was best to get out. But she would have one quick check under the bed. There she discovered a bundle of what looked like children's clothes. In the hope that it contained a secret stash of food she stretched her right arm under the bed as far as she could but could not reach the bundle. The bundle cried out.

It was the cry of a child, not a cat. Behind her the banister opposite the room erupted in flame. Lenka jumped up and put her hands under one side of the base of the bed. With one supreme effort she dragged the end of the bed towards the wall. She dived over the mattress and landed on the smothering floor on the other side. She threw her arm underneath, and this time she managed to retrieve the bundle. Pulling it apart, she discovered a baby. It was no longer breathing. She whisked the child up in her arms and in short, steady bursts, breathed into its mouth. The baby released an almighty scream.

Lenka wrapped the child in Olen's shawl. She climbed back through the gap between the burning wooden rafter and the door frame and found the stairs and the balustrade on fire.

Folding her right arm across her face to shield her from the flames, and tucking the child under her left arm, she scampered down the stairs, and bolted through the fire engulfing the living room. Olen's shawl, and her clothes were on fire, as she flew through the back door as the flaming ceiling collapsed. She spun in the air so as to land on her back, cradling her the precious bundle in her arms. Heaping snow over the flaming clothes she was relieved to hear it was still crying.

Lenka bolted towards the motorbike. Now mounted on it, she had one last look as the house. The main bedroom they had just escaped from was completed consumed by flames. In the snow, the glint caught her attention. It was the metal crib she had tossed aside. Grabbing it, she pulled the blanket from the floor of the sidecar, wrapped it around the terrified child, and tucked what remained of Olen's shawl around it.

Kick-starting the engine, Lenka wrenched the handlebar to the left. The motorbike pivoted around in one movement on the narrow path and sped off down the road with her passenger wedged firmly in the metal cradle.

It took twice as long to weave her way down the tight hairpin turns, as the moon had disappeared behind a large dark cloud. Lenka had to drive with her headlight on full. She knew that this bright beam of light would make her a beacon for any nearby patrol, but she had no choice. She kept glancing down and checking on the child with her hand. Despite her ordeal and cold cheeks, the uneven road had rocked it to sleep.

A motorbike appeared in Lenka's side mirror. As it drew close, she recognised his uniform, the *Fallschirmjäger*, the elite of the German parachute rangers.

Though she was driving with the throttle fully open, the Sokó was no match for the new Zündapp KS750. Its rider quickly drew up along her right side and made a grab for her handlebar. Rather than pulling away, she leaned sideways and grabbed Olen's singed shawl from the dozing passenger. With her right hand steered her machine towards their attacker, she threw the shawl across the rider's face. He threw his hands up. His machine flipped over to the right, firing him over the handlebar into the dark oblivion of the forest. In her right-hand side mirror, she could see the motorbike was on its side in the middle of the road.

As Lenka relaxed the throttle, a second Zündapp motorbike emerged from the woods to her left. The ranger was steering the motorbike and working the accelerator with his right hand, while blazing away with a MP40 submachine gun cradled in his left.

The moon arrogantly elbowed the dark clouds to one side, and lit up the long, straight road ahead. Lenka only had seconds to get off the road. Bullets whizzed around them. Turning the motorbike sharply to the left, it shot off the main road and into the darkness of the woods. She killed the bike's lights off and shot under the dense coverage of branches that blocked out the light of the moon. With considerable skill she manoeuvred the Sokó through the dense thicket. The bulky Zündapp was finding it hard to keep up, but ahead of her Lenka saw open fields, which meant that she and the child would once more be an easy target.

Lenka killed the engine. She leapt off and lifted the child who was crying once more, up into her arms. Lenka darted into the darkness with the baby, with their pursuer a few seconds behind.

The ranger pulled up, leapt from his vehicle with his submachine gun in his hands. He opened fire on the Sokó, riddling the fuel tank with bullets. There was no way out for them now. Metres ahead of him, he heard a baby cry in the darkness.

After what he saw happen to his colleague, he took no chances and opened his machine gun in the direction of the cries. He marched steadily forward, as the child's cries grew louder. The ranger was but a metre away, but the chamber was empty. He threw the empty magazine away into the night and snapped the new one in, before he felt a weight on his back. Glancing up, he saw the flash of the blade in the moonlight above his right shoulder, before it was plunged into his chest. He tried to grab it, but his hands were lifeless. As he fell on his knees in the mud, the blade was repeatedly thrust into his heart.

Though Lenka was sure the ranger was dead, as the black clouds returned to cloak the forest, she snapped his head back and plunged her dagger into his throat. Only then did she climb off his back. She stood up, wiping her knife on her sleeve and sliding it back into her right boot. She stepped over the corpse and trekked past her beloved Sokó. At least the Irishman had been wrong about it not lasting until lunchtime.

She trampled through the snow to make her way around the six-foot-high rock that stood defiantly between the dead Nazi and the child. Lenka crouched down to pick up the wailing child.

'Forgive me little one – it was all I could think of.' She brushed the dirt from its unblemished cheeks and whispered, 'I'll prepare you something a little less solid than Irish stew.'

She rubbed her nose against that of the frightened baby, stunning it into silence for a few seconds.

The Zündapp KS750 pulled up alongside 'The Sleepy Armadillo'. While everyone was finishing their dinner, Sean stood up and made his over to Lenka carrying a plate of mutton and vegetables.

'Eggs, milk and fuel I think you said,' as he bent down to smile at the child crying in one of his metal cradles. 'Well this beats Jack, returning from the beanstalk with a handful of beans,' as he inspected the bike she had commandeered. 'A top of the range German military motorbike, and a baby.'

'Her name is Molly. I checked with I gave her some milk. She's a healthy little girl'

'Molly?'

The children knew why, as this was the name of the calf they had lost in the fire. Sean lifted Molly from the metal cradle. He saw the blood on Lenka's right hand and sleeve, as she dismounted. He kissed her on the lips, 'Are you OK?'

'Always,' she replied.

Behind them the girls nudged each other, and the boys giggled. Leo looked even less impressed than usual. Ursula smiled at him and leant forward to kiss him on the top of his head, which only added to his discomfort.

The next morning, after a pitiful breakfast of reheated stew, they faced the most dangerous part of the route, the drive down the mountain pass. Sean had expected fresh snow, but the bitter cold snap that followed a surprisingly warm night, was far worse. Snow that had melted into slush, morphed into sheet ice. Looking at the smooth icy road ahead, winding down into the valley, he thought that it was apt the town's name was derived from the word glass.

Peering down at the treacherous road that lay ahead, Sean and Lenka quickly thought they should stay where they were until nightfall in the hope that the weather might improve. However, even though they were off the road, they were exposed and could easily be seen from the mountain opposite.

Once again, 'The Sleepy Armadillo' meandered down the mountain. Within a few metres, Sean was desperately trying to control the bus with gear changes rather than its brakes. Over the next few hours, the back tyres flipped around like a serpent's as Sean turned the steering wheel to make each hairpin turn. Twice the bus slid dangerously close to the edge of the mountain, when its snow-chains proved ineffective on the icy surface. Through luck and evasive driving, he managing to carry on steering the vehicle down the mountain road.

Shots ricocheted off the metal plates. Two bullets came through the windscreen and one tore through Ryan's leather jacket, grazing his right arm. The screams of several children only aided the sniper located trees only helped him pinpoint his targets. Lenka was on the motorbike in front of the bus. The first of the bullets to hit her gazed her forehead, the second one caught her in her right hip. It was the impact of the second bullet that spun the motorbike off the road. She rolled off before a bullet hit the fuel tank. It exploded into a fireball of metal that bounced down the steep sloping mountain side.

Ryan brought the bus to a halt under by a clump of trees. He leapt from the bus, rolling around the road as bullets pinged around him. Having reached the other side of the icy road, he sprang up and hurtled down the bank. He found Lenka crumpled up in the snow. Next to her was a Smith and Weston model .44 calibre revolver. She kept it hidden from him; she still did not trust him.

He swept her up in his arms, grabbed the firearm, and made his way back up the icy slope. Dodging more bullets, he zigzagged his way back to the bus. He vaulted inside and lowered Lenka gently down on the front seat next to Ursula.

'I need to get us out of here. Can you take care of her?' he asked, the anxious looking young woman.

Ursula nodded, and added, 'I have Leo,' as she pressed a handkerchief to Lenka's wound, causing her to groan.

Leo appeared with some towels and helped Ursula apply the iodine that Sean handed them. When Ursula indicated that Lenka would be okay. The boy raced back to his seat, removed a piece of newspaper from his bag and started to fold it.

Sean released the hand brake and continued to steer the bus down the icy mountain pass. As bullets ricocheted off 'The Sleepy Armadillo', Lenka lost consciousness. The first of the windows shattered above the children. Coming within range of increased firepower, delivered with greater accuracy, more bullets were able to squeeze between the metal plates.

When Lenka woke, there was an origami figure of what

looked like a lion on the seat in front. She looked at the serious little boy who was sitting on the floor of the bus in front of her. She blew him a kiss, which sent the blood racing to his face and he ran back to his seat. He looked around to check that no one was looking at him, but then he caught the Irishman's eyes in the driving mirror. Sean winked at him. Leo looked back sternly, but as the Irishman kept his gaze, he could not hold his smile in any longer. The solemn little boy stared at his feet, which were now swinging in a pendulum motion.

During the four hours that Lenka had been unconscious, the sun had confronted the snow and ice, and taken back control of the mountain. The bullet pinged off the metal plates but they were not a frequent at when the bus came under attack. The Sleepy Armadillo's passengers were so exhausted they hardly stirred. But the drop by the side of the road was perilously steep once more.

Though Ryan could throw the truck around the curves faster now the icy road was thawing, it brought new dangers. A tremendous explosion erupted on the mountain side only metres from the bus as it approached a wide hairpin bend. Large lumps of frozen soil rained down on the bus, one shattered the windscreen. Hearing the base of the mountain for the first time, 'The Sleepy Armadillo' was within range of the enemy's mortars. Explosions followed in quick succession as the bus made its way ungainly around each turn.

The children huddled together on the floor, crying as each explosion showered them with fragments of glass from the windows. Even worse, due to the impact of the shelling, all the remaining metal plates on the left side of the bus had broken free of their nail supports. The snow-chains too had broken away. More bullets pierced the shell of the vehicle, allowing small shafts of sunlight to explore the inside of the bus. Larger holes appeared as rocks ricocheted off the vehicle. Mortar shells shattered the foot-high stone wall that separated the road from the sheer drop down the mountain.

Beams of light entered the bus like searchlights seeking the children. The touch of one could expose them to sniper fire. Ryan remembered from his childhood Bram Stoker's vampire, and how he sympathised with the poor creatures' fear of the sun's rays.

The Irishman continued to drive at full speed, slowing only to negotiate when another large crater appeared in the road as the result of another mortar landing. The trees began to rise alongside the road, and the mortars fell silent.

From what he could see ahead and the speed he was going, he calculated that it would take another three hours to reach the foot of the mountain. Lenka was lapsing in and out of consciousness, while the children wrapped themselves around each other on the floor, near to exhaustion. Two of 'The Sleepy Armadillos' six wheels had been shot out. They were also low on fuel, so for over two hours he had turned the engine off and coasted down the mountain whenever he came to a straight stretch of road, even though that meant having no traction on the ice – with the engine turned off, the air in the brakes could not build.

Fortunately, none of the children had been hit, but it was only a matter of time now.

On the next hairpin bend, the road burst into a wall

of flame, as a mortar landed a few metres in front of the bus. Ryan lost complete control of the vehicle. Though it was not a direct hit, a lesser man would have made excuses, saying it was unavoidable – but Ryan knew the truth, he was as exhausted, as the children. Drawing on his last reserves of energy, he spun the vehicle around so that the right side, which still had a full set of metal panels, faced the forest rather than the sheer slope. This is where the final assault would come from.

Ryan motioned to the children to stay flat on the floor of the bus. He removed Lenka's revolver that he had left on the dashboard but found that the chamber of the gun was frozen to the body. With the tension of the drive, he had forgotten that he no longer had a windscreen. He tried to defrost it by rubbing it, but he could barely move his own fingers.

The Irishman stepped down onto the wet gravel road, the first time he had stepped on anything other than snow for days. He crouched on the ground by the front of the bus, to secure a good view of the forest. Lenka appeared behind him and uneasily made her way down the steps of the bus. She slumped beside him.

'Sorry, we've literally run out of road,' confessed Sean.

He put his arm around her and kissed her on the head to the left of the cotton pad covering the wound on her forehead. She did not rebuke him but put her hand on his to warm them.

Sean pressed her close, 'If they do not find us before nightfall, then when it's dark, we'll lead the kids down the rest of the mountain. On route, if we encounter the Nazis, we'll surrender, as we can't risk the children in a firefight.' He added, unconvincingly, 'If that happens, then as least they will take the children as prisoners.'

'I doubt we will make nightfall,' replied Lenka. 'Anyway, you'd have to carry me, and you look like shit,' she said, trying to smile. 'They will be here soon. I was stupid to think we could outrun them. But at least you have enough sense to know we cannot outfight them.'

'Yep, they will be here soon,' confessed Sean. 'If it was just us, we'd go out in a blaze of glory,' replied Sean.

Lenka pulled him close and smiled into his grey-green eyes before kissing him softly.

'Time for you to go. You have done all you can; there's no point in them capturing you, too.'

'All of us or none of us, remember,' replied Sean.

He looked away from her hazel eyes and down at her wounds. Ursula had stopped the bleeding, but her clothes were saturated with blood. He was not surprised when she fell unconscious in his arms.

Sean picked her up as carefully as he could and carried her back onto the bus. All they could do now was wait, as the sun disappeared behind the mountain. After their ordeal, the children were asleep, but not Leo, who joined Sean and sat on the top step at the front of the bus. The boy sat with his arms outstretched, with his hands on his knees as he had seen the men in cafes in Kraków often do.

Half an hour later, they heard the first of the rangers approaching on skis, followed by the roar of a snowmobile. Ryan got to his feet and placed the revolver on the steps of the bus.

'Too many,' he said, and smiled as he gestured Leo to return to the bus.

233

The Irishman stood up with his arms raised and stepped away from the bus in case they opened fire. Two rangers on skis appeared. They trained their rifles on him, ordering him to kneel. Ryan did so and put his hands behind his head. The first ranger shouted, 'Halt' and aimed his rifle and fired. The Irishman thought the soldier was toying with him, as he fired over to the left of his shoulder. Then, he heard the thud of the bullet hitting its target and a muffled cry from behind him. He turned to find Leo bleeding from a wound to his throat.

The bullet had shot away most of the cartilage. The boy's hands were still up above him, as they were when the ranger took careful aim. Ryan leapt up and dashed to grab the boy, but this time he failed to save the boy from hitting the ground. Ryan gingerly rolled the little boy over and looked down at the surprised look on the boy's snow-speckled face. Leo stared up at him.

Ryan knew there was nothing he could do, only hold the boy's face in his right hand, support him with the other and lie to him that all would be well. Even for a realist like the Irishman, human nature being what it is, he wanted to provide some comfort in the last seconds of the little boy's all-too-brief life. Leo's eyes were still open when they froze.

He shook his head at the lifeless little face, 'Ah kid, why didn't you stay on the bus like I told you, too.'

Ryan rested the child's head back on the frozen road. As he did so, the boy's right hand fell open and a little paper figurine tumbled onto a patch of snow. It was the figurine he had made for Lenka, but he had drawn a mane on it and added his name.

Both soldiers were shouting at Ryan. Still kneeling,

with his right hand out of view. He drew his knife slowly from his boot. He knew he could not reach both men before he was killed, but he might at least reach Leo's killer. Still in a crouching position, raising his arms, while slipping the blade into his cuff, he turned slowly. The distance between him and Leo's killer was about six metres. It was unlikely he would make it.

Leo's killer aimed his weapon as the man leaped up and sprinted forward. The knife that shot from the man's cuff hit him in the shoulder.

Lenka's bullet went hit the other ranger in the back of his head.

Leo's killer felt the other ranger's blood splatter over cheek as he watched him fall to the ground. Desperately he tried to raise his weapon, but the man was upon him. The knife was ripped from his shattered collarbone, only to be thrust back up under jaw.

A third ranger on skis flew out of the darkness towards Ryan. A shot rang out and he fell lifelessly to the ground next to Lenka. To his left, Ryan glimpsed driver of a snowmobile bail out before it shot into a tree and exploded into a ball of flames. Four bullets hit him before he landed in a heap in the powdered snow. Ryan turned towards Lenka. How could she do all this after being shot twice?

A tall blond man holding two Colt M1911 semi-automatic pistols in his hands, appeared. He spun round and picking off two more rangers on skis as they shot out from the trees. Ryan peered down as the rangers slid lifelessly either side of him.

The Irishman caught sight of another skier launching himself into the air directly at him. Ryan pulled his blade from the dead stormtrooper and sent it spinning through the cold night air. It met his attacker in mid-flight. The skier had tried to twist in mid-air to escape the blade, but it punched his chest. The ranger was limp by the time he landed on the ground, before he slid under the bus and off the edge of the mountain.

Another skier took off into the air towards him. He dived out of his path, as the ranger opened up with his sub-machine gun as he sailed through the air. As if in slow-motion, another man, using a nearby boulder as a platform, leapt towards the ranger. This new entrant to the fight caught the ranger in mid-flight and the two landed in a heap by the bus. With his right arm, the man took hold of the ranger in a headlock, lifted him into the air and swung him against the back of the bus, breaking his back instantly.

Ryan saw Lenka, acknowledge both men with a nod, 'Who the hell are they?'

'Friends.'

'Thank fuck for that,' he said.

The marksman with the blond hair strolled over to the Ryan, still scanning the darkness with his two semi-automatics.

'I'm Jake. You've met my pet bear,' he said, nodding in the direction of the larger man. 'Fucking animal's barely house trained.'

Sean turned to Lenka, who had staggered up and was leaning against the bus still in pain and trying to regulate her breathing, 'You never mentioned you were part of a circus.'

The American made his way over to Lenka. 'Hi Darling! Mother wants to know what to wear for our wedding?'

'Fuck off!' said Lenka, before throwing her arms around his waist.

'I'll just tell her we haven't set a date yet,' as Jake, returning her embrace. He said within earshot of the Russian, but without looking at him, 'In the end the better man always wins the girl.'

The Russian strode up to Lenka, as she turned and they wrapped their arms around each other. 'In the end the better man, always wins the girl,' proclaimed Vodanski, standing with his back to the American.

'Women, eh,' exclaimed Jake with a smile, as he turned to Sean.

But the Irishman was already walking away. For the first time, Jake and Vodanski saw the young woman cradling the body of the child lying in the snow.

The Irishman knelt beside the tearful Ursula as she gently rocked Leo. She stroked the freckles on his face. 'I will miss you, my serious little man.'

As Ursula began to shiver, he finally lifted Leo from her arms. He past the tear-stained little faces looking out of the empty window frames of the bus and found a small patch of earth that was out of sight of the road. After laying Leo down, he returned to the bus to remove a shovel from the boot. Returning to the spot he began to dig.

The other men did not know who the man was, but they left him alone. It was clear that this was something the man wanted to do alone.

Lenka, with her arm around Ursula, made her way slowly over to Sean. She put her hand on his arm, before whispering, 'It could have been all the children. They weren't taking prisoners.'

'Leo was one too many,' replied Sean, as he lowered the boy gently into the small, dark hole.

Using only his hands he gently covered Leo with chunks of frozen soil. With great delicacy, he bent down to rest the little boy's last creation on his grave. Sean trudged back to the corpses lying in the snow and unceremoniously lifted one of the dead trooper's up on his shoulder. He carried the body over and dropped it beside the freshly turned earth. Jake and Vodanski picked up the other bodies and helped spread them around the boy's grave.

Ryan was not a spiritual man, nor a religious one, but knew that the wolves would soon detect the scent. He just hoped that the easy meat that lay above the ground might sate their appetite and that the most serious of little boys would be left in peace, at least for a while.

Chapter 9: Vodanski's Story

May 1919, Kiev

The Cossack was an expert killer; an expert being someone who has discovered their one true passion and devoted themselves to it. Infantryman Vodanski Bulgakov faced Kemak, the White Army's 'Hero of Feston', to the enemy 'The Devil'. The men were standing in the middle of the house with the Cossack's foot on the torso of a man. You could tell it was that of a young man as the Cossack was still holding the head, with its frozen look of horror, in his left hand.

Vodanski had learnt that many of those who, in peacetime, would either be in prison or receiving treatment for psychopathic tendencies, were termed heroic alongside true heroes during war.

'Have *ya* gold in your teeth?' shouted the Cossack at the Russian.

Vodanski had no interest in conversation, only in bringing the man's butchery of hundreds of men, women and children to an end. 'Kulaks do,' continued the Cossack and then smashed the decapitated head against a support beam. 'It helps to loosen the gold in the teeth.'

The demonic eyes and manic eyebrows of the Cossack stirred in Vodanski a memory of caricatures of Rasputin, every Russian child's bogey man. This was to leave no doubt in the reader's mind who the enemy was –

like actors wearing black hats in cowboy films. The difference between the Cossack and the revolutionary drawings of Rasputin – who epitomised the corruption and brutality of the Tsarist regime – was that Kemak looked in robust health, powerful built and was far more terrifying.

Believing the young Russian infantryman's guard was down, the Cossack leapt at him, simultaneously throwing his knife. The Russian dodged the blade. Though only eighteen, and ten years younger than his opponent, he had been fighting for over three years and was braced for the attack. He moved the upper half of his body to the left and but left his right leg hanging. The Cossack sailed past him, tripping over the outstretched leg, as Vodanski brought the edge of his right hand down on the back of his neck.

Kemak was stunned not just by the debilitating blow, which seemed to paralyse his arms so he could not save himself when he landed, but also by the speed at which this mountain of a young man had moved. He rolled over, only in time to see the younger man descending on him. His right knee landing onto his chest. The Cossack heard his ribs snap like dry sugar.

The Cossack stared into the Russian infantryman's eyes and though he was in extreme pain, he smiled – to be so close to the most notorious fighter in the White Army was always a fatal mistake. The Cossack's powerful hands locked on Vodanski's throat. Kemak bared his thin yellow tombstone teeth as he tightened his chokehold. No one had ever escaped his death grip. A few broken ribs did not sap his strength, as he tightened his infamous 'death lock'. As immense as the younger man was, it would now take only a minute, maybe less, to strangle his foolish opponent and then he could root through his pockets. Kemak pulled the Russian's bulging face closer to examine his teeth.

'No gold,' grunted the Cossack.

Vodanski feared no man, even Kemak, whose method of killing his victims face to face was known to every soldier in the Red Army. The Russian used the man's method of killing to his advantage. He raised his lower body and worked his right knee up to the Cossack's broken ribs. Kemak roared as the Russian used his knee as leverage to pry himself free from the Cossack's vice-like grip. The Cossack screamed as his fractured ribs dug into his lungs.

The more the man tightened his hold on the Russian's throat, the more leverage the soldier had to apply further pressure on the man's broken frame. For the first time in his life – a life spent holding men, women and children up to his face to check for gold – he released his victim.

Kemak's rage pumped adrenaline through every part of his body. He flipped back up, as if his bones had somehow miraculously healed themselves. He assumed a crouching position, ready to pounce. His pain was subsumed by his one overwhelming desire: to kill the Russian and take with him the shame of being the only person to escape his 'death lock'.

Vodanski was amazed that any man could still breath after the damage and pain he had endured, let alone position himself to launch another attack, but unlike his opponent, his mind was clear and focused.

The Cossack judged that the man would side-step

him as before. The Russian was resting his weight on his left leg. Yes, that is the way he will go. Kemak threw himself on the man. The man did not move. Instead, he swung the decapitated head of the Cossack's last victim by its hair and caught Kemak across the face.

On the floor, the Cossack spun around and gripped the head by its horrified look. Vodanski had used the decapitated head to stun the Cossack and drew his attention away from the real danger; the kerosene lantern that had been on the table was alight in his left hand. He smashed it across Kemak's face. The Cossack's head burst into flames.

The Russian circled Kemak, who was aimlessly flailing punches as he staggered around the room, his head aflame. He fell to his knees. The Russian launched a kick to his chest, sending him to the floor. Vodanski stood astride the burning body and ripped the boots from the flailing man before they too went up in flames.

The Cossack's boots were far better than his, whose flapping heels were letting water seep through. To survive in these conditions meant not just defeating your opponent, but taking from him anything that would help you survive a little longer. Many he knew were brutalised by war and mutilated their victims, but Vodanski took no pleasure in the death of another, even in that of the most feared and brutal murderer in the Tsarist White Army.

Picking up his *shinel*, a thick, long, grey trench coat he had taken off while he waited for Kemal behind the door, and his empty rifle, Vodanski strode out of the burning house. He saw a dull green Austin Morris, one of many imported by the army of the former Russian Empire, meandering up the slush paved road towards him. The female driver sat in the car expressionless, as the man in the back, Captain Diminova, Vodanski's commander, stumbled out. He glanced down, unimpressed at the muddy pools around his feet. It was a cold, rainy night and he would much rather be having fun with his men in the farmstead.

'This was Kemak's base,' reported the infantryman.

'What! Is he close? How do you know?' replied the terrified captain, who took another swig from the brandy bottle he had commandeered from the farmstead. 'You were ordered not to go anywhere near him. Let's get out of here before he discovers us.'

Vodanski rarely obeyed his commander and had little intention of doing so now. He continued to rile his captain.

'Inside I found the body of a man who had been strangled, before decapitation. Kemak's work.'

The captain dived back into his seat. 'Get me out of here!'

Vodanski shook his head at the driver, who nodded back.

'Kemak's dead,' continued the young Russian, staring unimpressed at the officer crumbled up on the backseat. 'But his band of murderers will be close.'

'Can you prove it's him?' demanded his captain scrambling from the vehicle. 'No one has survived his 'death lock'. We don't even have a reliable description of him, only than he looks like Rasputin.' The captain was shouting, not to make himself heard over the crackling of the burning timber, but because he was terrified. He, like many others, believed the popular legend that The Hero of Feston, like Rasputin, was impossible to kill.

243

The flaming roof of the house collapsed behind them. Vodanski leaned into his captain, 'He's in the house; you can go inside and check if you like.'

'You were ordered not to engage . . .' he slurred, 'and to retreat if we encountered him and his men.'

Vodanski was aware that the order came from the highest level, perhaps even from Trotsky himself, the Commander-in-Chief of the Red Army.

'He wasn't with his men.'

'The White Army's pogrom to kill . . . bloody Kulaks,' yelled the captain, referring to wealthy merchants, 'has been a propaganda coup for . . . Mother Russia.' He continued to sway and shout at Vodanski, despite the proximity to the burning house – brandy always made him brave. 'Even that crazed imperialist Churchill, has expressed his revulsion to Deniken' – the White Army's General – 'at the thousands they butchered at Feston.' He stepped forward positioning his head beneath Vodanski's chin, and slurred, 'You disobeyed my . . . direct orders, Voo . . . Dan . . . Ski.'

The captain suddenly realised that the soldier's fists were clenched, which made him realise the limits of his brandy-induced bravery. He stood back and changed tack.

'Vodanski, I'm proud of you. Go and enjoy yourself. You have done a great service for . . .' he belched. 'Mother Russia. We have made our headquarters in the farmstead on the other side of the bridge. Your heroic comrades have corralled some girls . . . there.'

The farmer and his wife had not tried to obstruct the captain and his men when they had burst into their farmhouse two days earlier, but when the soldiers approached their daughters and they tried to draw their attention away, the captain had them put up against the dining room wall and shot. He condemned them for what he called their 'disloyalty to the defenders of the State'.

The captain would have had any other man shot for his insolence, let alone disobeying orders, but he remembered he only had five men left – not enough to take Vodanski prisoner. His men were in the homestead on the other side of the hill. Though drunk, he thought it prudent to report it to Moscow when he was some distance from the man. His superiors would have Vodanski court-martialled and then shot or, worse, sent to a gulag.

Vodanski strode past the terrified captain, who was relieved to see him go. His driver noted the smell of sweat as the captain threw himself into the back of the car. As she turned the car around, she gave a fleeting look at the infantryman. Vodanski did not bother to look at the car as he trekked down the hill towards the white house. Cowering in the back of the car, the officer finished off his bottle of brandy in three very quick gulps.

His courage returned – to an extent, and he round down the passenger window.

'I will head to headquarters immediately to report your bravery tonight. There could be a medal in it for you,' shouted the captain to Vodanski as the car drove away. 'Save some for me when I return, as two of the bitches are very attractive. You can do what you like with the oldest one,' he roared.

Vodanski still did not look at the car, and he

continued to march towards the river. The driver knew of the young infantryman by reputation – every Russian soldier in the Ukraine did – and she hoped beyond reason that he could save the young women.

Vodanski's mother and father were hardworking farmers; his three sisters and older brother took care of him, lavishing love and attention on their youngest sibling. But by the time he was ten, they had died from cold and starvation in the bitter winter of 1910. His mother's uncle, a kindly but quiet man, raised him. No one had ever taken the young boy to one side and told him he must protect the vulnerable. But no one had to tell the young Vodanski this. His family was poor and had little, like many throughout the Soviet Union, but he knew they had given a large part of what food they had to save him. Their love and sacrifice made him the man he was, a man who would use his strength not to coerce or bully, but to protect; he would treat every child as if it were his brother or sister, every mother, as if she were his own.

He had been conscripted into the Red Army at fifteen and was so innocent that he expected to be issued a uniform of similar colour. He knew nothing of Communism. It sounded good; everyone would be equal and all would have enough food to eat once the Communists had won the Glorious Revolution. That was three years ago. The trains laden with all this food never arrived. He had fought in over thirty engagements against the last of the Imperial forces of the White Army. It included several battalions of Ukrainians, and Cossacks, who were the toughest fighters amongst them.

The White Army had carried out several pogroms

across the country. The worst atrocities took place against the Jews in Kiev. No one had ever explained to the young Vodanski why the Jews were victimised, apart from one captured Ukrainian fighter who declared that the Jews were the leaders of the Revolution. This seemed strange to the young Russian, as many of the orders his unit received would refer to the enemies of the Bolshevik state as 'Jewish conspirators'. Vodanski was raised a Christian, but throughout his life he would witness weak governments looking for someone to blame for their mistakes, and the Jewish community would often be the scapegoat.

On reaching the river, Vodanski broke into a run across the footbridge that traversed the Dnieper River to reach the homestead. He opened the door of the white house. Over by the dining table were three drunken members of his unit, swigging wine and eating cold slices of sweet meats. On the floor by the table, illuminated by a blazing log fire, were the bodies of two young women in various states of undress, their clothes scattered around the living room like discarded laundry. Empty wine bottles lay strewn across the floor and the eldest girl looked like she had bled out after being cut across the throat by the broken bottle lying limp in her hand.

Vodanski placed his rifle by the door besides the other empty rifles – they had run out of ammunition a month ago – and made his way slowly over to the bloody woman. It was too late to do anything to help her, but he knelt next to her to examine her. The cut across her neck was clean, not jagged as you would expect from a bottle. Vodanski lifted the bloodied hair from her face. She was

247

probably only a year, maybe two, younger than him. He registered the horror in her brown eyes of the last moments as she had suffered. He gently pulled her dress down to cover her torn underclothes.

'I always knew you were a homo, Vodanski,' shouted the stockiest of the red, blotchy-faced men at the table.

His comrades laughed, as they drank wine and one applied his knife to the lid of another recent discovery, a jar of pickled green prunes.

By the fire, on her back on the stone floor, lay the body of an even younger girl. Vodanski stepped over to her and knelt beside her. She looked about fourteen. This time the wound to the neck was jagged. She was naked. Vodanski took one of the soldier's trench coats from a wooden dining chair and placed it over her body. The smallest of the drunken soldiers was about to protest, but Vodanski glared at the man, and he lowered his head to examine his wine glass.

The girl's glazed expression was almost peaceful. Whether the elder girl had killed her younger sister to spare her the ordeal that she would suffer at the hands of the men, or she had taken her own life or Vodanski's unit had killed them both, he did not know. As he stared solemnly at the frozen face, above the dried gaping wound, Solka, the corporal from his unit, staggered out of the kitchen. He held a bottle of homemade wine in one hand and a chunk of bread in the other gave. Vodanski was to have his questions answered.

'Fucking bitch; she went mad and killed the other whore before we could fuck her. We had to cut her throat to stop her killing the youngest girl. But with drink it all went to fuck, with everyone lashing out – you know how

248

it is.' He shrugged. 'We could have had a few days of fun and then saved her the trouble.'

The corporal spoke without shame, only with frustration. 'And look what she fucking did to me,' shouted over the red, blotchy-faced drunk once more from the table. The man glared at Vodanski, who could now see the scratch marks beneath his bloody eye. He looked once more at the body of the eldest girl and the dried blood on her nails.

Solka lifted his hand up and placed it on Vodanski's shoulder. 'We have saved one for the captain though,' he said and smiled at Vodanski, 'Well, we don't want to do anything that would put us in front of a firing squad, do we?'

'Where is she?'

'Over there,' replied Solka, pointing to the bare beechwood door in the far corner of the kitchen. 'You dark horse,' added Solka, nodding in the direction of the other four soldiers in the unit, though one was asleep on the floor by the stove. 'I thought you only liked women, but you like them young, too, eh!' He grinned up at Vodanski. 'No problem, you enjoy yourself, but don't do anything down below, or the captain will have us all lined up in front of a firing squad,' he added, tapping the side of his nose and giving him a knowing look.

'No fear, he's a fucking homo,' shouted over the flushed faced soldier.

Solka and the other two soldiers laughed.

'Is anyone in there with her?' asked Vodanski.

'No, but after you and the captain finish what you want to do, we will all go in,' tapping his nose again, and flashing a toothy smoke-stained grin. 'Eh!'

Vodanski strode over to the beechwood door at the far side of the kitchen. He gently turned the wooden doorknob and slowly opened the door. In the farthest corner of the main bedroom, by the unlit fireplace, was a little girl who was no more than eight years old, sitting and weeping on the wooden floor with her back to the bare stone wall. She held a blanket to her face.

The young Russian infantryman stood in the family bedroom and glanced down at the shattered picture frames on the floor and thought of his own family. He wondered about Katalina, the daughter he had never seen, and thought of Nicki, his wife, whom he had married two years ago. They did not know what they were doing when they married, but getting wed and having children was what everyone did. Both seized the opportunity to be happy when it came, as the lives they lived were brutal and short. He thought of her and once again wondered whether he loved her. He could not say for sure as he did not really know her. They were too young, without thoughts and opinions of their own. But that all seemed such a long time ago. He was a man now.

He slowly approached the child with his arms hanging down by his sides, trying to be as unthreatening as a man of his size could be.

'Put this on,' he whispered as he bent down to place his trench coat around her shivering body. It covered her like a tent. With great care, he picked her up in his arms.

'Where are my sisters?' she whispered.

'They have gone to a more peaceful place,' he replied softly.

It was a double lie. Vodanski had seen too much evil to believe there was a benevolent God.

'Are we going to join them?'

'Not for a while,' he whispered. 'I'm taking you out of here.'

Making their way to the main room, he tried to distract the girl with questions. 'Do you have any other family nearby?', 'Any friends we could visit?', and 'What is your name?' but the child did not reply. The big man had confirmed her worst fears about the fate of her sisters.

The little girl lay motionless and exhausted in his arms, as she prepared herself for what she might see. For two days, without food, she had listened to the horrific screams and bouts of maniacal laughter from the main room. But when they reached the main front room, on the other side of the kitchen, Vodanski lifted the collar of his coat over her eyes.

He whispered, 'Please, whatever happens, do not open your eyes until we are out of the house.'

Vodanski appeared in the doorway of the kitchen, cradling the girl in his arms. Solka was drinking from a wine bottle that he had passed around the others. They saw him: their laughter ceased.

'Where the fuck are you taking her?' yelled Solka.

'Out that door. Stand aside or I'll go through you. Your choice.'

Vodanski placed the girl behind him on the floor, ensuring his coat still covered her eyes. He positioned his feet on either side as he faced his unit.

'Diminova will have us all executed,' spat Solka.'

'Then die now,' announced Vodanski, as he picked up a half empty wine bottle in his left hand and, holding it by its neck, smashed it against the brittle doorframe. He removed the serrated dagger from Solka's jacket hanging

251

on the door and griped it in his right hand. He stood in silence, filling the frame of the door and facing the three men.

The men of his unit waited for one of them to make the first move towards him or out the front door. His comrades knew that if he left with the girl, their captain would have them shot, but taking on the best fighter in their unit, perhaps even in the entire Red Army, meant certain death. The three men rose from their chairs and edged towards the empty bedroom. Vodanski had calculated, correctly, that challenging them to make the first move that none of them would the nerve to do so.

'You win Vodanski, but God help you when Moscow hears of this,' declared Solka, stepping inside.

The young infantryman opened the door, grabbed each of the soldiers' rifles by the barrel and lobbed them as far as he could into the frozen river. He helped himself to the bullets in the corporal's inside jacket pocket that he knew would be hidden there. Then he gathered up the girl in his left arm. Holding his rifle with the same hand and grabbed the large bag by the door with his right.

'But that's all the food we took from the houses! We'll starve!' roared Solka, racing towards him.

Vodanski dropped the heavy bag, grabbed the corporal by the left arm and spun him violently around, tearing his coat from him with one swift movement. Solka landed on the floor, as Vodanski wrapped the corporal's trench coat around the girl. Vodanski checked to see if any of the others would make a move, but no one dared. He turned back towards the door and threw his right boot against it, kicking it off its hinges with such force that it broke into several pieces as it flew out into the snow.

'Thank you for the coat,' said Vodanski, without turning around. 'Wrap up warm though, the doors a little loose.' He glanced at the table. 'Diminova should return in a couple of days. It looks like you only have food enough for one, till then.'

With the girl wrapped up in his arms and his rifle and large bag over his shoulders, Vodanski set off across the bridge

Solka looked at the drunk lying asleep on the floor of the room and wiped his knife from his belt. He stabbed the unconscious man in the chest and glowered at his two comrades.

The snow drift cloaked them as Vodanski, carrying the girl, made their way along the riverbank, and up into the mountains. The town of Kaniv was a three-day march. It was their only hope.

Wearing his budionovka, a useless army issue cloth helmet, his coat and the leather boots he had taken from the Cossack, he waded knee deep through the snow and tramped through the forest growth where the overhanging growth was thickest. On the second morning, after traipsing through the foot-deep snow through the night, the girl cradled in his arms smiled up at him and said her name was Katalina. He smiled back; it was a good omen for the future.

The forest became denser as they made their way high up into the mountains. As the visibility grew worse as the snow became thicker, he told Katalina fairy tales he had learnt for the day when he would, finally, see his own daughter.

When the snowstorm was at its peak, he could barely feel his arms. As he trudged through the night, he kept breathing on Katalina's face to ward off frostbite.

The next day he managed to shoot a wild hog taking cover from the increasingly biting snow blizzard. Good fortune was with them. He found a cave where lowered Katalina onto a dry piece of ground and prepared a fire with some dried twigs. Pierced on the serrated knife, Vodanski roasted pieces of the pig over its flames. He smiled at sleeping girl: they would make it.

On the third day, when Vodanski tried to shoot a crow, the firing pin in his rifle broke. Perhaps it was frozen to the mechanism. It was the last of the bullets, anyway. He dug a hole in the snow to bury the weapon, just in case his captain, and what remained of his unit, had imbibed enough liquid courage to follow them. The food he had commandeered was all gone.

When he discovered an exposed burrow, he placed a simple loop of wire he always carried with him in his backpack, over its entrance. Three hours or more later he quickly wrenched the wire, trapping its occupant by its back foot. He skinned the rabbit and tore off its limbs with his bare hands before cooking it over a fire, using the empty backpack as its core. Vodanski rotated the skewered rabbit over the flames on his blade, while cleaning the blood off its pelt in the snow. As they ate, he tucked the animal skin inside his clothing, against his chest. Once he was happy it was dry, he tied it around the girl's head. She had not complained about the cold, but she smiled.

There was no lull in the snowfall that day, or the next. The Russian's luck ran out. The snowfall became a blizzard and even snow rabbits did not emerge for food. He continued to traipse through the storm with the girl in his arms. When he felt that fatigue and the sub-zero temperatures would finally bring him to his knees, he would glance down at Katalina. She always returned his smile. This simple act would replenish his energy and drive him on.

As he trampled through the forest, he sang lullabies that he hoped he would one day sing for his own daughter. Katalina seemed happy and even laughed, which was incredible as she must have been very hungry.

When they finally emerged from the forest, the plain was free of wildlife, but he looked at Katalina's smiling face. He knew that soon they would come across a house where food and warmth would be offered. Though they had come down from the mountain, the blizzard tore at the Russian, sending tiny razors of ice to slash at his face. His body was barely covered. He had wrapped the child in his overcoat, as Solka's had disintegrated, leaving two damp vests covering his arms and chest.

All that kept him going was the smile on Katalina's face, without which he knew he would have rested and death would have followed.

In the distance of the snow-covered landscape, he spotted a building. As he approached it, he could finally make out that it was a farmhouse, with smoke coming from its chimney. There was a paraffin light hanging from a window. A black and white border collie barked as they approached its owners' home. Then, having broken free from its kennel, it leapt over the front fence to meet them. The dog ran back and forth, circling them, trying to corral them in the direction of the empty sheep pen.

Vodanski saw a bright light streaming from the doorway. Then the silhouette of what appeared to be an elderly couple appeared at the door. He pushed open the gate leading to the stone path to the house.

He looked down at Katalina. 'We're almost there, little one,' he whispered, staggering forward.

The girl looked up at him and smiled.

The Russian's legs gave way. The woman was the first to rush to the aid of the half-naked man, who was still holding the bundle in his arms. Her husband and what appeared to be their son joined her. The woman looked inside the bundle and then handed it to the elder man and told him to take it into the house. Meanwhile, the woman and her son managed to lift Vodanski onto his feet and led him into the house.

The woman shut the door behind them and pointed to the older man to lay the bundle down by the open fire. Two younger women appeared and wrapped blankets over Vodanski. He lay on the floor, watching the others gather around Katalina. He heard the woman say something, but he could not work out what. One of the younger women was unfolding the bundle of clothes.

Vodanski tried to speak before he passed out.

His jaw was frozen, but he mumbled, 'Is Katalina alright?'

One of the daughters turned to her mother. Vodanski thought he heard her say, 'The child is dead. I think she's been dead for days.'

Chapter 10: The Blind Man

March 1938, Berlin

'Why did Lenka refer to you as "The Blind Man"?' asked Sean.

'You're impatient, Irishman. Your woman must find you a very disappointing lover,' noted the small, neatly dressed, middle-aged German man.

'That's the problem with women. They can't keep a secret,' replied Sean.

'You don't take yourself too seriously, but this is a serious business,' replied the diminutive German.

'If I took myself seriously, I'd be a basket case,' smiled Sean.

'How is Lenka?' asked the German.

'She is recovering from her injuries. That's why she sent me. But she'll be fighting fit soon enough, and I am sure the Nazis could do with the break,'

'My girlfriend, Jewel, is looking after her,' replied Chris, who spoke for the first time since the three had first been introduced ten minutes earlier.

'Thank you. You seem like a good man, so what are you doing with . . .' exclaimed the German, as he looked at the Irishman again and shrugged.

Sean smiled, for though he had just been introduced to Otto Weidt, he liked him the sharp-witted German.

The factory owner poured from a small battered white clay teapot, whose lightning cracks down its sides leaked tea, which made using it, as with everything else in Berlin, precarious. Over the next few hours, the two visitors were to learn that any money the man had was not spent on luxuries, or was even reinvested in the factory, but on keeping his staff alive.

Picking up his cup, Chris replied, 'Jewel, and I arrived in Berlin this morning. Lenka introduced me to Sean,' nodding at the man on the chair by Otto's desk, 'And we're here to ask for your help.'

The three men sat in the German's spartan little office, which seemed even smaller due to the size of his two visitors. If it had seen better days, there was no sign of it.

Chris continued, 'We have thirty children of all ages, most of whom have a disability, plus three babies, that we need to hide from the Nazis tonight, before we smuggle them out of Berlin.'

The German's tone changed, considering the seriousness and magnitude of the task. 'I will do all I can. Come with me.'

The two men strode along the corridor, either side of the owner of the broom-making factory, who trotted along between them trying to keep up. Sean decided to let Chris do most of the talking, as the German clearly saw him as the more sensible of his visitors. Otto opened the tatty and old battered door leading to the shop floor.

Sean had expected to enter just one room with a handful of workers, but there were men and women hurrying back and forth from several interconnecting rooms. In the wood-panelled main room, there were about ten men and women sitting at wooden desks. There was a faded cream clay-tiled furnace in the far left-hand corner of the first room, providing warmth throughout the workshop. On each desk, there was a vertical press with a handle on the right side, which, when lowered, pushed the threaded copper wires wrapped from a spool into each hole along with the folded coarse horsehair.

In the room on the left were two women folding strains of horsehair around wooden-handled lathes. The other rooms were further to the back of the main room. In one small room, tucked in on the right, were three men and a woman drilling holes into the wooden heads of the brushes. In the room next to that, there was a young man using a hand drill to make holes in lengths of wood that were flat on one side and curved on the other. In the room overlooking the backyard, another woman was turning a thick two-foot-long rectangular piece of wood on a large lathe. Sean noticed a little wooden box secured underneath her left-hand side for storing nails, darning thread and scissors, which also contained a tube of bright red lipstick. Thankfully, some people still try to lead a normal life, thought Sean.

He glanced back along the hallway. It was a superbly orchestrated operation to create the most basic of implements, a broom. The workers, about forty by Sean's estimate, delicately weaved their way around each other like ballet dancers, negotiating their way ably from room to room. A performance that was remarkable, for they were all blind and many were deaf.

Sean was reminded of Magdalena. If he had known of the factory's existence before, he would have brought her and Tóth here, but it did not matter now as they were

259

safe somewhere in England.

The Irishman smiled at the factory owner, before saying, 'Sadly, I don't think the Nazis are literally going to sweep across Europe.'

Chris raised his eyebrows at the decidedly unimpressed Otto by way of an apology.

'When did you first meet Lenka?' continued Sean.

'I've never met her,' replied Otto, 'But she writes many letters. Did you know that?'

'I've heard,' said Sean.

'She writes to those who may be able to help her children. I believe you can always tell a good person from the letters they write. Can you write?' he asked, but he continued without waiting for an answer. 'She used to write me to see if I had work for the eldest children when it was time for them to leave the orphanage. Many of them are also blind and mute, I believe.' With a broad smile, he asked, 'And what of the wondrous Olen? Lenka speaks lovingly of her. She's the beating heart of the orphanage, so Lenka tells us. My wife loves to read Lenka's tales of Olen's antics, and how she makes the children laugh.'

Sean replied solemnly, 'We had to leave her behind in Kraków to look after two of the children. I called the local doctor on our way here, but he has no news of her or the children.'

The German looked up at the Irishman. 'Lenka will need a friend and not just a lover.'

Sean was surprised to be referred to as her lover. The wily old man missed nothing.

'You're the first good German I've met.'

'Don't judge a race, a creed, or a religion by the

actions of a few, or you'll end up marching alongside the Fascists,' countered Otto. 'I may be the first, but that doesn't mean I am alone.'

In the smallest room, farthest to the back of the factory, Otto bent down and pulled on the brass handle of the safe in the wall. Chris and Sean moved forward to help, but he had already pulled it open with incredible ease to expose a staircase.

Sean looked down at the elderly gentleman. You probably would not notice him in a crowd. Yet, this unassuming man, with the resolute support of his wife Machla, had somehow managed to protect these blind men and women from the Nazis. To do this, right in the centre of the German capital, only a twenty-minute walk from the Reichstag and SS Headquarters, was incredibly courageous.

'It's locked to the floor, in case the Nazis try to look behind it, but if you release the locking mechanism, it's light as a feather as the casing is an empty shell.'

'How do you release the locking bars?' asked Sean.

'I must have some secrets,' declared the man as he pushed the safe back. Sean and Chris nodded to each other as they helped Otto up – the man had the heart of a lion and the guile of a fox. 'There are stairs that lead up two floors to the attic, where the children will stay tonight. They will be safe there. Even if anyone hears them, they will think it's the children of the workforce, who are at school now. They live with their parents on the floor above us.'

'Are all your workers Jewish?' asked Chris.

'Yes, my factory has officially been declared as of supreme importance to the war effort, as we supply brushes and brooms to the Wehrmacht. Therefore the Jewish men and woman who work here, are also deemed essential to the war effort.'

'How the hell did you do that?' interjected Sean.

'By using my brain; you should try it.'

'Sounds awfully dangerous; I might injure myself,' exclaimed Sean, before deferring the conversation once again to Chris.

The little man smiled and said, 'Plus, a little bribery of a few Gestapo officers.'

'Are you Jewish?' asked Chris.

'I'm a pacifist.'

The little bell rang excitedly in the office. Sean had noticed it and the string connected to it running down the wall of the stairway. It now being pulled by a woman perched on the front step of the factory.

Otto returned briskly to his office and removed a white band from a drawer and slipped it on his arm to indicate he was totally blind. Then he collected a white cane that was hidden behind a hat stand in the corner.

He turned to his visitors, 'The Nazis aim to set the world alight, but there's little spark in their brains. You have to make the signals explicit.'

'You fooled me,' confessed Sean, smiling at the man.

'You make it sound like a challenge,' replied Otto, smiling at the success of his ruse. 'I know this factory, as I know my darling wife's face. I do not need props to navigate it.'

Sean liked the old man even more for his mischievous ways and how he managed to keep a straight face when he was asked why he was called The Blind Man. Chris also enjoyed the verbal sparring between Sean and the German. It reminded him of Jake and Vodanski when he first stepped into the Banco de España and encountered Lenka's Rogues and Jewel.

'Either the Gestapo are paying us a visit or we have a "Catcher" in the alley,' snapped Otto.

A young woman hurried Chris and Sean back along the corridor and into the stairwell behind the safe. The two men noticed – now that they were looking for it – that the woman had pressed her heel down on a wooden slat nearest the skirting board.

'What are Catchers?' whispered Sean.

'Traitorous pigs,' she replied. 'Some of our own who are local, paid informers seeking out fellow Jews who are hiding,' before shutting the false safe door behind them.

Through a gap in the wooden panel, Ryan could see four men. They were not in uniform, but they were police of some sort, probably Gestapo. Two were dressed in long black leather coats, the others in light cream trench coats. All were wearing brown homburgs. They took their time to meticulously check the identity papers of the workers a few feet away from the two men.

'Don't kill them or you will bring this place down on these people,' whispered Chris, as they sat back against the bare stone wall of the hidden staircase.

'Look. I've no idea what Lenka or Tweedledee and Tweedledum told you, but I'm not a complete fucking head case,' whispered Sean.

'A couple of years ago, I read a story in the *Scottish Examiner* about a man called 'The Englander' said Chris quietly. 'The journalist said that when an Italian cavalry officer pointed a gun at him, he killed the officer's horse with one punch.'

'That's bollocks! The horse wasn't hurt. I only pulled the horse down, so I could unseat its rider. I love animals. It's people I have trouble with,' replied the Irishman in a low but irritated voice.

Chris's eyebrows almost came together.

After the Gestapo had left the building, Otto opened the door to the recess and glared at Sean, 'Thank you for not killing them.'

'Jesus, I need a new press agent,' replied the Irishman, crawling out on all fours.

Chris tried to hide a smile. As Sean walked ahead, as the Scotsman whispered to Otto. 'You don't like the Irishman, do you?'

'I do. He's deceptively clever and has wit, but he is a man who needs to be checked. He's a man who would fight the world, even if it brought carnage to all those who loved him.'

Back in his office, Otto outlined his plan for getting the children to the factory.

'Bring the children here about nine o'clock. It will be dark, but busy enough so as not to draw too much attention. But take the utmost care; there are spies everywhere.'

'You mean Catchers,' said Sean.

Lenka lay on the seat at the front of the bus and watched as the first of the snowflakes floated down past the transparent film that Sean had taped in the broken window-frame. They were the first of many white layers that would soon blanket the streets of the city. Spring was nearly upon them, but the easterly winds had Europe in its grip.

264

It was prearranged that when Jewel and Chris left Madrid, they would head to the British Embassy in Paris. When they arrived, a message was waiting for them from Lenka that she would be in Berlin on her way to London. They headed to Berlin, in the belief that whatever their friend was planning, she might need their help. It was fortunate that they did, for when Jewel examined Lenka she discovered, and then removed, a bullet which no one knew was lodged inside her.

Lenka knew that Jewel and Chris had expected her to have been happier to see them, but she just stared out at the buildings as the heat from their rooftops gave up its struggle and let the white powder settle. As a child, she loved the snow. Lenka recalled memories of snowball fights and building a snowman with the other children at the orphanage. She had always thought that the first day of snowfall was more exciting than even the first day of spring, as you did not know how deep the snow would be and how many mornings you would wake up to see a surreal white canvas. Its appearance now, stirred only painful memories

Watching to drift easily to the ground, she saw Leo lying motionless in the snow, cradled in Ursula's arms. She thought of Olen building a snowman the night before they had left the orphanage, and then standing and waving at the gate as they drove away. But there was no news of her or the two children. This was not how it was supposed to be.

It had turned nine o'clock when Chris, Jake, Sean and Vodanski led the children down the dark narrow alleyway leading to the factory entrance. The snow was building up on the smooth cobblestones. Jake and Vodanski were holding the hands of the most vulnerable children, while Sean carried Lenka, with Ursula following behind.

While the others made up beds inside the factory, Sean and Jake returned to the bus parked at the end of the alleyway. The Irishman had earlier removed the last of the armour-plates, gummed up the bullet holes, and replaced the clear plastic film covering the windows, so as not to raise the suspicions of Berliners hurrying home. The American kicked the engine into life, and The Sleepy Armadillo reversed slowly back onto the main street.

'Keep going. I'll jump off around the corner,' whispered Sean.

'I knew it was too easy,' replied Jake, as the Irishman opened the doors and leapt onto the icy pavement.

He did not look back as he headed back towards the alleyway and the bus pulled away from the traffic lights. Ryan turned into a doorway on the main street on the edge of the alley, waiting for the man to come out of the darkness opposite the factory entrance. Once the snow had erased the trail of tiny footprints leading to the factory. The man Ryan was waiting for emerged from the shadows of an alcove.

Ryan had a better view of the Catcher in the light. He was tall – taller than the Irishman – and in his mid-twenties. His frame was slight, his face gaunt. The man reminded of a skeleton he once saw in a medical school that was used as a coat stand. He had a narrow, aquiline nose. In fact, everything about him was lean, apart from the beginnings of a potbelly.

Like the Irishman, the Catcher had chosen not to wear a hat even though the snow was falling heavily.

As the Catcher scurried out under a streetlamp, Ryan saw that had a form of alopecia. With his stooped, gangly frame, carefully orchestrated steps, he now reminded the Irishman of Max Schreck's *Nosferatu*.

The Catcher failed to notice Ryan leaning back against the dark doorway and scurried in haste passed him and turned right as he entered the main road, toward the Brandenburg Gate. Ryan followed.

Twenty minutes later, the Catcher took a left turn towards a complex of nondescript grey concrete buildings. The man's pace quickened. He was no longer avoiding the glare of the streetlights. Ryan knew this meant that the man felt increasingly secure and was therefore near his paymasters. It was always in those last few moments when a man, however careful, would usually drop his guard. The man darted towards the back of a bland grey building. The street was deserted. Ryan sprinted towards him. At the final moment, the man turned to see who was running up to him, but he was too late to dodge the runner's fist smashing into his left cheekbone.

With one hand clasping the back of the man's head, Ryan delivered three powerful, rapid punches under the Catcher's jaw with the other. It was enough to break it. The Catcher was dead before the Irishman released him and let him flop onto the snow-covered street.

Ryan grabbed the Catcher by his ankles and dragged him onto a side road. He did not know that the building was the headquarters of the SS, but he knew that this was where the Catcher was going to report the arrival of the children.

He waited for the two guards in the front of the other grey imposing building to stop, turn around and goose-step back towards each other. When they met, the sentries stopped to light cigarettes. With the body of the Catcher draped over his shoulder, Ryan climbed the metal staircase that scaled the side of building, out of sight of the guards. Ten minutes later, he reached the third-floor balcony of the ten-story building unseen, but breathless.

Ryan pressed himself along with the body against the wall, as he waited for the sentries to turn around and march back to their respective corners of the building. When they did, he tied the dead man's belt to an outside handle of one of the closed double windows. He pressed himself once more against the exterior wall while holding the Catcher back into the shadow of the balcony with his right arm. He waited for the guards to do one more circuit. Seconds before they reached furthest corners of the building opposite, Ryan threw the Catcher from the balcony. The double windows behind the corpse burst from the frame.

Before the body and the windows hit the snow, Ryan swung himself over the rail and onto the neighbouring balcony. He climbed his way down a drainpipe running down the left-facing wall of the building, while the sentries, rifles in hand, raced towards the carnage. The Irishman waited until they bent down to examine the Catcher, before leaping over the light that came on in the room beneath him. He bent his knees, so he made hardly a sound as he landed on the snow.

Deftly he covered the ten metres of ground that led to the empty street.

Twenty-five minutes later, he was back at the alley that

led to the factory. To his great relief all was quiet, and there were no new tracks in the snow. After an hour, he was satisfied the authorities had not connected Otto's factory with the death of the Catcher. He made his way back to the bus, which was parked in an officially designated truck park, a kilometre from the train station. Ryan entered the bus to find everyone asleep. The blanket covering Lenka had fallen to the floor. He lifted it back over her and gently tucked it in. He slipped in beside her on the seat, cradling her sleeping body in his arm. He stared out at the snow – the snow, which once again began to cover the body of another man he had killed – but his only thoughts were when it was the backdrop of those last few seconds of Leo's life.

At dawn the next morning, The Sleepy Armadillo headed once again to Otto Weidt's broom factory. Vodanski pulled the bus over to the side when he saw a police car parked in the street opposite the alley. Chris and Sean were sitting on the floor behind him with their revolvers drawn. Meanwhile, Jake was making his way to the American Embassy to send a message home.

At the same time, Jewel was helping Lenka reach the British Embassy to meet Paul and finalise arrangements for the children to board the train that evening for England. An hour later, the police car drove off. Vodanski turned the engine back on and headed out onto the thoroughfare. The street was empty. He reversed the bus into the alleyway. Vodanski slipped in through the factory's front doors and a few minutes later he came back carrying Mala. He nodded to the others to give the all clear to go in, as he went up the steps of the bus and

269

slipped the girl carefully onto the front seat. He turned to Sean.

'Otto's not happy. It seems a man was thrown out of one of the windows of SS headquarters last night.'

'No finesse, these Nazis,' said Ryan, shaking his head.

'The man was one of the Gestapo's informers. Catchers, they call them, and this one used to watch this neighbourhood.'

'Oh dear, well, I'm sure they'll find a replacement soon enough.'

'Unlikely, it seems their network of Catchers are all in a panic. They think the Nazis are turning on them. Three were arrested this morning trying to board a freight train out of the city.'

'Good news does indeed travel fast. How does Otto know all this?'

'He likes to keep up with the latest events and listens in on police radio transmissions.' Sean smiled as the Russian shook his head. 'He thinks you killed him.'

'And you?'

'I don't think it was you . . . I know it was you,' said Vodanski, as he slapped his hand on the Irishman's shoulder before he strode back into the building.

Sean followed and was greeted by a hug from Ursula.

'How's Lenka?' she asked.

'The police entered the bus last night to check our papers. When they got to Lenka, Jake told them she had a fever that was likely to be contagious. It worked. They searched everyone else, but not her so they didn't discover wounds.'

'Where were you?'

'I couldn't sleep, so I went for a walk. But Lenka slept through it all, and she was the first one up this morning, so she's recovering.' He decided it was best not to mention that Jewel had to remove a bullet from her hip.

'Did they believe your story that you were all off to a circus convention?' asked Ursula.

'What's not to believe? Look at us.'

Vodanski trudged past with one of the girls up on his shoulders. He stopped to lift his arms up into the air and adopted the classic muscular pose of a circus strong man. The little girl above put on a stern face as she mimicked him.

Ursula embraced Sean and whispered, 'I miss Leo.'

Sean sighed and nodded as he helped her negotiate the snow towards the bus.

Otto appeared and strode up to the Irishman.

'Killing is not the answer. You believe you were doing the right thing, but life is not so black and white. The man had a family too.'

'You are a pacifist, and I'm about as far removed from one as you can get. Either way, it's a tough road we take. Most people keep their heads down, we don't. Every day we have to make tough calls, and one day we will be judged by them. I'll accept my punishment when it comes,' as he turned towards the bus, 'but not today.'

'Death follows you Irishman and despite your good intentions, the innocent will always suffer because of your recklessness.'

'Many already have,' confessed Sean. 'Will you at least shake my hand?' he said, offering it to the man.

271

Otto shook it. 'I bear you no malice, but for the sake of the people who are under my protection, I hope I never see you again.'

Chris appeared, carrying the babies in their metal cradles, and placed them on the front seat.

The Scotsman stepped back into the alley, 'After three weeks jumping from train to train, Jewel and I slept the sleep of the dead last night.' He scratched his chin. 'But we missed something, haven't we?'

He and Jewel had not stirred once they were cuddled up together, apart from when the police brutally woke them to check their papers.

'Sean, I have only just met you and though everyone gave you a hard time yesterday, you seem OK to me.' The Scotsman shrugged, 'Well, you haven't killed anyone yet.'

'It might be a little soon to employ a new press agent,' said Sean.

Chris spotted saw Piotr, a boy weakened by polio, standing by the door of the factory. He trudged through the slush, lifted the boy up in his arms and carried him onto the bus. As he lowered the boy gently into a seat by Vodanski, he recognised his knowing smile.

'I've definitely missed something, haven't I?'

Vodanski said nothing, but his smile broadened.

Chapter 11: Gathering of the Rogues

March 1938, Berlin

Though it was March and Berliners had thought they were emerging from a bitter winter, they were now in the middle of a snowstorm.

It was eight o'clock in the morning. Standing a block away from the Lehrter Bahnhof terminal, Jake was stamping his feet and flapping his arms as the bus pulled up in front of him

'Something's up, there are soldiers all over the train station,' said the American.

'Looking for us, no doubt?' replied Sean, as he stepped down from The Sleepy Armadillo.

'I don't know, but Lenka told me to help the children board the train and then we should find somewhere on the other side of town and keep a low profile.'

Sean heard a familiar greeting come from behind him, 'Err . . .'

Without turning to see who it was, he greeted the man: 'Good to see you, Paul.'

Chris, Vodanski and Jake looked suspiciously at the young man. He wore very fine quality clothing, but he was dishevelled in appearance and one side of his white silk shirt was hanging over his belt. Their unease was not placated when, as Sean shook the man's hand, a small

273

bottle of expensive Rioja fell from his coat pocket and smashed to the ground.

Jake turned to Chris and said, 'Something to steady the nerves. I'd say that he's worked with the Irishman before.'

The Scotsman smiled, and he noticed that even the Russian's lips turned up a little at the sides. That the Irishman was wild appeared to be the one thing they could all agree on.

Sean shook the man's hand as much to steady him as it was to acknowledge that he was pleased to see him. He stooped down to help him pick up the broken glass, while using the opportunity to find out what he had agreed with Lenka.

'You met Lenka?'

'Yes, first thing this morning. She, and an Australian lady,' he replied without referring to her scars, which was fortunate as Chris was not a man to rouse. 'She told me to come straight to you with the children's train tickets and their forged identity papers. Then I was to get children into the station . . . stay with them on the train . . . as I speak fluent . . . Ger . . . man.' He nearly lost his footing in the snow at that point, but Vodanski grabbed his arm. Composing himself, Paul continued, 'I left her and the Australian lady at the Embassy, as London told her to wait for further news. I have no idea what . . . that . . . news is. In the meantime, you are all to stay out of sight.'

The others knew it made sense that only Paul accompanied the children, as he looked more like a teacher.

'There is an underground bar . . . you must . . . sorry

. . . it would be best you go there . . . and she and her friend would join by midday. It's called The Bier Keller, on Hardenbergstrasse opposite the zoo. It's always open, despite the sign on the door. I'm sorry . . . but the train is not due to leave until 9:00 pm tonight . . . and it's the only place I could think of where you would not draw . . . suspicion.'

'I take it the bar is one you know?' asked Sean.

'Yes, it's the best place I can think of where such uncouth characters . . .' he paused as he looked at the four men, '. . . I mean . . . I-'

Sean saved the man from further embarrassment:

'We understand, just don't embarrass us by asking us to use a knife and fork.'

The other three nodded and shrugged their shoulders to express empathy and carried on helping the children off the bus.

The children huddled together on the snow-carpeted pavement, with their little knapsacks either on their backs or held in their hands. The large troop of children and four men would have attracted considerable attention, but for the bitter blizzard that pressed the faces of passing Berliners into their scarves, as they pulled their hats over their eyes. The children, led by Paul, set off towards the Lehrer Bahnhof Station. The four men waited in a side street and watched. Having been forced to stand out in the snowstorm for nearly an hour while the two soldiers checked their forged papers, Paul and the children were finally allowed inside the train station.

An hour later, on the other side of the town centre, the four men strolled past a sign that read *Geschlossen* (closed) and made their way down the wooden stairs into The Bier Keller.

Sean ordered four steins of Czechoslovakian Pilsner, while he surveyed the other customers. This was Paul's kind of place, all right. It was clouded in cigarette smoke, while the men spilled the contents of their glasses as they engaged in animated debate. Jake, whose German parents had taught him the language of their former homeland, listened in on the three very drunken academics at the table nearest the bar. He smiled as they were having a very noisy row about what had started the argument in the first place.

It might as well have been midnight. There was little light in the room, apart from the roaring fire in the centre of the floor, and a few paraffin lamps hanging above the bar and on the tables.

Lenka and Jewel arrived just after noon. Both women made their way slowly down the steps, but Lenka was gaining in strength as she no longer required support as they approached the men at the bar.

Sean knew what her first question would be, so he did not wait for it: 'Paul is with the children inside the station.'

'He makes me nervous,' replied Lenka, as she filled a wine glass from the bottle on the bar.

'No more than he makes himself,' replied the Irishman. As they picked up their drinks, Jake nodded, 'Come on, let's sit by the professors over at the back.'

The six made the way to the largest wooden table on the other side of the fire. The trio of academics spotted them and sobered up, but continued to argue in whispers.

Lenka had many questions for Jewel and Chris, as

she had been fully focused over the last twenty-four hours on getting the children to the train station.

'Tell us of Spain? Is it as bad as they say?'

Jewel knew that Lenka had delayed this moment as much as for Jake and Vodanski, so they learnt together the fate of those they had fought with.

'You were right to leave Madrid. The Communists purged even the most loyal of Republican fighters. If you weren't a card-carrying communist, you were arrested and put in front of a firing squad.' Jewel looked at Chris. He responded with a strained smile, which she took as a sign that she could continue with their story.

'With the Fascists on one side and the Stalinists on the other, anything in the middle was deemed as the enemy by both sides.'

For Lenka, Jake and Vodanski, they were not telling them anything they did not already know, but it did not lessen the impact of hearing it.

'And your patients?' asked Lenka. 'What happened to them?'

Chris held Jewel's withered hand while she described the final moments before they fled Madrid.

'We could hear the machine guns getting louder and the cries as the Nationalists surrounded Gran Via. My man here,' squeezing his hand, 'repelled the Fascists attacks, which gave Katherine . . .' she hesitated and looked at Chris. His head fell, 'And I time to prepare our patients to make the journey to France.' She put her right hand on Chris' arm. 'Chris found us a truck, and we managed to fit our last remaining eight patients, including a recently injured young girl, onto the back of it. But as we were leaving, the Fascists threw hand grenades through the windows.' She paused and dropped her head along with her voice. 'As Katherine tried to protect one of the children, she received the full force of one of the explosions.'

Jake suspected it, but he had been afraid to ask for fear of the answer. Vodanski glanced at the American, as he knew he cared for Katherine more than he would admit to any of them. Jake had suffered more than any of them during their time in Madrid. Chris knew that too, and he looked up at the American and gave him a brief nod as if to acknowledge their shared loss. Jake looked at Chris and nodded. The man had lost the only family he had ever known.

The sombre Scotsman rose from his seat and walked over to the bar to order another round. Chris was a man who would not speak of his grief, even to Jewel. It was not that he did not want to. He did not know how.

After a pause, Lenka spoke, 'Did you have a chance to bury Katherine?'

'No,' replied Jewel, 'we had no time as the Fascists were nearly upon us.'

'What happened then?' asked Vodanski.

'With the stretchers loaded onto the back of truck we drove straight out of Madrid.'

'What of the cordon?' asked Jake.

'The Fascists had taken most of the city, so they must have dismantled it, thinking it was no longer needed.'

'Or those manning it, had poured into the city to join in the looting, more likely,' added Jake.

'From there we headed to Barcelona, where we boarded a train to take us to the border. There Chris secured another vehicle, and we made our way through a lightly guarded pass into France.'

'How many are in the camps?' asked Lenka.

'The French Government say over half a million refugees are camped on the border. We just came from the one in Roussillon and there is no proper shelter, no food or proper sanitary conditions. Local gangs roam the area trying to extort food, stealing clothing and money.'

'Fuck! Is the world doing anything to help?' yelled Lenka, whose outburst silenced the three academics.

As Chris put the tray of drinks on the table, Jake spoke: 'The British and the French are taking in some refugees, providing they have skills, such as in medicine and teaching. I hear now that if you have experience of civil defence, you are welcome. Perhaps they are starting to realise that war is coming.'

Jewel too had questions: 'Jake, did you go back to America?'

'I flew back to see my family, but after a week I decided to return to Europe and help where I could. I hung out in Paris and went to the British Embassy each morning to see if Lenka had left any messages.'

'Why the British Embassy?' asked Sean.

'Lenka,' he said, nodding to the Polish woman, 'told us all before we left Madrid, that she would send regular messages to London. These would then be circulated through their diplomatic channels, saying where she could be found if we wanted her, or she needed us. After a few days, there was a message for me saying that she was making her way with a bus load of children to Berlin.'

'Why make Paris your base?' asked Jewel.

'Paris and Berlin are the main train hubs to reach

anywhere in Europe. I chose Paris, as I didn't fancy mixing with slaphappy Nazis in lederhosen.'

'Thank God you got my messages,' said Lenka. 'I couldn't risk sending the details of our route and it being intercepted. But I knew you'd all work it out,' added Lenka, before turning to Jewel. 'I was able to work out the optimal route you would take in a vehicle. I knew you wouldn't risk the trains.'

Jewel hesitated as she leaned towards Vodanski. 'Did you go home to your family?'

The Russian did not return her gaze or respond to her question. Jake took this to mean that the Russian's family was dead and that he would never tell them what had happened. When Jewel repeated her question, thinking Vodanski had not heard her, Jake caught her eye and shook his head.

Lenka shared Jake's view and moved the conversation quickly on with another question: 'How did you find us?'

Finally, Vodanski spoke. 'I was in Paris and I picked up your message saying you were driving a bus load of children to Berlin,' making no reference to the American having already mentioned this. 'I headed to the Polish-Czech border and waited. I knew you would try to circumvent the German Army massing on the border, so you had to head south.'

Sean got up to buy another round of drinks. He knew that for men like Chris and Vodanski, it was better to drink than talk about loss. With the Irishman up at the bar, Lenka turned to Jake and Vodanski, 'So where did you two meet up, before you started shooting Nazis out of the air?'

Before either man had a chance to answer, another man descended the wooden steps into the bar. He was in his early twenties, about five foot seven, balding and tubby, with little evidence of a neck as his ears were only just above his shoulders. His blotchy red cheeks gave one the impression that he was a man who enjoyed life to the extreme. He saw the solemn gathering and approached them.

'Ah, Van Gogh and the Septic Tank,' prattled the man, which united the antagonists, as the irate Russian lifted his hand to what was left of his ear and the American bridled at the man's rhyming slang for Yank. 'I haven't seen you two since Madame Jiggy-Jigs on the Rue St. Dennis?' shouted the new arrival.

The other drinkers took more of an interest in the raucous table at the end of the bar.

Jake and Vodanski looked away in opposite directions, now that Lenka had her answer. She looked disapprovingly at the newcomer, a look he soon got used to. Without embarrassment, the smaller of the Scotsmen commented on her frown, 'Pull your lip in, love. My name is Jocky.' He then turned to Jewel and said, 'Hi Gorgeous.'

Jewel turned her face away.

Chris grabbed his fellow Scotsman, lifted him by his jacket lapels into the air and rammed him against the wooden column by their table. Such was the impact that it sent the ornamental shields on either side of the column flying off in all directions. 'I don't know who the hell you are, but if you disrespect her like that again, I'll put you through the wall.'

Those around the table had never witnessed Chris

lose his temper, but none of the Rogues moved to intervene. In the background, the three academics rose from their chairs and edged their way along the wall leading to the staircase.

'I meant no offence, it's just my way of speaking. She has beautiful . . .' The taller Scotsman tightened his grip. This ended any further comment from the smaller man, who was dangling a foot off the ground, struggling to breathe.

Jewel put her hand on Chris' arm and said, 'I don't think he meant any harm. Please, my love.'

Chris released the man, who dropped to the floor in a heap.

'Jesus . . . hundreds of women just passed before my eyes,' exclaimed Jocky, holding his throat and desperately trying to breathe. 'I thought that was the end.' He glanced up at Jewel. 'Sorry, love, I didn't mean any offence. But *yer* have stunningly beautiful green eyes and I don't give a *shite* about *yer* scars.' He continued to massage his throat as Jewel helped him up. None of the others moved.

Lenka exploded, 'All this childish boys' stuff drives me insane. I've had two years of Jake and Vodanski tearing lumps off each other. Now God has burdened me with this Scottish halfwit, and that mad bastard up at the bar will probably blow the place up. God must hate me, to inflict me with my very own collection of arseholes.'

Much to her Polish friend's surprise, Jewel burst out laughing. Lenka loved to see her friend happy, but her mood was such that if anyone else had laughed at her outburst they would now be missing several teeth.

Though the man riled Lenka and Chris, Jewel found the new arrival to their table amusing. She had seen and suffered so much pain, that she enjoyed anything that lightened her mood, having spent a large part of her youth having rarely heard an unrestrained laugh. She had always enjoyed the repartee when the Rogues sparked off each other, providing it did not turn violent; though between Jake and Vodanski it often did.

'Terrible language, Gorgeous. *Yer* must be stressed, but if I can help relieve the tension?' said Jocky, winking at Lenka.

Lenka grabbed the bottle of wine on the table by the neck, but Vodanski stayed her arm.

The Russian leaned forward and whispered in Lenka's ear, 'Wait until the pygmy turns to me and makes some remark about my ear again.'

The smaller Scotsman continued, oblivious to how close to being hospitalised he was.

'Anyway, sorry I'm a wee bit late, but I had to complete the documents *yer* requested,' he said as he tucked the tail of his shirt into his trousers.

'You're either the technical guy sent by the British or you've been sent by the Nazis to kick the war off,' Lenka snarled, weighing the bottle in her hand.

'Look, I may be a total *fukwit*, halfwit, whatever, to *yer*, Gorgeous, but I'm a Valentino to many a lady and a technical genius to the rest of the world. Forging papers, getting anything with wheels on the road, securing supplies. I deliver the impossible. If *yer* ever find yourself naked in the middle of the high street, with *yer* thumbs up *yer* arse pal, Jocky will pull them out.'

'You'll be a big hit in Moscow,' replied Jake, 'I hear the streets are full of 'em', which set Jewel off giggling again, as she peered across at Vodanski's deadpan expression.

'I herald from Glasgow, a place of culture and refinement and not to be confused with that Scottish *shitehole*, Edinburgh.' He glanced at the wooden column that he had been pinned to, before turning back to look at Chris. 'No offence, pal.'

Chris did not mind what people said about him.

Jewel quickly looked at her man and was pleased to see that, rather than taking offence, he was smiling at her. She lost herself in thought for a while and squeezed his hand. It was the first time she had seen Chris smile since Madrid.

'Here's the proof that I'm more than a pretty face,' declared Jocky, as he handed out the forged papers he had prepared, including the ones he had been asked to produce for Jewel and Chris. This followed following Lenka's last minute request to London.

Lenka examined the papers. She had to admit that the quality was the best she had ever seen.

'I have another set – the ones *yer* wanted for the Paddy?' he imparted to Lenka.

'You can give them to 'The Englander' yourself.'

'An Irishman called 'The Englander'! Where is he from?'

'Cork.'

'Jesus! If you want to turn the world up on its arse, you can always rely on the paddies?'

Everyone at the table stared at each other, knowing that things were going to be a little livelier.

'Shift up, kilt lifter,' demanded Sean, as he deposited another tray of drinks on the table.

'Away and *shite*!' replied Jocky.

'Say hello to 'The Englander'!' said Lenka, stretching her hand out to Sean.

Sean ignored the new arrival and took a long drink from his metal stein.

Jocky was affronted, much to the amusement of the others.

'How did *yer* know I was Scottish?'

Sean winked at Chris, but out of view of his fellow Scotsman. 'I could read the signs from the bar. Within a minute of coming down the stairs, you were smashed up against a post and nearly strangled by the most decent men I've ever met, while learned men were legging it up the stairs, and a woman had to be restrained from knocking you out with a bottle. You might as well have come down the stairs blind drunk, wearing a kilt and a ginger wig, carrying a caber, while trying to play Scotland the Brave by blowing into a haggis.'

'*Fuken* bog-trotter,' cursed Jocky as he turned to the group. 'And, I'll get me *fuken* own drink, shall I?'

'Please. Take mine,' offered Jewel, who like Chris was not much of a drinker.

'Thanks, Gorgeous.'

Hearing this, Chris dropped his smile and clenched his fists as he leant forward. Jewel settled her hand on his arm once more and with a smile whispered into his ear, 'I think that's how he refers to all women. He's fun, and we have been through a lot lately. Especially you, my love.'

With that, she kissed Chris on the cheek.

Jake and Vodanski looked at Lenka; clearly a lot had changed since they had left Madrid. Lenka brought the conversation back to why they were here and turned to Sean.

'Paul certainly found a location where we are well out of the way, but God help us if the Nazis discover us.'

'True, but if we're discovered, no one here will interfere,' observed Sean, as he looked around at the few customers remaining, now that the professors had escaped.

'Why? They're German, aren't they?' replied Lenka.

'Not the Nazi kind. They're heavy on anyone involved in criminal activity of any sort, unless it's the result of their own homicidal tendencies. This is an illegal bar, as nothing opens this early to sell alcohol. So, if anything happens, no one here is going to say a word.'

Jocky turned to Lenka. 'The bogtrotter's got a point.'

Sean gave him a big beaming smile.

Lenka remained focused. 'London helped organise the train to transport the children out tonight, but I learnt this morning they are also sending a contact from the Admiralty.'

'Why? We have Paul, along with this Glaswegian town-crier,' replied Sean, who turned to Jocky. 'Seriously, could you attract any more attention, if you played the bagpipes out of your arse?'

'Bastard!'

Lenka agreed with Sean about the new contact. But she did not let the others know that she had warned London that morning, that new faces would only attract the attention of the authorities.

'The Admiralty contact has secured bona fide official papers from the Nazis for the children, providing all of them with safe passage to England. The contact is delivering the papers here.'

'Great news, so our work here is done,' noted Jake.

'This is Nazi German. I won't relax until the train reaches Holland,' said Lenka, staring at her glass.

Paul descended the stairs. He jumped from the second to last step onto the wooden floor of the bar in his haste. The noise of his landing made the drunk who was asleep on the bar, lift his head. The young Hungarian surveyed the bar, like a turkey checking the farmer's house for a Christmas tree. He bumped into a table, and had to stop himself from breaking into a run when he saw Sean. Paul furtively approached the intimidating gathering, but before he had a chance to speak, Lenka leapt up. But, as she did so, a sharp spasm of pain caused her to press her hand to the dressing covering on her hip. It did not stop her from confronting the man: 'Who's with the children?'

'Please . . . don't worry . . . I have some good friends from my university who are looking after them at the station. Everything is taken care of.'

'Why are you here?' demanded Lenka.

'I thought you needed to know . . . there has just been an official broadcast . . . by Joseph Goebbels, Minister for Propaganda . . . over the radio and over the public tannoy system . . .'

Lenka lost what little patience she had. 'Christ, if you had a stammer we'd be here until Christmas.'

This made Paul worse, 'Err . . . with . . . I'm . . . sorry.'

Sean intervened. 'Paul, you were right to come here. We need to know what the Nazis are up to. Take your time.'

Paul accepted the glass of red wine that Sean handed to him. He lifted it to his mouth. He then stopped, leaving it tilted tantalisingly close to his lips. 'The Nazis have marched into Austria . . .' Still holding the glass up to his mouth, he added, '. . . if the Austrians defend their sovereignty, the Nazis will be stopped in their tracks . . .' He fumbled for his cigarettes. 'If not . . .'

'In one swoop, the might of the German army doubles overnight,' muttered Lenka.

After a while Sean leaned forward and rested his arms on the beer-stained table, 'Well, it's a distraction we can use. The city will be celebrating, so hopefully will the police and the soldiers guarding the station and the trains'

'It comes at a high price,' whispered Lenka.

'In the meantime, it's best we stay here,' continued Sean. 'The longer the soldiers at the station have time to get drunk during the celebrations, the less likely they will be to take an interest in us and the children. And we can't go anywhere until we have the papers.'

'Well . . . I thought I'd let you know,' added Paul as he poured some more wine from the half-empty bottle on the table into his glass. 'I will head back now. I just wanted to make sure you knew . . .'

Paul got up, leaving his drink untouched. He did not shake anyone's hand but just gave a self-conscious shake of his head, as he always did when he attempted to leave. This was only marginally less embarrassing than when he would trip over something to announce his arrival, or his departure. As he made his to the stairs, he bumped into a stout man sitting at the table devouring chunk of meat off two large skewers. The man shouted at the Hungarian, covering him in lumps of masticated pork-belly. Paul apologised as he backed into the woman at the neighbouring table, spilling her drink.

'That boy reminds me of the metal ball in a pinball machine we had in my local bar back home,' commented Jake as he turned to Sean. 'You trust him?'

'He's the bravest of us, because he is terrified every moment of the day. But despite the risks, he has done all I have asked of him.' He watched Paul trip on the last step before he disappeared. 'I'd be a nervous wreck too if my family had just been murdered.'

'That's terrible,' said Jocky, then he brightened up. 'Right, any *girlies* around here?'

Chris shook his head. 'Is that all you care about?'

'No, when I'm not thinking about the ladies, I'm thinking about me. I have a strong interest in self-preservation.'

Sean looked at Chris. 'Don't knock our little friend; he just has a different perspective. He enjoys the simple things in life.'

Lenka turned on the Irishman, 'Are you saying women are simple?'

'No, just our little bundle of testosterone here.'

'Simple? Are *yer* saying I'm simple, *yer* Irish goat-fondler,' protested Jocky.

'You're even better at making enemies than I am,' noted Sean. 'The Pope isn't on your list, is he?'

'I hope so, the Fenian bastard.'

'Pope Pius XI is Austrian, but surprisingly you got the right continent.'

Chris was laughing and leaned over to Sean, 'So you admire our little friend here?'

'If all he wants to do is drink and make love, then good luck to him.'

'*Yer* decided to fight in a war that wasn't *yers*; I'm not harming anyone,' added Jocky, looking at Chris, Jake, Lenka and Vodanski. The remark struck home.

'I guess you sleep easily, my friend?' asked Chris.

'Unless I'm entertaining,' and at which point Jocky looked at Lenka and Jewel and gave them a wink and a broad smile, releasing a loud laugh from Jewel and securing a stony-faced response from Lenka.

Maybe it was the beer, but Chris was in a contemplative mood. 'Sometimes I stay awake all night. I see the faces of those I've killed, but I want to stay awake as the faces become more vivid when I close my eyes.'

Jewel lifted his right arm and slipped under it, allowing it to envelop her shoulders.

'We've all done things we are not proud of, but it doesn't mean we have to be happy about it,' replied Sean.

Chris knew what Sean meant and gave a toast to the new arrival.

'Well Jocky, here's to your simple outlook on the world,' he said, and he drained what was left from his metal container.

Vodanski rose. 'Drink?'

'Does the Pope shit in the woods?' declared Jocky, holding his empty stein out, but making it clear that his remark was directed at the Irishman.

'Jocky, I have as much interest in Catholicism as you do in social etiquette,' replied Sean.

'I'm not going to be in debt to the Holy Mary here, so out of the way, Boris. I'm getting these,' announced Jocky, as he jumped up and tried to make his way past Vodanski to get to the bar.

The Russian let out a genuine laugh as the little man tried to push him out of the way. Jocky stared up at the man, and decided it was prudent to amble his way around the Russian.

Jewel whispered to Chris, 'Do the Scots and Irish always fight?'

'Our countries have never officially gone to war,' interjected Sean, 'but that's only because we haven't stopped arguing long enough to go through the formalities of declaring it.'

When Jocky returned with another tray of beer and another bottle of wine, Jewel was drunk and confided to her new friends, 'You two would have been handy in Spain.'

She raised her glass in her right hand and made a toast, 'To Katherine and Dominique.'

Lenka, Vodanski, Chris and Jake nodded their heads and raised their glasses.

'Who's Dominique?' asked Jocky.

'No idea. I guess someone they lost in Spain,' replied Sean, as both men raised their glasses along with the others.

Everyone was drunk and laughing. Vodanski even slapped Jocky on the back, nearly sending him across the table along with his beer. 'Scotsman, I like the women too, they are my strength and my weakness,' roared the Russian.

'I love all women; if there are pretty, great, but if not, it's not everything,' wheezed Jocky. 'Give me a woman's kindness and love, over *yer* heroics anytime.'

Chris smiled at Jocky. The Scotsman really did see the beauty in Jewel.

Jocky turned to his former fellow client of Madame Jiggy-Jigs, 'Vodka, remember that big lass *yer* were with,

Claudia. She had the lot; twenty stone after a good *shite*, and her own teeth, bar the ones at the front, pal.'

The Russian abruptly stopped laughing and leaned into the Scotsman's face. He seized Jocky's head with his right hand and aimed it towards the table.

'Christ, Vodka! Just jokes!' pleaded Jocky.

The Russian rotated the Scotsman's head slowly towards him. He stared into his face and to everyone's surprise and the little Scotsman's relief, he released a mighty belly-laugh.

Lenka watched as Sean and Jocky, then Jake and Vodanski started trading insults again and despite herself, she looked at Jewel and Chris laughing, and smiled. This was a unique gathering, as she looked at her friends around the table, old and new. She was the link that brought these Rogues together. She knew that all of them, perhaps even the fiery little Scotsman, had lost someone they loved. Katherine, Dominique and Leo were but the most recent.

The world was on the cusp of war. If the Nazis succeeded in taking Austria, the war that would follow would claim the lives of many, perhaps maybe as many as the Great War, the war they called, "The War to End all Wars." There was still no news of Olen, Anzelm or Celestynka. She asked herself whether, with so many friends lost and so much at risk, was it right to get drunk together and laugh? But the children were on the train. It was only the middle of the afternoon and it was too early to head for the station; but still it was wrong. Perhaps those around her were drunk on the madness around them – maybe it was lunacy to think they were immune.

Looking around the table at Chris, Jake, Jewel, Vodanski, Sean and Jocky, this was maybe the one and only time they could escape the world around them, and the horror that would inevitably come.

Chapter 12: On the Roof of the World

'Do you mean it?' (**September 1937, Madrid**)

'But where is Katherine?' (**October 1937, Madrid**)

November 1937, France

Chris remembered those moments, which delivered him into the adjoining realms of love and pain. He and Jewel were now on a train from Toulouse to Berlin. The eight patients they had smuggled out of her makeshift hospital in Madrid were safe and being treated in a hospital inside the French border. Jewel was asleep with her head resting on his shoulder. Thankfully, she had been able to stretch her legs out along the empty seats in their carriage.

He looked out the dirty window into the night and thought of how much had happened over those two months since Jewel, Katherine and he had decided to remain in Madrid after the others had left. He thought time and time again of those moments in life that change you forever. The ecstasy of the first time you truly fall in love and the pain, the first time someone you love more than life itself, dies.

September 1937, Madrid

Chris was crouched on the roof of the Banco de España.

He was scanning the rooftops and the streets below, through Jake's binoculars – a parting gift. It was the best observation point to view all the main avenues of the city: Paseo de Recoletos, Paseo del Prado, Gran Via and the other main tributary, the Calle de Alcala. The Banco de España sat amongst its museums and libraries and was for many Spaniards the heart of Madrid.

The city was waiting for the Nationalists to launch their final push. Chris could do nothing to stop them, but with this viewpoint he might find the weakest spot in their attack and, taking the others with him, break through. He was sure that more seasoned fighters like Lenka, Jake and Vodanski would have developed a better strategy to transport Katherine, Jewel, and their patients to safety. But they were gone now, and he hoped that they had made it past the ever-tightening cordon thrown up around the city, had reached San Sebastian and led the convoy of children safely into France.

The make-shift hospital in the lobby on ground floor, was a labyrinth of actively. It was the largest room in the building, but it was also chosen because it was by the main doors. In war, seconds count; a casualty's chance of survival was said to double, if they receive treatment in that critical time known as, 'heaven's hour'. In the far-left corner of the huge reception area was the kitchen, where Lenka did most of the cooking while the other Rogues prepared food.

In the other far corner was a desk strewn with various maps and papers. This was where Lenka would marshal their defences, coordinate food and medicine distribution, and just as importantly, cleaning supplies. When Jewel and Katherine were not ministering to the wounded they were constantly cleaning, for disease and infection killed as many as the bullet in the sweltering heat of the summer.

He thought of the three people he had known for a matter of months, but who he trusted with his life. Jake and Vodanski had taught him how to protect himself, and those he was with, and how to kill the enemy, in that order. The men, separately, had taught him how to strip and reassemble his rifle with either hand. As both men explained, again separately, this was in case he lost a hand in battle. After his tutors demonstrated each action, Chris would have to repeat it until he was equal to his teacher. Surprisingly Jake, with his outgoing carefree manner, was as diligent in his training as Vodanski. After a month, he could reassemble his weapon with one hand while blindfolded.

Lenka had taught him how to use a knife at close quarters. She taught him how to read an opponent's next move by his eyes, his stance, and even his breathing – slow steady breaths indicated that an opponent was conserving his energy in preparation to leap. In one lesson, she combined the two. In all ten attempts to advance on her, he found the point of her blade pressed against his heart.

During these exercises, Lenka would never stray from the task at hand, Jake would talk about anything but the war, the topic usually being women, while Vodanski hardly spoke.

After one practice, held in the far corner of the makeshift hospital – in which for the previous two hours Jewel and Katherine had been trying to save a young woman – Chris asked Lenka if she could teach him how to disarm an opponent so he could take him as a prisoner.

'No idea. My objective is to kill my enemy as quickly as possible, not fucking dance with them.'

Her anger was palpable as they watched Vodanski and Jake lift the dead young woman off a blood-soaked hospital bed. Jake lifted his head to look at Chris before nodding towards what remained of the library.

'You might find your answer up on the shelves. If you do, keep it to yourself. None of us are interested.'

That summer, the young man from Edinburgh had fought beside the three of them. He had become, according to Javier, one of the Spanish fighters in Lenka's Rogues, one of the most feared fighters in Madrid. Chris neither believed it nor was he proud of it.

Compared to Jake, Lenka and Vodanski, the Scotsman was a reluctant fighter – not that they revelled in killing – but they did not seem to possess the doubts he did. They made instant life or death decisions, and usually they got it right. But killing a man never came easy to Chris, perhaps because, unlike the others, he had grown up in a world, relatively free of pain and death.

He did not judge Jake, Lenka or Vodanski. They were instinctively fighters – in battle, many thought the same of him – but he was a man of peace. Now that the other Rogues were gone, he stood alone at the forefront of the deadliest battle in Europe. His sole aim was to protect Jewel and Katherine until their patients were fit enough to make the journey to France. If either woman fell into the Fascists' hands, he had no doubt they would be executed.

Beautiful church steeples, the stone figurines of saints and cardinals and the grand dome of the cathedral, accompanied by the soundtrack of distant gunfire interspersed the skyline. Chris saw a plume of smoke appear to his right, in the north-west of the Paseo de Castellana quarter, as he scanned the roofs for snipers. It would be only two, maybe three, days now. With the serrated knife with an 'L' carved into the handle, another parting gift, this time from Lenka, he cut another segment from his apple.

When he saw a silent puff of smoke in the distance, he wondered how many were lying dead or injured beneath it. Perhaps a Republican, perhaps a Nationalist, or now that the war was fought from street to street, more likely to be someone who did not care either way and just wanted everything to return to how it was before the civil war.

It was two months since he first made the roof his bedroom and rolled out his sleeping bag under a little canvas canopy held up by a few wooden canes as its roof. Each night he watched the beautiful skyline, violated by spontaneous black clouds and the appearance of flames that spat, as if in spite, towards the sky. Javier would often come up to the roof to have a smoke and share the contents of a bottle of wine. Sometimes Katherine would come up too. She would sit beside him and tuck herself in under his arm and fall asleep. At those moments, he would think of that day, only a few months earlier, when he had been packing his bag to leave the orphanage in Edinburgh. That was the day he learnt he had a family.

Chris knew that he was accepted by Lenka's Rogues, but they all knew he was different. He had not come to fight for an ideal; he had not come to save lives, apart from his sister; he was not fleeing anything, nor did he seek adventure. He was a simple man who had come to find the only family he had, but he was also a man who had fallen in love.

He thought of earlier that afternoon and how life was similarly unreal in Jewel and Katherine's makeshift medical unit below.

'Hold the blood bag up higher, the blood is not going in,' demanded the Australian nurse, as she applied a disinfected bandage to the soldier's stomach wound.

Chris rested his rifle against the wounded man's camp bed and did as he was bid, but with his height, he only had to lift the bag up to his face for the intravenous drip to be at full stretch. He was not complaining, though he was also holding the other blood bag for Katherine, who was treating a wounded woman next to them. This summed up those summer months. If he was not defending the building with a rifle in his hand, he was supporting the women as they nursed their patients.

But the scene was even more surreal. His worlds had collided. It was he who had shot the mercenary when he opened fire on the hospital. The same mercenary whom Katherine was now trying to save. The mercenary had shot a woman earlier, a mother of four young children. It was she who now lay in the bed opposite.

Despite Katherine's efforts, the mercenary died. The dead man reminded Chris of a Nationalist soldier whom Katherine had found lying face down in the city's main park, the Parque del Retiro, in the summer before the others left. He had the same shoulder-length black hair, with wide curly ringlets sticking out below his green

Nationalist helmet. He too had been shot in the stomach. Jake had taken the shot from the roof the night before. Whenever there was a lull in the fighting, Katherine would leave the Rogues headquarters in search of the wounded.

With the help of Javier's two sisters, they carried the Nationalist soldier through the back streets to Jewel's hospital. The sisters were not as charitable to the enemy as Katherine and Jewel and wanted to slit the man's throat. Katherine, being a determined woman, not only persuaded them not to, but had the audacity to ask the women for their help. The Spanish women were furious, but they did as the Scottish woman asked as she had recently removed a bullet from their brother's groin.

Chris peered out over the rooftops of the city. He cut another segment from the apple. He knew that Vodanski would have killed the Fascist if he had found him, or at the very least left him to die. Jake and Lenka too, would not have thought twice about finishing the man off. It was no secret that the three Rogues did not agree with Katherine and Jewel, treating the wounded Nationalist soldier under their roof.

There was a clear divide between the humanitarian beliefs held by Jewel and Katherine, and those of Lenka, Jake and Vodanski who believed that humanity would only survive by defeating the enemy at all costs. But the hospital was a sanctuary for all. Despite their differences, every one of them would have given their lives to protect those inside it.

Three days later, the nationalist soldier, having recovered his strength, disappeared during the night. Katherine argued with the other Rogues the next morning, 'Okay! He stole some food – but he could have killed us in our sleep, but he didn't.'

Two weeks later Jake shot the same soldier, as he tried, with others in his squad, to storm the hospital. Katherine said nothing, which surprised her brother after all her efforts to save the young man's life. But after the shooting ceased, she zigzagged her way through the streets to see if anyone was left alive. Jake provided cover for her as always, which was fortunate, for one soldier that Katherine checked out for signs of life was feigning death and turned his revolver on her. Jake shot him between the eyes from twenty metres.

Perhaps the Nationalist soldier had no choice when he was ordered to attack the hospital, as many were summary executed without trail for disobeying orders on both sides. In a war, who was to know and who was to care why the enemy had to die. But the why always troubled Chris.

He once asked of his sister, 'Is it right to treat the enemy, knowing that as soon as they are well again, they will return to killing the women and children whom we defend?'

'Life is not so simple, little brother. Jewel and I are not here to decide who lives or dies. We will leave that to God, judges and snipers.'

Chris stared down on the contorted face of the mercenary he had shot, whose hands were still clutching a crucifix. He had no doubt the man deserved to die for shooting the woman, and mother of four, at point blank range, but did he have to be judge, jury and executioner?

The week before Jewel had saved the life of a French Republican fighter, Ratchet, who months earlier had raped a nun when he was part of a raiding party that attacked a convent on the outskirts of the city. A month later the man was drunk in a bar in town and boasted of this to a stranger – that man was Vodanski. This explained his admittance to the hospital some time afterwards, for in the fight that followed he was castrated with a broken bottle. Some said it was right to save the man, as he was 'one of our own', but Lenka and Jake shared Vodanski view that 'a rapist was rapist and should have his cock thrown to the dogs ''. Jewel and Katherine carried on with trying to save the man, but he died of severe blood loss. The man had missed 'heaven's hour', as he was left writhing on the ground while the Russian finished his drink, having fed the dogs.

On the day the Rogues left for the convoy, each presented Chris with a gift, Jake one of his Remington's along with the binoculars, Lenka's the serrated dagger, and Vodanski handed him a sack of hand grenades.

'The gun and the knife are precision weapons but use these when you can no longer be fucked with it all,' said Vodanski, without a smile.

The twelve wooden beds below, which until recently were full, only had a handful of patients. There were more mats and bedding folded up and stored in the corner, but there had been no reason to unfold them. The large metal bin where contaminated bandages and swabs were deposited no longer overflowed. The temporary medical unit was immaculately clean. There was much less blood, bile, vomit, excrement and urine for the Jewel, for the remaining Rogues to deal with. In the middle of the room, pieces of unpainted wood were nailed together and mounted on square wooden stands that supported

303

drips containing blood and glucose. Before, they would be pushed around the hospital beds like anaemic flamingos, dangling colourful treats. Now, they remained still.

But on the streets outside, the fighting had intensified. Gunfire and mortar attacks blasted the protective walls of slants and books from the windows several times a day.

The reason why the hospital was surreally quiet was because no one, wounded or otherwise, would dare enter. A recent internal communique circulating in the Communist held western quarter of the city, read: "Lenka's hospital is now in enemy-occupied territory. It is of no strategic importance to Moscow and is to be treated as a target."

In those summer months Chris watched the two women and still found it hard to believe how much and how quickly his life had changed. Katherine took care of him and fussed over him in a way he had never experienced before. When Katherine would have to sew up any fresh wounds and cuts that Chris had received, or re-bandage recent ones, Jewel would peer over his sister's shoulder in case she needed any help. She only seemed to do so when Katherine attended him, as she never seemed to fuss when his sister treated any other patient. He wondered if Jewel liked him, but he was afraid to ask, fearing the answer or risk causing her any embarrassment.

He envied the other male Rogues' confidence with women. Jake always had that spark that ignited any gathering, while Vodanski was the smouldering type; both approaches made them very popular with the women of

Madrid. Chris saw himself as an ordinary man, quiet and unassuming. Sarah was his girlfriend at the orphanage, but their relationship had evolved from the friendship they had had since they were children. He was not a virgin, but he was insecure. As he had once confessed to Katherine, he did not have a clue about women. She laughed and said that they were definitely family, as she did not have a clue about men, except that they just wanted to jump on everything.

'I don't!' said Chris, clearly affronted. 'I just want to be with one woman.'

'I know, little brother, that's why I'll wait until I find a man like you.'

Now here he was on the roof of a building in the middle of the final days of the war, while below were the two women he loved. A year ago, he had not known of their existence. It seemed so wrong to have found love, surrounded by so much pain and grief.

Chris admired his sister for her strength. She had a slim frame and was light on her feet, and with her love of nice clothes and lavender scent when she could afford it, she gave the appearance of being a 'girlie girl' as it was called in Edinburgh. But he had seen her plunge her hands into a girl's rib cage to try to remove a large piece of shrapnel close to her heart – and succeed. Many of the Spanish members of Lenka's Rogues had made a pass at his sister. Javier had once placed his hand on her backside and received a knee to wound she had treated in return – she later apologised when she had to replace some of his stitches. Jake too made repeatedly advances, but she always rebuffed him.

Katherine once confided to her brother, 'I like Jake, but I don't want to be another notch on his gigantic bedpost.'

Chris was surprised to hear his sister admit this, as she scolded the American more than any of them.

One evening, he and Lenka sat in the corner of the temporary hospital sharing a bottle of Rioja, as they watched Katherine berate Jake.

'Sometimes in relationships, there is not a lot of difference between love and hate,' said Lenka, taking another full measure from the bottle.

An hour earlier, Katherine had gone in search of a missing bottle of alcohol she used for sterilising her medical instruments. She discovered Jake and a female Italian journalist together in his sleeping bag. Beside them were two tin cups containing the remains of the missing bottle mixed with a small amount of freshly squeezed juice from oranges from the Parque del Retiro.

The day after Katherine had saved the wounded Nationalist, the little lieutenant from Communist headquarters banged on the doors of the Banco de España. This time he brought four very big Russian armed troops with him.

'We have come for the Fascist. Give him to us.'

Katherine, who was the first to pull open one of the huge oak doors, turned around to ask if anyone could translate. Vodanski appeared and delivered the diminutive lieutenant's message in English.

'No,' was her unequivocal reply. The others would have elaborated a little, but she disapproved of bad language.

'You are harbouring an enemy of the revolution.'

'Which revolution?' asked Vodanski, who was now standing beside Katherine.

The question caught the lieutenant by surprise. His standard reaction when this happened was to issue a threat.

'We will raze the building to the ground if you do not give him to us.'

Vodanski advanced beyond Katherine. 'I only care about a few people in Madrid, and you and the American are not among them. If there is an attack on this building, I will hold you responsible and I will tear this city apart to find you.' He scanned the faces of the four soldiers. 'If you do not pick him up and carry him off, I will tear the little fuck's head off and beat each of you to death with it.'

Chris and Jake appeared. Both had their guns drawn, but the fear on the faces of the soldiers told them that their weapons would not be required. Vodanski bent down towards the little lieutenant and pressed his forehead against the peak of his hat. He grabbed the cap and spun it into the street.

'Fletch!' roared Vodanski.

The five men retreated into their armoured transport carrier and sped off, zigzagging through the street.

'He's an animal, but he's our animal,' whispered Jake in Katherine's ear.

Chris heard the roof hatch open behind him, and he turned to find Katherine climbing up. 'How is the woman?'

She shook her head as she walked towards him.

He cut her a piece from another apple he had in his satchel.

Katherine realised she still had her blood-covered apron on, untied it and left it by the hatch. 'Four children and the husband are probably dead too.'

She would rest her head on her brother's shoulder whenever things were bad. Chris smiled and placed the slice of apple in her hand, which she failed to lift to her mouth. He slipped his arm around her shoulder and they said no more that evening. They never talked much. They did not have to. They just savoured the fact that they had found one another. A few hours later, as the furious sun slipped behind the horizon, Katherine kissed her brother on the cheek and walked back towards the hatch. It was time to relieve Jewel downstairs. She picked up her dried apron on the way.

They had their first admissions in weeks. A baby boy had been found alone in a pram on the street, by a young girl. Not knowing what to do, she brought him to the hospital. Thankfully, two recent mothers who worked in the Hotel Internationale, which was kept open by journalists' expenses, braved the back streets to take it in turns to wet-nurse the child.

A few minutes later, Chris could hear the roof hatch opening behind him once more. It was Javier. The Spaniard sat beside him and opened a bottle of Rioja and a fresh pack of Moroccan cigarettes. He could speak no English, but the Scotsman had picked up enough of the language to understand the man.

He thought that even if he were fluent in Spanish, it was unlikely that he could have got a word in edgeways as the excitable Spaniard had strong opinions on everything.

This time he was outraged as Katherine had ordered him out of the hospital; not for berating the corpse of a Nationalist soldier, but for smoking a cigarette surrounded by patients.

An hour later, having smoked ten cigarettes and emptied the bottle on his own, he slapped Chris on the back and gestured that he was thankful to him for his advice. Chris hardly spoke to Javier apart from, '*hola*' and '*adiós*'. The Spaniard nearly toppled down the hatch but caught himself at the last moment.

It was dark now, and the black canvas of the night had several stars pinned to it. A cool breeze occasionally brushed the warm air aside. Fires still raged at several points across the city. Each night the pattern of fires drew tighter and closer. Chris heard the hatch opening once more. He only ever had a maximum of two visitors each evening and they had gone. Chris jumped to his feet, knife in hand. Having left the Remington by the window facing the main street on the first floor, stealthily he lifted Lenka's gift from the black leather sheath that covered its steel blade.

It was Jewel. He dropped the knife but hurried over to the hatch to take her right hand in his.

'Is everything OK? It's not like you to come up here.'

'No problems; I just wanted to see your little Fortress of Solitude.'

'That's a strange term.'

'Just something I heard on the radio. The lead character reminds me of you.'

'I'm surprised to see you up here; the stairs could not have been easy.'

'I can walk anywhere, it just takes me a little longer,' she said.

She hobbled over to where he had been sitting as Chris folded his blanket for her to rest on.

The nights were getting colder now that summer was passing, but thankfully it was still early, so he judged that the best use of the only bed clothing he had was for comfort rather than warmth.

'I've never been in a man's bedroom before. It's missing something.'

'A roof?'

'I was thinking more of a woman's touch.'

Chris was always a little lost for words when it was just the two of them, so Jewels, reluctantly, decided the pace and subject of the conversation.

'At least the morphine allowed the woman to die peacefully.' He nodded and squeezed her right hand. 'I can see why you come up here. It certainly is beautiful.' Jewel looked out into the night, dotted by moths in a hurry to go nowhere in particular.

Chris glanced at Jewel. 'Yes,' he said.

'I came up to say, the nights are getting cold now. You can't just stay up here.'

He felt uncomfortable. He did not want her to know that one of the reasons he had decided to spend his nights on the rooftop was that he found it impossible to sleep when he could hear her working nearby or when she slept close to him.

'I like it up here; it's quiet and peaceful.'

'Is that all?'

'Well, I'm selfish too. I find it difficult to sleep downstairs with the cries of pain.' This too was true, but it was not the real reason. 'You and Katherine never have a break from the suffering, I'm afraid I need it,' and again he spoke the truth.

'We could never have survived here this long without you,' she said as she placed her head on his shoulder and lifted his right arm so he could wrap it around her shoulders. She had done this before, but only when she was tired or cold. He gently placed his arm around her, careful so as not to hurt her or to betray his feelings.

After a few minutes Jewel had pressed her face into his chest and he felt her breathing quicken. 'Chris, can I say something?'

'Of course.'

'I know nothing about relationships, apart from family ones.'

'Funnily enough, Katherine and I had a similar conversation.'

'Do you have a girlfriend?'

'Once, but that was some time ago. She married a vicar, I hear.' Then he heard that wonderful giggle of hers, and it made him relax a little. 'Jake once said that after him, all the women he met became lesbians as no man could ever match up to him. Vodanski said that the American's old girlfriends became lesbians because he put them off men for life. My one and only girlfriend fled into the arms of the Church.'

He felt her face press harder against his body, as if she were afraid of something. He felt the warmth of her breath quicken on the skin exposed between his shirt buttons.

'Do you like me?' She paused and pressed her head

311

closer to his chest, 'I mean more than just as a friend?'

'Yes,' and as he said it, what surprised him was not only that he had said it but that he had not hesitated.

Jewel lifted her head and looked at him for the first time that night, and she put her hand over the scars on her left cheek. 'Do you mean it?'

He lifted her hand away from her face. 'I mean it.'

October 1937, Madrid

The next morning, the first day of October, Chris and Jewel were woken by the makeshift canopy collapsing on them. Chris looked to see who was violently shaking his blanket. But there was no one there. He realised that everything was shaking, including the building.

He turned to Jewel. 'Stay here.'

He jumped up wearing only his grey canvas trousers and covered her with the blanket.

'How did the Fascists reach us so fast? The Soviets must have fled during the night,' he shouted, but as he looked over the edge of the building, he had his answer. Below was an armoured Russian transporter wedged in between the huge oak wood doors of the building. He reached for Vodanski's bag of grenades. But he could not throw them down because of Katherine and the others below. He looked again and saw the little lieutenant appear out of a hatch at the front of the armoured car.

Chris weighed up his options. If the grenade bounced off the lieutenant or the vehicle, then he would blow up all those in the hospital. But if it dropped through the open hatch and exploded in the armoured car, it might give him a chance to descend the stairs before any more soldiers attacked the building. If he did nothing, they would kill everyone before he even got down the stairs. He looked at his hand. It was steady as a rock. He looked over, and a second hatch on top of the turret opened. Now was his chance.

The Scotsman held his arm out from the edge, glanced down, measured the distance and allowed for wind and opened his fingers to send Vodanski's grenade back to the army that supplied it. Chris raced to the hatch as he signalled to Jewel to stay where she was. Opening the hatch, he heard the little lieutenant scream, followed by an explosion.

Chris leapt down the stairs, covering the two floors that separated the roof from the ground floor. As he landed at the base of the staircase that brought him to the first floor, he grabbed the Remington and dived towards the open entrance hatch above the medical unit. All he could see was a cloud of grey and white plaster and dust.

'Katherine!' he shouted, but there was no response.

Ignoring the steps, he leapt through the hatch and landed onto an empty bed in the centre of the room. A figure came towards him, but he could not make out who it was. A rifle appeared. He grabbed it by the nozzle and pushed it away just as it fired. Chris thrust Jake's rifle into the mist. It pierced something. He pulled the trigger of the Remington. A groan was followed by a thud. A knife appeared from the side and Chris dropped so the arm holding it and the weapon sailed passed his neck. The Scotsman reloaded and fired his rifle to the left of the flaying arm. The second invisible assailant disappeared back into the white cloud. A third hand appeared from the other side and Chris turned his rifle to his left, but it was a woman's hand.

'Chris!'

It was Katherine. She searched for his face to make sure it was him and threw her arms around him. As she did so, he dropped them both to the floor so they were now a smaller target, as a strong wind blew through the oak doors to scatter the white and grey cloud.

Chris held his sister close as the cloak of dust dispersed. Though the patients were moaning, some crying and others screaming with pain, thankfully, none of them appeared to have fresh injuries. Even the armoured car looked surprisingly intact. It was built to withstand grenade attacks – though it was never the designer's intention that it should survive the impact of one landing inside.

The raiding party had not been so fortunate. As the dust settled on the floor, Chris could see the bodies of his attackers. One was face down and lifeless and the other a torso as he had been hot at point blank range. Chris walked over to inspect the armoured transporter. The bottom half of the little lieutenant was gone, while his upper half was bolt upright on the floor, like a plaster bust, and covered in white powder.

Chris turned to Katherine, 'Don't move, I'll check to see if it's clear.'

'The child,' yelled Katherine, as she rose and stumbled towards the cot that was only a metre from the front of the armoured transporter. Thankfully the child was crying loudly and on closer inspection, though covered in dust, was unharmed. Chris returned to the breeched oak doors, when the first of the Soviet standard RGD 33 stick grenades flew over the armoured car. It bounced and then rolled along the stone floor towards Katherine and the cot. Chris did not hesitate, springing into the air, he landed on top of it, and pressing himself flat down to absorb the explosion.

He waited, praying that Katherine would survive. A second grenade came through the blown-out window on the other side and rotated towards the pram. Chris heard it when it first bounced onto the wooden floor and he looked up to see his sister standing by the pram.

'Katherine!' he screamed.

She turned and seemed surprised to see her brother lying on the ground, then heard the grenade rocking towards her and the child. She looked down and saw it by her feet. For one brief moment, she stared at her brother.

Chris looked at her face. It expressed neither fear nor panic, but the composed look of someone who knew exactly what they had to do. She turned from her brother and with all her might she launched her hands against the holding bar of the pram, pushing it to the far side of the armoured car. She looked down and kicked the grenade away. Second later, the pram was on the opposite of the armoured car when the grenade exploded.

Chris opened his eyes to discover that once again a white cloud of dust had shrouded the room. Jewel's face appeared above him. He wiped the dirt and tears from her face as he rose. A metre or so away lay items of blood-soaked clothing. He crawled towards what appeared to be his sister's blouse. Beyond that he could now see cloth from her skirt and the base of one of her plimsolls. They were covered in what looked like blood. Jewel crawled over to him. She wrapped her right arm around him as tightly as she could. He could feel her tears dropping down onto the back of his neck. The air was warm and sticky. Her tears felt nice.

Looking at the assortment of torn and charred clothing, the young man stretched his arms and swept the items of clothes into a pile in front of his face. He tried to focus on each item to examine them, but his vision was blurred as the dust had settled on his eyes. That would explain Jewel's tears. Yes, the piece of material was from a skirt that looked remarkably like his sister's. Then with relief he exclaimed, 'It's not her, Katherine would never wear anything this dirty,' and almost as an afterthought he added, 'But, where is Katherine?'

Chris looked through the dirty glass window at the French countryside, as the train propelled them to Berlin. He remembered that morning in Madrid. After the explosion, nothing was real. The world was a theatre set. The train rocked from side to side, but the train did not seem to be moving forward, rather that the French countryside was whizzing past in the opposite direction. Shortly, the painted canvas would be quickly changed to that of Germany's landscape, carried past the carriage by unseen technicians.

He remembered that Jewel had cried whilst trying to provide him with some words of comfort, saying he was lucky that the grenade beneath him had been a dud. But he did not count himself lucky. The child in the pram appeared at first miraculously unscathed but was later diagnosed as deaf by a doctor when they crossed over the French border. The eight patients, along with the child, had been loaded on the back of the open flat-bed truck by Javier and his sisters and people from nearby buildings, whose faces and names he no longer recalled.

For the first few hours Javier and his sisters took turns driving until Chris took over without asking. He needed to free himself of his thoughts. Apart from toilet stops, he drove non-stop towards the Catalan region, up through Barcelona and through the Basque region before crossing into France. He could not remember talking to anyone during the journey or even saying goodbye to Javier and his sisters when they parted.

Only Jewel was real. Her head was resting in his lap as he stroked her blonde locks. Now that they had boarded the train for Berlin, he now had time to think. He wished he didn't. Why had the Communists attacked them? Perhaps the little lieutenant had been ridiculed too many times. How ironic it was it that in the end it was those they had fought with, rather than the enemy, who had inflicted the greatest pain. On that last night in Madrid, he had felt the happiest he had been since Katherine first found him, when he kissed Jewel hard on the lips for the first time. He remembered when he did so, she panicked.

'Chris, please don't. I can't make love . . . I can't have children. I can't . . . be a woman . . . I can't . . .' and then she could speak no more as her tears consumed her.

Chris just gently held her face in his hands and lifted her head up slowly, so he could look her in the eyes. 'It doesn't matter.'

The courage that had finally brought her up onto the roof, vanished. Turning her face away, unfettered tears streamed down her ravaged cheeks. She had never cried like this. Her defences, seemingly impregnable to every horrific attack, collapsed under the weight of years of pain, frustration and rage.

'They hurt me Chris . . . and . . . it's not just my face and body . . . I'm broken . . . I'm so . . . sorry.'

'It's Okay,' he said, and he pressed her to him and kissed her hard on the lips once more. He was always so gentle, but passion overcame his caution.

Jewel had never been held so close. Most people never saw beyond her scars. Chris saw a woman.

The carriage door shook Chris from his memories. The conductor made an announcement that Chris could not understand, apart from the word Deutschland. He handed the inspector their papers and turned back to the dirty window. The scene this time was of an orchard that swished passed almost immediately. Chris remembered when he first arrived in Madrid, the apple tree by the Parque del Retiro cloaked in the vibrant pink blossom of spring. In the summer, he would set out to collect apples from its generous branches for the hospital under the cover of darkness each night.

When they drove passed the tree when they had driven out from the city; it was naked and vulnerable. He remembered saying to Jewel, Javier and his sisters that once they were over the border he would double-back to find Katherine. He had found her before, and he would do so again. This time he would not take no for an answer and he would bring her back to Edinburgh.

Chris looked out once more through the dirty windows of the train carriage. The empty fields were bathed in the moonlight now that the orchard had disappeared. Even the glass was cleaner now. The theatre technicians had departed for good. Katherine was dead. He must have known this as they drove out of the city, but his mind refused to let him believe it. If it had, he would never have left her.

Chapter 13: City Without Pity

March 1938, Berlin

Sean noticed the black stiletto appear on the top step of the stairway. Then the other shoe dropped down to the step below. Two firm but shapely calves appeared below an elegant cream-coloured winter coat. The pale, manicured fingers of a young woman's right hand glided down the balustrade. The outline of the woman's breasts, larger than her figure had indicated so far, projected from her open coat. The woman bent down to view the occupants of the bar before reaching the base of the staircase, the most beautiful face they had ever seen came into view. The woman had unblemished, pale porcelain skin that you would find only in the most flattering portraits of princesses.

When she reached the bottom of the stairs, she spotted where the Rogues were sitting, straightened up and briskly headed towards them. As she got closer, Sean could see that her eyes were green and bright, but her eyelashes were unnaturally thick, black and long. Blonde hair escaped out from under a blood-red hat, matching the colour of her Chanel lipstick, which was as glossy as the most fervently polished car. Everything about her was perfectly symmetrical apart from the hat which she wore at a jaunty angle. The svelte woman approached the table, keeping her eyes locked on Sean.

'*Fuk* me,' exclaimed Jocky, and if he had not made his interest perfectly clear, he followed this with a wolf-whistle.

'Never an option,' replied the woman, coldly.

Jewel and Lenka looked at each other. Jewel smiled, and Lenka raised her eyebrows. The woman seated herself on a chair that Jake whisked from another table. She did not say thank you, and her look of indifference indicated that she expected it.

Lenka was the first to speak, 'I'm Lenka. You must be the courier, as you are exactly as London described you. I . . .'

Lieutenant Amelia Brett addressed Sean, 'You're the Irishman?'

Jake kept his eyes on the two women, but leaned towards Jocky and said, 'I think our new friend might out do you in the social skills department.'

'I couldn't give a *shite* if she had just walked over to me and kicked me in the bollocks,' replied Jocky. She's Helen of Troy, Cleopatra and Aphrodite all in one – and I don't mean she's fat, pal.'

Without waiting for an answer from Sean, the lieutenant lifted some documents from her satchel. 'Here are the papers for the children.'

Lenka leaned forward as Sean opened the folder. There were papers for every child, bearing the official stamps of His Majesty's Government and the National Socialist Workers Party of Germany.

The Irishman found the one he was looking for, which bore the name LEO THOMACKI written in black pen. He folded it and placed it inside his leather jacket. He nodded to Lenka, 'For Ursula.'

The lieutenant dropped her voice, so it was barely audible to those sitting around the table. 'I also have new ID papers for you all.'

'No need Gorgeous, I gave them their papers,' announced Jocky cheerfully.

'Scrapped. We got our best on to this,' she said as she put a smaller file containing the identity papers and train tickets for all of them on the table.

'Away and *shite*!' retorted Jocky, though he was still leaning to his side as he had not taken his eyes from her long slim legs.

'Have you heard of the term, '*Kindertransport*?'

'Yes,' interjected Lenka, but the lieutenant appeared not to hear her.

The others watched for their Polish friend's reaction, but she seemed unperturbed. Sean had noticed over the past few weeks how so-called 'respectable women' kept Lenka at a distance, though some whispered disparaging remarks.

'*Kindertransport* is the name being used for trains being organised across Europe to transport Jewish children to new homes in friendly countries. These trains are not financed by governments but are resourced and coordinated by various benefactors. However, these can only take place if a friendly government agrees to accept the children as refugees. Thanks to your American's efforts,' she said, without looking at Jake, though the others did with surprise, 'the British Government has agreed to accept your children.'

She examined the faces at the table, before continuing, 'The standard conditions are that a guarantee bond of fifty-pounds must be to cover the living expenses of a child refugee. Each child must also have in their possession the address of their confirmed foster home in England. Again, in the case of these children these have been covered already.'

Apart from Jocky, no one was drinking anymore, including Jewel, though she was still a little giddy. It was time to sober up, as they would need to leave for the station soon.

Jewel squeezed her friend's arm. 'For a blond, you're a dark horse, Jake. So, you pulled some strings in London, before meeting your ladies in Paris. You must have some pretty powerful contacts in the States?'

'I just knocked on a few doors in Washington and got some money together to provide the bonds that the British require. Then I heard from a mate in the State Department that some "old British bulldog" in the Parliament was pulling strings to find families to foster children.'

'*Yer* a legend, pal,' interrupted Jocky.

'I'm flattered,' replied Jake.

'I mean *yer* and the Russian were already legends with the ladies of Madame Jiggy-Jigs, but this is something else indeed. I'm proud to know you, pal.'

Jake and Vodanski registered Lenka's look of disapproval, and though neither man looked at each other, each wore a smile of satisfaction rather than one of embarrassment.

Lenka returned to the reason why they were all there. 'So, these trains are being set up only to evacuate children to England?'

'Not just England. My home country, Australia, and I hear that even Palestine will provide safe havens,' replied Jake.

'How many trains are there?' continued Lenka.

'I don't know,' sighed Jake. 'I just pray there will be enough.'

The British officer scanned the faces of those around the table, apart from Jewel's. The Australian starred uncomfortably down at her wittered hand.

She continued, 'There is an Englishman, a stockbroker called Nicholas Winton who is currently organising trains for Jewish Czech and Slovak refugee children trying to flee Prague. For weeks now, there has been a severe refugee crisis in Czechoslovakia. The fear is that the Germans will march through the northern region of the country, the Sudetenland, at any moment.' She raised her head, 'Did you hear that the German army marched into Austria today?' No one expressed surprise. 'There are also a number of trains leaving the Netherlands taking Jewish refugee women and children across the Channel.'

Turning to Sean, the lieutenant continued, 'The woman and the boy you brought to Vienna were booked on one of those trains.'

'What do you mean 'were'?' snapped Sean.

'They are here in the city,' replied the lieutenant, matter-of-factly.

'What?' shouted Sean, attracting furtive looks from the other drinkers in the bar.

'I don't know all the facts, but they never made the boat train. It seems the woman was taken ill with a fever shortly after leaving Vienna. Her forged papers fooled the Germans who did not realise who she was, and they brought her and the boy back to Berlin for treatment. She has been in hospital ever since. She discharged herself yesterday and disappeared with the boy. We have no information on their whereabouts.'

'Does Paul know?'

'I only found out myself when I arrived at the British Embassy an hour ago to pick up *some* woman's message about where to find you all,' replied the lieutenant, tartly. Sean glanced at Lenka, but again she appeared indifferent to the woman's barbs. 'Messages can take a while in these times and let's not forget we are dealing with foreigners.'

Again, her comment did not stir Lenka, whose thoughts were of the children.

Jake leaned towards Jocky and smiled, 'The Brit really is a charmer, isn't she?'

'Oh God, yes,' responded Jocky, missing the sarcasm in the American's words, as he still had not lifted his eyes up from her silk stockings.

Sean had a multitude of questions, but not for the British officer.

'Time for me to leave, my mission here is done.

'Before you go, can you take a message to Paul?' asked Sean.

'I'm in a rush.'

'Tough,' snapped Sean. 'I take it you're leaving on an earlier train from the same station that we are?'

'No, I'm taking a flight from Berlin airport actually, as you can meet uncouth ruffians on trains as well as in bars.'

'I apologise, your highness,' which was as near to an apology from Sean as one was ever likely to receive. 'Please, can you take a message to Paul and ask him to use his contacts to find the woman and the boy and take them to the train we're on tonight.' He did not wait for a response and spun around to Jocky. 'Can you sober up and knock out some paperwork matching this for a woman and a boy?' he asked as he handed over Leo's papers.

'I'm a professional, pal,' and, looking at the papers, he added, 'It won't take much to alter this for the boy and I'll draw up something for the woman, though the paper quality I have, won't be an exact match. But it will do.'

'Okay, your Highness?' The lieutenant glared at Sean, unimpressed at being asked to do anything by a civilian, let alone the Irishman. 'Of course, your ladyship, I can go to the station myself in broad daylight and risk the whole fucking operation if you like.'

Lenka dug her fingernails into the table. This was a high stakes game the Irishman was playing.

'But, of course, as you clearly need help!' replied the lieutenant with a wry smile.

Abruptly, she rose from the table, turned around on her high heels and made her way back towards the staircase. There was not a man in the room, including the drunk who had been previously asleep with his head on the bar, who did not stare as she disappeared up the stairs.

Fifteen minutes later fourteen men in black uniforms, wearing black peaked caps adorned with the Death Skull motif of the Gestapo, stomped down the steps leading into the underground bar. They were followed by another man, a stormtrooper from the SA, who lumbered down the wooden steps. He was eager to see what his Gestapo brothers were up to – brothers he was eager to join. The

327

Gestapo fanned out in a semi-circle cutting off the stairs, the only exit point, while the stormtrooper, taller and broader than any of them, watched impatiently.

The SA man, in his dull brown jacket that matched his shirt, lederhosen and white knee-length socks, jutted his head like a large hungry chick, restlessly shuffling behind the black crows in front of him.

Jocky whispered to the Irishman, 'I guess they've rumbled it's an illegal drinking den?'

'Sadly, I wish that were true, my little bundle of testosterone,' answered Sean, not bothering to lower his voice. 'But this is something else. Illegal drinking dens operate when the right people have received a payoff. But you don't turn up in uniform to collect your payoff, and you don't bring half an army with you,'

'*Yer* not speaking in whispers, so I guess *yer* think we are the "something else" . . . *shite*!'

The officer at the front of the group wore the SS insignia of three silver-coloured diagonal squares above two horizontal silver stripes, which declared he was the Hauptsturmführer, the equivalent of the rank of captain. He strode over to the table and as he did so, he yelled at all the other drinkers, '*Raus! Alle raus!*'

The barman grabbed his coat and ran up the stairs, leaving it to his customers to lift the drunk who had once again fallen back asleep at the bar, and carry him up the stairs with them.

Jocky sat back and took another swig of beer from his metal tankard, smiled and moved his chair a little away from the table, 'Don't damage the uniforms. They will come in handy.'

'Uniforms!' shot back Jake. 'Are you out of your

fucking mind? These are Gestapo, not a little girl's collection of Kewpie-dolls.'

'Look, I heard in London that *yer* are all lethal killers, so do what *yer* do, but don't damage the uniforms, pal. They might help us get to the station.' He leaned further back as if he had taken a front-row seat prior to a boxing match.

Now that the room was clear of other drinkers, five of the Gestapo officers stepped forward to form a circle around those sitting at the table.

The captain directed his curt questions at Lenka, 'Purpose of your visit to Berlin, business or pleasure?'

Lenka explained in fluent German that they were circus performers on their way to join an international gathering of fellow performers. She had noticed a poster on a lamppost when they drove into Berlin. Then she hurried to the British Embassy, where she contacted London to ask for papers to be manufactured accordingly, vouching for the Rogues new occupation. Her urgent request was relayed to a British Naval commander based in Room 39 in Admiralty Arch. He sanctioned it immediately.

Jocky remembered the words of that same commander, when he had handed him Lenka's message the day before: 'You're my best "fixer" Jocky. I need you to prepare these documents forthwith. Then fly to Berlin, as I need you to deliver them in person.' The British officer slipped a Morland of Grosvenor Street cigarette into his Asprey holder. 'Once there, do whatever expedites the safe arrival of the children in England.' Jocky examined the book on the desk. It struck him as unusual. It was entitled

"Birds of the West Indies".

'I'm a bird man, *meself*,' said the Scotsman, picking it up.

'It's for a little project I have in mind. I may write a book, or two, once we have vanquished the Nazis. I'm looking for a name for the lead character, something bland. Perhaps the author's name would suffice,' replied the sombre old Etonian.

Jocky looked at the author's name on the spine. 'Commander, *yer* succeeded.'

'Papers?'

Lenka handed hers over first to the captain.

The story that they were circus performers had worked last night when the police checked the bus, but this was the Gestapo.

The captain glared at Lenka as he opened her documents.

'I expect to find the "J",' he sneered.

He was referring to the latest decree by the German government that all Jews over the age of fifteen had to have the letter printed large on the cover and on each paper of their identity papers. A further decree made it mandatory for every Jew to have a new photo taken for their identity papers, with the left ear visible. This was because Nazi anthropologists had recently released 'irrefutable' scientific research that the size and shape of a person's ear determined if they had Semitic roots. The scientists did not elaborate on what was so distinctive about a Jewish ear, but the German Police, the SS and the SA forensically examined a person's photo as if they knew.

The SS officer turned his attention to the Russian, 'What is it like to fuck a Jew whore?'

Lenka raised an eyebrow and addressed her former lover, 'Well, answer the man.'

Vodanski could speak German, but he did so with an unmistakable Russian accent. Knowing this, Lenka might as well have stepped out onto the snow-decked pavement and announced that hostilities were to break out below. The Russian rose until he was standing near a foot above the SS officer. In an exaggerated comic Russian accent, but in German, deliberately unhurried to add emphasis to each vowel, he replied, 'She's better than your wife, but lacks the experience of your mother.'

Before the SS officer had time to draw his gun, the Russian smashed the heel of the palm of his right hand under the man's chin. The force was such that it lifted the SS captain off the floor and forced his jawbone into his brain. He was dead before he landed.

Ryan sprung from his chair and bolted headfirst into the next man, an SS lieutenant, driving him across the sawdust-covered floor, into the open-fire in the centre of the bar.

Jake grabbed the arm of a third Nazi and wrenched him towards the knife he had slipped from his right boot. The silver steel blade disappeared into the man's neck, as a torrent of blood shot across the table.

Lenka threw herself backwards off her chair in the direction of a fourth member of the Gestapo troop. As she did so, she pulled the knife from inside her left sleeve and with both hands gripping the handle swung it up over her head and into his groin. The impact made him fall to his knees, bringing him nearer. His head fell forward, and

331

she slashed the blade across his throat and delivered the killer thrust by stabbing it into his eye.

Chris spun to his left and caught the Gestapo trooper behind him by his right arm. In one swift movement, he wedged his right shoulder under the man's secured arm, lifting him into the air, and flipped him over his right shoulder, smashing him head first on to the edge of the table, breaking his neck.

In the mayhem, Jocky dived under the solid oak table, dragging Jewel down with him. While shielding her, throughout the brief but brutal encounter, he shouted commands at the others.

'We need the uniforms!' 'Don't get blood on them.' 'Don't stab the bastards where *yer* can see a mark!' and, 'No guns, or we'll have more of the *fuken* robots down here!'

Having eliminated the first tier of their attackers, the Rogues took defensive postures with knives in hand, waiting for the next line to advance.

Four SS men ran at the Rogues, while the SA man stood where he was, scrambling to remove his Luger from his holster. Behind them, the remaining five men drew their Lugers. But in the dimly lit bar, and with the Rogues moving so nimbly, they feared killing one of their own. It cost all five their lives. The Rogues had registered the immediate threat. Their knives were airborne. Each Rogue had aimed their knife at the nearest Nazi training their pistols on them, with such precision that it missed the advancing wave of SS men running at them. Lenka's dagger connected with one Nazi in the throat, while Vodanski's weapon prised open another's forehead. Ryan, Jake and Chris' knives hit their targets in the heart.

The four attackers were now upon the Rogues. The first dived at Ryan, but the Irishman bent his left shoulder down, pivoting himself so his right-arm landed on the back of his neck. His attacker stumbled and landed in the on his lieutenant, who was frantically trying to escape the flames.

Jake moved forward to meet his attacker but dropped onto his knee, as his assailant raised his dagger. The American wrenched Lenka's knife out of the head of the dead Nazi lying with his mouth open on the ground. His attacker saw the blade and seized the American's arm. But Jake was the more powerful of the two and barely moved as the man powered into him, knocked Lenka's knife from his hand. The American seized his assailant's arm holding the Nazi dagger with his left hand and grasped the man's throat with his right. Swinging his right leg behind the man, he knocked him onto his back and followed him down. Jake tightened his grip on the man's throat, until his eyes popped and his windpipe shattered.

Vodanski's attacker pulled his Luger from his holster. The Russian used table that Jewel and Jocky were hiding beneath as a shield and rushed the shooter. The thick oak absorbed two bullets before Vodanski rammed the man into the stone wall.

Jocky screamed, 'Vodka. *Yer* mad Cossack, bastard!', as Jewel threw her arms around the terrified Scotsman.

Though the back of his head was split open, the Nazi Vodanski had pinned to the wall, was as huge and as powerful as the Russian. He was barely stunned, even though all that remained of the table were two legs that Vodanski was holding in his hands. Vodanski's opponent reached up to seize a wine bottle from the bar by its neck

333

and smashed it off the counter. But the Russian delivered several blows to the man's head with the wooden legs. He only stopped when the pummelled head of Nazi slipped down the stone wall and came to rest in the expanding pool of blood on the floor.

At five foot-eight, Lenka's opponent was the shortest in his unit. Her attacker smiled, as his opponent was an unarmed young woman. Repeatedly, he jabbed his dagger towards her face. His smug smile disappeared as she parried his arm holding the SS dagger and leapt towards him. The man was seized by an excruciating pain through his temple. Unbeknown to him, the defenceless woman had extracted two skewers from the serving of pigs-trotters that had been on the table behind her. He raised his hands and felt the handles of the steel skewers that were now embedded above each ear. He collapsed onto the floor.

The SA man saw that the man who was aiming punches down on the faces of the two Gestapo troopers in the fireplace had his back to him. He rushed towards Ryan.

The Irishman heard the clambering boots behind him. He spun around, and now that the man was upon him, he smashed the heel of his boot into his knee, breaking his kneecap. Ryan grabbed the man by his dull brown tie and wrenched him forward. The stormtrooper toppled forward and landed face down on top of the two men who were frenziedly trying to escape the flames. Ryan seized the SA man's head from behind and began to smash it against the faces of the other two Nazis underneath him. Now all three men were screaming as the flames engulfed them.

If it were not for the flames flaying their bones, the three men might have noticed that their slayer's grey-green eyes were now a piercing glacial blue. The dying men's screams and violent convulsions made Jocky bury his face in Jewel's arms.

With their opponents lying dead in several horrendous positions around the floor of the underground bar, the Rogues helped themselves to whatever arms and ammunition they could gather.

Jocky looked up at Jewel, 'Sorry Gorgeous, I hope I didn't hurt *yer*.'

Chris gently clasped Jewel's right hand and pulled her up. Together they then helped Jocky up on his feet. She smiled at the smaller of the Scotsmen, 'Thank you. You are more of a gentleman than you give yourself credit for.'

Jocky turned on Sean, '*Yer* stupid Irish bastard, I told *yer* we needed the uniforms. *Yer* haven't left enough material on those bastards in the fireplace for an ant to wipe its arse with.'

The Irishman ignored Jocky's tirade, but turned to Jewel, who had made her way to Lenka's fallen opponent and was applying bandages to the man's head. She delicately wrapped some fresh dressing from the medical kit that she always kept in her bag around his wounds, avoiding the ends of the skewers protruding from either side. He was shaking violently, but his vocal cords must have been damaged somehow as he tried to speak but could not.

'If you save him, I'll only have to kill him,' said Sean.

'That is what you must live with, but not me,' she replied, and continued to wrap the bandages around the man who looked in his early twenties.

The dying man seemed bewildered, as he looked at the scarred face of the blonde woman tending him. She left her right hand on his forehead in his final moments, and then she gently closed his eyes with the scarred fingers of her left hand. Chris stepped forward and lifted her up. All around her were dead bodies and the smell of blood and burning flesh. As he pressed her to him, she looked at the others. 'You do what you do, but I can never accept taking a life.'

'Never accept it,' said Chris. 'It's people like you who offer the world hope for a better future, not people like us.'

He bent his head down and rested his head against her hair.

The others started to strip the dead bodies of their black uniforms, looking for the best fit, but without looking at him they knew that Chris was right.

Sean knew from what Lenka had told him up in the mountains, that it was the Australian nurse who had kept them sane with all they had witnessed in Spain. When they reached Berlin, Lenka had collected the message from the British Embassy, which read that Jewel was arriving the next day with Chris. On reading the message to Sean, she went further and described the nurse 'as her conscience'. In Spain, Jewel had been the one who challenged them, particularly the time when they all sought vengeance after the death of Dominique. She had taken Jake in her arms and whispered to the grief-stricken man, 'That vengeance did not absolve him from doing what was right.'

What Lenka, Chris or any of the others did not know was that a few months after Dominique's death Jake had confessed to Jewel, 'If you had not stopped me that day, God knows what I would have done. Dominique wouldn't have wanted that.' Jewel had placed her right arm around him, and held the powerful, though troubled man, as tightly as her body would allow. Jake whispered, 'You saved me, or at least my soul if it exists, as I probably couldn't have lived with what I was about to do.'

Jocky, being by far the shortest of the men and even an inch or two shorter than Lenka, was having trouble finding trousers on what was left of the Gestapo officers to fit him. Sean pointed to the lederhosen on the body of the SA man that he had dragged out of the fire. There was nothing to extract from the bodies of the SS men beneath him. The SA man's flesh above his chest had burnt away, but what was left below his waist was intact. But the shorts looked ridiculous even on an average-sized man, let alone the colossal SA man who was trampling around in the snowstorm earlier.

Sean held the man's shorts up to the disgruntled Scotsman, 'I can turn them up for you, if you like?'

'Potato picking bastard,' grunted Jocky, but he still grabbed the shorts.

He slipped them on. The hem was below his knees. However, he did not require the man's belt though, as the Scotsman was about the same size as the late SA stormtrooper around the waistline.

With the carnage all around them, it was an absurdly surreal sight, Jocky, wearing the shorts of a man who was

337

nearly twice his height. The image became even more ridiculous as Vodanski marched over to the Scotsman and placed his hand on his shoulder.

The Russian had first met the man as he strolled down the corridor of Madame Jiggy-Jigs with his arms around Lissotte and Marilynn. At that moment, the volatile little Scotsman was ejected by one of the women from her room. He was followed by a woman screaming, '*Sale pervers.*'

Months later, in the illegal underground bar, the Russian once again towered above the other former guest of the Parisian brothel. He bent down so his nose was less than an inch from the Scotsman's eyes. 'You're a good man to have in a fight.'

Jocky knew he was up for ridicule, but for once he decided to keep his opinions to himself.

'Next time we fight the enemy, send a postcard and an address, so we can find you later,' added Jake.

Jocky's self-restraint did not last long, 'Bollocks to the lot of *yer*. I'm a lover, not a fighter!'

'Thank you Jocky for protecting Jewel,' said Chris, stepping forward and held his hand out to his countryman, who shook it warmly.

Ryan, Chris, Vodanski and Jake slipped on what Gestapo uniforms they could salvage. But every item was splattered with blood, despite Jocky's protestations during the fight.

Sean turned to Lenka and Jewel. 'We'll pretend you're our prisoners.'

The women nodded. However, any suspicion that might be aroused by the poor condition of the uniforms, would be countered by the fact that only their colleagues in the Gestapo would dare challenge anyone wearing the feared black uniform.

Jocky realised that the SA man was the only one to enter the bar without a jacket. 'I'm wearing short trousers belonging to seven-foot Nazi built like a gorilla with no *fuken* jacket in the middle of a snowstorm. I'm going to be the centre of attention, no matter how many lunatics in bloodstained SS uniforms surrounded me. I look like I'm auditioning for the part of a *fuken* Munchkin in *The Wizard of Oz.*'

'Let's hope it's not a speaking part, or they'll give it an X-certificate,' said Ryan, wryly.

'Funny, bastard!' cursed Jocky, as Lenka suggested that he stay out of sight by sticking between her and Jewel when that got outside.

Sean added, 'With the rest of us surrounding you, just pretend you're the Pope in St. Peter's Square surrounded by his entourage. Just don't wave to your flock, Holy Father.'

This was met by another torrent of abuse from the fiery Scotsman.

In their various guises, the Rogues knew it was time to leave before the Nazis started to look for their missing colleagues.

Before they left, Ryan stuffed a napkin into a brandy bottle, lit it from a lantern hanging above the bar, and threw it at the shelf that had the most bottles of spirit on it. The back wall of the bar erupted in flames.

'Jesus Christ, *me* heart,' screamed Jocky, who grabbed two bottles of brandy and a handful of cigarettes, just as blue flames began to dance on the beams above.

As Sean walked up the wooden steps, Lenka met him at the top.

'You're a lunatic, but it might work as it should confuse the Nazis for a while. Hopefully, they'll think their men died in an accident?'

'Maybe,' muttered Sean. 'It gives us time, anyway. A fire in an underground bar shouldn't raise suspicions until they extinguish it and wonder why the only bodies in an illegal den are of their own. Let's hope the children will be in England, or at least Holland by then.'

The Rogues entered the street to be met by the now blinding glare of the sun. The snowstorm had moved on to inflict havoc elsewhere, but it left a thick white layer of powder a foot deep on the ground in its wake.

Following the events of the last fifteen minutes, the Rogues were perfectly sober and ready to fight but were relieved that there was no reception committee to meet them. The people of Berlin were carrying on with their daily business, and it was hard to believe that fifteen of their countrymen lay dead beneath their hurried feet.

The unkempt, but intimidating squad of Gestapo drew furtive looks as they led their prisoners along the street. Suddenly, passers-by turned shuddered. A loud explosion was followed by flames leaping up from a basement in the middle of the line of houses. Though frightened by the eruption, when they realised where it had come from, they were not surprised. The underground beer keller was well-known for attracting disreputable types and was frequently raided by the police.

The prisoner escort continued toward the train station located on the other side of town. Jocky, who did as he was told and hurried along in between Lenka and Jewel, flapped his arms frenziedly to keep warm.

Lenka observed the men wearing the bloodied uniforms of the Gestapo. As an experienced fighter, she understood the nuances, undetectable to most, of their different fighting styles. Ryan and the Russian were ruthless. When the fighting broke out, it was always short and brutal, knowing that the longer a fight lasted, the greater the risk of injury. Her technique was similar to theirs, for she had only lived this long by killing the enemy, usually men, as quickly as possible. But their styles differed from hers in one respect, they could call on their immense strength. Her naked hands could be used to hold a weapon or to block, while they could use theirs to kill. Their punches were aimed not at making a powerful impact on an opponent, as most combatants do, but delivered as if to punch through an opponent. Both men could, and had, force broken bones into vital organs.

However, there was one strange anomaly that separated the men. Lenka noticed that in the fight Sean's eyes had turned icy blue. She shrugged – perhaps she imagined it or the heat from the fire had played tricks with the light.

Jake was more deliberate; his approach was that of a trained marine, to immobilise his attacker as quickly as possible and then kill them. Chris was a little like Sean in some respects, in that he was a street fighter, using anything to hand to beat an opponent, but like Jake he would immobilise his enemy first. However, unlike Chris, Jake always finished his opponent off. Vodanski and Chris had greater height and bigger in build, Sean and Jake were slightly shorter, but Sean was the more agile of the men. In a fight between the men, Lenka found it difficult to say who would be the last man standing. She peered over at the big Scotsman, perhaps Chris, if Jewel's life was at stake.

For twenty minutes pounding through the snow, they had not been challenged. In fact, on two occasions as they marched past, the crowd burst into applause and shouted out '*Scheißkerl Juden*'. Jocky's idea about using the uniforms and Sean's refinement to the plan that the women would pretend to be their prisoners had worked – so far.

They turned into the main thoroughfare, the Kurfürstenstrasse, and were met by the sight of a man being pushed to the ground. His attackers were not the thugs of the SA, the SS, or the police, but, as they later learned, his neighbours.

Men and women were kicking the elderly man curled up in the snow. The mob was shouting angry expletives, some adding the word *Juden*. Similar attacks were taking place throughout the city, with Jewish families being forced from their homes, their possessions seized by German families. The crowd gathered around the old man was in a frenzy.

A savage metamorphosis was taken place on streets throughout Germany. Soon, similar outbreaks would occur in Austria and neighbouring countries. Minutes earlier, the gathering crowd had been merely curious when two men evicted the elderly man from his house. Now, like sharks detecting blood in the water, the eyes of the crowd rolled back. They were consumed by the instinct to maim, even kill if no one intervened. One woman, who earlier would be judged as perfectly respectable in her flowery dress and a pink silk scarf suitably tied around her bonnet due to the increasing wind, was now on her knees, biting the man's wrist so he would release his satchel.

Despite all the horrors they had witnessed, Jewel and Chris were shocked at the brutality of the attack on the old man. His shirt was ripped open and one man was waving the sleeve of his coat in the air like a trophy. One woman held her daughter high above her shoulders so she could see the man being kicked. Another woman broke her way through the throng to spit on the wretched man on the ground. The mob rolled the man over with the soles of their shoes into the slush-covered road, and into the path of the on-coming traffic.

Vodanski turned to Lenka and whispered, 'Am I the best lover you ever had?'

'No,' she replied in a similar low voice.

'Do you trust me with your life?'

'Yes.'

He seized her throat with his plate-sized hand and lifted her from the show. Ryan had not heard what Vodanski had whispered to her, and not knowing the Russian as well as the others, went for his knife.

Jake stayed his arm, 'He's as thick as a brick, but I trust him.'

Lenka glanced at Ryan and lifted her hand to indicate that she was a party to whatever the Russian was planning to do.

Jocky grabbed Jake's arm and snuck off.

With Lenka held like a rag doll, apparently semi-conscious in his vice-like hand, Vodanski brutally pushed the crowd back. With his free hand, he roughly grabbed the old man by the nape of his torn, but good-quality, long tweed coat, and dragged him off the road and up onto his feet. The man had a bloody gash in his forehead.

The crowd stood in stunned silence, as the huge scruffy Gestapo officer dragged the man and the young woman along through the soiled brown-grey snow toward the prisoner escort. None of the elder's man's abusers uttered a word, as the woman and the elderly man were thrown into the middle of the other Gestapo captives.

One woman whispered to her friend, 'If he treated the woman like that, what will he do to that old Jew?' He friend whispered, 'You'd think he could have been issued with a jacket that wasn't busting at the seams.' Another man commented, 'Now the Jew will receive a proper beating.'

Jocky drove up in a truck, launching a tide of slush over the escort party's boots.

'Where did you find this heap of shit?' asked Sean.

'All thanks to the Yank. Kind of . . .' Jake was sitting next to him and just smiled sheepishly. Jocky continued, 'Well, when Vodka set off, we thought we'd better find some transport for when he came back with the old fella.'

In full view of the crowd, Vodanski threw his female prisoner into the back of the vehicle. But, with his broad back to the mob, he lifted the old man gently up onto the flat wet wooden floor of the lorry.

'Lenka, thank you for trusting me,' said Vodanski.

'You make it sound like I had a choice. You nearly fucking choked me!'

The others quickly leapt up into the back of the truck. They knew, and Sean realised now, that though

344

Lenka mistrusted the Russia for centuries of abuse of her country, she trusted Vodanski. Otherwise she would have stabbed him in the throat with the knife she always kept in her boot.

Jocky was able to secure a good view of the road as he found a cushion behind the driver's seat to place under him. He let out a deep sigh of relief, 'Haemorrhoids: the Nazis of the arsehole.'

'Charming,' noted Jake.

Jocky drove through Berlin's streets in the direction towards the station. Jewel was on the floor of the open-backed truck, wrapping a bandage around the old man's head wound. Sean, Lenka and Vodanski sat on the snow-covered wooden floor. For the first time since they had arrived in Berlin, they could sit back and simply view the streets of the city, without fear of challenge, protected by their feared persona.

It was a beautiful city, especially now as it was carpeted in snow and bathed in the resplendent radiance of the evening's blood-red sun. Its historical buildings were magnificent, but all that was new was base and crude.

There were posters everywhere, emphasising German superiority in body, mind and spirit. The people depicted had healthy, smiling faces. Even factory workers, standing beside farmers, had similar bronzed faces and tanned, muscular bodies. The Aryan ideal of what men and women should look like was a common theme which resonated throughout a city that two years earlier had hosted the Olympics. Every poster expressed vigour and prosperity, and in the background was always the *Hakenkreuz*. All were filled with bright colours, apart from those that depicted communists or Jews; these were grey and black.

Berliners were making their way through the streets at a fast, but orderly pace, as you would see in any civilised city. But as the Rogues travelled on the back of the vehicle, the random outbreaks of public violence continued. Sean remembered when he was a child, coming across a man on a Dublin street who had been tarred and feathered after being tied naked to a lamppost. A sign was tied around his neck with 'INFORMER' scribbled in large letters.

Sean knew that during war, or when there is economic turmoil, someone or some section of the community becomes the conduit for a nation's frustration and anger. But what made the events he witnessed as they drove through Berlin even more shocking was that this was not a city at war, nor was it poor.

The truck passed through the streets, as clothing and other personal items were thrown from several windows. Outside a school, a child wearing a kippah was tripped by his classmates and toppled into the snow. A young man was being checked for papers by a policeman, but without warning, another policeman smashed the young man's face into a brick wall.

The Rogues were more unsettled by the inaction of passers-by who skirted around those attacked, than by the actions of the perpetrators. Most gave a passing glance, while others crossed the street with their chins raised defiantly as if they had intended to walk that way all along.

The police and the army stood by, only intervening if the victim put up too much of a fight. The Nazis had a sweeping term for this policy: Aryanisation. The hatred of the Jews had lain dormant in German culture, and until recently it was only expressed in the home or in bars by Berliners within their own social circles. But now the Nazis had created a society that rejoiced in hatred. This was where the true power of the Nazis lay, for across Germany, they released the vilest base hatred for Jews, along with Slavs, homosexuals, gypsies, Freemasons, Catholics and the mentally and physically disabled. Soon it would spread across Europe, accompanied by prejudice and intolerance of what was different. Disquiet grew to dislike, then to angry outbursts, then denouncements, then murder, and ultimately genocide.

As the Rogues travelled through the streets, it was as if they had entered a new and horrifying world. A world where the furies had been released and had violently torn away the humanity of its inhabitants. It was a city without pity.

When they were about a mile from the station, the engine overheated.

'*Shite*! All out!' cried their Scottish driver.

'Can't you fix it?' asked Jake.

'Lucky we got this far. Of all the places to smash a driver's head, *yer* dick. *Yer* not of Irish descent, are *yer*?'

Jake shrugged, as Sean and Vodanski examined the bloody hole in the grill in front of the radiator. It was the size of a head, a notion supported by a German soldier's felt cap wedged in it. Vodanski gave Jake another of his frequent looks of disdain.

Though the elderly man was still recovering from his terrifying ordeal, he staggered to his feet. He thanked

Jewel profusely, but he was eager to leave. Nervously, he offered his thanks to the uniformed men and shuffled away through the snow. He still could not work out why these slovenly dressed members of the Gestapo had saved him, and he rightly believed that his family would not believe him. Later, when he paid a visit to his rabbi and explained how he was saved by the kindness of the Gestapo, he was told, 'Shlomi, it is not for us to question the methods that God employs to protects us; just be grateful that he does.'

Over on the right-hand side of the street, Sean noticed a young girl, maybe thirteen or so, running whilst dragging a younger girl by the hand. Behind them were six SA stormtroopers who had broken into a run.

If the SS were the disciplined torturers and killers of The Third Reich, the SA consisted of equally brutal, but blunt, sadistic thugs.

Lenka spotted them as she jumped off the back of the vehicle into the slush, 'For Christ's sake, don't interfere, we are nearly at the train station.'

The other Rogues knew she was right, and they set off in the direction of the station, but all kept looking over their shoulder at the pursuit. The first of the SA squad, a corporal and the senior of the group, caught up with the older girl, caught her by the arm, swung her around and slapped her across the face. She fell to the floor just in front of a display sign mounted on a stand outside a shop:

JUDEN
VERBOTEN

Another of the pack grabbed her by her hair and dragged her from the snow-quilted pavement into the dark alley. Another of the SA thugs joined him, lifted the barely conscious girl up by one ankle. The smaller girl ran after them, but one of the men still in the pack and was met by a fierce blow from the back of the man's hand, knocking her dazed to the ground. As the little girl struggled to her feet, another man pushed her towards the alley with the heel of his boot.

'Keep walking,' ordered Lenka, as she dropped back alongside the Irishman who was at the rear of the group.

'If they are taking her out of view, then they intend to do something that might even disturb the sensitivities of the average Berlin mob,' said Ryan.

That was when he saw the eldest girl hit and about to be dragged into the alley.

'You don't know that,' grabbing Sean's arm.

'Really, that's the entrance to a police station, is it? I don't see any of the bastards waving around handcuffs.'

Then the younger girl was hit across the back of the head.

'Sean don't,' cried Lenka.

'Bollocks!' announced Ryan, veering off into the road in the direction of the alley.

The Nuremberg racial laws, imposed by the Nazis, forbade a German from having sexual intercourse with a Jew. You could kill a Jew on the street and not be punished, but to rape one could result in severe retribution – not because it was the brutal violation of a woman, but because the act might produce a child of mixed race. Ryan could see from the men's faces that they had no interest in upholding that law, perverted as it was.

'I'll meet you at the station,' shouted Ryan over his shoulder, as he made his way across the road, navigating the slow-moving traffic and jumping over the troughs of grey snow.

'You don't speak German,' shouted Jake.

'I'll just shout and look angry, that'll be enough,' the Irishman yelled as he entered the alley behind the pack of men.

'I speak German,' exclaimed Vodanski, as he set off in the direction of the road to the left, which ran parallel to the alley.

Jake drew the two Lugers he had salvaged from the bar from his black leather belt and followed the Irishman towards the alley without a name.

'Fuck!' whispered Lenka, turning to the others, 'Come on.'

Chris held Jewel gently by her arms, 'I'll stay as back up, and make sure that if more Nazis arrive, they don't block off the entrance.'

Jewel turned to her best friend. 'Lenka I'm sorry, but there may be wounded. We will meet you on the train. I promise. You have Jocky and Paul to help you with the children if we don't.'

Rather than scold them, Lenka grasped their hands, and shook her head, before heading after Jocky, who was running towards the station.

The Irishman entered the narrow alleyway. Two of the men, including the corporal, were kneeling over the distraught and barely conscious eldest girl. The corporal

350

ripped a silver Star of David from the chain around her neck and lifted it up to the sky to peer at it. The other four members of the pack formed a circle around their two colleagues and watched. They were all powerful, fearsome-looking men, apart from one who was five-foot-four and slight of build. He was laughing gleefully.

A shout startled the pack. They turned to discover a Gestapo captain at the end of the passage. He was yelling incomprehensibly at them and banging his fist on a metal sheet covering a window. The two SA men jumped up as the officer was clearly angry over something – the Gestapo was not to be trifled with. The black-uniformed officer approached. The six stormtroopers exchanged nervous glances.

The severe-looking man would have been an imposing presence, even without the uniform. But, to the six men standing in the snow circling the girl, his uniform added to their perplexity. His peaked cap was crunched on one side and his ill-fitting jacket was torn, and a few buttons from the top of his grey shirt were missing. The buttons on the front of the jacket were also gone and held together by a black leather belt.

The Gestapo officer walked up to the youngest girl who had crawled into the alley. She looked up at him, petrified. Sean gave her the briefest of smiles, as he passed her. He stopped when he reached the semi-conscious girl. He crouched down and addressed her in a strong and assured voice, as he asked her to take his hand, *'Bitte fräulein.'* Dazed she slipped into the snow. Sean slipped his hands gently under her limp body and rose with her in his arms.

The pack now had a closer look at the dishevelled

captain in the Gestapo. The men backed away a little, as the large intimidating figure in the black shabby uniform stood silently. The laughing trooper was no longer laughing. He advanced towards the upright Gestapo officer, as the pack, apart from his corporal, reformed behind him. The little trooper took another pace forward but froze when he saw the man's chilling blue eyes. They held him and only him. The trooper lost his nerve and stepped back. The Gestapo officer glared at the pack, before turning and striding back towards the youngest girl who was kneeling in the snow.

The corporal moved forward to apologise to the Gestapo officer. The captain ignored him and continued to trek through the snow with the young woman locked in his arms. The corporal saw the large patch of blood in the middle of the man's black tunic.

The corporal yelled, '*Achtung kapitänin! Achtung!*'

The officer did not stop, nor did he increase his pace, but continued to trudge through the alley with the girl gripping his left lapel of his jacket.

Sean offered his left hand to the girl on her knees. She stretched out her trembling hand to take it but froze when she saw that the SA draw his revolver and was pointing it at them. What strength she had ebbed away, and she fell backwards into the snow.

Ryan turned his head away from the younger girl towards the corporal. The Irishman smiled at the man who was pointed the Luger at his head. He gently laid down the elder girl on the virgin snow beside the younger one. With his eyes on the corporal, the Gestapo officer slowly took out his Luger and pointed it at the younger girl. The corporal, seeing the smile on the senior officer's face, grinned broadly as he too turned his Luger on the girl. The man in the blood-splattered black uniform made his way over to the corporal, keeping his gun still trained on the little girl. Both girls were now crying, clinging to each other. The corporal looked at him, and still wearing a large grin, spoke to the senior officer as he nodded. But, the man in the black uniform only recognised two words, *Sturmabteilung* and *Schutzstaffel* the names of the SA and the Gestapo.

Ryan turned to the corporal, and winked, said, 'Dysfunctional lunatics, the lot of them!'

He swung the butt of the Luger into corporal's face breaking the bridge of his nose man, before grabbing the back of his head and smashed his face into the wall killing him instantly. The two SA men behind him attempted to reach for their Lugers but Ryan grabbed the knife from his belt and with his right hand plunged it into the chest of the first man. Jake's blade, which he launched from some fifteen metres away, hit the second in his throat, sending his limp body to the ground.

The shortest of the SA men grabbed youngest girl and stabbed the barrel of his pistol against her head. He was laughing hysterically again, until the second of Jake's knives entered his left cheekbone, nailing his tongue to the inside of his right upper cheek. The younger girl screamed leaping up towards her sister, as the man fell face down into the puffed-up snow, narrowly missing her.

The last two stormtroopers, one far fatter than the other, ran towards the evening light at the other end of the alleyway. But just before they could escape into the street, a huge silhouette in the moonlight and barred their path. The Russian caught the thinnest stormtrooper by his left arm. In one powerful swift movement, he yanked the man forward, as he delivered a fist into his face, breaking neck. The stunned rotund stormtrooper stared at the man who immediately delivered a right-hook to his throat. He dropped to his knees, clutching his smashed windpipe before slumping into the snow.

Jake strode forward to help Sean carry the girls, as a car pulled up abruptly behind him. The American turned to find a dull-black Mercedes-Benz 260 D had blocked the entrance to the alleyway as its occupants, two uniformed officers of the Gestapo, stepped out. The shorter senior officer on the right of the two fell face down in the snow. Bewildered, the other officer peered down at him. Before he could gather his thoughts, a hand cupped his mouth, and a knife was thrust up under his jawbone.

Chris released him, as he slumped down beside his dead colleague, before grabbing their ankles and dragging them into the shadows. Fresh snowflakes once more starting to drift down to shroud the array of bodies in the nameless alley,

Sean picked up the eldest girl who for the first time had a proper look at her saviour. Upon seeing the black uniform, she screamed. Vodanski appeared and in German tried to explain to the terrified young woman that they were not Nazis and that they were here to help them. The appearance of the large Russian, his hands and uniform covered in blood, did not allay her fears, but she stopped screaming as she fainted.

Jake turned to Sean, 'We've done it now. It won't be long before the place will be crawling with police. They'll probably cordon off the train station. Even if we escape,

Lenka, Jewel and Jocky will be arrested, and god knows what will happen to the children?'

'There's a history of rivalry between the SS and the SA, so let's take advantage,' said Ryan, retrieving one of the Gestapo officers Lugers before it disappeared under the building snow drift. He hurried through the alley, pressing the barrel into the chests of the SA corpses to muffle the sound, as he fired it in turn into their hearts. Then he dragged them by the ankles, through the snow, and laid them by the other two Gestapo corpses. Ryan knelt and, once having judged the angle, he stabbed each officer in the neck with the knives from two of the SA men. Each handle was adorned with the black circle and a black criss-crossed arrow, which he left sticking out of their throats.

Ryan stood up and spoke to Vodanski who appeared next to him.

'It doesn't look like many pass this way, so with the snow covering the bodies they won't be discovered for a while. When they are, the authorities will want to hush this up until they work out the facts. By then, hopefully, we'll be well gone.'

Vodanski lifted up the younger girl. She could barely grasp what was happening, staring bemused at the other Gestapo officer with the blood on his back who was carrying her unconscious sister.

Jewel entered the alley and made her way over to the smallest girl as quickly as her body would allow. She asked Jake to translate for her. The American did as he was asked. The little girl was transfixed but was not afraid of the kindly woman whose face was terribly scarred.

'What's your name?' asked Jake.

'Golda.'

'And the other girl?'

'My sister, Hannah.'

'You will be safe with us. We will look after your sister,' added Jake.

This seemed to calm Golda, who reached out to touch her sister's limp hand as they emerged from the alley.

'Very hospitable of the Gestapo to send a car,' noted Sean, as he placed Golda in the back of the immaculate black vehicle. He trampled back over to the shop next to the entrance to the alley and lifted up the standing wooden sign. Snapping off the top section and placed it at the entrance to the alley. It now read,

VERBOTEN

'Before everyone jumps in, I need to apply some iodine to Hannah's cuts,' said Jewel, placed the girl on the footstep of the car, as its pungent odour began to revive her. Hannah woke was a start. Immediately, she turned and embraced her little sister sitting on the back seat, and gently rubbed the lump on the back of her head.

Jake and Vodanski looked at the car and wondered how the seven of them were going to squeeze in. Without admitting it to the other, both men thought of their first and only flight in The Flying Yellow Casket.

Chris knelt next to Jewel, 'Please, we must go.'

Jewel asked Vodanski to find out where Hannah and her sister were heading. He did, and Hannah replied that they were part of a group of families who were heading to the train station to be taken to England. But the SA arrived and attacked their families with wooden truncheons, and they were separated from their mother.

Hannah stared anxiously up at Vodanski, who was hiding his blood-stained hands behind his back, 'I hope our mother made it to the station.'

'If not, I will find her,' replied the Russian, with a nod.

Chris pleaded with Jewel, 'You can nurse them on the train, please let's go,' as Vodanski jumped into the driver's seat, while Jake leapt in beside him.

Jewel nodded as Chris slipped into the back seat, lifting Hannah onto his lap, so that Jewel would have more room. No one knew better than he that she was permanently in pain.

Sean jumped in through the passenger door facing the street. He lifted Golda onto his lap. Ripping the Death Skull motif off the front of his battered black cap, he tossed it into the road. Plopping the unmarked cap on her head, the girl chuckled.

Not for the first time, Sean thought how incredibly resilient children are.

Chris offered Jewel his hand to help her in. Jewel smiled as she bent her head down to climb into the back of the car. Then time seemed to stop, as blood oozed from the left side of her lips.

'Jewel?' whispered Chris as the two drops landed on the black leather seat by the open door. 'Jewel?' he cried again. The drops became a trickle as she stared vacantly up at him. 'Jewel!' he screamed.

She lifted her right arm as if to wave at him. The trickle of blood flowed freely now, working its way down the left side of her lip and neck and spread across the white cotton blouse, he had made for her in Madrid.

Jake, Sean and Vodanski turned to see Jewel's death play out in slow motion. Chris tried to grab her as she flopped backwards on to the fresh powder, as if she were relaxing into a bed of goose feathers. When she landed, she rolled on her side and only then did the others see the handle of the knife wedged between her shoulder blades.

Chris plunged Hannah on the seat before throwing himself out of the car, as did the three other men to cover him. Sean carrying Golda in his arms. Chris dropped to the ground. He looked into Jewel's eyes, as he had done that night on the rooftop in Madrid. He peered into her beautiful light brown eyes before they closed for the last time.

Jake was the first to see the laughing SA trooper, his face now frozen in a horrifying bloody smile created by the dagger pinning his cheeks back. He ran at the man and rammed the barrel of his gun into his mouth, breaking what was left of his front teeth, to muffle the gunshots. The American emptied the chamber, and only then did release his head and watch his body fall back into the alley. He made no mistake this time.

Pedestrians and motor vehicles seemed oblivious to the death that surrounded the entrance to the nameless alleyway and carried on with their daily routine. If anyone had noticed what had happened, they must have decided that did not want to get tangled up in an incident concerning the Gestapo and the SA.

Jake and Vodanski loved Jewel, but they knew they must leave as the authorities could arrive at any time. Together they tried to rouse Chris. Sean placed a blanket over the two girls in the back, now wrapped around each other and crying at the death of the kind lady. The Irishman looked on powerless at the three friends crowded around the body of the young woman.

'We must go, Chris, please,' pleaded Jake.

'I'm not leaving her,' he whispered. 'Go. All of you!'

'Jesus, man!' begged Jake, placing his hand on his friend's shoulder. 'Don't do this. She would not have wanted it.'

Chris only moved to cradle the dead woman, as her frozen face rested against his chest.

Vodanski held his left hand out to the Scotsman, 'Goodbye, Chris.'

Chris looked up, nodded and without a word he took shook his friend's hand. As he did so, the Russian jerked him upwards and landed a right-hook to his jaw. Jake removed the knife from Jewel's back, and he held her withered hand gently in his for the last time, before raising her in his arms. Vodanski threw Chris over his shoulder, and both men returned to the car.

Once they were all inside, Sean kicked in the engine and they set off to cover the last mile to the station. In the back, Hannah, her arms wrapped around the silent Russian, she sat on his lap. By the other door, Golda was sitting quietly on Jake's knees. Between them sat their unconscious friend. On the front passenger seat, Jewel's head rest against the window as if she were asleep.

With its *Hakenkreuz* flags waving erratically on both wings, the black Mercedes sped through the side entrance into the station, drove across the platform and came to a halt beside the train destined for the Hook of Holland. The guard who manned the approach to the platform, though surprised at seeing a Gestapo captain, a slovenly dressed one at that, greeted him with a Nazi salute. Out of the corner of his eye, he spotted a woman and a shorter, red-faced man descending from the steps of one of the carriages. As guard was about to reproach them, he was met by a stern look from the captain. He decided that with the arrival of the Gestapo that all was in hand, and it was best that he went to stand guard at the gates to the platform.

Normally, the arrival of the Gestapo would have caught the attention of even the most inattentive of passengers, but no one cared as the whole station had a carnival atmosphere. News had not reached the station guards of the events at the underground beer keller or of those in the alley a mile away, but everyone had heard that Austria was now at one with Germany. Apart from those on the train, all the other soldiers throughout the station were smoking and chatting animatedly with giddy young women. Around them the artificial silk flowers given away freely by a vendor, were strewn across the crowded concourse.

Lenka eavesdropped on the flower seller's radio, before breaking the news to the others: 'Goebbels has just announced that the Nazis have taken all of Austria unopposed. They're calling it the Anschluss, which I think means, annexation, rather than an occupation.'

Her unspoken fears were reality. The Nazis had finally secured their paramount objective, Austria, and with it more willing troops for its army, along with access to magnesite, timber and water resources. Harnessing the entire power of the Rhine for the first time, Germany was entirely self-sufficient in energy. Its neighbours were impotent as nothing could stop the Nazis from building the largest military force in Europe.

Lenka turned on Sean. 'We have over a hundred children on this train and you risked everything for the sake of two more.'

Sean was in no mood to apologise, 'When you start weighing up who to save in terms of numbers, you soon forget that you're talking about people.'

Jake, Vodanski stepped sluggishly out from the vehicle carrying the girls.

'And where did you get the car?' glancing at the vehicle.

But as soon as she said it, she saw by their forlorn faces. Something terrible had happened. She watched as Jake and Vodanski help ease the unconscious Chris from the back seat.

'Where is Jewel?' she asked softly, as she uneasily walked towards the car. 'Where is she?' she repeated quietly, as Jake lowering Golda on to the platform and, walked over to her. He took her by the hand and led her over to the driver's seat. Lenka bent her head and saw that Jewel was lying across the front seats. She eased herself inside, put her arms around Jewel and rested her best friend's face on her chest.

Jake and Vodanski eyed the guard, only to see him disappear into the crowd celebrating in the bar at the far corner of the station. Then they saw Paul running towards them across the concourse. If the Germans were not celebrating, he would hold their attention now, as he slipped over on the polished tiles, bathed in the slush from passengers' shoes. He quickly lifted himself back up and unsteadily approached them, a little more flustered and sweating than usual.

Sean steeped forward to challenge him about Magdalena and Tóth, but the young man was in a panic. 'I called the British Embassy . . . and they say the SS have rescinded permission for the train to travel to Holland. They are diverting it somewhere else but taking the women and children on board . . . with them.'

'We can't risk a fire fight with the children,' said Sean. 'We need a diversion, something to lure the rest of the guards off the train. After a few moments thought, he issued instructions to the others: 'Paul, grab some glasses from the bar and take the booze Jocky swiped from The Bier Keller and start a little celebratory drink with the train guards. Try to lure them away from the train.'

'What if I don't wish to share my booze with the Krauts?' asked Jocky.

'I can drink it at your wake.'

'I was only asking. I hope the bastards choke on it,' responded Jocky, as he handed the bottles to Paul, who was even more terrified.

'You want me to board the train . . . and . . .'

'Yes,' said Sean, making it clear there would be no discussion.

'For those who you can't lure away, make sure they at least have alcohol in their hands. Then in our guise of Gestapo officers, we'll appear, accuse them of drinking on duty, order them off the train and tell them to report to headquarters immediately.'

Sean turned to Jake. 'Best leave the speaking to you, when we do?'

The American nodded.

Sean could see that Paul was on the verge of collapse. 'Look, they wouldn't argue with us in these uniforms, even if we ordered them to do naked laps around the station.'

Sean walked over to Jocky. 'You're the technical genius, can you drive a train?'

'It's a machine, isn't it!' he retorted, and quickly set off towards the front of the train.

The Irishman's plan worked better than expected. Most of the guards accepted Paul's offer of brandy and after consuming a couple of shots they jumped off the train to join the party in the bar in the corner of the station. Minutes later Jake confronted the last of the guards on the train with Sean and Vodanski standing behind him. Catching them in the middle of making a toast, he reprimanded them severely and ordered them off the train. However, before Jake could order them to report to headquarters, they scurried off down the platform to join the other guards.

In the bar, soldiers were singing the latest songs, as approved by the tone-deaf Joseph Goebbels, while Jake threw Chris over his shoulder. He carried him to the train and placed him on the floor of the luggage carriage.

Gently but firmly, Vodanski eased Lenka away from her dead friend, before carefully lifting Jewel up in his arms. After crossing the platform, he mounted the luggage carriage and lowered her down on the wooden floor beside Chris. Vodanski saw a blanket and for some reason, he placed it under Jewel's head. He rested his hand on her silken hair before he rose.

Lenka led Hannah and Golda to the other children

in the first of the five passenger carriages. All the seats were occupied, but the young girls were happy to sit on the floor in front of Ursula. She handed them some chunks of bread and removed the blanket from her shoulders and wrapped it around them.

The leader of the Rogues bent down, and though her heart was heavy, she put her arms around both girls, and said, 'You are part of us now,' and smiled.

Rising she looked at the faces of the children in the carriage. No one spoke. Everyone was tired and tense, all wondering if the train would ever leave the station and take them to freedom.

Lenka returned to the luggage carriage, to find Jake and Vodanski standing silently, staring at their two friends lying on the floor. She knew that neither man would cry. Perhaps she would one day, but not today. When she did, it would be somewhere on her own away from anyone.

Despite the recent change in orders from the headquarters of the Secret Police and the SS, the train was now under the control of the Rogues, and the Nazis were none the wiser. Paul re-joined them, soaking with sweat and looking on the verge of nervous exhaustion. He had just led an equally distressed woman whom he had met when she burst into the bar in search of her daughters, into the first of the passenger carriages. Now reunited with Hannah and Golda, she could say goodbye knowing that they had made the train, though as an adult she could not join them. She hugged them, cried and promised them both that she would join them soon. She never did keep her promise for, as with many of the mothers who said goodbye to their children that day, her future was no longer in her control.

'Did the lieutenant give you a message to see if you could find Magdalena and Tóth?' asked Sean, seizing Paul's arm.

'Good God . . . I nearly forgot . . . Yes, but I had no need to find them . . . as they were already on the train. I spoke to them earlier, they are fine. But . . . when the SS came on to do some checks, I made myself scarce . . . and I waited outside the station until I saw you . . . arrive in the black Mercedes.'

'Which carriage?'

'Err . . . carriage two, or three . . . maybe four . . . sorry, I can't think straight.'

Sean turned to Lenka, 'Is there a list of who is on board?'.

She passed it to him without a word.

Quickly scanning the list of passengers, he found that Magdalena and Tóth Schreiber were in coach C. He dropped the list and ran through the carriages until he got to the fourth coach, but there was no sign of them. Desperately he began to ask the children in the carriage if they had seen a blind woman who had a young boy with her. None of them were from the orphanage and none of them understood English.

Paul appeared. The Hungarian repeated the question in German. A boy at the back of the carriage shouted. Paul turned to the Irishman.

'The boy said the SS got on the train and were checking papers. When they got to Magdalena and Tóth they took them, no one else . . . I don't understand any of this. Why do the Nazis want them . . . so . . . desperately?'

Sean shook his head. 'Ask if anyone knows where they have been taken?'

This time a young girl sitting by the window replied to Paul's question.

'She says a black and red Mercedes pulled up by the train and the woman and the boy were bundled inside. She overheard one of the men order the driver to go to Anhalter Bahnhof Station . . . It's for trains to the Eastern corridor, just take a left at the Brandenburg Gate . . . and it's . . .'

'Don't worry, I know the area.'

'She says they mentioned . . . Himmler's Fortress. It's . . . it's just outside Berlin . . . to the north.'

Sean shook Paul's hand. 'Thank you.'.

He left the anxious young man and headed back to the luggage carriage. As he entered, Vodanski shook his head. Jake's hand was resting on Chris' shoulder, who was conscious, sitting silently with Jewel's face resting on his lap. Lenka was sitting directly in front of then, her head resting on her knees.

Sean stared at the faces of the last surviving members of her band of rogues. Would hate and revenge now consume them now? Chris had not shed any tears or expressed grief. He was a shell. When the pain is too great, the mind shuts down in self-defence. Sean remembered his parents' funeral and that of his brother, when an old woman walked over to him and his sister. 'You must be numb with grief,' she said. As clichés go, it was an apt one. Numb was the best term he could think of. Something inside him had died and what was dead could not feel.

Though he knew he had to leave, Sean looked for a few moments at the pale scarred face of the woman he had only recently met, but whose wonderful unrestrained laughter in The Bier Keller, he could still hear. He knelt on one knee beside Lenka.

'I have to find the woman and the boy.'

She said nothing; she did not turn her head from her late friend to look at him. Sean went over to Chris and crouched down, 'I'm so sorry Chris; it's my fault.'

Chris did not move. It was as if he had not heard him, as he tucked the blanket around the dead woman's neck.

Jake walked over to Sean, 'You're on your own. We must protect the children. When the Nazis realise we are heading west rather than east, we will have to fight our way out of Germany.'

There was no debate as the men, apart from Chris, understood what was demanded of them.

Sean walked past Lenka and slid open the door to jump from the carriage. She raised her head and stared across at him. She spoke without emotion, 'You didn't kill Jewel, but more of those I love will die if you come back to us.'

For a few moments they held each other's look, but there was nothing more to say. Sean knew she was right. He nodded and smiled, before turning away.

Chapter 14: Train to Hell

March 1938, Berlin

Outside the train station, Ryan looked for transport to take him to Anhalter Station on the other side of the city. There were about thirty army motorbikes in various spots, mainly Zündapps and BMWs, even a British Triumph. Six had their engines running and three of these looked in very good condition, with good tread on the tyres. Ryan selected the NSU Motorenwerke, which was not the most powerful as it was more of a cross-country bike, but in these treacherous conditions he judged it to be the most manoeuvrable, plus its tyres were slightly below pressure so it would have a better grip on the snow and ice. Of course, as the engine was running, that meant its rider was still on it.

Ryan marched over to the fat policeman sitting on the NSU Motorenwerke, who was devouring a very messy sausage and mustard concoction.

Upon seeing the feared uniform the Irishman was wearing, the man tried to stand to attention, forgetting he was still astride his machine. The startled policeman was about to give the customary salute, when the Irishman grabbed him by his ear and wrenched him from his motorbike. No further force was required, as the policeman lost his footing and plunged headfirst into the snow, still grasping his dinner rather than using his hands to save himself. By the time the policeman got back on his feet, aided by four passers-by, Ryan and his motorbike were four blocks away.

The roads were treacherous as the snow was falling heavily again. Three of the fat policeman's colleagues were in pursuit of Ryan and the stolen motorbike. One was on a Zündapp and the other on a BMW, with the third policeman in a sidecar armed with a mounted machine gun. The three police motorbikes dodged and weaved through the slow-moving traffic of Berlin's snow-carpeted main avenues, like large rabid hounds pounding through its streets. Their growls grew louder each time there was an open section of road and their riders opened the throttle. Ryan checked his driving mirror to assess the closest rider on the Zündapp. The Irishman slammed his brakes on. The rider lost his nerve, shot off to the left, hit the kerb and was launched himself towards the window of a butcher's shop. As he crashed headfirst through the glass, he unwittingly removed the JUDEN VERBOTEN sign, which had been added recently to increase the passing trade of its growing Nazi clientele.

Ryan took off once more. The other rider, though late to the pursuit, had a more powerful BMW R75 supercharged, two-cylinder 500-cc engine racer model, and he rode it with greater nerve. His passenger was blazing away with a 7.92mm MG34 mounted machine gun. He was holding nothing back. Pedestrians dived for cover as the bullets whistled past and caused little puff grey clouds on the granite walls of surrounding buildings. Despite the weight of an additional passenger and gun, the powerful machine was gaining on its target. The rider of the Zündapp rode his machine nervously, but the

BMW rider's Achilles' heel was not so easy to spot. Then Ryan saw it.

Ahead of him Ryan could see first the road sign and then the magnificent building that was the gateway to the east, Anhalter Bahnhof. A stream of bullets sprayed passed him with one skimming the left shoulder of his black jacket, spraying blood onto his left cheek, but the Irishman focused on the road ahead, waiting for his moment. Another spray of machine gun fire ripping through the back tyre, but as his bike buckled under him, he held the handlebars firmly in his grip.

Ryan was metres from the spot in the road he was gunning for, as the powerful bike behind bore down on him. Now, just before the main entrance to the station, he made a sharp right turn. Without any major loss of speed, he headed into the dimly lit little arch that provided foot-passengers with access into the station. With only one front tyre, it was a major feat to able to carry out the manoeuvre without falling under the motorbike behind him.

The second rider was as fearless and as expert with his motorbike as Ryan judged him to be. He manoeuvred every turn at great speed and with superior control. But, as the Irishman had calculated, the rider had taken the turn so expertly and as fast as he could, that he had given himself no time to slow down when he saw the metal bollard that was to be found at small public entrances to stations to stop vehicles coming through.

The Irishman had read the rider well. He had realised that his pursuer was following exactly the path he had carved out in the falling snow, wary of the ice that lay beneath the virgin powder. He rode it like someone negotiating a minefield, by following in the footsteps of those in front. It was not the impact of the sidecar on the fixed metal post that killed both men, but the rider's failure to focus on the road ahead and take command of it. His weakness was to concentrate solely on his prey.

If Ryan had slowed down as he drove through the three-foot gap between the metal post and one of the walls, the explosion behind him, when the BMW's fuel tank ignited, he would have been engulfed in flames. He opened the throttle, as he could see that the only train in the station was pulling out.

Cerberus leaned forward on the bare wooden chair, 'You will tell me about those who helped you and your son escape . . .' he paused and smiled, as he thought of the one question that really interested him, but that would be after he had gone through the formalities. The woman mumbled incoherently, but as he knew the answers, he reclined and thought of his achievements over the last two years.

His Alpha Wolves had killed and tortured hundreds across Europe. Their victims were opponents or declared to be opponents of The Third Reich. The Alpha Wolves had led covert raids into neighbouring countries to goad them into war, or at the very least sow resentment amongst the people against their governments for not coming to their aid.

More importantly, he had compiled incriminating dossiers on politicians, senior military officers, and other influential leaders that would be released to their national press prior to invasion. Cerberus' masters in Berlin were especially pleased when they heard of the extent of the

372

information discovered or manufactured. Democratic governments would fall, or at least be in turmoil prior to Germany's advance.

Cerberus leered at the injuries he had inflicted on the semi-naked body of the woman. Though he regretted that there was never enough time, he did not like to rush anything – particularly when the outcome was not in doubt. He had enjoyed torturing the Jewess the first time, but for him it was a rare privilege to return to a subject and examine some of his earlier work. He was keen to see what techniques would work on the woman and apply these to her son to test if any particularly weak points were genetic. He had experimented with families before, but the new science of genetics enthralled him. The major yearned to contribute to the pioneering work of the brilliant doctor Josef Mengele, and his study of heredity defects and the potential for genetic modifications.

The Major saw himself as a pioneer amongst his fellow officers, for though they carried out his instructions, left alone they carried on with the same tried and tested methods. He remembered the difficult decision he had to make when he burnt her eyes with a heated spoon, as there was the risk that the shock would kill her. He was not a man who took risks, but in this case, he deemed it an acceptable one to advance the study of genetics. Now, he would enjoy the dividends as the Jewess had survived, and he believed he was entitled to a little satisfaction, and he admired his work for a minute or two before proceeding.

Cerberus moved his face within inches of the woman so he could examine the muscles on her face contract, knowing that she could feel his breath on her cheeks. As a boy, he had been intrigued to see how animals behaved after he burnt or sliced parts off them. He would also do this in the presence of other animals to see if it heightened their fear seeing in advance what he would do to them. The man returned the still red-hot welding prong to the heating plate. Her questioning, what there was of it, was over and she had told him nothing he did not already know. But now he could move on to what really excited him.

Cerberus held her jaw in his clammy right hand and used it to move her head around, so he could survey how well the nerves that had once connected her eyes had healed. The bandage that he had removed very slowly, with leather gloves, was stained with blood and pus. Remembering he murdered General Vaux in the forest, he was pleased that he commandeered the farmer's leather apron, that he now wore, as this was going to get very messy.

He held the scalpel in his gloved left hand, waiting to explore if the woman still had any feeling in her optic nerve. As the blade, Grossmann stood behind the woman, holding her face firmly in his gargantuan hands.

Cerberus laughed, which surprised the captain and the four Alpha stormtroopers in the room. He did not explain why, but he suddenly remembered that it had escaped his mind to go through the process of asking questions; especially the one that *did* interest him.

'Tell me of 'The Englander'.'

Though still in Grossmann's vice-like grip, Magdalena tried to turn her head towards Tóth's muffled cries. Not that she could see anything; it was instinctive. The carriage was cold, but she no longer felt it. She hardly

374

felt the burns that her captor had inflicted on her. Thankfully, she still had her undergarments on in front of her son. Cerberus insisted that his victims were always to be stripped, but only to their underwear, as he found male and female genitalia disgusting.

With all the other children on the train this morning, she had finally thought that this time she and Tóth might escape Germany. Then, just before they were dragged from the carriage, she heard the voice of the man who had taken her eyes. As the man probed her injuries with a cold sharp instrument, her one thought was to stay awake in the belief that if she passed out, the man would turn to her son. She knew that Tóth was being forced to watch, and his muffled cries only stopped when she guessed he had finally collapsed from exhaustion. She slipped into unconsciousness.

Cerberus was disappointed that the nerves had sealed. While she was conscious, her brain, as if sensing it was being threatened, panicked and her violent spasms were only controlled by Grossmann's immense strength. Frowning, Cerberus looked with disdain at the insentient woman as he wiped the scalpel with a beautiful white embroidered handkerchief. He turned to the boy, knowing that in an hour, maybe less, they would receive 'treatment' in the fortress. Yes, in the time remaining, he would concentrate on the boy. The woman bored him.

He wiped his black leather gloves on the brown leather apron that he had commandeered on the same day as the handkerchief. That was indeed a day to remember. Once again, he recalled the farmer. He shuddered. He despised the sight of the man vomiting on his porch. Surely, he did not throw up every time he slit the throat of one of his pigs, so why was a human being any different? He regretted not having the man killed.

Magdalena's torture was taking place in a carriage that had been built to Cerberus' specifications. For over two years it was an integral part of the special train that Himmler had sanctioned for the major's use so he could operate anywhere in Europe.

Cerberus slapped the boy across the face with his glove, but he refused to wake.

'Frustrating. Perhaps, I should take refreshment and return to the boy before we reach the fortress. Grossmann, prepare a pot of Earl Grey.'

'Certainly, Sturmbannführer. Would you also wish to take lunch?'

'I'll dine in the fortress.'

He turned to the captain standing behind Grossmann. The captain was tall and smoothly handsome, with short, sun-bleached blond hair. Several times, the captain had been asked by artists commissioned by Goebbels to pose for sketches for propaganda purposes. He was viewed as a healthy unblemished poster boy for the Aryan race – apart from the distinct scar over his left eye, which was airbrushed. He, along with his men, four other members of The Alpha Wolves, had stood to attention throughout the woman's interrogation. The men did not flinch as the major committed each act of violence on the woman. They seemed removed from what was taking place right in front of them: if they held an expression, it was one of indifference.

'Cable the fortress and tell them the furnace must be

ready to treat our patients before the second train arrives. Queues are a sign of inefficiency. The second train with the children should have left Lehrter Bahnhof, by now, and arrive at the fortress an hour after us. This is a defining day,' added Cerberus.

The captain turned to one of his men and ordered him to go to the radio transmitter in the far right hand corner of the carriage and send the message immediately.

Grossmann made his way along the snow-decked metal walking gantry that ran along the side of the coal wagon that separated the carriage from the galley. As he entered the galley, he noticed that the guard on the platform at the rear of the carriage was no longer at his post. The bald goliath stepped towards the door at the end of the carriage. He opened it and was surprised to discover a police motorbike wedged on the platform between the security rail and the carriage door, exactly where the guard should have been.

If Grossmann had not been so quick to follow his master and their prisoners into his special carriage as the train pulled away, he would have seen the Irishman drive a motorbike at full speed onto the station concourse. Then he would have seen the rider take a sweeping turn away from the train, nearly toppling as the wheel without a tyre frantically tried to get traction on the smooth tiled floor, before turning sharply to be at a right-angle to the train before it reached the end of the platform.

The guard, who was standing on the wooden safety floor at the back of the galley, lighting a cigarette, had his back to the empty station concourse. He did not hear the roar of the motorbike above that of the steam engine, as

Ryan drove at the moving train, throttle fully open, and launch the motorbike into the air with the use of a luggage loading ramp. The motorbike landed on the back of the guard, knocking him off the train into a concrete pylon where he now lay motionless, wrapped around the base.

Bemusedly by the damaged NSU Motorenwerke, Grossmann, hearing something behind him, spun around to face the galley. He was met by three quick blows with the edge of a steel frying pan to his face. Though blood flooded his eyes from the gashes to his forehead, he caught the frying pan before the fourth blow landed.

It was enough. He caught his assailant's arm and spun him around to launch him back into the galley, and right over the marble-topped kitchen table. Grossmann grabbed a cleaver from the rack and launched the first of a series of attacks on his assailant. However, he could barely see his target, who delivered another slicing blow with the sharp edge of the frying pan across his left eye and another to the bridge of his nose. The man-mountain continued to lash out blindly at the large but fleeting shadow.

Grossmann glimpsed the shady outline of his assailant leaping onto the table, but he missed him with the cleaver. The man leapt over him again, landing behind him, but he must have had a chain in both hands as he did so, for Grossmann felt the cold shackle pulled back sharply across his throat. He twisted around frantically to grab at the blurred figure, but the man continued to jump around, wrapping the chain tighter around his neck. Grossmann flew his hands up to his throat to remove it, but this only trapped his hands as more lengths of chain coiled around them like a boa constrictor.

Unbeknown to Grossmann, his adversary had thrown the end of the chain over the meat hook bolted into the reinforced section of the ceiling. The giant threw his arms towards the silhouette, but the man lifted both feet and smashed them into his chest, using the chain to support him. This pulled the chain taut and to Grossmann's amazement the shadow turned upside down and was yanking it tighter, by pressing both feet against the roof. The Nazi tensed his neck muscles and pulled himself down onto the floor, as Grossmann calculated that the enormous effort would either break the chain or pull the mounted hook, which he could just about see, from the ceiling.

The hook and its moorings broke away, tearing a foot-wide hole in the roof. Snowflakes drifted down into the carnage. Grossmann was kneeling on the floor and tried to rub his eyes, but only then did he notice that by wrenching down on the chain, he had severed several fingers.

The captain and two of his men burst into the galley, Lugers drawn. Ryan threw himself backwards into the door, smashing it against the two guards. One of The Alpha Wolves had fallen beneath the wheels of the train. The other was on his back on the connecting platform that linked the galley with the coal wagon. But the captain had dived through the gap and opened fire at Ryan as he did so. A bullet hit the Irishman in his left side.

Ryan grabbed the captain's arm, forcing his pistol into the air. But the officer landed several short, powerful punches to the Irishman's open wound. Ryan lifted the officer into the air and ran him into the marble-topped table. The captain toppled over Grossmann, who was frantically tearing at the chain around his neck with what digits remained.

The captain landed on the floor. Ryan followed arm with a left hook. He tried to grab Ryan's neck, but the Irishman caught the fingers of his right hand and snapped them back. Appling more pressure downwards, he broke the Nazi's wrist. As the officer screamed, Ryan wrapped a second chain around his neck, before leaping towards the open back door of the galley. As he did so, Grossmann swung the cleaver in his left hand, hitting the shadow, but he had no idea where.

The captain who was still on his knees looking at his broken wrist, heard a clattering metallic sound, followed by the blast of a train about to pass them. He tried to remove the chain from around his neck, as his adversary kicked the motorbike off the off the platform.

To the captain's amazement he saw his opponent grab the lip of the carriage and in one swift motion he swung himself forward and up on to the roof. The chain on the floor shot up and he felt the sudden stress of the chain on his neck. In the second that remained, he realised that the other end of the chain was still attached to the motorbike, now snagged on the front of the train heading in the opposite direction. The captain's head was ripped from his body. It struck the marble-topped table and then the left side of the open door before bouncing off down the track, still held by the chain, towards Berlin.

Ryan swayed on the roof of the galley, as he made his way to the carriage behind the engine. That had to be where Magdalena and Tóth were. But he had lost a lot of blood.

The eight-inch opening across his back, where Grossmann had sliced him with the cleaver, hurt more than the bullet wound in his side. Looking down at the blood on his trousers, his shirt and on the roof of the carriage, he had to stem further loss quickly. The Irishman tied his belt even tighter around his black jacket pressed the leather against the wounds on his back and on his side. Ahead were the first of the tunnels. He threw himself down on the roof as the train quickly entered and exited four short tunnels. More would come, he thought, as the rail track ahead would transport them further into the mountains.

Leaping from the roof of the galley onto the open top coal carriage would take an almighty effort. Ryan launched himself into the air but had not expected the guard he had smashed with the door to grab his ankle. The momentum of his jump meant he landed face down on top of the coal wagon. The other man leapt up and onto his back. The stormtrooper's Luger had fallen from the train, but he held the weakened Irishman in a stranglehold.

The Nazi was not practised in the use of a knife, as it was still in its sheath hanging from his belt. Ryan moved his hand back, undid the black leather flap securing the man's dagger and grasped the handle. With quick rapid thrusts, he drove the dagger blindly into the man's thighs and groin. The man's grip around his neck loosened, as each thrust released more blood until he collapsed lifeless onto the coal.

A third stormtrooper appeared at the end of the coal wagon. He opened his sub-machine gun at the injured intruder at the other end of the coal wagon. The train entered a tunnel and was only lit by the light from the continuous burst of fire from the machine gun. The machine gunner glimpsed his killer's glacial blue eyes as suddenly all was light as the train emerged from the tunnel. All went dark as the handle of the blooded knife was all that was left to see as the metal was buried in his throat. His killer launched him from the train into the ravine.

Ryan could barely stand and the pin securing his belt buckle had broken in one of the struggles and his jacket was open again, exposing his wounds. His strength was ebbing away as more blood dripped down onto the slippery, snow-covered metal gantry. He tried to negotiate his way along it to reach the carriage ahead, but he had to stop and rest against the metal plate of the coal wagon and try once more to stop the flow of blood. Breathing slowly now, trying to control his heart so he could lessen the blood loss, he staggered along the open metal walkway, using the side of the coal wagon for support. If he could save his last reserves of energy, he might at least be able to smash through into the last carriage to free Magdalena and Tóth.

Something moved above him. A single drop of blood landed on his cheek. He looked up to find Grossmann's crazed and bloodied face peering down at him. The meat cleaver flashed in the moonlight, before descending towards his face. Ryan tried to move, but the bloodied palm of the man's right hand caught him across the throat, pinning him to the body of the wagon. The blade cut through his jacket and shirt and sliced open the skin across his chest. Still pinned to the wagon, Ryan knew several ribs were broken, but as he could still breathe, it had not reached the heart. The one thing that saved him was the tenuous grip that man's left hand had of the cleaver – having only a thumb and an index finger. Ryan had lost his knife, but he threw his arms up to grab his attacker, but the man was already falling towards him.

Grossmann did not have a clear view of the shadow, but he knew that once he could secure his opponent under him, he did not need to see him to kill him. The German landed on the Irishman, as lumps of coal fell around them. He could now make out the outline of the man trying to lift himself up by grabbing the side rail. Grossmann rose and seized the man's right arm with his left, as did so. Holding the man firmly, he raised his right foot and brought the heel of his boot down on the arm. The Nazi released a loud shrill of delight, as loud as the shadow's painful scream, as he broke the man's arm. Once more he fell on to the man and pinned his good arm down with his knee. Grossmann grinned broadly; now he could pulverise the man's head.

But such was his frenzy, that with his first blow of his right hand, he realised that he was hitting the man with a bloodied stump. The pain tore up his arm, and he screamed once more as he leapt up, as much as from surprise as with the pain.

The Irishman saw the steel cleaver lying in the snow-covered gantry glistening in the moonlight. He grabbed it with his right hand and swung it upwards into Grossmann's groin. The man screamed even louder this time. He toppled back holding onto his crotch, with what remained of his hands. Grossmann lay on his back on the gantry, but as his eyes were filling with his blood once more, he moved his hands towards the pain in his pelvis.

He felt first the warm blood streaming through his two fingers and through the opening in his trousers he found his testicles. Both slipped from what fingers he had. Shock turned to uncontrolled rage.

The German had only one thought now, to seize the shadow. Grossmann screamed for the last time and flew at the shadow. The impact launched both men into the air.

Chapter 15: The Fortress

March 1938, Brandenburg Forest

In a little clearing in the Brandenburg Forest, two men lay motionless, gradually disappearing beneath the thickening blanket of snow. For a moment, the clouds moved briefly aside to allow the silvery light to bathe the landscape. But if the moon was squeamish, it would have pulled the clouds back in front of it. Violence and horror were spreading across the world. Even in that small clearing in the wondrous snow-covered forest landscape of the Kutschenberg Mountains some sixty kilometres outside Berlin, where man walked, he brought barbarity with him.

Ryan woke up looking at the night sky. The snow had settled an inch deep on his face and he slowly lifted his right hand up to clear it. He lifted his head to look down out of the one eye and saw he was totally covered in blood. He could not feel his right leg, and he already knew his left arm was broken. He hoped that he was temporarily deaf, as he could no longer hear the train. His thoughts were of Tóth and Magdalena. For a few minutes, maybe more, Ryan lay there looking up at the snowflakes and thought of them both and all they had suffered. He thought of the Budgakovs, of Leo and of Jewel, and wondered if Olen, Anzelm and Celestynka had made it to safety.

To his right, he heard a groan. Ryan rolled his head

to discover Grossmann's bulging bloodshot eyes fixed on him, a few inches away. The man was covered in snow, and what was visible was covered in blood. The Irishman with his right hand felt around in the fresh powder and found what appeared to be a black rock; it was coal. Ryan dropped it and sent his hand to search beneath the snow. He found what he was looking for. The jagged rock was about the size of his hand. Unsteadily, he lifted it up and gradually turned back to Grossmann's flickering eyes. The Irishman summoned all his strength and swung his right arm across his body, bringing the rock down on the German's forehead.

If the blows did not kill him, as least they might reopen his wounds so he would bleed to death. Ryan had little strength, but every few minutes he had enough energy to raise the rock once more and bring it down once again on the German's head. It must have taken an hour and about thirty blows – he counted to keep himself conscious – but feeling the man's jugular for a pulse after releasing the rock after every five blows, he was finally satisfied that the man was dead.

Ryan lay there thinking about the fortress, and he once again thought of what had happened to Magdalena and the boy. Himmler was based in Berlin, and he guessed that his estate was not far outside the city. He must have been on the train for maybe thirty minutes, maybe more. He needed to know what was at the other side of the hill. He knew there was only a slim chance of the fortress being there, but he had to know. With his right hand, he inspected his body, moving his fingers over what bones he could feel.

His right leg was broken, as was his left collar bone,

and his left arm was fractured in at least two places along with all his fingers on that side. He could not feel for breaks on his rib cage, but from experience he knew they were broken on both sides. The bullet in his side had gone clean through and the cleaver that had landed above his heart had only broken the skin but not hit any vital organs. Strangely, the cold may have saved his life by slowing down his heartbeat and reducing the loss of blood. It had even frozen his clothes over his wounds, stemming the flow of blood.

Ryan's thoughts returned to Magdalena and Tóth. He must move his broken body to save them. He thought of how he needed to turn, and braced himself for the pain, for any movement would tear open his wounds. Somehow, he summoned enough strength to roll over.

Every part of his body screamed, pleading with him to never move again. Ryan looked up at the hill ahead. By alternating working his way forward with the use of his right hand and left leg, he began dragging himself through the snow. It took him ten minutes to cover the five metres to the base of the slope. Each movement released spasms of pain through his body. Each time he rested, it allowed the cold of the night to attack him and freeze his face and hands once more. The sight in his right eye was returning, but his left leg was numb; perhaps frostbite or even worse paralysis was setting in. He relied solely on his right arm for traction.

After four hours, he had crawled to the top of the hill, but it was still dark with no sign of dawn, but for the first time he saw the silhouette of Himmler's Fortress against the backdrop of the full moon. Above it, dense grey plumes of smoke were rising from the chimney stack and disappearing into the night. He did not know why, but he knew that Magdalena and Tóth were dead.

Ryan lay there as a rainstorm began to pummel the snow, but he did not notice it. The rain cloud was hurried on by the wind, and within minutes it bent the trees to its will. He did not move. He just stared at the fortress. For the first time, Ryan saw the flag carrying a swastika, as the violence of the wind prevailed over the other elements and began to unfurl it.

He knew that after the events in Berlin, there was a spy amongst them; he did not know who. He knew that the enemy was using methods previously thought unimaginable. He knew that Berlin had sanctioned a covert unit, but he did not know why it had targeted a young woman and her son – a family he had failed to save.

The flag bearing the swastika above the menacing fortress, was flapping proudly, lifted by the thermal current from the chimney to its right.

On a snow-covered slope in the distance, lay the motionless broken body of a man. His face and exposed limbs were bloodless and as deathly grey as the icy slush around him.

If the man was not already dead, he could not survive in such a desolate place for much longer; the crimson trail that led up the frozen slope to his still seeping wounds would only confirm that death was close. But the man's eyes were wide open and fixed firmly on the flag flying arrogantly above the fortress in the distance. If you came across the man's body but looked only into his eyes. Those piercing glacial blue eyes would convey only one message – the man's fight had only just begun.

NOVELS BY JOHN RIGHTEN

ALL AVAILABLE ON AMAZON

The Rogues Trilogy: *Churchill's Rogue; The Gathering Storm* & *The Darkest Hour*

....

The Lochran Trilogy: *Churchill's Assassin; The Last Rogue* & *The Alpha Wolves*

....

The Lenka Trilogy: *Heartbreak; Resilience* & *Reflection*

....

The Englander

....

The Benevolence of Rogues

....

The 'Pane' of Rejection

I hope you enjoyed my novel. Reviews are always welcome on Amazon. If you have posted a review, I have limited edition sets of postcards of The Rogues Trilogy, The Lochran Trilogy and The Lenka Trilogy covers, plus *The Benevolence of Rogues* and *The 'Pane' of Rejection*, which, stocks permitting, are available free of charge including p&p. If you would like a set, please send me a personal message via Facebook, Twitter or Instagram with the name of the novel you reviewed, so that I know which set to send, your name/pseudonym and postal address/ PO box no.

"An author writes in isolation – it has to be. But when they receive a kindly review it brightens their world."   John Righten

What the critics said . . .

The Rogues Trilogy

Churchill's Rogue – The Rogues Trilogy Part 1
December 1937. Winston Churchill asks a former adversary, Sean Ryan, for his help to save a woman and her son. Ryan agrees to help, but on his own terms. They, and other refugees, are being hunted by a specially formed SS unit, The Alpha Wolves. They are led by Major Krak, a psychopath, known by his enemies – he has no friends – as Cerberus.
Ryan encounters a formidable woman, Lenka, and other Rogues who have their own personal reasons for helping those trying to escape their Nazi pursuers. The Rogues were born of struggle, each forged in the flames of the

Irish or Spanish Civil Wars, the Great Depression or the Russian Revolution. We learn how each fought, suffered or lost those they loved.

Despite their bitter rivalries, the Rogues join forces in a desperate race to save as many families as they can. But for each of the Rogues the struggle comes at a terribly high price. Meanwhile, Churchill stands alone, ridiculed by governments desperate to appease the evil stealing towards them.

Thus, begins the story, leading up to the outbreak of war, of the men and women who dare to challenge the Nazis. *Churchill's Rogue* is the first in a rousing trilogy, followed by *The Gathering Storm* and *The Darkest Hour*, which chronicle the bloody encounters between the Rogues and Cerberus' executioners.

Churchill's Rogue reviews

"This is British author John Righten's debut novel following the first instalment of his non-fiction autobiography *The Benevolence of Rogues* which brought to the fore some of the real life 'Rogues' he's met during a multi-faceted life spent in some very dangerous places. John isn't someone who has just had an exciting, precariously balanced life; he also has a talent for transferring such existences to the page. Anyone doubting this should certainly read *Churchill's Rogue* – and hold onto your seats!

Churchill's involvement is interesting as, in an era when the UK and US were dithering as to whether the Nazis should be fought or be expeditiously befriended, the future Prime Minister was a lone voice of almost prophetic warning.

Although there are other factual characters appearing (e.g. Himmler and the Fuhrer himself) the most compelling are the fictionalised. Sean Ryan is almost a 1930s Irish Jack Reacher and yet, as much as I love Lee Child's work (and I do love it!), John Righten adds rugged, scream-curdling realism and a pace that would render Jack Reacher an asthmatic wreck.

Speaking of scream-curdling brings us to the most wonderful baddie in the Earl Grey drinking Cerberus. His real name – Major Krak - may give rise to a smirk or two but we don't laugh for long. He enjoys torture and, to give him credit, he's certainly got an imagination for it.

Indeed, earlier I described the novel as 'bloody' and for a good reason; it's definitely not a story for the delicate. However, the intensity of violence isn't for gratification. It reminds us that in the real world shootings and explosions don't just produce a tidy red dot on victims' bodies; death can be a messy business!

The other thing we notice is that this is doesn't suffer from that usual first in series malady, set-up-lull. As we follow the pasts and presents of Australian, Russian, American and British Rogues we back-track them through other conflicts like the Spanish Civil War and the Russian Revolution. The more we come to know them, the more we can't help loving them while also realising why it's best not to get close to anyone in this line of work. We're at the mercy of an author who will kill at will (in literary terms) but having started on the emotional roller coaster, I don't want the series to end. Bring on *The Gathering Storm* – I'm braced and more than ready!"
The Bookbag (UK)

Nominated for the inaugural Wilbur Smith Adventure Writing Awards

....

The Lochran Trilogy

Churchill's Assassin – The Lochran Trilogy Part 1
New Year's Eve 1964 and a young Irishman, Lochran Ryan, is being transported by Special Branch to a secret rendezvous with Sir Winston Churchill. Just as he arrives, a sniper tries to kill the statesman. But why kill a man who the world knows is gravely ill? This is the first of many questions that Lochran tries to answer. His quest for the truth takes him from New York, to London and Moscow, where he encounters the most ruthless criminal gangs, including Delafury – a one-man execution squad – who warns Lochran that a new force is rising that will change the world.

Churchill's Assassin review
"A riveting political thriller. Due the strength of characterization and plotting, the story reels you in immediately. Although Ryan and Churchill make for strange bedfellows, the concept nevertheless works brilliantly. *Churchill's Assassin* is a fine mixture of historical detail, thrilling action, and detailed characterization, making for a riveting spin on one of the world's greatest statesman that will have readers eager to pick up the next book in the series."
Editor, *Self-Publishing Review* (US)

....

The Lenka Trilogy

Heartbreak – The Lenka Trilogy Part 1
1990. Lenka Brett, a smart but unworldly young Irish teacher, volunteers to deliver medical aid when the world learns of the horrifying plight of children in Romanian orphanages. An English naval officer, Captain Simon Trevelyan, volunteers to be her co-driver. Together, they join a convoy of humanitarian aid drivers known as the Rogues, the last hope for those in areas where official charities cannot enter. Lenka falls in love with one of the drivers, but when the Rogues become the target of mercenaries, tragedy follows, and she discovers her lover is not who he appeared to be.

Heartbreak reviews
"Righten's novel is a revealing and emotionally charged account of the political volatility in Romania, where orphanages overflowed with traumatized and abandoned children in the aftermath of dictator Ceausescu's genocidal reign and Bosnia, torn apart by war and hate. As the title of the book suggests, images of such human frailty and suffering indeed cause immense heartbreak, yet Righten effectively uses camaraderie, humour, and bantering dialogue between his characters to lighten the effects of what might otherwise have been a fairly daunting read. There's also plenty of action and several good twists to make the novel work at the pace of a thriller.
Righten's protagonist, Lenka, is compelling from the

start. Having inherited many of her dead parents' sensibilities, including a heart condition and a formidable sense of resolve, she's formidable without being menacing, forthright and above all, loyal to those she loves. At times veering towards being overly heroic, she's nevertheless easy to root for - quick on her feet and using her intelligence to outwit her adversaries, rather than resorting to overt violence. Viscount Arbuthnot "Foxy" Foxborough, on the other hand, is the perfect foil for Lenka's serious demeanor. Flagrantly irreverent and always ready with a witty retort, he adds just the right amount of sass and pompousness to an otherwise very serious story.

Heartbreak is both thrilling and poignant, and a strong start to The Lenka Trilogy, with a surprise ending that will have readers asking for more."
Self-Publishing Review (US)

"*Heartbreak* is a work of action and adventure fiction penned by author John Righten and forms the first novel in The Lenka Trilogy. Written for mature audiences due to some moderate references and language, this exciting and enjoyable novel takes place in the year 1990. Taking the form of a recent historical thriller, we follow central character Lenka Brett as she embarks on a mission to give foreign aid to orphanages in Romania. With the assistance of a motley crew of former officers, alcoholics and general lunatics, the humanitarian quest begins, but there are even more dangers than one could imagine as the group is targeted by mercenaries with totally ulterior motives.

Bucharest comes alive in this thrilling work as author

John Righten paints a poignant picture of tense political aftermath, terrible poverty, and a fraught atmosphere that only the bravest souls dare navigate. Lenka is an instantly likable character despite her initial naivety and overconfidence and, throughout the novel, the narration enables us to see right into her heart and connect with her motivations for wanting to help. The more she gets sucked into the dangers of the world, the more formidable and stronger she becomes, adapting intelligently to situations but also remaining vulnerable to tragedy, like anyone else. I particularly enjoyed the inclusion of Foxy, whose witty repertoire lightened even some of the darkest, most grim moments of the tale. *Heartbreak* is a harrowing but also hopeful story that sets up a powerful trilogy: a highly recommended read."
Readers' Favorite (US)

"There are certain periods of history that often feel too close for writers to establish the right perspective, but author John Righten digs into one such recent era with *Heartbreak*, the first installment of The Lenka Trilogy. The 1990s might not have the same distant ring as the 1960s or 1930s - the subject of Righten's two other well-received historical trilogies - but the author's personal experience in critical areas of Romania, Bosnia, and South America during the 1990s provide him with unique insight and a confident pen, making this book a solid start to what portends to be a strong series.

Drawing on those all-too-real experiences, *Heartbreak* is an intense dive into the war-torn hearts of both Bosnia and Romania, seen through the eyes of a teacher delivering aid to orphanages in desperate need of assistance. Volunteering for such a dangerous task, one that takes main characters Simon and Lenka face to face with tragedy and horror, demands a very special kind of person, and these characters certainly make the cut. Fiercely independent but loyal, confident, cautious and occasionally bristling, the dynamics between this pair make the dialogue in the novel sing, and bring the story to life.

These characters on a mission that few others would undertake, but there is also a relationship developing between them - one of mutual respect and trust, and perhaps something more. Violence and heartache are not strange bedfellows, and Righten manages to weave emotions beautifully well in these pages. The personal reflections for both that are revealed through the narration give the characters real depth, and encourage readers to engage in their lived experience, their shock, and their impassioned responses. Whether Simon is learning about AIDS being spread amongst orphanages as a result of unclean supplies, or encountering places of supposed refuge running out of food or building supplies, readers are brought to the frontlines of a humanitarian crisis.

Some authors stumble and overly romanticize horrific situations, but Righten has a strong clarity of memory, and at times it is difficult to tell where the author ends and the man begins. Such authentic and gripping writing about modern history is uncommon, and *Heartbreak* provides a genuinely powerful experience for readers, particularly those who are unfamiliar with Eastern European conflicts of the 1990s. There is factual history woven brilliantly throughout this novel, demonstrating both a dedication to the truth and a rare gift for storytelling.

This book is an impressively researched and powerfully depicted tale from an author who can write equally well about fictional characters and historical events. While John Righten proved his storytelling mettle in his previous historical series, The Lenka Trilogy is shaping up to be something far more personal, and for that reason it his most powerful writing yet."

The Independent Review of Books (US)

Resilience, The Lenka Trilogy Part 2 review

"*Resilience* is a work of fiction in the action, adventure, and recent history sub-genres, and was penned by author John Righten. Forming the second novel of The Lenka Trilogy, the work does contain the use of some explicit language and is more suited to mature audiences. We revisit our heroine Lenka in 1992, where she sets her sights on her next mission to provide aid in war-torn Bosnia. Her interpersonal drama continues as secrets are unveiled about a former lover, whilst the brewing conflict spills over and threatens to quite literally explode onto a global scale, with Lenka and her delivery missions right at the center of the storm.

Author John Righten continues The Lenka Trilogy with style and flair, developing the protagonist as our young Irish girl once again finds herself in deep danger and put to the test. One of the things which I really enjoyed about the work was the inclusion of so many other essential characters who aid in her missions, which gives a good sense of how these operations work during wartime. The dialogue too was excellent for conveying the realistic experiences of the piece, and for establishing the time and cultural setting of the work. In terms of the plot, the novel eases us in gently and provides a good catch up from book one, which then rockets towards a very exciting story with plenty of new twists and turns to enjoy. Overall, I would definitely recommend *Resilience* to fans of the existing series and action/adventure stories set in real conflicts."

Readers' Favorite (US) 5-Star Award 2020

Winner of the 2020 Page Turner Spectrum Publishing Award

....

The Benevolence of Rogues

The Benevolence of Rogues reviews

"Aid worker's missions find unlikely support from prison forgers, gangsters' henchmen and sympathetic police... John Righten has been in the wrong place at the right time since the 1980s. Then, he was in Romania, delivering medical supplies to orphans suffering from Aids. Subsequently he was in Bosnia in the 90s, sneaking in medical supplies and in South America – Brazil, Chile, and Peru – during the 2000s. Righten is now back and has put together his experiences in his autobiography, *The Benevolence of Rogues.*"

Hampstead & Highgate Express (UK)

"This is not a memoir for the straight-laced, politically correct or faint of heart: massive

quantities of alcohol are consumed, many teeth are knocked out and sarcasm is in generous supply."
Kirkus Independent (US)

Printed in Great Britain
by Amazon

70418125R00234